Bones

Rebel Wayfarers MC
Book #10

MariaLisa deMora

Edited by Hot Tree Editing

Cover image by Eric Battershell Photography

Cover model: Stefan Northfield

Cover design: Debera Kuntz

First Published 2017

ISBN 13: 978-0-9983267-4-0

DEDICATION

The intricacies of life are but common to all; it is how we untangle these twists that paints our individuality in the canvas of destiny. – Dodinsky, *Labyrinth*

To the readers who never fail to make my days brighter: Thank you. A special thanks to Wendy Ihnat, for her fan-favorite entry in the "Lie To Me" contest. Check out the chapter titled, "Tell me your story." Hope I did you proud.

Contents

What Came Before   1

Life in transition   9

Ester   16

My beauty   25

I wanted to be saved   28

Things of value   35

Change in progress   48

Thirteen   53

Vengeance   59

Transformation   76

A warning   84

The coat   89

Ruined   92

I did that   95

Cherished   97

Prizes and givesies   98

Bonesday   108

Gone   111

Wake the monster   115

Aftermath   118

Lost   125

Patience   127

What you've got   129

Too damned far   131

Needings   135

Found   138

No doubts   142

Dark angel   143

For a reason   146

More than matters   149

Close to hand   154

Never enough time   162

Apt student   167

Settled   174

Forged in fire   178

Most precious   193

Gone to war   196

Distractions   212

Missing him   218

Eye for an eye   220

Hey, gorgeous   224

Never again   229

Come home   239

Tell me your story   241

My beauty   248

Making love   253

Rescued   254

Our time   265

Make a play   269

Faded memories   274

Beauty and her Bones   284

Matching needs   292

Brothers   304

Catch the fever   313

Morgan's in Arkansas   322

My Ronnie   331

Forever Rebels   334

On the cusp   353

Movie mirrors   356

Best in the history of ever   361

ACKNOWLEDGMENTS

Inspiration comes from all places. We just have to be open enough to receive.

Out of town for an event, I stopped for breakfast with friends. Several of us were sitting at the kitchen table chatting when a 6-year-old little girl came to me and climbed up into my lap. No words, no fuss, no muss, she simply climbed up and went to sleep. Her father told me he'd never seen her do that, and explained why this tiny person, adopted out of a horrendous situation, had good reason to not trust people. Yet, she trusted me.

Then he motioned to one of the guys I hadn't yet met and said, "Only other person she's like that with is Raven." I looked at the man patiently flipping eggs at the stove and immediately was struck by how much he looked like Bones in my head. Covered in tattoos, black and grey, hardly any inch of skin left bare, his skin was an oft-painted canvas. He should have been frightening to a girl like her, fearsome to a woman like me. But he wasn't. He isn't.

I'd written scores of words about Bones before I met Raven, but I didn't really understand who Sal Ramos was. Not until I spent time sitting in the kitchen of a biker clubhouse while an abused six-year-old child slept peacefully in my lap, giving me the brilliant opportunity to pick the brain of a man who intentionally self-isolated in a way that is permanent, defining, and hard for many citizens to see past.

When I look back, it's interesting to track the transition in my awareness and comfort with Raven over the course of a few hours. By the end of the day, I didn't even see his tattoos anymore.

No, by then—I just saw Raven. His expressive, dark eyes that crinkled at the corners when he laughed, and he laughed a lot. His hands that patiently folded paper airplanes only to see them crumpled and destroyed. Over and over. His teeth that were white and square, and made his smile so very real. He was imbued with serenity and grace, gifted with a striking intelligence and a sense of deep loyalty. A lover, a brother, a father, a man. Raven transformed Bones in my head, and made me long to write his story.

I am blessed. (BIG sigh.)

The list of thank yous for this book is long, so bear with me, yeah?

I am thrilled to have worked with Eric Battershell, Stefan Northfield, and Debera Kuntz on this cover. I met Eric two years ago, and his smiling approach was so sweetly kind he made quite the impression. Fast forward to spring of 2016 when I was searching for the right model to portray Bones. I had spent hours looking at portfolios from various photographers and models, found nearly a dozen guys who were not quite perfect, but backed away from licensing any of those. I needed this character to seem as powerful, larger than life, enigmatic, and awe inspiring as he was in my mind.

I did find a model who was perfect, but due to distance, scheduling, or other commitments, not an option. That was until I saw a post from Eric that my perfect guy, Stefan, was making a whirlwind trip from his home in the UK to work a photo shoot in Ohio. Several fast-flying messages and a few hours later, they captured my vision. The result speaks for itself, and is the artistry you see on the cover. Working with Debera Kuntz on the cover design is always amazing, because she is unbelievably talented. We toss ideas around until something gels, and what comes back to me is magic. Thank you all!

My editor, Becky Johnson, is one of the most patient people I know, and I appreciate her willingness to put up with my insecure demands for updates. She and the gals at Hot Tree Editing have done Bones proud, and I thank you.

I have the most talented of critique partners in my diverse crew. MirandaPanda, Kori, Megan, Jamey, and Kelsi: Thank you for not being afraid of calling me on my bullshit. Y'all rock.

The men and women of the RWMC have developed a very loyal following, and that fact is both thrilling and terrifying all in the same breath. For the readers and fans of the series, I hope you enjoy reading this story about Bones and Ester half as much as I did writing it.

Beyond Raven, I had occasion to call on the expertise of a select group of men and women. My friends, the folks who roll twos, and chase the sun on the winding backroads of America. Y'all are amazing, and I appreciate the chance to get my knees in the breeze alongside you.

Shiny side, yeah? Muuwah! <3

Woofully yours,

~ML

What Came Before
1984, Chicago

Emilio Salvador de Villa Ramos was laughing when his world changed. From the moment that laughter died in his mouth, he remembered how it felt before things descended into madness. Before his life's path was altered. Before Estrella died. Before.

He was outside, two blocks from their apartment complex when he heard the noise. He was doing his duty, walking old lady Donella's terrier mix, waiting for the dog to take a shit so he could use the bag to pick it up and drop it into the dumpster behind the pharmacy. He did this twice a day, and every day he thought the same thing: how insane it was the dog ate enough to shit twice a day when old lady Donella was thin as a rail. Every day he wondered how he could talk her into buying more food for herself, less for the dog. Even Sal didn't crap twice a day.

Tomorrow's my birthday, he thought, tilting his head to one side, shoulder lifting slightly. *Maybe she'll eat more for my birthday.* He laughed aloud at the thought because twelve wasn't a special age, no parties for him, which meant no extra meal to tempt the old lady.

This meant his laughing focus was on the dog at the end of the cheap, dyed-leather lead, watching so he didn't trip over the dog when it

1

hunched up to crap. He saw when the dog's head came up, twisting over its own back like an owl, looking back in the direction they had come from.

That was when he heard it, a series of pops, which could have been a car backfiring. Could have been a door slapping into place, again and again, pushed around by the steady, hard wind off the lake. Could have been a dozen things, but he knew it wasn't. Those pops, he knew what they were. Gunfire. Gunfire echoing down the streets, off the corralling building walls, directed and deflected until there was no way he could be certain of the location. Except, in that instant, he absolutely was. He knew in his gut where they came from. Back by the apartments.

The dog barked once uncertainly, then slowly untwisted itself as it turned to line up with its head, ears slicked back, flush with its skull, caution written in every line of its body, still looking back the way they came. Another noise came, thin and wailing on the air, snaking its way to his ears, bending around the corners of the businesses and houses. Sal uncoiled his own body, turning to face the sound that battered at him. There was no way he could recognize the noise as anything other than pure sound, but somehow he knew. And, he knew he was right.

"Mama," he muttered, forcing his legs to move, lengthening his stride until he was running. The dog bounding alongside him, distracted from the noise, curious at this new locomotion Sal demonstrated. They always walked sedately, Sal considerate of the dog's age, so this, this running, was entirely new to their walking partnership. Bounding and bouncing, the dog bumped against his calf, nearly knocking Sal over, then the dog's head came up again, ears back, and suddenly the dog wasn't running with him, but sprinting ahead, barking as it ran up against the end of the lead, choking sounds pouring from its mouth.

As he ran, listening to the noises from the dog, the sounds still rolling through the air, the punctuating *pop, pop, pop* one last time, Sal did something he hadn't done in...ever. He prayed. *"Dios. Dios, por favor deje que nada malo suceda.* Please, let nothing bad happen. *Please,* God."

He glanced up, seeing most of the sky was still cloud-covered, as it had been for days, winter threatening to come on them in force, keeping any sunshine at bay during the day, deepening midnight so it was thick with shadows. Now it was early evening, nearly night. The clouds broke for a moment, thinning and then opening, exposing the silver shining moon, half-full and dim, brightening as the clouds separated and moved, the moonlight turning the thin clouds brilliant white and silver. Feet slapping on the sidewalk, he ran into the growing noise, knowing it for what it was now, the wailing pain of a woman. His mother.

Crying, screaming at God to take it back, threatening God with her hatred, her howling agony was on the wind. It crippled him, causing his legs to move more slowly with every step. The whole time, the dog still fought at the end of the lead to get home, to get back to its master, back to old lady Donella. Choking itself with every leap, the dog fell back to the sidewalk, each bound shorter and shorter as Sal slowed, holding back, keeping the dog with him.

His mother's screamed words were unintelligible but filled with such pain it took his breath. Urgency boiled in his blood, and his belly cramped with fear. Stride lengthening again, speeding up once more, he took a single step for each long sidewalk rectangle, eyes still on the sky, watching the moonlight turn the clouds brighter and brighter. That circle around the half-circle of the moon was like a spotlight above him, highlighting the dog lunging at the end of the leash, pulling him forwards and taking him into the sound splintering the air around them.

Rounding the last corner, still running flat out, he took in the scene at a glance, seeing the crumpled piles of fabric in the bleak courtyard. The space more cement than ground and grass, more dirt and trash than a happy place to play, but it was where Estrella and her friends spent their time. Even in the chill of winter you could find them there, because having the sky overhead was infinitely better than being cooped up inside the too-small apartments. Walled boxes that always smelled like someone else's cooking, smelled like a mélange of dishes, none of them complementary to the other. Sounds traveled between the units, too, ricocheting down the hallways and stairwells, arguments or fights, making up, or worse.

Four men stood between the street and the onlookers, the women of the apartment unit holding and supporting his mother. Without their hands on her, he knew she would have fallen to her knees, opened hands beseeching the heavens before fisting and shaking in her anger. "Mama," Sal cried, and every head turned to look at him.

"Get down," one of the men shouted, but he didn't understand the words, couldn't comprehend what the man needed him to do. The dog still pulled hard at the leash, choked yaps now sounding hoarser than anything he'd ever heard, like the dog had been strangled for days, dangling at the end of a rope like a piñata. So near the apartments now, Sal gave a quiet cry when the leather slipped from between his suddenly numb fingers. The little dog tore away, body gathering into itself with each leap, then stretching and elongating as it soared, then landed and gathered, then soared again. Finally free.

Pop. Pop.

Pop.

The first gunshot took Sal's legs from under him, and he fell face first into the small strip of bare ground running parallel to the sidewalk splitting the space.

Eyes open as he plowed the dirt with his hands out to break his fall, he saw the second gunshot without knowing what it was. A blinding white mark appeared in the cement just ahead of him, instant newness in a four-inch strip of otherwise dingy and stained sidewalk.

He tasted the rancid, oil-filled dirt in his mouth, covering his tongue with dryness. Until that moment, he never realized dryness had a taste, but it was rotten and foul. Unmistakable. Unforgettable. Then the dry went away, and it was wet and metallic tasting, flooding his mouth and flowing over his lips.

The last gunshot went wildly astray, off and up into the apartments. From his own experience, Sal knew the residents would be cowering in the back rooms, flattened to the floor, praying silently for the trouble to pass. Much as people around the world had done for centuries, they'd be begging their gods to take the suffering from them, to allow them to breathe another day, to let this trouble, this thing happening right now, in the present, to let it slip past without a mark.

Sal wondered for a moment if the gunfire had taken his hearing, if the loudness of the gunshots had deafened him because it was silent, eerily so. No running footfalls to check on the fallen. No panting and barking dog. No shouts of anger and grief.

Then he coughed, and there was a thick liquid in the noise he made. He groaned at a tearing pain in his side, and in a rush, it all fell back in on him. The dog whimpered, sounding pained, and Sal turned his head to see the old dog belly-down in the dirt not far from him, head on its paws, lying next to one of the piles of fabric with too-thin old-lady stick legs poking out from under it, the apron unmistakable on the unmoving body. Old lady Donella.

"*Mi hijo.*" He heard his mother's cry just before hard, strong hands hit his back, gripping his thin shirt to lift his torso. The grip adjusted and Sal heard a ripping noise, felt a chill from the air as the fabric of his shirt tore along the shoulder seam, then the hands dragged him roughly across the surface of the sidewalk and behind the short cement block wall. "My son."

Gentle hands, no less hard than the previous ones, but their touch was so different they could belong to no one other than his mother. They turned him, lifted his head, neck bent at a painful angle, and Sal coughed again, pain battering at his hold on consciousness, it felt as if his insides were ripping apart. "My baby."

Gaze directed down his own body, Sal saw a brilliant red staining the front of his shirt, and noted with astonishment the complexity of the patterns the courtyard dirt made in the wet where they stuck, looking like the incomplete layout of a maze. Anyone walking on that path would be doomed to failure, wandering forever because there were no exits. A design on his body, lines drawn in blood, shapes and forms swirling through his mind in response.

Beautiful. Stark and terrifying all at once.

Wailing ripped through the air again, inhuman and harsh, precisely delivered outputs of sound. Bouncing against the walls of the buildings surrounding the courtyard, the siren's Doppler Effect confused distance, and direction, volume set to intimidate and stupefy. Reflections of alternating red and blue lights rippled across the curtains blowing out of the now-opened windows as residents leaned out to see the aftermath of the events. Red and blue faded to black in the corners, absorbed into the shadows lining the courtyard.

"Ma'am, we need you to step back. Let us see to the boy," an unknown male voice said, his accent so different from the people Sal lived around as to be from another world entirely. His clipped consonants enunciated in a way that Sal knew the speaker was not his people. Speech patterns provided dividing lines and this was the first time he had realized those lines could be moved.

His view shifted, and Sal lost the beauty of the marks, but his mind held the shape tight, impressing it on his memory in a way he hoped to God that he would never lose it. Staring up at the sky, he saw the clouds begin to close in, now streaming across the face of the moon, dimming, and reducing the glitter and gilt of the moonlight. He blinked, darkness sliding down, down, down, deepening, snagged hooks pulling him deeper. His lids were reluctant to open again, but he forced them up. The clouds were thicker now, the opening less distinct, crowded and frayed.

His eyelids sagged closed again, and he felt hands on his body, was lifted and moved, placed on a firm surface, with hands on his shoulders and ankles holding him in place. The cold fabric underneath his back caused an immediate shiver to sweep through him. His muscles jerked and shuddered uncontrollably, the pain of movement overwhelming. Cold. So cold. A cold more bitter than even the wildest storm sweeping off the lake in February.

More movement jostled him, taking Sal along with it and he fought to open his eyes again, barely parting the lids a scarce sliver before he gave up, catching a brief glimpse of the cloud-covered sky, dim light framed by the bars of his eyelashes before they closed again. Darkness swirled and sucked him down even as they got closer to one of the unrelenting sirens, the wail louder and louder until he thought it might split the skin from his bones.

Everything around him began to fade away. All sound muting, the light behind his lids fading, even the air around him seeming to die down, warming, growing softer. The surface underneath him shifted, tilted as those impossible hands held him tightly at his shoulders and ankles, pressed him down firmly. Radio noises fled through the air, making him think of a television cop show: muted hisses and crackles followed by words and phrases, call signs and names. Oscar, alpha, beta. Salvador, Estrella.

He felt the cold press of metal moving up and across his body, and then at the waistband of his pants, down the sides of his legs. An exposed feeling was followed by a bone-deep chill. Then, and then—*Dios, how good*—warmth enveloped him, wrapped him from the waist down in a heat that began to fight back the cold, calm his jerking muscles.

Voices came at him from all sides, talking, saying things he could not understand. The pain in his chest swelled and then receded, his arms going cold at his sides. Motion jarred him, an undulating shift as the fabric of the sheet slid across the flat pad on which he lay. The sound of movement beside him, then he felt the clasp of a hand, hot and hard on his. *Mama*, he thought. He tried to say but his mouth would not cooperate, and he did not know why. Then, he did not know anything for a very long time.

Life in transition

2011

Sal raised his head and scanned the inside of the bar, searching for pockets of discontent which could so easily become trouble. He'd gotten good at sussing it out over the years. With a shake of his head, he thought, *Decades of practice.* After nearly forty years on earth, these past few months had pushed him harder than ever before to make difficult, instant judgments, so many of which had lasting consequences for those around him.

In the years since leaving the barrio behind, Sal had found himself in need of this skill more often than he wanted. Growing up as he did, not even realizing how dangerous the streets were—not until he'd died— he'd tried to learn everything anyone had to teach him. A skinny boy, like smoke, able to slip in and out of parties and stores without being noticed, he'd traded in information. As the son of who he was, ridicule had followed him, people thinking they knew who he was just by laying eyes on him. Back then, he'd been easily turned away, nothing more than a child seeking information about his sister's killers, always coming up empty handed.

Street gangs had not interested him, and his own father's path of dealing drugs was not one he'd allowed his feet to follow. Remembered terror of the giant guns tucked into loosened fabric on the backs of chairs and couches, lying beside plastic-wrapped bricks of cocaine and heroin, while children played on the rug in front was a deterrent. It was not for him, that life of keeping watch over your shoulder, peering out the door, seeking to see who was watching, who else was looking too close. Sal's exit from his father's world had been paid in blood long ago, blood and death, with only one resurrection. As soon as he'd managed it, Sal had turned his back on that part of his family and never looked back.

It was as if he'd lived three lives so far. From the iron-barred apartments of his childhood, he had moved west, into a suburb, seeing a lucrative trade in supporting the local don. Each transaction involving bags of money handed over to the contact, meaning Sal would receive a folder in return. The entire process a simple, easy transfer, in-and-out, tucking the goods inside his jacket as he exited. Walking out each door with scant information, still he knew there would be lives cut short by marks on flat paper.

That second life had never been a long-term solution, and even before he'd reached legal age, he'd known it, staying only for the money to be had in convincing people to turn a blind eye on discrepancies. Staying for the flash and cash, the cars and women, the prestige of being who he was, and working for the don. It had been good for a time, and he'd been excellent at his job.

Sal looked around the bar again, comparing, liking where he was now so much more than twenty years ago. Where he was now, this third life he currently lived, was something he'd stumbled into, quite literally.

Out on the town clubbing, ready to call it a night, he shoved past the bouncer and stumbled, rebounding off the flat surface of the door as it unexpectedly slammed into the rear tire of a motorcycle parked on the sidewalk.

Rolling his eyes, he moved to step around it, caught the toe of his loafer on the kickstand and was in the process of falling on his ass when a hand grabbed his arm. Lifted back to his feet, he turned to find the largest man he had ever seen standing beside him. "Thanks," he offered, ducking his head, feeling his aloneness acutely yet not wanting to be recognized if this man had a beef with his employer.

"You needa bike." Gruff and deep, the man spat the words as if they were distasteful. "Got it on good authority. This is for you." Sal looked at the black and chrome monster, easily weighing more than six times his own weight.

"Thank you, but I have a car." Sal jerked his thumb over his shoulder to where he had parked his upscale sedan.

"Not anymore, you don't." With that, the man tossed a jangling clump of keys Sal's way and turned on his heel, walking into the darkness before Sal had even caught them.

"What the hell?" Sal asked the air, twisting to see an empty space where his car had been parked only an hour before. He looked down at the keys in his hand, then up at the bike, thinking furiously. Phone in hand, he dialed to find the number used to report in for work was disconnected. He knew how this worked, had been the one delivering the news more than once, and it only took him a moment to accept the inevitable. As easily as that, he was cut out of everything he'd known for the past handful of years. Keys in hand, Sal turned to look at the machine parked on the sidewalk in front of the club.

With a series of jerks and starts, stalls and frequent wild careening from side-to-side on the road, he managed to ride the motorcycle back to his apartment. Opening the door, he found a note slipped under in his absence, advising he look for new accommodations immediately. Right next to it was the title for the motorcycle. Well and truly done.

Over the next week, his skills on the motorcycle had increased, and his search for a solution on the job front bore quick fruit. A local motorcycle sales and repair shop was looking for a repo guy who would be unafraid to face down the kind of men who purchased bikes. *Right up my alley*, he remembered thinking. The third repo job assigned to him was for a bike belonging to the president of the Skeptics.

Skeptics were a Chicago-based motorcycle gang. He didn't know it then, but the fact they were in their second generation of members indicated they were well established, which meant they had contacts in all kinds of places. Sal had only done cursory digging into the gang, believing they didn't factor in the recovery of the bike with past due payments.

Black Jack was Bones' first introduction to the world of real outlaws. He hadn't recovered the bike on that trip; in fact, he had taken an ass kicking which had left him bruised and hobbling for more than a week. His second attempt was only slightly more successful, as he'd at least started the motor before a trio of Skeptics members caught sight of him. The third attempt was now legend.

Sal pressed his back against the outside wall of the Skeptics clubhouse, listening to the voices floating out the window over his head. "Asshole thinks he can just come in and take a man's bike." That voice belonged to Jack Crandell, the man in charge of this particular gang of criminals. If he were here, it nearly guaranteed the bike would be. Sal grinned and settled in to wait. If tonight followed the usual schedule, every man in the building would be totally soused by midnight. That would leave his way open to repo the bike. "Asshole thinks wrong." Sal scoffed, keeping the sound quiet because he knew he was the asshole this asshole was talking about.

"Think he knows we can see him?" A different voice, raspy with years of smoking, asked a question that flooded Sal's veins with adrenaline. "Fuck, Jack, he's a ballsy one. Got some stones."

Jack's voice was nearer the window when he responded. "Stones aplenty. Bastard can take a hella beating, too. It'd be nice if he were interested in having men at his back. Too bad—"

A hand gripped Sal's neck, and he felt the painful press of a gun's muzzle into the ribs underneath his arm. The window above his head was flung wide, and twisting his neck, Sal looked up to see Jack's face poking out as he finished his sentence, "—he don't have no interest. We'd be willing to entertain the idea."

Glaring up, Sal took an inventory of his position, the murmurs on either side telling him more men had approached. "You would have room for a man like me?"

"What does a man like you need?" Jack waited, hanging half out of the window, elbows propped on the sill, staring down.

"A purpose."

Jack grinned and laughed aloud. "Life's a crap shoot. You don't get handed a purpose, you gotta find it in yourself."

Sal reached into the front pocket of his jeans, pulling his hand out slowly, trying to be nonthreatening. He balanced a pair of dice on his palm and stared up into Jack's face. "Then let us roll the bones."

That was what the legend had grown to say. The real story had significantly more fists and less witty repartee. That first interaction still brought him to today, in a place where he was the current president of the club. A few years ago he'd reluctantly taken over from Black Jack, a highly intelligent man who had first been an enemy, then a friend, finally a brother and mentor. And the rest, as they say, was history.

A history rich in blood, betrayal, and bullets. Bones looked down at his inked arms resting on the table. Pierced by a thousand needles, he wore his life on his skin. The path from Salvador Ramos to Bones, writ for anyone who cared to read. There were a few strategically placed voids remaining on his body. One an area so sensitive Bones didn't know if he would ever seek ink there, since the thought of having his dick tattooed made him grimace. Others reserved for either the right moment, or the right person.

Fortunately, right now, there were no issues to be sorted, no challenges to his world. He sat comfortably bounded on all sides by men who trusted him. In chairs at the table on either side were men he called brother, men he believed in, and who gave that back to him in a thousand ways. He felt one side of his mouth tip up as he listened to a story Shades was telling. He and Shades went way back; they'd become brothers in the barrio, and followed that path to here. Sal had been breaking bread with this man for decades, helped carry the man's mama to rest, a place of honor to stand among the six selected to bear the casket.

When Black Jack had tapped Bones as his successor, Bones had, in turn, tapped Shades to come into the club as his second.

We have been through much together, he thought, tuning back into the conversation when asked a question. "Bones," Shades said, calling Sal's road name, "What do you make of this new club out by Joliet? Diamante."

Bones shook his head, glancing around the table to see all eyes on him. "I think placement is prophetic, putting their clubhouse within sight of the prison there." Laughter from all sides, and after it died away, he finished, "Flash in the pan. They will implode at the first sign of a real test. No *cajones*, those ones. Got no stones."

***

Tipping his chin down, Bones eyed the look of concentration the whore wore. Face buried in his crotch, cock deep in her mouth, her tongue roughly caressed the throbbing length of him. Pulling back momentarily for breath, she immediately bent to her task again and forced him down her throat, fingers curling into the blankets on either side of his legs.

Her eyes rolled, and she looked up at him, lips locked around his shaft, hair shifting and moving with her bobbing action. Hot and wet, lots of suction, as she'd been instructed. He knew she was hoping for a warm place to sleep tonight, and he would hand her off to Shades when she'd gotten him off, knowing his brother wouldn't turn her away. Bones didn't share his bed.

Urgency rose, and he told her, "Deep again, suck hard." If she could be taught, he would use her another night, and she could possibly earn a place into the club's stable. Contrary to his orders, she pulled him shallow, tonguing the knob of his cock playfully.

Without warning, he gripped the knot of hair at the back of her head and shoved himself into her throat again, then with a growl, ripped her off when he felt the threat of teeth scrape his cock. He used that hold to set her away from him, leaning over and pushing his face into hers. "You think to fuck around with me like this? Not smart, bitch."

"I'm sorry. Sorry. I didn't mean to." Slobbering, she panicked and twisted in his grip, apologizing and reaching out to try and get her fingers around his cock. "I can do what you want. Let me do it. I want to do it. I'm sorry."

"Using your teeth on me was not smart." Bones released her, spreading his knees wider, making a come-here motion with his hands before resting them in fists on either thigh. He hated the look of fear she offered. *This one will not be a repeat*, he thought, keeping his eyes on her as she swallowed his cock again. Deep and hard, as ordered. He closed his eyes, letting biology take over, wanting nothing more than to have this encounter over with.

Ester

A drumming noise came from deeper in the alleyway than I cared to go. Echoing, metallic in nature, I found myself listening more intently. Were those feet pounding for freedom, trapped inside a metal box, a body discarded but brought back to life, unexpected imprisonment something to be railed against? A hand, perhaps, the heel striking an urgent percussive accompaniment to something only the owner could hear? Footsteps shifting, paper and other garbage shoved aside to find a more stable surface upon which to stand, that noise came from beyond the last in a line of four dumpsters.

The first had been my destination because it was Wednesday, the night the grocer discarded overripe fruits and crusty bread from the display case kept on the front walk. A case rolled inside through the just-wide-enough door at night. Normally on a Wednesday I would be able to saunter the thirty paces, carefully counted so I could retrace them quickly, to the dumpster and shift it out from the building slightly. Barely enough to turn the caster wheel, creating a space of about eight inches. Two spans of my palms.

I looked down, palms up, considering. Perhaps six inches.

The drumming noise came again, and I heard a grunt. Not a pained grunt, not something caused by having a knife stuck in your gut. I'd heard that before. This wasn't that. It wasn't a dying grunt, not one expelled without conscious effort as a body lay motionless on the ground. I'd heard that, too. This was a staccato grunt, a series of sounds, stuttering together to nearly be inseparable from each other, like children on a playground with arms linked, fending off an assault of Red Rover. This was the sound of a man expelling his seed, noises pumping out of him as the white fluid pumped from his member.

That drumming, though, had no place when associated with that sound.

I'd heard those grunts many times, so many times it didn't bear counting because the weight of the number would surely pound me into the ground. Near or far, you never unheard that sound. Not when you were a girl, unprotected, intended to be cherished but instead found yourself facedown on the baseline that stretched from third to home. Not a home that was safe, even if that was what the black-attired men said when the players made it to touch the blemishless white bag with the barest graze of their toes. *SAFE*, they shouted, but I hadn't been safe, not at all.

The grunting stopped, and I leaned against the brick wall, feeling the grit of the decaying mortar rub my cheek raw. Not as raw as I'd been once, but it hadn't been from grit or grime or anything other than the staccato movements of the gang of boys I didn't see in time. I didn't see them because my eyes were fixed on the toes of my just-bought shoes, scuff-free, unblemished. New. With shouts and shrieks, they'd boiled out of the framed-in depression just off the baseline, the place where they'd been dug in, building up their ideas and their courage in ways that caused them to cover me like lava from an island mountain. Covered and changed, scarring and leaving blackened waste in their wake.

That drumming, though, as much as it didn't fit here in my head with what else I'd heard, had stopped.

More shuffling feet, moving, shambling back and forth, then another sound, the exhaled rasping, coughing breath of repugnance. I knew this sound but had never heard it quite like this. Raw and fresh. I'd heard it from behind closed doors where the white coated people stood and discussed what should happen with me, where I'd stood with the woman who carried a satchel with her. I'd seen her before, standing at the table on the trapped side of the handrail in the big room where the women cried, and the children cried, and the man with the black dress was bored. I'd seen her at the house where the man and woman stood, eyes fixed on me in a dare to tell about what their blood child had done. A hard sound of repugnance, ripe with rebuke there on the sidewalk as she took my bag and carried me to the car.

Coughing and ripping sounds, then a voice, "You promised a twenty." Soft and slow, weak with illness or fear, a woman's voice. Not a child, now, but she held the child she had been inside her still.

"You get what I give you." Grunted again, but this not smoothly, this was a dangerous grunt and one which reminded me of where I was and what I needed to do. At that moment, I elected to remove myself from the situation. Those words given to me by a case worker who offered advice she didn't expect me to take. I'd been eight then and unlearned, but I remembered and held those words to me for a long time. Nearly two years before I embraced her counsel, words I'd come to live by and words that always worked.

Retreat, shouted my feet, and I agreed, but before we could make good on this new decision, movement in the alley startled me. A woman, half again as tall as me, darted out of the shadows and up the alley, something clutched in her hand. Her throat was a mass of red marks, deep weals wrought into her flesh, dark bruising with white between and half-moon blood-filled craters on one side.

"Hey." The guttural shout startled me, and I looked past her to see a man. A giant of a man. He dwarfed the woman in height, breadth, and sheer size. Trundling out of the shadows, his measured movements were in stark contrast to her darting dance of evasion, her shoulder a finger's-width ahead of his grasping hand. "Hey," he shouted again, and I recognized the dangerous anger in his voice.

Anger I knew very well, and tried to stay away from as best I could. For nearly thirteen years I'd been reasonably successful, but there he was. His anger bubbled over, eyes fixed on me and not the woman who had now turned the corner and was away up the street. I stared at him coming towards me knowing he was an inescapable force. Even if I tried to move, his anger would draw me in, closer and closer, like a dark star I'd seen a movie about in the planetarium where they offered heat on a cold winter day, and people threw away half-eaten hot dogs and candy bars when the show was over. Sometimes taking pain was the only way to avoid it.

Then "Hey" came from behind me, and the man pulled up short, blood-crusted nails so near my face I could make out the splits in the tips, see where the cuticle had been scuffed back. The circumference of his fingers matched the fat, red weals on the woman's neck, and I knew his was the hand had been wrapped around and choking. I tore my gaze away from his hand and glanced down, sagging pants buttoned but not zipped, plaid fabric sticking out of the opened enclosure like a flag telling everyone who cared to look that something had escaped recently.

"Do not touch her." Words came again from behind me, and I saw the man move, watched his knees bend as he prepared to jump, forwards or back I could not say, would not say, should not say, then the voice said, "You will make me a happy man if you pursue that thought."

I wasn't sure if the voice was talking to me, but if this was how it sounded when happy, I surely didn't want to make it unhappy, so I followed the thought I'd had about the man, and told it so. "I can't say if he's going to jump on me or over me, but he is definitely about to move."

A laugh, the voice closer than before. It was a man's voice, but not frightening. The sounds were as crisp as if we stood in Lincoln Park at 5:00 a.m. with only the joggers' footfalls to hear us talking, where you can nearly hear the trees growing at the height of spring when the leaves are unfurling from the branches, and he said, "He is about to move, little one, but his direction should be away, if he wants to remain healthy."

"Most people want to be healthy, but they are afraid of what it takes to get there, or stay there. Watch at the gym sometime and see which are the ones who look inside the windows longingly, because they want to be back there, or if they stare at their shoes and hurry past, because they fear who they could become."

I hadn't said so many words together in a long time, and I thought I should share that, too. "You make me want to talk."

"This is good, little one, because I like to hear your thoughts. You should not keep them bottled up. Let it out. Let the world hear you." The man in front of me lowered his hand, and I lifted my eyes to look into his face, impressing his features into my memory. Avoidance required knowledge, after all.

"Bones," the hulking man said, and that didn't make any sense because while I was thin, I was far from boney. I'd seen bones and skeletons inside the museums, and I had far more flesh than they did. "Don't want no trouble, man."

"Do not make trouble, then, Charlie. Walk away."

"Bitch took my wallet."

Something flew past my head, and I flinched to the side so hard I landed against the wall, expelling a huff of air that wasn't a groan, but a grunt, but not like the ones from before. The big man fumbled with what I saw was a wallet, cursing as it landed at his feet, spilling the contents to the dirty pavement of the alley. I was near the dumpster so decided no time like the present. Putting my shoulder to the metal, I pushed. An inch, another inch, and then a hand appeared in front of me and gripped, pulling the metal box so effortlessly that I stumbled forwards. I didn't fall because another hand gripped my upper arm, holding me upright. Restraining but *not* restraining, I was merely suspended between falling and standing until I got my toes back underneath me again. Without looking up, I jerked away, the grip falling to leave a chill behind on my arm, and then I had the bag in my hands. The grocer always put a bag out for me, and that was why I happened to be there at this exact time on a Wednesday. I decided to tell him that, too. "This was all I was here for. I can go now."

"Where will you go, little one?"

Heavy footfalls moving away, down the alley and towards the street marked the departure of the grunting man.

Boots underneath dark jeans were planted on the pavement right in front of me. I clutched my bag tighter because he had somehow moved closer without me knowing. Not the grunting man, but the quiet man with the musical voice, an accent dancing along the edges of words like the flags fluttering over the hotels on the Magnificent Mile. Flipping noises this way and that, so they came at you from unexpected directions, the sounds beautiful in their randomness.

"I go where I want."

"But where do you want to go now? I can give you a ride, *preciosa*." Rolling vowels and consonants made up the same words other people said, but when he let them free of his mouth, they forced me to shiver.

I saw slim hips topped by a metal belt, entirely made up of links of chain. It had to be heavy, but he bore the burden without complaint. A wide chest with broad shoulders, elbows to the side with his fists planted on those hips.

I stared.

Every exposed inch of skin told a story. I could see the flow of some of them, like the glyphs at the Egyptian exhibit they'd thrown me out of because you weren't allowed to touch the things. I found my fingers clenching the bag fiercely, trying to deny myself the knowledge of what his skin would feel like with all those stories. Would it read like braille to my fingertips, a learned language of experiences he would be willing to share with me? Would it be grooved and stroked with music like a record, where only the finest of needles could decipher the surface? I found myself leaning towards him, as if the whorls of blackness were drawing me closer, whispering their secrets only for my ears.

My gaze lifted involuntarily, and I looked at his face. Something I'd trained myself not to do, something most people found uncomfortable, an action that could provoke the evil that lived inside so many of us.

That was when I knew him, knew why his name was Bones, knew everything I would ever need to know about him. All the things he kept locked inside a room hidden in his head and didn't let anyone see. Everything I needed to know was plain on his face, covered in ink to distract and dissuade people from looking too closely. Words and symbols and lines and pictures and color—and all of it so people wouldn't see him.

"I see you." I told him this straight out, not wanting any lies between us. "I see you, and I know you."

"What do you think you know, little one?" One corner of his mouth lifted into an easy grin, and I saw how the lines rearranged to tell me this wasn't comfortable for him, the idea of someone seeing him behind his disguise.

"I won't tell anyone." That promise was something I would keep until the day I died. He would never know how soul-deep it ran. "I promise." That too, I gave him straight out.

The grin fell away, and I saw him again. Bones. He was so beautiful it tore my heart in two, and I felt the fluttering clasp of it dancing through my chest, edges mending back into something different, a more whole heart than I'd ever known. I had no idea how long we stood there, staring at each other, but it was about an eon too short a span of time. His expression softened, and how such a softness could live on a man who needed to be hard astounded me. I reveled it was turned my way, loved how it felt to bask in sweet softness, knowing few had ever been granted that place. "I need to go."

"I know."

He narrowed one eye, tilting his head ever so slightly. "You do?"

"I do." My reassurance was quick and firm. I'd heard the motorcycles in the distance, and I knew from the symbols on his vest that he was out of place. I urged him with words and a nod, wanting him to be safe, but not knowing why. "You need to go."

The rumble transferred up my feet and into my legs, and I knew he felt it when he grimaced, and this expression screamed discomfort to me. "I fear I have left it too late."

I smiled, because I knew a secret about that alley he didn't know, and the thought of teaching this man something pleased me. Quoting one of my favorite movies, seen a dozen times one weekend at the dollar theater, I told him, "Come with me if you want to live." Holding out my hand, I waited as a look of surprise and then pleasure danced across his features, fear washing it away far too quickly when the rumbles started to die off, signaling the bike engines were being unengaged and then stopped. His painted hand lifted, fit itself to mine, palm to palm, and I pulled him deeper into the alley, towards the space where it turned back on itself into a tiny courtyard. A courtyard where a fire escape ladder was drilled and mounted and secured to the wall. Leading to the roof, only two stories up, easily scaled by me, even more easily for him.

I felt a hundred feet tall when he trusted me, felt rewarded by a thousand kings when he grinned his silent thanks at me, and then felt cherished beyond a million sunrises when he pushed me up the ladder ahead of him, marking my safety with his own body. Once on the rooftop, he paused, staring down at me. "I see you, too, little one." With such a gracious gift, he left, running swiftly across the rooftop and away.

My beauty

Bones rolled the bike to a slow stop, scanning the benches in the park. It was the third one he'd been to in the past hour, and with each approach, he had felt his pulse speed in anticipation. *There*, he thought, satisfaction and relief sweeping through him. She sat on a bench, head cocked to one side, listening to a boy tell her a story. Arms pumping, the boy seemed to be miming every aspect of the tale, from running while looking frantically over his shoulder, to leaping across an obstacle, finally collapsing back onto the bench with arms lifted in victory. The woman's own arms raised in shared jubilation, and Bones heard her laughter ringing through the air.

He had first met her months ago. A chance meeting which intrigued him so much, he felt compelled to seek her out again and again. That first time had been in a section of town belonging to neither Skeptics, nor Rebels, and his very presence there carried a certain danger if discovered. Alert to any oddness, the bolting exit of a woman from an alley with a man's wallet in her fist had caught Bones' attention.

One moment later she continued on her way sans wallet, and he'd walked into the alley to see what was transpiring—just in time to see a man lifting his hand to strike the whore in front of him. Bones thought surely the skinny woman must be a whore like the one who'd just escaped, finding out moments later he had been wrong. Reading wrong meaning into circumstances, he had judged as surely as every person on the street judged him. The knowledge had stung.

Defending her regardless, that defense had granted him far more than anticipated. Such had been his introduction to his nameless friend. Standing with a bag of spoiled fruit clutched to her chest, she had squeezed so tightly in her fright the peaches had left pink stains on her shirt. Bright eyes looking out from underneath a wild mass of hair, she had gifted him with a wide smile when she stretched out her hand, quoting a ridiculous movie. With her actions and words, she'd shown him she had mastered not only her environment, but also was a master at observation. She'd taken his measure in a glance, and not found him wanting. Something for which he was eternally grateful, because she somehow made his life richer.

Destitute, homeless, she was filled with a giving nature the likes of which he had never seen. He had watched one day as she took a loaf of bread given to her by a shopkeeper and divided it down so her portion was the least. Half given to a woman with a child, half of what remained to a legless veteran on the street corner, half of what remained to a dog that whined and twined around her legs, making her laugh, and half of the last piece went to the clutch of pigeons that landed at her feet the moment she took a seat on a bench, happy to stuff a single bite into her mouth, laughing again as the birds strutted and preened at the attention.

The boy stood, and she tilted her head up to look at him, then they simultaneously twisted their necks to look at a red-faced woman shouting, standing on the path. Bones watched as the boy shrugged, then ducked his chin to his neck at another shout. Embarrassed, it seemed. Seated, she shooed him away, releasing him from the niceties of society and the boy ran backwards a few feet, waving madly until both of her hands rose above her head, pivoting in a wild wave at the ends of her arms.

My beauty, Bones thought, checking traffic before he pulled back out, slowly increasing his speed, riding away from her and no longer caring when she had become his. She simply was.

I wanted to be saved

Ester

It wouldn't be until the fifth time I saw him that I told him my name, which took nearly a year. For someone who liked to keep his fingers on the pulse of things, he seemed reticent to learn me. Much later I found out it wasn't what I had thought, which was that I was rather less interesting than anything else he had to learn, but because I was *more*. If that made sense, and I didn't think it did, but what did I know? I was just me.

Time two had been in a tiny park behind a movie theater. I didn't expect to see him, hadn't yet conceived of a plan to find him. I had the desire to, but lacked the ability. Not that I couldn't find him if I wanted; that was preposterous. I could have recited the edges of his territory from memory based on the words and letters and symbol on his black vest. Chicago was strictly divided, and those divisions were defined by who owned which section of our city. In some cases, the city was owned by a family, and there were suits and cars, and trucks backed up to docks and men watching with guns hidden behind boards and barrels and lapels of those suits.

In some cases those divisions were more fluid, with lines which shifted nearly daily as they flowed back and forth between anger-driven surges of energy and effort, and a belief of *this* or *that* mattering more than *that* or *this*, but in the end, didn't it all matter? Didn't we all matter? But in their self-appointed positions of wisdom, they only saw the one-sided oppression and suppression, and repression and depression. Everything gave them freedom to feel validated because what they worked for and towards, any idiot could see the rightness of what they were fighting to change or defend or prevent or encourage. Their talking and conversations were bursts of static on a radio dial, and as they swung back and forth between the ends of reception, their message became more focused and loud, or weaker and scattered until nothing was left.

Parts of the city were separated by iconic divisions drawn by streets or train tracks, a river or bridge, and if you were from this side, you couldn't go to the other side without incurring the wrath of whoever was trying to keep you out, trying and wanting and needing to get over *there* could tear you apart. Iconic and ironic and because the very things that walled you in were what you fought so hard to say didn't matter, but they did matter because they'd been there forever and the weight of history made the pendulum hard to turn. So you fought and you railed, and you rallied and raised awareness for this cause or that cause, but the cause was inherent in the division which was immovable by nature. Laid in place so long ago people overlook the reasons.

Then there were the parts carved out by effort and strength, bound to the will of men who knew what they wanted and would fight and die to keep it, because it was simply who they were. Bones was one of those kinds of men, and the men he was friends with all felt the same. So, I knew where I could most easily find him, but I also knew those places would be where he was least himself. Where he was guarded, and painted onto the canvas he'd assigned himself. This meant I didn't want to go looking for him because I wouldn't find him, I would find Bones. And while that was his name, it wasn't who he *was*.

Who he was, was the man who had climbed the ladder behind me without making a single comment that would make me uncomfortable even if I were bare underneath my skirt. It wasn't something I thought about until much, much later, or I would have thanked him for not trying to reach, or touch, or penetrate even with his words, because it mattered a lot to me once I remembered.

Who he was, was the man who had smiled so freely at me before taking the escape offered. While I knew he was too powerful to have died at their hands, he would have hurt if those other men, who felt their territory had been dishonored, had found him. He had intruded into something precious according to them, sneaking in and the breach would never be healed without blood to pay for the desecration.

Defiled was a state of being for them. A constant they railed against. Not something which poured down your throat as those grunts came from above you and blood beaded on the back of your head. Hair torn away at the follicles in a swath but it grew back, thank God, it always grew back, covering the memories. The pain on your scalp faded, but you never forgot *that* feeling, of being shamed for all your life. Sullied, and corrupted.

So, the second time I saw him was a surprise for me but not him because he didn't see me.

I had left the building by the back door so I could escape the grasping, groping hand of the man who wouldn't watch the movie. I didn't miss anything. It was the fourth showing of the day and my third day in a row to go there, but the rain had finally cleared. The weather breaking outside meant I didn't have to stay inside, and so I didn't.

Bones had backed his motorcycle into a parking space meant for parallel positioning. While he wasn't positioned parallel to the curb, his motorcycle was entirely in the space, so I supposed it was nearly the same thing. Because if the lines were simply there to create divisions and boundaries for narrow-minded people and not to define the thing parked within them as a rectangle of this precise size or that specific orientation, then that was fine. Just like I wasn't defined by where I lived or what I wore. I was just me.

It would be like Bones being defined by the lines and divisions and boundaries on his skin, and *that* was so ludicrous I laughed aloud. Something I hadn't done in so long the sound itself frightened me. Before he could look to see where the hideous sound was coming from, I had left, turning the corner and walking away from Bones.

Away from where he was supposed to be, but still bound by the man he had made for others. Which meant he wasn't the him I wanted to see.

The third and fourth times were equally random, his placement within the city correlating for a few moments with mine as we crossed paths. Those came with words and smiles, and I tucked away the memories created with him. Letting my brain pull them out at night when cold wind battered at the sides of my place, allowing Bones to warm me from the inside out.

Then came meeting number five and seasons passed between so it was true chance and not design. Because if I had designed a meeting, it would have been very different and not included me tripping and falling in front of a bus. Wouldn't have required me being dragged out of the way of the unslowing vehicle. Unslowing because it would be easier for the driver to hit me and fill out one report than to crash the bus while avoiding me and fill out a dozen reports.

On my hands and knees, I froze as the huge metal box bore down on me, and while there weren't any scenes from my past that performed a parade for me, I could see how it might happen for people who had long moments in which they realized they are going to die so their brain tried impossibly hard to remind them how much they wanted to live and they needed to move in order for that to happen. But I didn't have anything to live for—no family, no friends, no pets, and no possessions which owned me. Patience Pilgrim's wisdom didn't apply at that moment because I would have given my next breath for anything to have mattered to me enough that it called me back from the brink.

Not that I'd fallen on purpose, not at all. This wasn't a seeking on my part, but an avoidance because I'd seen a group of men, boys really. I'd seen the way they worked hard to posture and pose, strutting for each other to make themselves older and stronger and meaner than they really were. I had learned long ago to avoid those encounters at all costs, but never thought the cost would be my life. Cut short by thugs and a twisted ankle in the middle of the street.

Then a voice I knew—would never forget, could gladly hear in my dreams for the rest of my life—and for the briefest of moments, I wondered if this voice was the sole thing my brain felt was worth living for, but then a hand grasped the waistband of my jeans and jerked me sideways. We slid between the bumpers of two parked cars as the bus plowed past. A plow without a blade, but it would still have scooped me up and tossed me aside like fallen snow. The shiny chrome on the car reflected the surface of the man behind me, the one who saved me not once but twice, and I didn't know then, but he would save me many more times, even times he didn't know he saved me, but he did. This was time number two, and I would take it and be grateful.

"Thank you." Gratitude offered, I expected his grip to loosen and leave, but it tightened instead.

"That was close. Too close, beauty," Bones murmured with fear in his voice and the next breath I took carried joy into my chest; it must have because my heart reacted violently, trying to leap from my throat.

"You saved me." Those words didn't seem like enough. I needed him to know I wanted to be saved and his efforts wouldn't be thrown away at the next opportunity. It was crucial he understand, because I'd seen how the firemen could be beaten down, helpless with the knowledge that the one they cut from the rafters in time today would be leaping from a bridge the next. Even if they knew the lifeless body fished from the river

32

would finally bear a peaceful expression, that helpless feeling would beat at them all their lives, so I wanted to spare Bones that. "I wanted to be saved."

His breath was faster now, and I didn't expect his next words to expose so much. I couldn't read his expression in the reflection, and when I tried to turn, his arm slipped around my waist, and I was anchored in time, in space, and definitely in place. "I wanted to save you."

No one had ever wanted anything with me.

My mother had left before I held any memories of her, erased so completely from our lives that my father never spoke of her. No pictures, no mementos, no tottering around in shoes I would one day long to fill. Mother's Day was a void in our world, a day sucked empty with angry silence and holes in the walls that were fixed before the next Sunday came with visitors who wanted to see how he was getting on with the little one. There weren't any Brother's Days, which was a shame, because I had memories of him.

My father had been the person those firemen saved. Each time meant I had to stay with strangers for no less than three days, sometimes more. One of my first real memories was of his feet kicking wildly in midair, toes tracing the edges of the upended chair, curling and stabbing and trying to pull it back into place. The back of the chair had smashed me to the floor as it tipped over, and my vision blurred with red that splashed onto the rug, and it scared me. Seeping liquid had darkened his socks and dripped to the floor. That smelly mess made before my screams called the neighbors.

Our neighbor had circled my father's hips with his arms, shouting for help and had stood there holding my father until the firemen came.

Picked up and placed against the wall by the neighbor's wife, I'd been told to stay out of the way, so I had. It was a fireman who'd seen me and shouted down the house in his anger because there I was, wanting to live, and there my father was, throwing it away.

I was six when he succeeded. I told Bones some of this, because it was a profound truth and part of who I was. "My second memory is of my father's attempted suicide. I want you to know I wanted to be saved."

His arms tightened, not painfully and not in a frightening way, just a better anchoring than before, and he told me a truth, too. "I saw you fall, beauty. I saw your face. I could not bear to see the world without you in it. It would be so bleak without your presence. You needed saving. So"— a squeeze, and I liked the squeeze nearly as much as I liked him calling me beauty—"I saved you."

I liked everything he'd called me, like beauty and little one, and *preciosa*, but he needed to know I had a name. I didn't require one loaned out by him, one that could be taken back at any time, returned like a book to the library, the idea of it in your hands and mind the only thing remaining. The shape of it defined by memories, subject to warping and changing with time. So, I told him mine, because then he had an always thing to call me, even if it had been nearly a year and a half of days since I'd last heard it spoken on the air. Four hundred and eighty-nine, but I wasn't counting, and today the count started over, anyway, and I liked the idea of that.

"I'm Ester." And that was what made meeting number five so memorable, because I had all of him and I knew it, from the very first time he'd gripped my hand I had him firmly fixed in my mind. And with those five letters, I fixed the idea of me there, too.

Things of value

Bones

Dios, he thought, head bent over her knee, dabbing gently at the bloody scrape with antiseptic. Listening for her hiss of pain, he leaned in, blowing a stream of air gently across the stinging flesh. His nameless beauty, nameless no more. *Ester*.

She sat on the edge of a picnic table, arms wrapped around her knee, pulling her leg tight to her chest. He was working on her injury through a fresh rip in her jeans, and from this angle, he could see another rip high on the inside of one thigh, fabric gaping to expose her bush, pretty pink pussy lips peeking out of the dark hair. *Dios*. His cock fattened, trying to uncoil in his jeans, pushing against the fabric. *Right here. She is right here.* He pushed down the feeling, needing to possess her more than anything he'd ever felt. *I cannot.*

With the rain, he had known better than to look for her in a park, seeking her instead at her favorite indoor activities, finding her by description at the third theater he'd checked. The manager had looked at Bones sympathetically, shaking his head as he commiserated, "I got a crazy sister, too. Good luck, man." Amused at the man's mistake, Bones had paused a moment to consider if his mystery woman had a family.

From her stories, disjointed as they could at times be, he didn't think so. It sounded like she had landed in the foster care system at a young age, and he was yet unclear if she had escaped by aging out of the system, or simply escaping.

As he had stood at the back of the theater, eyes slowly adjusting to the dimness inside the large area, a piercing brilliance had appeared from the exit door near the screen, and he had seen a small form slipping out. Something told him it was his beauty, and he had followed.

Thank God I did, he thought, remembering again the terror that gripped him when she had fallen to the street with a cry. She had crouched there, staring at the twenty tons of metal and captive flesh bearing down on her. He trembled to think if he'd been even a handful of seconds later. The memory of her voice told him she knew how close it had been, too. Even as distracted as she sounded, the sharing of her story impressed on him how much it mattered to her that he knew she had things worth living for. Himself counted among them, it seemed.

"There," he declared, leaning back slightly so he could look up into her face, "all done." As it had from the beginning, her unexpected beauty struck him hard. Her hair tangled into an impossible rat's nest, he still saw the gleaming health so at odds with her life and diet. Sable in color, she had twists of paper and twine braided into the sides. At times, she would catch the whole of it back into a single hank hanging down her back, but even then he had noted she would leave the bright bits in place. Her jaw was strong, too sturdy for traditional beauty, but that jaw supported the width of her lips, which, when stretched into a smile as they were now, carried a loveliness the like he had never seen. Her eyes were unique, a deep green at the outer edges of the iris, fading to a light blue along the inner border around her pupils. Set wide on her face, they were a match to the jaw, balancing perfectly in his opinion. One cheekbone was slightly lower than the other, a minuscule amount, but when paired with the crook of her nose, he knew these features shared a history of damage.

Why someone would hurt her, could have hurt her, and he knew this to be true from her stories, boggled the mind. "Does it yet hurt, beauty?"

As always happened when he used that word to refer to her, those eyes widened in pleased surprise. Without thinking, he lifted a hand to stroke her hair, pausing without completing the action when she flinched away, eyes closed tight in preparation for an expected blow. "Beauty, I would never harm you." *Dios, what her life must be like.*

Her bottom lip moved side to side, and he knew it was because she gnawed on the inside. She did this a lot when she thought she had displeased him. Eyes still clenched shut, she whispered, "I know."

The phone in his back pocket rang, and she moved then, clattering across the table and gaining her feet on the opposite side. He had seen this reaction before, but it startled him nonetheless. For someone who spent a significant amount of time in exhibitions, theaters, museums, and anywhere there were free classes or instructions to be had, she feared the technology of telephones and computers with a bone-deep terror.

"Wait," he called, knowing it was useless, and as always, by the time he had pulled the phone from his back pocket to silence it, she was already on her way. She limped on what must surely be a sprained ankle he hadn't noticed, too caught up in his glimpse of her hidden beauty to properly care for her. *Shit.* The call connected, and he spoke into the phone, "Yeah?" A moment later he ignored the caller when Ester turned and shouted at him, hands cupped around her mouth.

"Bones."

Head up, he watched her, knowing she didn't need a response from him to understand she held his full attention.

"We keep saving each other." Ill-tempered buzzing echoed from the phone, but he didn't care, pulling it away from the side of his head as he nodded at her. "That's a good thing, right?" He nodded again and she returned the gesture, her hands falling to her sides. Staring at her, his waif in too-large clothes, dirty and torn, so beautiful and at risk from every fool who thought to take her for themselves, Bones realized he was half in love with her. "I wanted to be saved," she reminded him, her words still audible without the megaphone of her hands. He nodded again, thinking to himself that he wanted to be the one to save her. She turned, and without looking back, limped down the block and turned the corner. Gone.

Lifting the phone again, he cut off the angry words with a single word. "Silence." Quiet for a moment, and he broke it with, "Begin again."

***

Bones stood, watching as the door of a dream closed on his friend. He and the Skeptics hadn't been invited but came anyway, and as was her generous nature, Mica Scott-Rupert hadn't turned them away from her wedding party. Mason stood to one side, facing away from the dancefloor where a beaming bride swayed in the embrace of her husband, Daniel Rupert. A woman Mason had wanted for himself, or so Bones had thought. He now regretted spewing those ideas and misgivings to their mutual friend, Watcher, vowing to devise a way to retract his words at the soonest opportunity, even if Mason never knew of them.

Another mutual friend walked across the room to stand at Bones' side, Slate. Andy Jones when Bones first met him, years ago, nearly fresh off the Wyoming prairie, Slate was a man Bones had worked to win for his Skeptics, losing out to the Rebels while still counting it a win because having another good brother for Mason meant more strength at both their backs.

"She's happy," Slate remarked, and Bones nodded. "Gonna miss this crew." That comment surprised Bones, and he must have revealed this without concern, feeling for once that he was surrounded by only friends, not having to guard his every thought. "You didn't know?" Slate laughed through his words, reached out to grip Bones' shoulder, fingers digging deep with an emotion he didn't understand.

"Since I do not know what I do not know, then I am compelled to say I do not know."

Slate smiled at this and nodded.

"True enough." A heavy sigh preceded the pronouncement, telling Bones that Slate didn't know for certain if he wanted this thing to happen, whatever it was. "I'm gonna be taking over Fort Wayne. Bingo needs to pull back, take care of personal business. I've found a muddied mess there, and we've been sorting shit out."

"I knew you were out of town, but had no idea there was trouble in the Fort for the Rebels." This didn't bode well, because it was a strong chapter for Mason. "The distance is not far. Are you expecting this business to consume all your time?"

"For a while, yeah. We had yellow in the club, had to cut deep to get it out. I've been dealing with all kinds of fallout, and...other shit." Avoidance was second nature to them all, and Bones did not take offense at Slate's reserve. "Headed back down in a couple hours. Just waitin' to see if Mica's little sister is okay."

"She is ill?" That was not good to hear, because Molly had been dealt a hard hand by life already, her life precariously pitched against the wall of happiness time and again. He liked the sweet girl, most recently working as a round-bellied pregnant waitress in the Rebel bar, Jackson's. "Is the babe all right?"

"Gonna be entering the world any minute now." Slate turned and pointed at a convoy of vehicles pulling out of the parking lot and grinned, and Bones found an answering happiness inside him and returned the expression.

"Good luck to be born on such an auspicious day," Bones murmured, turning back to see Mason still standing across the room from them. "You wouldn't know it to see his face," he gestured towards Mason with the point of his chin. "Angry enough to raze this tent."

"Not angry," Slate muttered. "Fuck me." He sighed. "He's more resigned."

Mason turned when Mica walked up beside him, her hand on his arm, and Bones and Slate watched as she pulled him to the dance floor, demanding his attention for the span of three minutes. After the dance, when Rupert reclaimed her, Mason turned and walked to them, his step lighter in a way Bones didn't quite understand. "Mason," he greeted his friend, "you will let me know how Molly fares, yes?"

"Fuck, yeah," Mason responded immediately, hand out for a wrist clasp. "Glad to see you found the place."

"I understand you are losing Slate." From the way Mason glanced around, Bones decided to curb his curiosity, understanding the reticence of discussing anything in an open venue. "Will you be traveling to Fort Wayne often?"

The expression on Mason's face changed, becoming sly. "Often enough to figure out what has the man drawn to that town. Thinkin' it's DeeDee's gal, but I'm not sure." Slate had stepped to the buffet table, and Bones turned in time to see him stare through a woman who was apparently making an approach. "You see that shit? Turnin' down pussy. Ain't like him, so I suspect there's a reason with a rack."

Bones snorted, nodding. "Are you going home or to your clubhouse tonight?"

"House, why?" Mason lifted an eyebrow, and Bones grinned.

"Thought I could come and chat. Share a bottle." He wouldn't come out and say it, but he really wanted to make sure Mason was okay with tonight. Losing Mica would do more than sting, even if it had been orchestrated by Mason himself.

"Not opposed. Roll in ten?" Bones nodded and turned, lifting a hand to Mica, who returned it with a quick wave of her fingers. She raised her arms again, slipping them around Rupert's neck, flowing with his movements as he swept her back to the dancefloor.

An hour later, a nearly-empty bottle of bourbon between them, Bones quizzed Mason. "Truly you want to shift your colors west? The Rebels are solidly set in the center of the nation, Mason. What gain is there to spreading yourself thin?"

"Yeah, I'm sure. The more we control, the better off every chapter is. Look." Mason pointed to a map pinned to the wall behind the bar. There were flags and pins in ten locations, each marked a Rebel Wayfarers chapter. "You see?"

"I see a network. As I have said, it's a robust network, Mason. You have locked down many key cities. Interstate and highway junctions, where traffic in and out is easily disguised. Why—" He leaned over, picking up the bottle and pouring into the two glasses sitting on the table. "—do you need more? Is that just gluttony?"

"Fuck, Bones. There's a need, man. Just leave it at that." Mason took the glass Bones had extended, sipping at the liquor. "Fuckin' leave it."

"What you do stands to disturb clubs. That turmoil will have an impact on me and mine. Of course, I am not going to leave it." Bones scoffed, taking his own measured drink. "Your Rebels are too big to do things on a whim."

"Not a whim, man. Wanna contain shit if I can. The only way to contain is to build borders." Bones squinted, looking between the man and the map, considering. Mason repeated his words with a firm nod. "Only way."

"Shooter is west." Bones knew this wasn't lost on Mason, but needed confirmation. "You want to launch into areas that butt up against Outriders territory?"

"Fuck, yeah. Pin him to the west coast. Control his motherfuckin' damage." Mason sipped from the glass cradled in one hand. "He's dangerous, but you know that."

"Better than most." Bones agreed.

Justice Morgan, Shooter's father, had run a chapter in Mason's home county in Kentucky for a long time, keeping the club's activities local, playing it smart and maintaining a low profile. Then, unfortunately for all involved, Morgan had been lost in an accident in Utah more than a decade ago, leaving Shooter as his sole heir to the expansive Outriders club.

The shared hatred of Mason's half-brother wasn't news to either of them. Bones had intervened many times over the years, defusing arguments and fights on both sides, but what Shooter had done recently was beyond the pale.

Shooter's members in Kentucky had gone into a local strip club and rampaged as if they were Vikings, raping and pillaging at will. The aftermath had shuddered throughout the entire motorcycle community, and more voices than just Bones and Mason were raised in dismay, not wanting any kind of attention turned their way from the authorities, but most certainly not that kind of attention.

Shooter had laughed it off, pointing to clubs of old, saying it was nothing more or less than had been done before. Truth, in some cases, but not for decades. There was a reason for biker rallies, those parties where citizens were discouraged from attendance, because the less those sheep knew the better, and rallies allowed men, and women, of like minds to gather and celebrate the life they chose to lead.

Not those working-class citizens. Women and men who had shown up to their jobs like any normal day, only to have their world turned upside down, pain and humiliation raining down on them without hope of rescue. Some of the stories Bones had heard told of the Cynthiana chapter's actions were so rancid they turned his stomach.

"His bullshit's dangerous. Dangerous to all of us. If I can keep him contained—" Mason shrugged, "—we all come out winners."

"I do not disagree. Should we engage other clubs?" With that word, the single "we," Bones told Mason his actions with the Rebels would have any active support from the Skeptics that he needed.

Blowing out a breath, Mason shook his head. "I got friends. Rebels have friendly relations with a dozen clubs who would benefit from this. So many ways it can go, brother." He lifted his glass and drained it. "We'll circle back around in a couple of weeks. See where we want to aim. Glad you're here, Bones. You'll stay the night."

"That was not a question," Bones noted, lifting his glass to where Mason offered the bottle, carefully lining up the weaving rim to catch the pouring liquid. "And is an astute observation."

"You and your bullshit way of talking." Mason lifted the bottle to his lips, taking a long pull. "Like you think people won't notice it keeps everyone at a distance. Yeah,"—he grinned—"it's a fuckin' astute observation. You're fuckin' wasted, brother." Reaching out, he tapped a finger against the side of the glass. "Drink up, you're among friends. Got your back, brother. Always safe here."

"I know." He locked gazes with Mason and nodded, getting a chin lift in return.

"Bed for me. Room at the top of the stairs for you, if you can get there." Setting the bottle beside his discarded glass, Mason heaved himself off the couch and stood, looking down at Bones. "Shiny side."

"Shiny side," Bones agreed, lifting and draining his glass. *I will sit here for a time*, he thought, stretching one leg out, easing the muscles in his back complaining of an old injury. A few minutes later, or it could have been hours, because in his ease at the company he kept, he had fallen asleep, Bones startled awake when a hand touched his belt.

Chin down, he looked at the woman who knelt between his knees, squinting to see her clearly. Still half asleep, all he could see was how the dark hair haloed her too-pale face. He blinked, surprised, thinking for a moment it was his Ester, then was disappointed as her features resolved. She was just one of the women who lived in this clubhouse, sheltered by the club, servicing members as they desired.

"What do you do, girl?" He was gracious with his declaration of her age; she had passed girlhood long ago, but it cost him nothing to be kind.

Her fingers rolled the hidden latch, unhooking the tines from the links of his chain belt. Eyes lifting to his, she smiled. "Wanna blow you."

"You desire this?" Unbidden, his cock stirred under her hands, and she felt it, palming the length of him, stroking him through the fabric of his jeans. Nails scratching lightly against the swelling head, she nodded. "Then enjoy yourself." He granted permission, placing his palms on the tops of his thighs, a threat or promise, because they were in close gripping proximity and she recognized this, glancing at them, then back up at him, her small smile slightly larger.

Less than a minute later, she had extracted him from his jeans, and set to her self-appointed task. She licked the length like a sweet, the tip of her talented tongue darting around the rim of his mushrooming head until she drew a groan from his throat. Her hand a vise, clamped around his shaft. She stroked quickly, focusing on the root with her fingers, her knuckles bumping his belly with each movement of her arm.

Taking him into her mouth, she kept his cock shallow and suckled hard, flicking the slit and drawing out droplets of hot liquid. He felt the tiny tremors that accompanied this with anticipation and clenched the muscles of his stomach, jerking his cock against the roof of her mouth to escape the sensation.

"Suck me," he hissed, and found she took direction well, hollowed cheeks marking her immediate response. "Yes," he rewarded her and groaned again. "Suck me hard. Feel me in your throat? Is that what you want?" Her head bobbed, and he took it as an invitation, threading both hands into her dark hair, feeling it dry and sticky with what he hoped was gel. Not wanting to lose the beginnings of pleasure to his imagination, he pulled and lunged up with his hips at the same time, feeling the chill of the metal belt hit his exposed hip. That contrasted with the heat of her mouth along his length, and he lunged again, pushing her head down, feeling her hands clutching at the muscles of his thighs.

Knowing her experienced, he waited until she gave two fluttering slaps before he released his hold, letting her draw him out, noting she didn't lose the knob from her mouth as she sucked air around his soaked cock, then she volunteered her throat again, shoving her mouth onto him, nose grinding the hair in his crotch before he even had a chance to repeat the motion.

He rewarded her again. "Good. Fuck, yes." Grunting, he thrust deep, feeling the muscles at the back of her throat clench around him. "Hot and wet, suck me." Two fluttering slaps again, and he released for a moment, hands tight in her hair. Not giving her more than a handful of breaths before he shoved her back down, pumping up and into her throat. An image of Ester's hair came to mind, and he looked down to see the raven locks of the club whore dancing across his hip. "Beauty." Eyes closed, he saw Ester's mouth, saw her chewing on the inside of her cheek, saw the sweep of wet left behind on her lip when her tongue trailed across.

With a groan and Ester's name on the tip of his tongue, he came, holding the whore in place, uncaring of her struggles until he finished shooting ribbon after ribbon of white heat down her throat. He let his hands fall away, hearing her pant for air as she rested her cheek on his thigh, exhausted from the ten minutes spent under his hands.

Afterward, he leaned his head against the cushions while she licked and cleaned him. "Very good, girl. Was there anything you wanted?" He wouldn't insult the Rebels by offering to pay her, but if she asked, he could reward her.

"Warm your bed?"

Tucking himself away, he shook his head as he refastened his belt. "I sleep alone. Aught else?"

"Whiskey?" she asked, and he knew her drinks were free here, so he raised an eyebrow. She smiled as she answered, "They don't keep good stuff here."

Arching up, he gently pushed her out of the way as he dug out his wallet. Two twenties tucked into her hand earned him a smile. "Should buy a bottle or two." She nodded. "I am headed to my bed. This is my reminder I sleep alone. Tell the others." He gestured towards the other club whores gathered with the Rebel members at the pool tables or bar. He handed her another twenty. "My gratitude."

"I'd a done you for free." She gave him that, and he took it as the compliment she intended, nodding.

"But I value your charms more than that." Bones rose from the couch, shoving his wallet back into his pocket. The unspoken words "you should too" were between them, and she moved away quickly, leaving him to make his way to the empty room upstairs.

***

Bones twisted his head, staring over his shoulder at the artist working on the back of his arm, checking her progress. "Silly," he called, a thought striking him. She tossed a glance up at him, then back to her work, that single look her response to urge him to complete whatever thought he interrupted her with. He laughed and obliged. "I have thought of a theme to tie the shoulder to my chest. You need to put on your cap of thinking."

"Thinkin' cap," she muttered, shifting so the angle of her thumb drew his skin taut for the needle, "got it. Tell me."

"Redemption."

The ever-present buzz of the tattoo gun stopped, and she lifted her head, staring into his eyes. "Say again?"

"Redemption. I've enough to anchor the idea." And he did. His shoulder was covered by a massive cobra, delineated in fiery reds and oranges. "Naja haji," he named the snake, "is grace and speed, and hidden wisdom. And draca"—he jerked his chin, indicating the dragon wings on his chest—"is passion. Hidden wisdom and a hunger for life can easily be drawn to wishing for a long life." *I wanted to be saved.* "Redemption will give one a good life, for as long as you are breathing." He twisted his head, staring at his shoulder. "Hidden wisdom is a blessing. Think on it."

"I'll do that," she said, and shifted, the buzzing returning as she tucked her chin, eyes to her work. "I'll think about it."

Change in progress

Bones

"Diamante." Bones spat the word like a curse, and surely that was what they had become. Thorns in his side no longer, they had driven a wedge deep into the Skeptics' territory, an insult he could not allow. So he had made the call to Mason. A man he counted as a friend, a man who was like a brother to him, for all they labored under different patches. Now Bones sat across a table from Shades, as they plotted the demise of a rival. Nodding at the closed door, Bones underscored the importance of discretion with a phrase. "Need to know." Shades lifted his chin, message received. He reached back and pulled a small box off a shelf, turning a knob on the front so it emitted a small hum. Provided by Mason's man, Myron, a tech genius, this was supposed to block any listening devices.

"Mason will do as I suggest," Bones started without preamble, knowing Shades would fill in any blanks needed, or ask if he couldn't. "By tomorrow, Dominos and Disciples will be no more. We will use the distraction to sweep Diamante up, everywhere they exist. And allow me to be clear, I want them to exist in Chicago no more."

"Isolated?" Shades grunted the word, and Bones felt his mouth stretch in a humorless smile.

"Southern Soldiers will be conducting the same maneuvers tomorrow. As will other clubs in Louisville and Birmingham. Chicago will have no one to call on for timely assistance. Isolated—" He paused, the slow smile spreading across his face pulling a mirrored expression from Shades. "—and dead."

"About fuckin' time," Shades muttered. "You got specifics for what we need to do, man?"

"I do." Bones sat and looked at Shades, then sighed. "We will kill them where they stand, to a man, if they stand. Every patch belongs to me, I want them stripped and carried to my hand. If they do not stand, then we hunt them in the alleys and bars. We search the homes of friends and any family they have. At the end of the day, Diamante Chicago will be no more, and we will all breathe the easier."

"Ain't anyone gonna have problems with this, Bones. We're solid." Shades reached across the table, gripping Bones' wrist. "Skeptics forever, brother."

"Forever Skeptics." Inwardly Bones winced, because that saying would not be true always. For now, it held, and he could meet the eyes of his second, and plan the death of a club.

***

Breathing hard, he uncoiled the metal links of his belt from his fist, unwrapping it with quick shakes of his hand so the buckle dangled towards the ground. Reaching behind him with his other hand, he slipped the still hot pistol into the holster there, flipping the leather lock into place around the grip.

"Sound off," he heard Shades yell and began the count with his number.

"One." Sweeping the warehouse with a glance, Bones strode across the open area, hearing the men still standing in the room counting off. He noted the two holes in the numbers, each void matching a member he'd seen fall. Swallowing hard, fighting off nausea from the smells in the enclosed space, he knelt next to the first unspeaking member, fingers pressed to the thick neck. "Pulse, call Doc." Their on-call medic was supposed to be positioned just around the corner, and Bones trusted Shades had made the right arrangements. Up, and moving to the next man, Bones was gratified to find this member yet lived as well. Noise at the doors and Bones looked up to see a man with a toolbox coming in. He called, "Doc, here first."

Standing, Bones ran the length of his belt through his fingers, unconsciously checking for damaged or misaligned links. He used it as a flail, and a trapping weapon, dragging opponents closer than they liked when the chain wrapped around an arm or neck. Threading it through his belt loops, he waited for Shades to come and report, but already knowing what he would hear.

Five Diamante dead. This meant at least eighteen had fled, if their intel on the numbers was correct, and Bones had a great deal of confidence it was. His phone buzzed, and he brought it out from a vest pocket, looked at the screen, and grinned, feeling a fierce satisfaction. Rebel Wayfarers had grown in numbers, and chapters, as expected.

Shades made it to his side, and he gave him a chin lift, raising the phone so Shades could read the text. "Glad he came through for us," Shades said, and shook his head. "It's 'bout fuckin' time." Without giving Bones a chance to question the statement, Shades swung immediately into his recitation of the battle's outcome. "Cage rolling for two, got another van comin' in for the trash. We'll be here another twenty, then we can set the alarms like it's any other night. Got our fuckin' warehouse back, Bones."

"Clubhouse afterwards. We will need to discuss." Shades nodded agreement with Bones' statement and turned to walk away. "I will be there soon. I have an errand to run."

Swinging back to look at him, Shades frowned. "Not a fan of you heading out on your own tonight, Bones. We got a dozen and a half of 'em on the run. Based on check-ins, they're down past Gary now. Still not likin' the idea of you roaming."

"Shades,"—Bones spread his hands wide to either side, indicating the men and the warehouse around them—"the enemy is defeated. This is ours." He lifted the phone, shaking it back and forth. "We have strong allies. I think I can take a ride safely."

"Not a fan, Bones." Shades sucked in a breath. "Lemme roll with you."

Bones sighed, realizing he wouldn't get what he wanted. Not tonight. He knew if he were honest, if put in Shades' place, he would be insisting on the same thing. He also knew he had to let someone else know his secrets at some point, and it might as well be tonight, and flush with victory, he gave in with grace. "Rolling in five."

"Gotcha."

Thirty minutes later, they were parked outside a twenty-four-hour diner, their bikes tucked into the shadows at the side of the parking lot. Inside, framed in the window, her reflection dancing across every shiny surface inside, was Ester. She was laughing, talking to a waitress who had taken the booth across from her, the cook coming out from the kitchen and leaning, elbows to the counter so he could take part in their conversation. Ester concentrated on the table for a few minutes, positioning things in places that illustrated her story, then flung her hands out in a voila motion, and she grinned broadly at the two people laughing along with her. They were friendly with her, they liked her, and Bones made a mental note to come back and find out what they knew. Leave money for food.

"Who is she?" Shades paused, and when Bones didn't immediately respond, he expanded the question. "She the reason you been different?"

Without taking his eyes off her, Bones asked, "Different how?"

"Less pissed off."

With a chuckle, Bones nodded. "Probably."

"Who is she?"

"She is mine." Bones left the statement between them, unwilling to give her name. He drank her in with his eyes. The cook left, coming back in minutes with a plate he handed to the waitress. She slid it in front of Ester who lifted her hands, seeming to argue for a moment, then she smiled brilliantly and nodded. Bones watched her eat, fork to the plate and then to her mouth, her head tipping back as she savored each bite. He wondered what it would be like to see her eat food made with his hands, see her in his house, at his table. *Cobweb dreams.*

Finally, he motioned to Shades, and the two men started the engines of the bikes they rode, and Bones saw Ester's head swing towards the window. Unsure if she could see him in the darkness, he still lifted a hand in farewell.

Thirteen

Ester

Diamonds sparkled at the wrists and necks and ears of the two women leaving the museum party, and I watched the lights playing across the surface of stones so valuable people had killed to own them, died to find them, and I was amazed these people wore them so carelessly. Didn't they see the men in the shadows beside the car park, the dark shadows where the street lights didn't fall as brightly?

I pushed up from the bench where I'd decided to sleep, because it was close to the twenty-four-hour store where they had a shower in case of chemical spills. The graveyard shift worker would let me use the bathroom, so I was guaranteed to be squeaky clean in about five hours. Standing on the curb, I tracked the women's progress with my eyes, looking between the women and the men. Those men now milling around in agitation, ready for this thing to get moving, ready to get it on like Donkey Kong so they could move to the next scene of violence they would create. I was vacillating in my mind and my body, shifting back and forth from involved to uninvolved, moving from foot to foot, dancing in place. One step forwards, one step backwards, one step forwards.

Involved. Uninvolved.

The men moved and metal glinted.

Involved.

Decided, I shouted my warning. "They'll injure you to possess those diamonds." I lifted my hand and pointed towards the shadows, watching with one eye as one of the men disappeared into the pitch darkness beside the building. The women stopped and looked at me, so I shook my hand, trying to emphasize the danger. "You should avoid that location."

My words weren't what I wanted to say. I wanted to shout and scream. Wanted them to see the blood in their mind like I did, wanted them to anticipate the fists falling and rising. But my mouth, as it ever did, failed to cooperate. "Returning to the party for an escort is highly advised."

This was why I didn't talk a lot, because what I wanted to say and what actually emitted from my lips were hardly ever the same thing.

I heard motorcycles in the distance, tracking them with my ears effortless now, because I did this kind of thing all the time. I was on the edge of Bones' territory, and I liked knowing I was at least on the fringe of being his, because everything within his borders belonged to him and so if I was inside the boundary, then it meant in some small way I might be his, too. The engine sounds grew louder, and I anticipated when they would sweep into view.

Distracted as I was, it shouldn't have been a surprise that I lost track of the disappearing man because there was a lot to watch. The women returning to the museum, slowly at first, then quicker when the remaining men shouted their anger.

The motorcycles could mean I would see Bones again, this the thirteenth time, a not particularly lucky number sequence, but you couldn't skip numbers, not like floors in a hotel where they ignored the fact that renumbering thirteen to fourteen didn't actually change the count. Lighted numerals in circles in an elevator could lie just like a person, this not even an omission, but a commission because it boldly stated twelve, and then fourteen, as if the elevator car could will the thirteenth floor away.

Even staff elevators told the same lie, and the thirteenth time I talked about it as I carried dirty linens to the basement to stuff into the bins and baskets for the laundry staff to deal with, the man with the key who ran the elevator slapped me. So thirteen meant blood to me.

I was thirteen a decade ago, and for me, that number had been no more or less lucky than any other year, so maybe this meeting wouldn't be bad. Then a voice appeared in the air right behind me.

I would say the man appeared, but he didn't. He had traveled the full distance in the usual methods. I'd heard his footsteps but lost them in the idea of seeing Bones again. So, the man's appearance was startling, and I jerked, but not fast enough because he had my elbow. Pinching fingers unable to be pried away and I saw the hit coming so I tried to move with the swing, failing miserably when the hand those fingers belonged to tilted me back and into the blow. Bad luck falling on my face with force.

***

Bones

"*Christos.*" Bones cursed, seeing the woman knocked to the side by the power of the blow, the man not pulling his strength but striking with a closed fist to her face. Without thinking, without considering, which was very unlike him, Bones pulled his gun, and still traveling about thirty miles an hour, shot the man's hand which was pulled back for a second blow. Her attacker fell at the woman's feet.

Ester stood there, staring down at the man as Bones pulled to a stop behind her, sleeve of her shirt ripped at the shoulder, not even lifting a hand to her cheek. The women she had warned away screamed at the gunshot, running pell-mell up the sidewalk towards the museum's exhibition party, those attendees now spilling out into the street in reaction to the noises.

***

Ester

The man screamed as if touching me had injured him, had bloodied him, had wounded him deeply, and I wanted to tell him the injury was mine, my face stinging with an imprint of his knuckles. His hand had fallen away from my arm. Then a blazing heat hit me with velvet strokes on my skin, far less painful than his fist had been, but that fist was fallen with his body to the gutter, and he gripped the trunk of his wrist with his other hand, the holding one, now fisted as a constrictor to hold in velvet liquid. My eyes stung, blurring red, so I closed them.

"Should not have hit her." A hand at my back, searing hot, but not a hit and I finally heard the report echoing from the buildings. "Ester, are you well?"

"I'm lucky." Luckier than thirteen would make you believe, luckier than blood diamonds would let you know.

"Let me see your face." Eyes still closed, I turned and didn't have to use my eyes to know he was smiling, because it was in his voice. "Beauty." A piece of fabric, soft from years of use which meant he was touching me with something he frequently touched himself which made me giddy with glee. He touched my face, brow to chin, one side of my nose, then the other, eyelids, left then right, gentle over my cheekbone where I felt the swelling already making itself known. "You will need some ice, Ester."

"I've four and a half hours before I shower. I can get ice then."

"This needs ice now, baby."

The world stopped spinning, held in place with that word. My ears rang with the force of things clashing against time as it tried to push forwards, locked tightly by his gift. "You give me the nicest presents."

A puff of breath danced across my skin, scented with beer and pot and perhaps ice cream. I wondered what flavors he liked, because vanilla was my favorite and wouldn't it be cool if we liked the same ice cream? "I do like vanilla. I will get you some, but I would like it if you let me get you some ice, too."

Mind readers didn't exist, so I knew he hadn't lifted the word from my thoughts, which meant my lips were traitors to the cause of keeping myself secret from everyone. "You're not everyone. You're Bones. I'd know you anywhere."

The touch stroked, surging upward along my hairline, then back down. "I would know you, too, Ester."

Sirens sounded, and I sighed because I would have to find a different place to sleep. "My shower will wait."

"Yes," he said, agreeing with me. "We shall both have to wait." A finger curled under my chin, lifting my jaw, brushing along the edge of the bone there. "Will you open your eyes before I have to go?" The shouting, hitting man had moved away, with assistance it sounded like, dragged back to the darkness near the building on this side of the street, opposite his previous placement by the garage. Men were talking to him, using words and force to impress something they felt it important he know. Sounds muted, their bodies a fortress between him and me and I knew he would no longer threaten me even in my dreams.

I blinked, my eyes tearing after being in the darkness behind my lids for so long, then I slowly focused on his face. Right there, not twelve inches away.

I considered a moment. Maybe thirteen.

"You got a new picture." His lips, lines drawn so near them with needle and ink, lifted in a broad smile. They were full, the bottom one bowed down gently, and I wondered if they were as soft as they looked.

"I like you noticed, Ester."

I notice everything about you, I thought, and my lips for once stayed faithful, and sealed.

Vengeance

Bones

He folded the bandana he had used to wipe her assailant's blood from her face, tucking it into an inside pocket of his vest. Entirely trusting of him, she didn't falter in her gaze upwards into his eyes. Not the first time he had touched her, but the first where she had given herself to him in this way. Following his directions without question.

"Prez," Shades shouted, and Bones heard bike engines starting behind him. A reaction to the quickly approaching police presence. Security assigned to the museum had likely called, perhaps even before the bikes showed on the scene. Bones nodded, indicating he understood. Lifting a hand, he whirled a finger, the clear command followed by all except Shades. All but one bike roared off, passing as they moved up through the gears, gaining speed and distance from the man they had just killed on his demand. "Prez, we gotta hit it."

Ester, her eye already nearly swollen closed, smiled up at him, making no indication it ached to do so, even if he knew it must. "You gotta go." She urged him earnestly and took a half step backwards, likely thinking space would return his sanity.

"Come with me." At his plea, her face turned to stone, and the half step became three, a river of separation she didn't want him to cross. "Ester...."

She allowed the trailing sound of his voice to clear the air before she spoke, and as ever, her words were confusing, something he would spend hours deciphering, counting it worth the work. "Thirteen's my luckiest of the luckies." She pointed to his face, where he had the set of numerals inked just two days ago, then to his vest, where they resided inside a diamond, positioned to the side and underneath his 1% patch. "Means you're my lucky, too."

"I would be honored to be your lucky any day of the week, Ester," he called across the distance between them. "Ice."

She mouthed something, a word, and then snapping a sassy salute, she grinned and he winced along with her as pain from her cheek made itself known. Ester whirled and with footsteps light and quick, raced between buildings, lost to the dark in moments.

"Bones," Shades clipped, and Bones reacted, moving to his bike. They were away in moments, mirrors reflecting the lights rounding the corner behind them a few seconds later. Down the street to the first major intersection, then a right that took them across the bridge, into the part of town where they had grown up, where they had the upper hand over the cops.

Twenty minutes later they rolled through the wire gate of the Skeptics' compound, a prospect lifting a hand as he swung the gate closed behind them. Backing into his parking spot nearest the door, Bones was ready, and Shades didn't hesitate to give it to him.

"Are you fucking insane, Bones? Are you, huh?" A hand lifted, pulling the bandana from Shades face, bringing it down to his neck before going to the back to work at loosening the knot. "Sitting there on the posh side, citizens watching from the lobby as you fuckin' shot a man. Wearing your vest like it's a goddamned tea party and you don't care who knows you're there. And then—" Shades shook his head, disbelief in every line of his body. "then, you stand and chat, like it *is* a party."

"He hit her." Bones didn't get off his bike, didn't shift, didn't give any indication that having a screaming 230 pounds of club member in his face made him uneasy in the least. Bones had ample practice at this last, having worked at it his entire life, where controlling his responses was how he lived. "Struck an unarmed, unprotected woman in the face with his closed fist. It would not have mattered the who, the wrong is the same. Then I saw the who and determined he would never again have the opportunity to take his frustrations out so. You did not protest until you failed to leave as ordered." Bones leaned forwards an inch, crowding into Shades' space. "An order, my friend."

"Like I'm gonna leave you uncovered, boss." Shades sighed, shaking his head, then changed the topic slightly. "That's the girl, right? The one from the diner?"

In the months since he had first met Ester, Bones had shared only small pieces of their encounters, and with no one except Shades. Watcher was the only other person who had seen her, and like with Shades, only from a distance. Ester had followed Bones to a meeting, not willing to be dissuaded until she had her chance to tell him about the beauty of a rare flower blooming at the botanical gardens she had seen the day before.

Bones had noted her appreciation of small things before, in her rapt stares at the power of a storm as it swept offshore on the lakefront, her drenched in the downpour, eyes to the clouds as they raced away. In how she slumped in disappointment after the sun rose, colors bleeding from the sky with the strengthening of its rays, turning to Bones to tell him, "Don't be sad. They're still there. We just can't see them right now." Words she used to comfort herself, brought out to ease a sadness she imagined echoed in him.

Now, he was faced with a dilemma, to confirm what Shades had already sussed out, or play his interest in her false, in an effort to keep her off any compiled lists of people interesting to his enemies. Neither felt right, so he chose a third route, that of confession. "Yes, that is her." He sighed, then offered even more trust to this man who had earned it a hundred times over. "That is Ester." Then Bones stepped across a line he never expected to see in front of him, but in his mind knew he had already crossed long ago. "My Ester."

"Snuffed the guy," Shades told Bones, and he knew it, because he had given the signal for terminal force. "She worth it?" It being the potential heat, because they hadn't time to deal with the body, hadn't time to pick a place and time with no witnesses, hadn't time to look for cameras and disable surveillance. This had put the entire club at risk, because Shades was right; they were all wearing their vests, the leather with the club patch proudly displayed on the back.

"A thousand times over." Bones statement gave her worth in Shades' eyes, and he knew it when the man pounded his fist to his heart. Even without the Rebels' words, the action alone told Bones he understood. "Let us go inside, see where the threat will come from, impede progress if we can."

Two days later, Bones had a brief interview with the police, ending with him walking out their doors, shoulders back, lawyer trailing behind. His casing had been picked up by one of his men, leaving no evidence he had fired at the scene. His weapon was registered, and he was licensed to carry it in all the ways Chicago hated.

Mason's man Myron, a tech wizard, had assisted with the museum's video feed, rendering it unusable. This left a group of privileged people who saw a group of men, all wearing the same apparel, and a dead body which was not connected with either group. As the club's lawyer pointed out, the police hadn't called any of the fete attendees in for questioning, which begged the question if they were profiling in a way that was outside the narrowly defined laws associated with such a thing. In the end, the police were glad to see the back of him, and Bones was just as glad to leave.

But he knew, and it burned in his stomach, that he had put the club at risk for Ester. It burned even more to know he would do it again, without hesitation.

***

"Why would he do such a thing?" The woman sitting at the table across from Bones wept into her hands. He waited, and her sobs slowed, hands falling to press against the surface of the tabletop. They sat at her kitchen table, in her kitchen, in her house, in a western suburb, and Bones had just given her proof her husband was a pedophile. In the backyard, her two daughters played with a neighbor, the singing bounce of the trampoline springs testifying to their activity. Aged seven and eight, they were innocently beautiful, sweetly obedient when ordered outside by their mother.

"That I do not know, nor will I ever understand. But—" He leaned forwards, seeing her inch away, maintaining the safety of space between their faces. "—a leopard cannot change their spots. If he was driven to do this once, if he were so compelled, then he still is. This is not something that simply goes away. You have seen, or sensed things." Bones watched uncertainty combat with fear on her features, and set himself to ensure fear won not only the battle, but the war. He would accept no less. "You have daughters of an age his foster sister was." Digging a deep hole by using the familial words, he hammered the doubt home so it seated well enough to last. "He was nearly thirteen. She was a child."

Shaking his head, Bones wove truth for her, nothing but truth as he had discovered it. "She was injured already. His friends had jumped her the week before. Of a surety, he knew what had happened, because he used their abuse of her, used their actions as a way to shame her." When she averted her gaze quickly, glancing down and away, he knew she had felt the edge of the same blade from her husband, Ester's former foster brother, and rapist.

Once Bones cobbled the story together from the bits and pieces Ester let drop, he set Myron to find her in the system. The attack at the baseball field more than enough to warrant long memories, Myron had found everything. Bones now knew more about Ester than he suspected she did. Mother running off with Ester's uncle, estranging the brothers. Mother and new husband dead years ago, victims of an ice-covered road. Bones thought it was that death that pushed Ester's father over the edge; his first recorded suicide attempt was only a week after. Following Ester's path through foster care was more difficult, but Myron had attacked the task like a dog with a bone, worrying at the edges and ends of the puzzle until he had enough data to build a model.

Foster care when she was six, when her father was finally successful in his quest for oblivion, leaving behind a daughter who was too tender for the mercies of the ones she wound up with. Shuffled from household to household, she'd finally settled in the foster care of a family. Seemingly the perfect situation for a then eight-year-old, until she was attacked and left for dead on a baseball field.

The faceless, nameless target of reform, her case hit the news in a national way, held up as the product of a flawed system. She was labeled as quiet and compliant by hospital staff, whose testimony seemed to speak of a different child than her foster carers. They had branded her a troublemaker, a manipulator of the highest order. Of course, that was only after their son raped her in her own bed, and she dared tell her case worker her stitches were bleeding. Carried out of the house with her head covered by a blanket, news reporters shouting questions and snapping pictures. Bones had seen those images, thin legs dangling below the arm of the case worker, head curtained by a blanket covered in pink and purple roses, taken from the bed in which she had been defiled.

The son proclaimed her a liar, which brought the earlier accusations into question until a judge saner than most shut it down, reminding the court attendees of the brutal nature of the attack. She had been beaten, raped so viciously her bladder had been ruptured, and her assailants had left the broken handle of a wooden baseball bat wedged inside her rectum.

Charges dropped, the boy skated, leaving the media focus back on the ones from the ballfield. And as they were caught out in lies, one by one, justice saw them sucked into the maw of the juvenile system. After being released, most of the guilty had moved out of state, their families mortified, unable to bear the scrutiny of neighbors and friends who now knew what kind of monster lurked behind their child's face. Myron was working to track them down, two were dead, but there were seven men who would not be expecting a visitation at this late date, and Bones was determined.

All of this meant her foster brother had gone free, until now. Bones sat across from his wife, talking about the possibility of him molesting his own daughters, and saw the doubt he had seeded already growing into a living thing. Something the man had done or said made her believe him capable of perpetuating such a thing on his own flesh and blood. *This is done*, Bones thought, standing with a fluid movement, marking that she flinched less than before. *People can become accustomed to nearly anything.* "You are those children's mother, their only advocate. What you choose to do with your own life is one thing. Their lives are a different matter. I pray you choose well."

Out the door, on the bike, and away, Bones breathed a tiny bit easier. Vengeance was a tasty bitch when she played along with his game.

***

"Gotta say, I'm enjoying the hospitality." That was Watcher, president of the New Mexico club, Southern Soldiers. Bones had met him years ago in Kentucky, when Mason dragged Bones to the funeral of the Soldiers' previous president and Watcher's brother, Danger.

That had been the trip when Bones found his calling. Before that time, he had often turned a blind eye towards activities he did not find personal interest in, allowing his members to partake as they willed, as long as it didn't reflect badly on the Skeptics. Things like prostitution and weapon running, not sanctioned, but not forbidden. The Skeptics had a healthy drug trade, thanks in part to Bones' connections from his youth, and as long as they were the middleman, he was fine with the lucrative results.

After that trip, however, he wrote a manifesto, read it in an open meeting, and had it voted into club law, forbidding flesh trade. Meeting Juanita, Watcher's woman, had opened his eyes to an entire world he had known about in a nearly academic way, but she brought it to life. Seeing her cowering at a man's laughter, watching as she turned herself inside out to please Watcher, feeling her pain as she struggled to cover the brand her owners had left on her, gave him a focus he had lacked before.

He had forged a close friendship with Watcher in those few days spent in his company, and maintained his bond with Juanita. Had rejoiced with the couple when their daughter Isabella was born, laughed at her antics as a child. Supported Watcher's decision to fight human trafficking, keeping an open conduit between their clubs at not only an officer level, but so every Soldiers' member knew they could call on his members in any way.

"I am glad, my friend," Bones told him truthfully. They sat in the back courtyard of the Skeptics' clubhouse, an area decked out today with picnic tables and a blow-up pool for the children, grills on two sides of the area giving off an array of aromas that made the mouth water. "You should get up this way more often."

"I'm up here enough as it is for Mason. Don't tell me I gotta start makin' special trips for you." Watcher's humor was cutting, and Bones knew it for what it was, a question.

"I have encountered issues of my own, and you are aware of this. I cannot take on more for Mason at this time." Bald honestly was preferred between friends, and Bones knew him well enough to share more if asked.

Watcher lifted his beer, tipping the can to his mouth and drank deeply. Bones waited, knowing this for the thinking pause his friend typically utilized, quietly pleased with his discernment when Watcher next spoke. "We both know what's coming. The writing's on the wall for us, brother. The question is, who's gonna take the first step off that ledge, trusting Mason to have a net waiting at the bottom."

"I will," Bones said quietly, having decided it was nearly time. "I always enjoy being out ahead of you. This is one more example when you will follow my lead, eventually."

Watcher snorted a laugh and took another drink. Then without looking at Bones, quietly agreed. "I usually do, brother. I usually do."

"How is your Bella doing?" Cautiously, Bones worked the question into the conversation, not wanting to expose the anger he carried. Watcher's only daughter had been abducted a month ago, buried alive, found by one of Mason's men in New Mexico. Bones had heard about the event through club gossip, calling Mason to verify, only finding out then that Mason's woman had birthed his child. Out of the loop, and left in the dust, it had made his quip to Watcher sting a little more than it would normally have.

Watcher was silent a moment, then bowed his head, eyes to the beer dangling from his fingertips. "You know I'd a killed her?"

Startled, Bones barked a laughing, "*Qué?*"

Leaning over, Watcher set the beer on the ground next to his chair, then righted himself again. He spat to the side, and sucked at his teeth, then bit his lip nearly hard enough to draw blood. Bones saw all of this for what it was, another stalling tactic while he regained some measure of control. In a rough voice, Watcher told him, "I went to Mexico. So fuckin' convinced I knew what I was about. So convinced I knew who my enemies were. I went to Mexico and was three hours away when Duck found her."

Not looking up, Watcher sighed, still speaking to his hands as they hung lax between his knees. "She nearly died. My Bella. Nearly died, and I wasn't even in the fuckin' country. Damned Lalo, took her and buried her." Tipping his head to one side, Bones felt the weight of his stare. "You know Mela was nearly taken just weeks before? I had that tip in my pocket, and I still let Bella out there."

Carmela was a young girl who had lived with Watcher and Juanita for so long, she might as well be their adopted daughter. Slate had played a part in her rescue from an unbelievable situation years ago, a girl whose father was now the leader of one of the most powerful Mexican clubs, the Machos. Watcher had long ago tied his strings to the Machos, much as he had the Rebels, and Bones could not fault him for it. Always smart to play corner against corner, coming out the winner in the middle.

"I did not know. How did Estavez take it?" Raul Estavez had stripped power from his own brother, Carlos, the former Machos' president. It was Raul who was Mela's birth father, something which undoubtedly tied those strings even tighter.

"Not well, I can tell you that. Especially since he was *incommunicado* when it happened, so he only learned about it after Bella was taken. You know I didn't call him, right? Estavez got a tip, called me. Me not callin' you, it wasn't personal. I just didn't think. Couldn't think. Couldn't fuckin' *breathe*, man. Didn't call anyone except Mason, All I could think of was Myron and his network and know-how. Got the call, made a call, and barreled out the door without a single fuckin' plan in my head." Chin down, Watcher heaved a sigh that spoke of his guilt. "Mason even told me he didn't think it was the right play, and all I could see was fuckin' Lalo. Fuckin' Lalo had my baby girl."

"Did he...?" Bones trailed off, not certain how to word his question delicately, but Watcher took his meaning.

"No, thanks be to God Almighty. He put his hands on her, beat her, tormented her in ways that are gonna mark her for life, but he spared her that, at least."

"Small blessings," Bones murmured, not sure Watcher heard him.

"She's doin' okay. Not great. I didn't see her this trip because she gets so...upset. Wants to go home, but Lalo's back in the wind, and I—" Heaving another sigh, Watcher paused and swallowed hard, then continued his confession, "I couldn't keep my baby safe. Trust Mason with her more than I trust myself at this point."

"Lalo is in the wind? I thought he was held by the DEA in Florida?" Bones was surprised and glanced across the yard to where Shades stood, calling the man to him with a tip of his head. "My last intel had him shuffled from safe house to safe house, and none of them were safe enough to protect him from the anger of those he had betrayed."

Shades stood in front of him, and Bones asked, "Were you aware Lalo was no longer in custody?" Lalo had been president of the Diamante chapter Watcher had shut down in New Mexico, so the man's ire at the Southern Soldiers was at least understandable. The Skeptics had treated with the man's cousin, Chismoso, a name Bones had difficulty saying with a straight face. So Chismoso was equally displaced and angry, and the Skeptics kept close tabs on his travels. "Chismoso still resides in Kentucky, correct?"

Fury, a Rebel now, a Diamante then, had moved his chapter from Kentucky to Fort Wayne, disbanding after only four months in that city.

His men had moved en masse to the Rebels, something Bones knew for a fact had been a calculated and strategic move on Mason's part. Chismoso had been granted leave from Diamante to begin a new chapter in Kentucky, to fill the void left behind there. Power grew to fill the boundaries of the territory available, and even the minds behind the Diamante club understood this fact. Divide the territory by chartering new chapters, and you restrict the reach of all chapters in the area.

"Yeah, Bones. Chismoso is in Kentucky. I'll verify, though," Shades admitted his lack of knowledge with some ire, finishing with, "Since I didn't know fuckin' Lalo wasn't still wearin' a fuckin' bracelet." He looked at Watcher, who stared up at him. "When did you hear this, brother?" That designation made Bones smile, glad to see the fostering he and Watcher had done bearing fruit still.

"Couple days ago is all," Watcher reassured Shades. "That's all, man."

"Still," Shades said, turning on his heel and stalking towards the clubhouse.

"Unhappy man," Watcher observed, shaking his head.

"You have no idea." Bones smiled when Watcher laughed, as he'd intended. "Tell me what I can do to help, brother."

"Not a thing, brother. She's gotta shake it on her own, sort it out and settle in. They'll move her to Mason's house now, since he's officially in Fort Wayne." The corner of Watcher's mouth quirked, and he asked, "You see Garrett yet?"

"Not yet," Bones admitted, "I shall be making a trip in a week. I wanted to give them time to settle into the routine at home before I dropped in with my men. I will definitely be going down to see the new prince, though." This gave him pause, and curious, he asked, "How old is Bella?"

"Eighteen, God help me." Watcher shook his head. "Seems only yesterday she was gap-toothed and grinning. Time flies, Bones. Time flies."

"How is it possible you and I have been allies so long, my friend? Surely you are mistaken. It's been only a handful of years since I met you and the beautiful Juanita. Do not think to pile your years on my shoulders." Bones laughed with Watcher, but the idea had stuck with him. All around him were men with families they had fought for and won, things they were honored to protect and keep. Precious lives held in their hands, cradled in their arms, lessons taught and learned. Family.

He looked around the yard, seeing the same here, as his men played with the children of their brothers, and as their wives and women gathered along the edges of the group. Support and love for anyone under his patch were a given for Bones. *My bed, however, remains cold.*

Shaking off that thought, he asked Watcher another question about the Southern Soldiers, and together the friends passed another pleasant evening. But the question of Lalo and Chismoso continued to circle through his thoughts.

***

Swinging his leg over and off his bike, Bones glanced around the lot, seeing his five men already off and stretching. Things had been busy, and this was the first chance he had to come to Fort Wayne. With a tip of his head, he indicated the clubhouse, and they walked that direction as a unit. Opening the door, Bones was startled to see Chase waiting. Mason's oldest boy looked polished, wearing a button-down shirt, and stood with shoulders slouched against the clubhouse hallway, face and fingers focused on his phone. He only looked up when Bones greeted him.

As with so many things of import in Mason's life, Bones had been present the night the boy's mother shuffled him off on a father he scarcely knew. Chase, at the time a scrawny sixteen-year-old who'd been frightened out of his mind, had stood alone in the back of a biker's party in a loud and rowdy bar.

"Look who is waiting for us." Bones knew his voice was warm as he walked towards Chase with a hand extended, wanting to offer a silent acceptance of Chase's growing adulthood. He was surprised but pleased when the boy circled his shoulders in a hug, and gladly returned it, allowing Chase to gauge when he was ready to release. "Is everything well with Willa and the babe?"

"Uh, yeah, s'all good. Dad said you were coming in, so I was waiting on you." Chase stepped back, grinning down at Bones. It took him a moment to realize their height advantages had changed position.

"You have grown." Bones observed, reaching out to grip the boy's bicep. He squeezed, and Chase made a muscle, flexing proudly. "Quite the man, Chase. I would suspect you are beating off women with a stick." Chase looked down and to the side, and Bones wondered if he had hit a sore spot. He decided to ease past it if he could. "Is your dad here at the clubhouse? I thought he was at home."

"He is, but he said to tell you that you can come over anytime. Just limit your guys to fifty or so." Chase laughed at the look Bones gave him. "Kidding, kidding. Geez. Bring whoever you need. Here—" Digging in his back pocket, Chase brought out a slip of paper. "Wrote the address down. It's easy to find, just watch for the line of bikes on the street and the sea of bikers in the yard. Willa's about crazy being locked down like this."

Bones accepted the paper, finished chatting with the boy, and went in search of Shades to tell him they would be heading over to Mason's home within the hour. He was sidetracked along the way by Slate, who nearly earned himself a bloody nose by catching Bones around the neck unexpectedly.

"Shit," Bones shook his head. "Are you *loco?* Keep your hands off me."

"Oh, yeah." Slate nodded, his grin belying his serious tone. "I'm crazy all right. Ruby's making me absolutely insane." He put on a falsetto tone, rolling his eyes. "Get me a pickle, Slate. My feet are swollen, Slate. Allen and Dani need their diapers changed, Slate." His voice dropped back to normal when he said, "Though she usually says Daddy for that one, not Slate." He clapped Bones' shoulder twice. "Good to see you, man. You don't get to the Fort often enough."

"Am I to take from what you have said your Ruby is expecting again?" She'd given birth to twins not long ago, or at least he thought, and realized time had again gained the upper hand, getting away from him.

"Uh, yeah." Slate used nearly the same tone Chase had earlier, and Bones grinned to hear it. "We're on the sixty-day countdown because it's twins again. You didn't hear about my super swimmers? Fuckers are in beast mode, alla time." He flexed his arm, and Bones laughed aloud. "Since she went early last time, the doc's got us jumpy as shit, man. Every time she passes gas, I'm sure it's labor. Works better for her if I get outta the house some of the time. Today is one of those times, so here I am. And here you are." Slate slung an arm around Bones' neck. "Gotta say, I expected you weeks ago."

"I never thought I would long for the days when you held me in awe," Bones said, unwinding Slate's arm from his throat. "I find that is true at this moment, however." Slate burst out laughing, and Bones smiled. "Congratulations, brother. You will call me when the children come, yes?"

"You know it. Gotta get a present outta you some way." Slate sobered, and asked, "You hear what's going on with Watcher?"

"I saw him last week, yes. Unless there is news since then?" Bones followed Slate into the office off the main room of the clubhouse, closing the door behind them when Slate tipped his head at the opening. "Is there news, brother?"

"Yes, and no. We know Lalo took Bella, how he took her. Duck dug her up, know all of that. Knew Lalo was in Florida. Did not know when he got clear of the DEA there. But Lalo was on Duck's land a few days ago, and that was the first we knew he'd been cut loose. Someone's blocking info, and I gotta tell you, it's pissin' Myron off." Slate shot him an amused look. "Pissin' him right the fuck off. Never seen the man so riled up and set to find out who's fucking with his pipeline. Geeks and their tech, don't get in the way, man. Worse than a meth head."

"Lalo was in Lamesa? Does Watcher know? He did not speak of the proximity, just that Lalo was 'in the wind.' With his anxiety over Bella, I am surprised he did not mention it." Slate was already shaking his head in the negative.

"Nope, definitely 100 percent on the negatory on that one. Mason's protective of Watch, and we all know that's true. They go way the fuck back, and Mason's decree was the info would be need-to-know. I'm decidin' you need to know. Skeptics pissed Diamante off nearly as bad as Soldiers did. If Lalo is out roamin', then you and your men should take care." Slate lifted his boots, resting them on the corner of the desk. "Lalo's crazy, man. Between Bella's story and what Duck had to say about how the dude acted? Sounds like he's flat crazy."

"Crazy is not good. Crazy is not predictable," Bones observed, leaning one shoulder against the wall, staring out the window of the office. "My men have families to protect. Are you telling me I need to warn them to expect something like what Watcher has endured?"

"No fuckin' idea, brother. Just wanted you to know." Slate maintained his position, but his body tensed and Bones watched him carefully. Something big was coming. "This is need-to-know, too. I'm gonna step down. Pull back, be a member. If Mason lets me, I'll do it easy." He shook his head as Bones held his breath. "Four babies in diapers at once. Fuckin' crazy ain't restricted to fuckin' Lalo. Ruby's blood pressure is high." He sighed. "Was high. Until I told her. Now it's better. She'd been carrying that worry the whole pregnancy. Eased her mind, made her healthier. Fuckin' love her, man. My every breath is because of her. So." He dropped his feet, leaning forwards to rest his elbows on the desk. "Mason doesn't make it easy, I go anyway. Take a beatout if I gotta. Make her life better."

"Mason will not ask that of you." Bones kept his voice low, protecting Slate's secret for now. "He will allow this, I am certain. A loss for the Rebels, but I am very happy you have that, brother." He shook his head, deciding to give Slate honesty. "I find myself somewhat envious. Very envious."

"Get an old lady," Slate shot back, standing and reaching out for a forearm grip. He grinned, leaning close to whisper, "Get a fuckin' life."

Transformation

Bones

With the words from the phone, an image of the old man's face swam up in Bones' memories. Gray, grizzled beard, an elder in the community, a man he had respected. "We are poorer for his loss, Mason." Silence for a moment, then Bones asked, "When will you have the services for Bingo?"

"Two days, maybe three. Gotta give his brother time to get here from Wyoming, and if I know Harddrive, he'll be ridin'. Gonna be a fuckton of brothers here, man. Lotta folks wanna pay respects, lotta clubs rolling here." Mason's words didn't surprise Bones. Neither did the unspoken warning. Which was to watch himself, because so many men representing so very many clubs could lead to anything.

"Yes, Bingo was well respected. We can only hope those in attendance will hold that respect close, and allow the family their time to grieve." Running members through his head, he had a question about one, and decided it would be best to get this out into the air. Spoken and exposed. "I would have Shades come with me."

No secret that Shades and Mason were not friendly. It wasn't the Rebels as a whole that Shades had problems with, just Mason in particular, and Bones had never asked why, not wanting to dig too deep, in case the thing needed to remain buried.

"Bring him." Mason's response was curt, brusque and angry. That anger had flared from nothing, before Bones' words Mason's tone had been entirely filled with loss and grief. Now, there was an edge of rage.

"If I were to ask what had happened to earn such enmity between two men I hold in such esteem, would you tell me?" Bones listened, and heard the rumble of bikes in the background, but nothing from Mason. This lay deep, then. "Never mind my question. It does not matter as much as your loss. I will see if Shades wants to come, or not. Perhaps he did not know Bingo as well as I, or others. I will watch to see the date for certain, and bring my men to pay our respects."

"Appreciated, brother."

Three days later Bones stood with fifteen Skeptics in a windswept graveyard, listening to a eulogy given by a man who wept through it entire. Shades had not made the trip, pleading a need to remain close to home, and Bones did not try and dissuade him. Weeping as he spoke, Preacher's words were eloquent and heartfelt, but it was his emotional reaction that took many of the men present nearly to their knees. One thing in particular stood out for Bones. Near the end, Preacher indicated the survivors seated in the chairs near the grave. Bingo's brother, along with that man's daughter and son. Bingo's sister's children. Blood, for certain, shared and diluted in places, still blood. But no heir of his own.

His poetry fulfilled him, Bones thought, and knew this for fact, having seen Bingo caught in the thrall of his muse more than once. Oblivious to anything around him, seated at a table with a notebook in front of him, short pencil clutched in a tight grip as he poured everything in his heart into words on the page. *I do not have even that.*

The service was over, and groups of people began to drift towards and away from the gravesite. Some wanting to give condolences, and others, no doubt, wanting to escape the knowledge that death comes for all. Bones and his men held their position, waiting for Mason to give an indication it was time to leave for the wake at the clubhouse. Movement in the distance pulled Bones' attention and he watched as two of Mason's men held a short conversation, then parted ways, one leaving with far greater distress than the other. Fury, his trademark red hair giving away his identity, even from a distance, stomped his angry way down the small hill and to a group of men Bones recognized as former Diamante. As a unit, they wheeled and headed for their bikes, not waiting on the signal from their local or national president.

And that is who Slate favors for his successor, Bones thought, wondering. He looked back to the other man, recognizing Hoss, a member who had found himself tested recently when his stepson was taken by the boy's biological father. Retrieved by force, the boy was home and safe, which was a blessing. Hoss had found a family wholemade, and made them his.

Bones snorted silently. *If I were a superstitious man, I would see augury and signs in these thoughts.*

***

Bones stood, listening to Slate, hearing the things that lay between the words his friend was saying, feeling the pain. Another death. Essa, a girl Slate was once enamored of. Essa, cousin to Mica. Molly, Mica's sister, a one-time target of Duck's brother. It seemed fate, these east Texas girls had been destined to come to the attention of the Rebels.

Bones let Slate talk, listening as he worked through the details. Bones frowned as Slate circled around again and again to feelings of guilt for an imagined role in her death. Finally, convinced he had the right of it, Bones interrupted. "Did you pull the trigger, my friend?"

"Fuck no." Nearly a shout, because this cut to the core of what Slate feared.

"You bear no burden of guilt for this death, Andy." Bones thought, *Let me bring him first to understand the man, then we will tackle the brotherhood.* "You were in this girl's life for a mere span of weeks. Was it six, eight? Less?"

"We traveled together for a few weeks." Not done, Slate tried to argue. "But that don't matter, man."

"Truly you believe that while in her life for less than six weeks, you had such a profound effect on her that this sorry event belongs to you? That you bent the fabric of her future, bringing her to this event, more than three years in the making? Vengeance, I can see and would approve. She meant something to you. Eons ago, in terms of a life, but she was an important pivot point for you. But out of the hundreds of weeks, the thousands of days she lived, you hold that the span spent with you the most critical for her? That is a weight of self-importance I did not expect." He clucked his tongue, mimicking the sound his mother had made when as a child, he had disappointed her. "Essa was important. I will not argue that. Mica's cousin, and the reason you found your Ruby."

Slate made a noise, but Bones talked over him. "Do not gainsay her role in that. If it were not for her immature ways, you would not have been in a place to recognize the beauty you found in Fort Wayne. So named, by you. Ruby, not as some believe for her hair, for all it is lovely and distinct. No, you named her Ruby even before she would have you, because you recognized the giving and loving nature she bore inside. Mica's blood was not your destiny, but Essa made it possible for you to find and keep your Ruby.

"Your Ruby, who is a treasure who loves you, gifting you again and again not only with her trust and an unexpected delight in your company, but who has also given you beautiful children. So hold on to the sadness for Essa's life cut short, before she found the one she was destined for. Hold tight too, to the vengeance in your soul, because I see the importance of this. Our families should be proof against involvement in club business, yet time and again we find them drawn in where they have no expectation or training to be. This is such a case, and cannot stand.

"Vengeance, not guilt must drive us forwards. And we, Mason's closest confidants, must guard him." Bones paused, waiting, and Slate filled the silence.

"Whadda ya mean, guard him?" He sounded sincerely puzzled, and Bones was surprised, but then not, because until this moment, Slate had been focused on what he saw as his culpability.

"We know who did this thing, do we not? A man we both saw stripped of rank and recognition in the Rebels, that exile earned for his behaviors. Abomination, among clubs, for a man to go against the known principles of the President. Tucker did this thing, yes?" Bones waited, and Slate made a noise of agreement. "Who deemed it right for him to be cut from the club, and yet allowed him to walk away a breathing man?"

"Fuck me," Slate muttered, and Bones knew he understood.

"Take your guilty feelings and magnify them by a thousand, and I suspect you will not yet tap the depths of Mason's. First, he allowed Deacon to live, and that is a death for which he wishes with everything that is inside him. Deacon partnered with Morgan, targeting women closest to Mason. Even if Judge did not know Bethy was Mason's blood sister, you and I know Morgan did. Did, and allowed her captivity. We know what happened to Willa, and I am confident that a test would prove Mason her babe's father, but that does not change the violation pressed on her by Mason's nephew. A man who slipped the net cast by Mason in California, only to breathe his last in Utah. With Deacon—if any moment in time could demand the ability to return and make a different decision—I know Mason would give much to be able to change that day. So you and I must guard him, or he will take this on, and a man can only bear so many stripes of guilt before he collapses underneath the load."

Silence for a minute, then Slate sighed. "I gotta make a couple of calls."

Bones immediately gave him what he knew Slate needed. "You are a good man, Slate. I could not ask for a better brother and friend. You do not wear the same patch, we do not work within the same club, but you are my brother. Never forget that."

"Back atcha, brother." Silence for a moment, then a quiet, "Fuck me, I can't imagine how Duck's dealin' with this shit. His woman is hurt, sounded like touch and go for a bit. Essa dead. *Jesus.*"

"Indeed." Sounds swelled in the background, first one, then another baby crying, the volume and pitch enough to note the difference. "You are at home, then?"

"Yeah, I don't get out much these days."

Bones smiled, looking down at the toes of his boots.

"Your words might lead one to believe that isolation at home with four little ones is taxing you." He paused. "I have a different belief, though. If you are not careful, my friend, I might think you enjoy this noisy and smelly phase of fatherhood."

"You just might be right, brother." Soft words told Bones his attempts to lighten the mood had worked. "Mason's got the same bug, man. You hear he and Willa are tryin' for kid number two?"

Bones blinked. "I had not. Already? Garrett is less than three months old."

"No time like the present." Slate's quiet words struck a chord and Bones straightened.

"You are right." Thoughts of Ester chased through his head. "We are not guaranteed anything beyond our current breath."

***

"Truly, this is done?" Bones lifted a hand, scrubbing it across his skull. He had recently started to grow his hair back, after having shaved his head for decades. Ester had made a comment about his hair, and he wanted to see what her reaction would be. So far, at two weeks in, it was less attractive than itchy, and he was not confident it would see another dawn. "And this is what you desire, Slate?"

"You know it, brother." Bones didn't really need the confirmation; relief was audibly present in Slate's voice, and had been since the initial hello before he told Bones he had officially stepped down as Fort Wayne president of the Rebel Wayfarers. "Been ready for a while, just things kept us from making the transfer."

"Smart move on your part, as well as Mason. When there is already turmoil in a club, a leadership change would be like throwing gasoline on a fire. Is Fury ready for this? Nearly outside his experience, yes?" He had just finished dinner when Slate had called, and strolled the block as he listened to his friend. Entering a park near his home, he paused and sat on a bench. Tipping his head back, Bones watched the first stars of nightfall appearing in the night sky. "I know he held the president title before, but even he had admitted that was a short-term thing."

"Yeah, he's more than ready. Mason's been moving him around, getting him to meet most of the leverage members, sending him here and there on missions that required he get cooperation at the local level. Mason's the master at this shit, man." Slate snorted a laugh. "Fury ain't afraid of making the big decisions, either, you know that. Witness how he wound up here, man. He's gonna be what the chapter needs right now."

Bones asked, "And you, my friend, what do you need right now?"

"Right now? I need to get to the store because we're low on diapers and wipes. I need to go to PBJ's place and check out his puppies, he's saving a female for me, although why I'd want to flood my place with more estrogen is beyond me, man. I need to get going so I can get home, hold my babies. Make memories for my woman, who had a shit set of parents, so she's entirely fucked up about how to parent herself. I should buy stock in that online bookstore. She buys so many books about what not to do." He sighed again, this one a happy noise, one that made Bones smile. "Right now, I got nothing except my old lady and my babies on the horizon, brother. I'm ready for the change."

"Then you should go," Bones told him, seeing movement at the back of his park. Slowly it resolved into a figure, and he tensed, then recognized the silhouette. "I have someone waiting for me, too."

"Yeah?" Slate's voice expressed more than a passing interest. "This gal got a name?"

"Ester."

A warning

Bones

Always a staunch supporter, Shades had been the first to toss his white marker on the table when they voted to join their Skeptics with the Rebel Wayfarers. Honored, Bones had thanked Shades with his own vote when it came time to vote in Bones' replacement for the new chapter. Bones himself stepped down, moving to the main chapter in Chicago as president, because Mason, their founder and national president, had plans he had laid out in a closed-door meeting. For years, the two men had shared a friendship, built on trust and a belief they walked the same road of honor. Now, their paths were truly united, and Bones couldn't be happier.

Sitting at his side, equals in this as never before, Bones listened as Shades talked to the assembled Rebel presidents. The meeting was held at the original clubhouse, the Mother chapter, a patch Bones proudly wore on the back of his vest, and all were in attendance, along with their nationals like Mason. Shades' argument held merit, and everyone knew it, but none would say it, Shades becoming more agitated as his speech went on without any questions or support.

In for a penny, Bones thought, laying his hand palm-down on the table. Shades paused, and Bones spoke into the quiet that followed. "We all know who is behind the recent events. None of us fear to call his name. He is not a boogie man set to frighten children. Deacon is a canker in the mouth of all clubs he has ever associated with, just ask the Florida club he betrayed." He took a breath, looking around at the faces he knew well, seeing fear he didn't expect there.

"Justice Morgan is another who is proof that blood can run true in the veins of children. Shooter is a wildcard we do not need, even jailed as he is." He repeated his words, using grave emphasis to make sure none mistook his intent. "We all know who is behind the recent events. The newsmakers do not, so they look to vility any who ride. It is up to us to police our own. That has long been the way of the code."

He paused for breath, making certain he had the right words. "The first part is known by all who ride, leave no one behind. The second is known by the chiefs who deal out the justice, leave no opening. Because as certain as you do, there will be those who do not honor the first and try to wedge in and make a mockery of everything we stand for. If Shades needs a vote to put together a task force—" There were snickering laughs at his use of that phrase, and he answered those with a grin. "—to hunt these two men, then I vote *yes*. I will shout it if needed. I would ink it, but that phrase is already on my chest." Real laughter then, and he knew the vote would swing their way. "Shall we discuss more, or can we put this to vote now?"

"Vote," Mason growled, and the anger in his voice surprised Bones. "I vote yes, too. I don't like it, but I see the need."

After the meeting had concluded, Bones sought out Mason, to find out the reason for his emotion. Mason didn't keep him waiting, turning from half-a-dozen men who were talking to or at him, and walked to where Bones waited patiently, two beers in hand. "Don't start your mind tricks. I can already see you working at how to pick my brain. Stop it."

Mason didn't smile, and Bones felt off stride with this opening. Then Mason grinned, and proved he was playing with Bones, "Jesus, your fuckin' face is priceless, Bones. Gotcha."

"Fuck you." Bones huffed out an insulted breath, then flipped him off, pulling a chuckle from Mason. "Why does the idea of hunting them cause you angst?"

Mason's expression sobered and his lips twisted to the side. In anger or guilt, Bones couldn't decide. "Shoulda killed Deacon when I took the club." Mason's words were blunt, but they were something Bones had thought a thousand times in the years since Mason turned the man out of his own club, patchless, but alive. That was when the Rebel Wayfarers was birthed, rising from the ashes of the Rebel Fiends, brought to life by Mason's determination to make a better life. *We all have a calling*, Bones thought and shook his head. *That is Mason's*.

"You disagree?" Mason asked in surprise, and Bones shook his head again.

"No. I told Slate the same not long ago, that it was one of your greatest regrets. You well know if it were me, I would have killed the man without qualm or hesitation. But, that is who I am." Mason turned, facing him squarely, waiting for what he clearly expected to be a personal hit. "You want better, and you work tirelessly for that to happen. Weaving people in and out of the paths you choose for them, making them better as you go along. You praise loudly and blame softly, favoring the carrot over the whip, every time. You wanted better from Deacon, for years, and he failed to deliver. You letting him walk out of that clubhouse and mount his bike to ride away, that was you giving him a last chance to want better for himself. Unfortunately,"—Bones shrugged—"that is not who he is. So, in his ignorance, he has tainted more people. You cannot dish that to your own plate, Mason. He was granted mercy, and chose to respond to that mercy with poison, making himself a mockery in the process."

Mason opened his mouth, but Bones kept talking, knowing if he allowed Mason's self-doubt to rise to the surface, it would be a mistake. "Morgan is not someone I can speak about in a profound way. I know the man by reputation more than personal experience. But I have had great experience with his son, and you and I both know the kind of man Shooter is. The kind of man he molded his son to be." Only months ago, Mason had killed his own nephew, son of his half-brother. "Judge chose his own path. The man had every chance to change. We have only to look to Eddie to see that." Judge had been Shooter's son, Eddie was his daughter, and the two had grown up to be as different as any siblings could be. Judge had enjoyed acts of torture as if he had invented them, and Eddie was happiest when working with disadvantaged children, helping them make the most of the world in which they had been born into. *Would that Ester could have had an Eddie at her back.* "This is overdue, Mason. Long overdue. Shades is methodical, and with the resources of the club, and the brains of Myron and Gunny, I expect he will be successful in sorting things out."

"I hope so," Mason said. "Ready to put this behind us, move on to better things."

"Your wife is well? Willa happy with her found life?"

Mason nodded, his face relaxing and that told Bones far more than a smile would have. She was his peace. "Yeah." He sighed, muscles loosening as his shoulders dropped. "We're good. I'm leaving in an hour to ride back to the Fort. She likes our doc there, so we're settled there for the duration."

"Blessings, my friend. They come when we need them, not when we ask." Bones remembered Mason's face at Mica's wedding, and mentally compared the two expressions. When Willa had been in danger, Mica was too, but Willa was all Mason saw. Two women in nearly the same situation, and he'd had only had eyes for Willa. "It's up to us to hold on."

"Agreed." Eyes crinkling at the corners, Mason cut him a glance, and Bones braced, not knowing what was coming next. "Heard you got a gal, too. Am I gonna meet her anytime soon? This Ester that's got Myron so worked up he's putting in eighty-hour weeks?"

Bones winced. "I did not know it taxed him so to look into things for me. I will talk to him, put a pause on the process." He very carefully didn't answer Mason's question, expecting Mason to call him on it, and he wasn't wrong.

"Myron does what he wants, regardless. If he didn't think it worth pursuing, he'd drop it like a hot potato and tell you so. He's got his teeth in this, and all I hear are mutters for justice. You ain't gonna get him to back off now. But my question is"—he leaned over, grinning as he bumped Bones shoulder with his own—"when do I meet Ester?"

"You do not." With a slow shake of his head, Bones rebuffed Mason's attempt to lighten his mood, standing firm in the face of another jostling shoulder bump. "Do you remember the words you spoke to me when I first met Willa?"

Mason would; it had been a turning point in his pursuit of the woman. Though living in Fort Wayne, she'd been in Chicago at Jackson's, looking for Mason without saying so. Bones, not knowing her, had seen a pretty woman confident enough to brave a biker bar, but smart enough to befriend the bartender, and intelligent enough to use mirrors and other tactics to watch her own back. Intrigued, he had been making an approach, in the process of being rebuffed when Mason called him from behind the one-way mirror that spanned the back of the bar.

Mason recoiled, then repeated his caution of more than a year ago, word for word, "Back. Off. You leave her the fuck alone. She's *mine*."

Bones nodded, knowing those for the exact words. "Consider yourself similarly warned."

The coat

Ester

I followed Bones often, trailing after him here or there, using jumps and shortcuts through alleys and buildings and stores that allowed me to keep him in sight as he rode his motorcycle through the streets with his friends. I noticed the symbol on the back of his vest had changed about three seasons ago, and knew his territory had moved, shifting, expanding like a deep sigh upon waking, when you pulled in a fresh breath to make fresh memories and greet a fresh day.

He looked more like my Bones these days, less the bound and gagged version of himself he'd become for a time. That was when things hadn't been working in his favor, when I'd overheard him tell someone there was strength in numbers, and strength in joined purpose and he was right. The sun alone couldn't make the world a habitable place, because on its own it would kill all life, scorch the earth, and nothing beautiful would be found. Not even a sigh, if you could believe a sigh beautiful.

Bones' sighs were beautiful, the inrushing breath that coasted over his lips. He would look at the sunrise over the lake or the sunset over the skyline and exhale a sigh filled with such deep longing I wondered if his soul needed something it wasn't getting from air alone. I wondered if he needed something that could be found close to hand. So I tried to stay close to hand to help him find it.

We talked and talked, sitting for hours wherever I found him. Or if he found me. Him buying me coffee, and water, and tea, and milk, and shakes, and those were good, but I had lactose intolerance, so the aftereffects were not so good. But, when I told him, he laughed and found a place that had special ones, and he got me vanilla shakes from there every time he saw me for two weeks. Which meant I had nine vanilla shakes in fourteen days, a good ratio.

He fed me, and told me I was too thin, and brought me a coat but it was too nice, so I couldn't accept it.

There was a fine line about nice things where I lived. Too nice earned you attention, and I didn't like attention. I liked to fade away, become background noise, that kind of quiet, white noise no one noticed so I could stay safe while I did my favorite things. Watching people, listening to their stories, learning from their lives. Leaning on their strengths to bolster me, dividing my fears by cracking a nut of wisdom. That knowledge given to me by people not me, who had earned it at the gristmill of experience. This meant I could be a student and learn, without having to brave those tides myself.

So, the coat was too nice, and he'd frowned when I'd told him, but he took it back. Bundling it into a bag, he'd shoved it into the locking box on one side of his motorcycle. Every bit of his bridled actions and movements told me he was hurt, even as his voice soothed me, so I tried to soothe him in return.

"I could take one that was less nice."

At my words, his head had come up and he speared me with a look. I would never have thought a person could be speared by something that wasn't tactile in nature, but speared I was. Pinned in place. "You would accept such a gift from me?"

I tried on a smile, something I didn't often do—I'd lost control of those muscles for the longest time. Only recently had I practiced again, wanting to earn another smile from him in return, so I tried on a smile, and it worked. His lips tugged sideways in a clear invitation to give him more, so I did, hoping my smile was as wide as my joy at knowing he was pleased with what I'd offered.

His lips had tugged the other direction, and he'd said, "Beauty."

That single word never failed to make my heart stutter, never failed to make it skip in my chest like a little girl playing hopscotch on the front walk of a home where her mother and father watched out the windows, keeping her safe even as they let her test her limits. Wants and needs, lost on the wind.

The sun needed a balance, needed the moon to keep things in sync so the earth could live. Things had their place, and as long as they stayed in their place, everything would be okay. No scorched earth threat, just a requirement that things remained as they were.

My heart wanted me to try more, to push more, to explore the feelings of happiness that radiated from Bones each time I saw him. Instead of telling him any of this, I'd nodded. Then he gave me the best gift of all and I didn't know if it was real mind reading or if my lips had betrayed me again, but whatever. I'd take it. "Ester, you make me happy."

I saw him the next day, and he had a different coat. This one was perfect, not new, not too warm, not too much of anything that anyone would want to steal. It was right in the middle of everything, like a bed, a chair, and a bowl. Fairy tales could be real.

I wore that coat for a year.

Ruined

Bones

When he'd reacted badly to Ester's rejection of his gift, the way her face filled with fear haunted Bones. He'd felt driven to make it right, and not just by gifting her with a coat of enough quality to keep her warm and healthy through the coming winter. He'd needed, and this feeling had boiled through his blood, to keep her safe. Safe, as no one had done throughout her entire life. That fear she felt and carelessly exposed said she wanted him in her life. Wanted him enough that she gave an option immediately, one he had leaped on, and that very speed revealed his own need for her.

Something she'd welcomed, if the pleasure that had shone from her eyes were real. Their friendship had grown strong, and she never turned him away when he sought her out, never claimed exhaustion or more pressing business. Something he wouldn't have considered part of the life of a homeless person, but in the cold months, time held meaning even for the displaced. One that was hammered home for him when he spent the afternoon with her weeks later.

He'd seen her in between, of course, visits here and there as their paths glanced across the other, or he'd looked for her, or she'd looked for him. They'd shared meals, when he would stuff her with as many calories as she could eat every time. Coffee, snacks, candy and protein bars shoved into the multitude of pockets she'd crafted into the coat, stocking her up for the times he wasn't around.

Everything culminating in their meandering trip through the zoo today, where she brought laughing tears to his eyes with a recitation of what she thought the animals were thinking. Her recounting of their trials while hilarious were made more so by her patent joy at his enjoyment of her pandering play. The harder he laughed, the more farfetched her stories became. Bones didn't know when he had spent more pleasant hours.

So, when the clock over the gates chimed and she looked up to see the time, the disappointment that rushed across her features was jarring, and her sigh of distress shook him to his boots. "Well, shoot a monkey. I'm late."

"What are you late for, beauty?" He looked at the clock, seeing it was half past six. "Where did you have an appointment today?"

Eyes to the sidewalk, she stepped sideways, avoiding a crack that zigzagged across the block of cement. With a cry of delight, she squatted, picking something up from the ground, and he squatted beside her to see she'd found a peacock's feather. Tattered, with the vanes clumped together in more than one spot, she lifted it and waved it through the air like a wand, cheering on her own antics with peals of giggles. Wafting it left, then right, she conducted a symphony only she could hear, then told him, "The shelter. They stop intake at six."

That meant she would be on the street tonight. He eyed the sky, remembering Shades had mentioned snow was expected. It had held off so far, but the clouds were pregnant with it, the wind biting as it slipped underneath the waistband of his jacket.

Standing, he held out his hand, waiting for her trust. She gave it, clasping her palm to his as she always did, and he pulled her to her feet. "Come," he told her, turning to the parking lot. She'd ridden with him before, enjoying the moments of free movement in a way that made him appreciate it even more, bending backwards at the waist, head tipped to laugh at the trees and clouds moving overhead, fingers woven into the belt at his waist. She would ride with him tonight. "Let us go."

"Where?" Her laughing question came with a tug, and he stopped, looking back at her, surprised she balked.

"My house. You will be warm, and safe, and I can finally cook for you." He tipped his chin down, telling her, "I have wanted to do that for a long time. See you in my home."

"*No!*" Nothing could have prepared him for her reaction when, with a scarcely stifled scream, she jerked her hand free of his, features twisting as she shouted, "You'll ruin everything."

"Ester," he called, and stepped towards her, stopping when she took two matching steps backwards. Panic gripped him, something was breaking between them, and he didn't know how to make it better. He took a breath, tried to read her face, but she had turned half away, hiding from him. Her posture shouted as loud as her mouth had that she was terrified. Of him. *Of me.* Heart in his throat, he pleaded the only argument he knew, "Ester, please. It is cold out. If you have no shelter, you will freeze. Please."

She took another step backwards, rejecting him and his offer with her movements. Bones didn't understand. He struggled with his instincts to reach out and pull her into him, hold her in place until he could argue sense with her. Make her safe, keep her with him.

I did that

Ester

"Ester, please." Bones' tone was sweetly cajoling, and I laughed.

Laughed aloud, but only for a moment before I clamped my lips on the braying sound, backing away. I whirled, preparing to run and I would have, because he had just asked the impossible and I couldn't imagine anything other than terrible things, so I needed to escape. Saliva evaporated from my mouth; dry and thick, my tongue lay mute in its fleshy cave. No sounds to drive him forwards, no arguments to bring me back. *Nothing good comes of trust*, I reminded myself of the *hims* who taught me that. All the *hes* that came before. The *thems* who tore my belief asunder. Shredded, I needed to escape. Before I could do anything, however, the tips of his fingers brushed my shoulder.

He didn't grasp, didn't clamp down, and didn't do anything to feed the fear gnawing at my gut. He simply touched me.

Touched me as if he thought I was a ghost, something ethereal and gossamer, like the woman's scarf I found once in the gutter. It was wrapped around a stick and had gotten stuck on a grate, or I'd have never noticed it. Dirty and dingy, I could still see the glorious colors embedded in the fabric when I'd picked it up.

Unwinding it carefully, gingerly, tenderly, until I held the length of it in my hands. I'd taken it with me, taken it home, and carried it with me for days, touching it lovingly. When I'd showered, I'd draped it over my body, letting the water wash over it as it washed over me, hoping the scarf would imbue me with the smallest iota of the beauty it had inside it, woven into it, always to be there, never lost because it entirely belonged in that article, that thing, the created beauty.

No matter what happened to it, how covered in gore or dirt or filth, it was always and would always be gorgeous.

"Ester, just consider it." I was frozen, tottering between what terrified me and what was real. Real won out. "You should have better options, baby. Let me be that for you. Let me..." He trailed off, and the anchor was set adrift. "Please."

Even with those words tugging me back, even with the grazing touch of his fingers pleading on my shoulder, I walked away. Quick time. Double time. Running time. Things were never the same after that. They were worse, and then they were worse again, and then they were better. Never the same, though, and I did that to us.

Cherished

Bones

A solitary diner, he sat at the table in his home, staring down at a plate of food, steam rising from the meat. Hot and nutritious. *I did not even feed her dinner*. Elbow to the table, Bones' fingertips traced a path across his brow over and over. Thinking.

He had relived the ending to their afternoon a dozen times already, trying to find where he could have decreed a different outcome. One where she sat at the table beside him, laughing. One where she slept warm and safe in his bed tonight. One in which he did a better job of showing her how he felt about what they had.

Leaning back, he threaded his fingers together on his stomach, staring out the window into the twilight. He looked for a long time, watching as the large flakes of snow falling from the sky multiplied, accumulating into tiny drifts. Tiny growing into larger, the wind swirling the snow around, packing it into every crevice. A scene that would have been picturesque before, now filled with menace.

If she were here, I could show her.

The discarded feather lay on the table to one side, saving her place.

Prizes and givesies

Bones

Things were different between him and Ester after the day at the zoo. He saw her just as frequently, more so perhaps, as he actively sought out her hiding places. Saw her, meaning he caught glimpses, but seldom more. Because now, by the time he parked and got off the bike, instead of waiting for his approach, she regularly disappeared. Even when she did delay, she didn't allow them the same time together as before. He could count their time together in minutes, not hours. Quick, brusque in her way, it felt as if she were punishing him for a transgression he couldn't understand.

Then, one day when they were approaching the outer limits of the time she would now allow, he caught her looking at him. The pain in her gaze told him this was intended as a punishment for her, not him. Bones didn't do helpless well, but without knowing what had triggered the withdrawal, without understanding, he couldn't see a way to repair things.

Any attempts to question her, to discuss the rift always resulted in her rapid retreat, so he stopped, trying to force himself to be willing to take whatever she allowed. Never as much as he wanted, but as much as she gave him, he would take. Not contented, no, far from it, but afraid down to the soles of his boots she would drop out of his life entirely if he did aught else. So, like a beggar with an empty palm upraised, he took what he could get.

Christmas loomed, and he teetered on the cusp of panic. If a coat could be cause for her to pull away, and the offer of a meal and a place to stay make her feel she had to build a wall to protect herself, Bones had not the first clue of what he could get her for Christmas that wouldn't send her into even more of a tailspin.

Seated at the bar in Jackson's one night, he had occasion to talk to Mica, finding her an unlikely sounding board, but a wise one. He hadn't considered her background, where she had left her entire life behind, brutally stripping herself of family and home to keep them safe. An endeavor which proved unsuccessful, and her sister's first child the result. Still, she had knowledge of making oneself invisible, and he believed this was what he needed to understand.

"So what you are saying is I offered too much." Frustrated, because he was too late learning some things, Bones tapped the bar, pointing to Mica's glass and his own beer, requesting refills.

"No, the offering isn't the problem. That's in her head. She loved that you thought about her, how you must have imagined her in the coat. But for her, in her world, it would make her a target." Mica shook her head, dark sheets of hair swirling with the movement. "From what you said, she's been living on the streets for a long time. I never had to do that, but I still had to be careful so I could hide. Nothing too flashy, because it might get someone's attention. Nothing too plain, because that would stand out, too." She laughed. "The best presents weren't things, though."

Picking up his fresh beer, Bones tipped his head and arched an eyebrow, waiting.

"Jess, she knew everything about me. She'd work connections to get me things from home. Things that reminded me of home. Food, souvenir T-shirts from places around Texas, even pictures of family, as long as she could get them in a quiet way." Mica's mouth pulled into a sideways smile. "Always the best friend I could have asked for."

"Mica, I feed her as often as she will allow. Her family, I do not think pictures of them would bring back pleasant memories." At the haunted look Mica gave him, he lifted a palm towards her. "I will not say more on that, just know her childhood was unpleasant before her father passed, and afterwards became horrific. I cannot see a way through what you suggest to find a gift for my Ester."

"I like that you call her yours, but you're not listening to me," Mica complained, setting her half-emptied glass down. "You heard things. It wasn't what Jess got me, but how they made me feel. I'm talking emotions. What does she like?"

"I do not know. She does not ask for anything." His torso jerked back when Mica slapped the bar top.

"*Things* are not emotions." Pushing her hair back, she let it fall from her hand, reaching out to use one fingertip to thump his bottle. "The beer is a thing, but it's nothing on its own. Just a puddle. Is the bottle the beer? No, the beer is inside. The bottle is just the way to hold it in, until you can take it out and enjoy it. Jeeze oh *Pete* you're thick."

"Mica, you make no sense."

"I make complete sense. You just aren't listening." Sitting back on her stool, she huffed out an exasperated sigh. "When you were at the zoo, that wasn't a thing, but she liked it, right?"

"Yes. It was a good day, until I...I do not even know what I did."

Ignoring his frustration, she pushed ahead. "The times you sat with her in the park, were those things?" Irritated at himself for telling her so much, Bones shook his head at Mica. She squinted at him, a matching annoyance clear on her face. Mica said, "Damn straight, they weren't things. They were doing, being, feeling, not things." She leaned forwards, elbow to the bar again. "She needs doings, you get me?"

Shaking his head slowly back and forth, Bones offered no other answer.

"Jeeze oh *Pete*." Head back, Mica looked up to the smoke-stained ceiling. "You said she's talked about classes, exhibitions, openings, and you've even gone with her to a few, right?"

Beginning to think he could see where she was headed, he said, "Yes, several times. We've gone to outdoor movies in the park, the amphitheater to hear the symphony, the butterfly exhibit—"

"*Exactly!*" she shouted, reaching out to grip his arm and shake him back and forth. "Doings. Not things." Chewing on her lip, she was silent a moment, then observed, "Outside stuff, yeah?"

"Yes, she is most comfortable outside. She will endure being inside for a thing in which she has keen interest." He shook his head again. "Mica, it is deep winter in Chicago. My options for outside entertainment as a gift are very limited."

"Not if you do wintery stuff. Skating, tobogganing, stuff like that." Dusting her palms together, she looked self-satisfied. "Done deal. Outside doings, no things."

"I am unsure if you helped or not, Mica. But I thank you for your time." Leaning towards the bar, her arm around his waist took him off guard, and he jerked around to look at her.

"I helped, trust me. You're at least thinking instead of moping. Everybody's been talking about it, and I'm sick of hearing about poor ol' Bones bein' all stressed out. I helped everybody."

***

From his elevated perch, Bones called a command to halt when he found Ester at the first place he looked. *She wanted to see me, too*, he thought, knowing she had made it easy for him. Hoping. He was choking on the idea that this woman had become so important to him, and yet did not know how precious she was. Standing on the sidewalk, he watched her for a moment, conscious of how caught up she was in whatever she was looking at. He swept the area with his gaze, noticing how the light glittered on the snow that lay drifted along the edges of the baseball field. He didn't know why she came so often to this field, a place of torment for her, but it was Tuesday, and he knew she would be here.

Crunching through the frozen crust of the snow, attention fixed on her form, he knew the moment she heard him. Saw her body twist on the cold cement of the picnic table, saw too, the quaking fright in her eyes before she recognized him. Then he saw the now-familiar pain, quickly masked by a forced smile, bright and fragile. "Bones," she cried, lifting a hand and crooking her fingers in a mitten-encased wave. *At least she's wearing them*, he thought, and recognized the coat, drawn tight around her throat over the mismatched scarf. *And that*. "I didn't know it was Bones' day. Did I miss something?"

"Bones' day?" he questioned, carefully keeping his tone light as he climbed up to sit beside her, wincing at the chill that bit through the fabric of his pants. "I did not know I had a special day. Thank you for the gift, Ester. I love Bones' day."

"Dork." She smiled brightly, apples of her pink cheeks lifting, eyes dancing. "Wednesday and Sunday. Those are Bones' days. All day, those days. Not limited to a slice, you get the whole pie." She sighed, turning to look out at the snow again. "I like pie. I like Bones' day pies best. Gobble 'em up, can't wait for the next bite and the next, then I have to wait days before I get another piece. Pie days are the best."

"Can't you eat pie every day?" She wasn't retreating, wasn't slipping towards the edge of the table before leaving. Her words struck him, though, because Wednesday and Sunday were the only days she would usually stay. Without fail, no matter how early he showed, they would spend those days together. "Pie is good for you. Builds strong bones and teeth."

"You're thinking of milk. I like milk, too. I'm intolerantly tolerant." Neck twisted, she grinned sideways at him from under a curtain of hair, eyes bright. "But pie is so yummy. Never a chance of badness when you have pie in your mouth." Blowing out her cheeks, she mimicked bringing a full fork to her lips, pretending to talk through a mouthful of food when she said, "Tastes so good."

"It does indeed." Bones hesitated a moment, wondering If he should take this and no more, holding his surprise for a Bones' day when he would be assured of her company. *I can do this again, if she balks and the only reason is an imaginary boundary on the time we spend together.* "I like prizes, too."

Clasping her mitten-covered hands together, she lifted them to her lips and smiled around the tips. "Prizes are the best." She nodded vigorously. "Especially this time of year, when everyone is excited to receive them. I love to give prizes all the time, but this is the best." Her chin dipped as if she were apparently struck by an idea. "What kind of prizes do you like?"

"Prizes that mean something to the giver. It opens a window onto what they think about when they think of me." He offered her honesty, and found a place to drop a guilt bubble he could use later. "That is when you know refusal is not an option, when it matters to them."

"True dat," she muttered, lips pushing up into a moue, her face a study in seriousness. "When the prize is a better gift than they know, because it shows a thing they can't share. Hot dog mistakes or buttered toast and bacon with your eggs."

"Hot dog mistakes?"

"Yeah." She sighed, the tip of her tongue darting out to wet her top lip. "When you have change for a dog alone, and it comes with cheese and chili and onions and peppers and all the best things because 'oh look, Ester, I made a mistake' and you know it's not a mistake, it's a—" She leaned close, whispering, "—prize."

"That is indeed a prize." He watched her, glad she wasn't discomfited by his study, knowing the hot dog vendor and the waitress hadn't made mistakes, but had taken it upon themselves to feed his Ester. "So you cannot give prizes back. You have to take them, correct?"

"Oh, yes." Nodding quickly, she had a childlike excitement that made him smile. "Takesies only, no givesies."

"And if I had a prize for you, what would you say to that? Would you accept?" He held his breath, waiting, and he wasn't disappointed.

"Have to." She twitched her nose, uncomfortable with this answer, but trapped into it by their conversation and her sense of rightness. Staring at him, dread shining from her eyes, she whispered, "What have you done, Bones?"

"You do not like things." Scrunching her brows together, she narrowed her eyes, and he felt something brush his hand on the table, glancing down to see she'd placed her hand beside his. Mica's words sounded right, and he let the feeling resonate through him, praying they left no room for rejection. "You like doings."

"True dat." She repeated her earlier words, eyes now open wide, and he felt her hand creep closer, her little finger draping over his, the mitten warm against his skin.

"Doings which let you see." She nodded. "Ester, have you ever been around horses?" Another quick nod. "Do you fear them?" A quicker head shake. "Then turn around, baby, and see."

She stared at him, all seriousness and he watched her jaw work as she swallowed. "It's not a Bones' day. Not anymore."

Trying to infuse confidence and certainty in his words, he assured her, "You may have pie today, Ester." She swallowed again, and her hand moved to cover his entirely, the touch making his heart leap. "Any day you want, you may have pie. But today, you get a prize." He worked to fit his mouth around her words, wanting no mistakes. "Only takesies, no givesies. Turn around and look. See what doings we are about to do."

She closed her eyes, sealing the brightness behind her lids, and it almost looked as if she were praying as her hand tightened around his, clasping to him. Then, eyes still closed, she twisted towards the edge of the trees, where he had flattened a path through the snow from the carriage, the horse half-asleep at the wait. A moment later she flung herself at him, and his arms came up to capture and hold, as he had wanted to do for so long, while she squealed in his ear about pumpkin being the best pie ever in the world of pie.

He agreed, wholeheartedly.

***

Halfway through the planned four-hour ride, Bones' phone vibrated with an incoming text. He had learned enough about Ester to know to silence it before approaching her, and to understand not to take it out in her presence. She appeared to be entirely terrified of them, still, and he was enjoying himself too much to want to risk her taking flight if he even looked at the display. A single text, not repeated, so likely of nonurgent nature.

Delighted as he had ever seen her, she had crawled out of his lap to clamber across the table, nearly dragging him off with sharp tugs at his hand and shouted commands to, "Come on! He's gonna leave! We'll be late!" With a good-natured impatience, she had suffered through him swinging off the table on the side where she waited, bouncing from foot to foot. "Come on, Bonesy." He sucked in a breath at that, the sharp cold stinging his throat. She had never called him anything but Bones, and as she often said of his words to her, this was a gift.

At the carriage, the driver waited with a grin as she spoke quietly to the horse, thanking him for his work and hoping she wouldn't be too large a burden. She pulled a granola bar from her pocket, and at the driver's nod, she unwrapped it, offering a third of it to the horse at a time, nimbly avoiding his smacking teeth and giving him a good scratching along his cheeks while he chewed. "Are you ready now, Ester?" Bones held out his hand, and she put her empty mitten into it, laughing when he pretended to scowl at her.

"I'll take two pieces to start." She had hauled herself up the steps and watched as the driver folded them away. "Mine." She showed him her mitten-covered hand, waggling it side-to-side, then she reached out, and when Bones started handing her the other mitten, she surprised him by reclaiming her hold, wedging both their hands down into the soft fabric, stretching it to fit, her fingers clasped around his. "Ours." Sighing, she looked at his other hand, and said, "Yours is coldest. Cold pie."

Leaning in close, he pulled a blanket from beside him, draping it across their legs, loath to lose her in any way, loving how she snuggled into his side. "Warmer," he told her with a smile, and she grinned up at him, squealing when the carriage rocked as the driver returned to his high seat, and they were moving down the street. They sat on the seat facing forwards, Bones' feet propped on the cushion across the way, the straight-backed posture of the driver leading them ever onwards. Bones had laid the path with him on their way to the park, and he would carry them without instructions unless Ester decided a different route for their journey.

"Tell me what you think of this prize," he whispered, watching as she stared upwards, eyes trailing across the Christmas lights displayed in the office buildings, floors organizing their decorations to arrange the lighted windows into a tree, or in one case a snowman.

"Best ever. No one's ever gotten me happy as a gift before. Not before you. You give me happy all the time, even when you don't know it, Bonesy." Leaning forwards, she turned her head in first one direction, then the other, marveling at streetlights draped with color. Looking into his face, she whispered, "Best. Ever." Her gaze fell to his chin, and she chewed on her lips, wrestling with what she wanted to say. Bones waited, hoping whatever caused her such visible turmoil would be worth it. "Every day can be Bones' day again?" The question was barely audible, and the moment the last sound escaped her mouth, she was actively chewing on her lips again, agonizing over his answer.

"Every day is Bones' day," he agreed, and she pulled in a deep breath, then coughed as the cold air bit at the back of her throat. "As many days as you will allow, beauty. Every day sounds excellent to me."

Bonesday

Ester

I wanted to kiss him. There, I said it, even if just to me. After he didn't care I mauled him, I pushed and pushed, wanting more, holding on so tight I could feel every twitch of his fingers. When he held me, and I knew he didn't like to be touched by people, but he'd liked his arms around me and that's when I was certain I wasn't just people to him, and that made me want more, too. Me mauling him like that, not biting him like a dog, and that was good of me even if mauling wasn't but he didn't care. Didn't care about the hugging and the handholding and the sitting so close he had to put his arm around me. Or maybe he did care, but in the other direction of not liking. Maybe he wanted more, too. *Maybe he wanted a kiss?*

He was so much of everything I'd thought he would be that I nearly didn't care about anything else, until I remembered the grown-up pumpkin waiting at the curb. I didn't know the horse, of course, not even by a different color, so I took the time to introduce myself like the church ladies did, hand out with a sweet, ready to pull my knuckles back at the first sign of madness. But he wasn't mad, he was a she, actually, and the man with the hat told me her name was Madeline. I thought it was pretty, and told her so, and she agreed, soft lips plucking the treat from my palm.

Then I mauled Bones again, and he didn't care again, holding my hand the entire time we rode through the wonderland. Forgiven, it seemed, and I hoped, I hoped, I hoped it so. I'd never seen the buildings shine so brightly, never seen so much of everything be beautiful. I looked at it and then looked at him and he was staring at me like I'd done all of this for him, when he was the one handing me the prize. Not even mad about the wrongs I'd done him. He looked happy, and happier yet when I told him he'd given me happy.

When we got out of the carriage, the man with the hat offered to take me where I needed to go, but I didn't have anywhere to go, so I smiled and told him, "Pumpkins change back all the time, and you need to keep yours safe." He didn't understand, but that was okay. I did. I knew, pumpkins were dreams come true, but where I lived would kill his dream, and so I didn't let him take me anywhere. Bones stood and listened, chin down, and I saw his hair had grown in, thick and dark and soft and beautiful. I was out of tries, having stopped myself—except for the two times when I mauled him—and I reached up, teasing a lock of it free of the rest, letting it drift through my fingers. It felt so good, I did it again. A third time I allowed myself, and he was looking at me from underneath that hair, eyes bright and breathing uneven, and that was when I recognized what I'd felt earlier.

I reminded him of the new truth, that I'd not be avoiding him anymore. I'd taken my licks, and waited out the pain, not crying. Never crying, because big girls didn't cry. "Every day is Bones' day." No more Sunday or Monday, just Bonesday.

It wasn't until I got to the culvert where I'd stashed my things that I realized I had the blanket in my hands. Mitten to blanket, the warmth had masked the knowledge I had stolen from him. Then I remembered him telling me it was a doing prize, but we'd agreed you couldn't turn away gifts, either. Giving it back would be taking his joy from him in the giving. "No takesies," I whispered as I snuggled into the blanket that smelled exactly like Bones. "No help for it. 'S mine, now." That was when I told myself the truth I'd learned tonight. I wanted to kiss him. Wanted with every fiber that was stuck inside my body. Every non-escaping fiber of my soul. *Needs, not wants, that's what we address first*, the court lady had said more than once. That was when they gave me clothes too new, a bag too new, shoes too new, and the other fosters fell on me like ravening wolves. Mad, and no curled knuckle to turn aside those bites.

Maybe I needed this thing. "Maybe I need Bones." My heart agreed with my throat, and they should; they'd spent the entire night getting well acquainted, what with occupying the same place in my body for the whole time. "Maybe he needs me, too." That was the best sleep in a long time, and my dreams were filled with pumpkins and pies.

Gone

Mason

Bike skidding to a halt, Mason was off it and pelting through the mess Watcher had left behind him on his kamikaze run. Gun in a one-handed grip in front of him, he lifted and aimed in the same motion, clearing his path of Diamante who thought to engage. *Aim to maim*. Behind him, he heard Opie's voice, yelling orders, commands only half the men would understand, Mason's Rebels following a different hierarchy when it came to leadership. They would have followed Watcher, because he had been part of them for as long as most could remember, skirting the edges, but theirs in a way that Opie wasn't. Yet.

Another Diamante stood in his way, cleared by a round from behind Mason, the man's own shot going wild, bullet ricocheting and impacting a bike. Then Mason was through the smoke from Watcher's mangled bike, handlebars nearly torn from the forks, a single boot lying near the twisted front wheel. With laborious running steps digging through the sand, Mason got to where the dirt was roiled, cleared down to rock in some places, bloody swaths left behind. Two paces more and an explosion nearly lifted him off his feet. Glancing back, he saw what looked like a dozen men down, affiliation unknown. *Fuck*. Not certain if it was a tank on a damaged bike blowing, or something packaged in a saddlebag, and for now, he didn't care.

Still, he held to hope. Hope that miracles happened, that good men lived beyond what normal ones could survive. On his knees next to Watcher, Mason felt all of those hopes fall away, torn free with each battered injury identified on his friend's body. A rattling cough and Mason's heart leaped in his chest. Ignoring the story told by the dark sand surrounding Watcher's lower half, he reached out and grasped his shoulders, seeing hands come into view to cradle and support the head and neck. He glanced up, and together he and Opie turned Watcher to his back, and Mason cringed at the damage. One leg nearly severed just above the knee, the other mangled beyond repair. His fingers went to the buckle of his belt, ready to fashion a makeshift tourniquet, but the blood pumping out had already slowed to a trickle.

Lifting Watcher's hand with his, a squeeze startled him, and he stared down into eyes bright with pain, knowing they didn't see him when the word whispered was a woman's name. "Juanita."

"Gonna take care of her, boss. Promise. She'll never want for anything, brother." Mason scarcely recognized Opie's voice, ragged with pain. "Promise you, man. Not her, not the girls."

His chest seized painfully as Mason stared down into eyes now gone glassy and fixed. Eyes he'd seen laughing not an hour ago, poking fun at Mason's repeated calls home to check on his pregnant wife. Eyes he'd seen smiling with pleasure as a story was recounted that told of the honor the Soldiers always brought to the table. Eyes he'd known his entire life, raised in side-by-side fashion on the shoulders of Kentucky mountains.

Too much to think of, too much to process, Mason knelt and held his friend's hand, grinding down, knowing he was clutching it too tight, but unable to stop. Wanting to provoke a response, any response, anything to let Watcher know he wasn't alone. He held on, long after the blood stopped flowing altogether. Opie stepped away, making a call.

Head tipped down, neck bent, taking in a series of hard, deep breaths, Mason tried to marshal his thoughts. Calls and decisions to make, if the sounds behind him were what he thought they were. A journey to finish with at least one empty spot in the line. At that, he realized he didn't know if any others of his Rebels had been injured, and then grasped he was no longer considering them two clubs. Watcher might still wear a Southern Soldier patch, but that was only going to be until they got to Las Cruces, this much he and Mason had already decided. Stability demanded Watcher not drop his center until the rank and file did, and Mason would now have to see this through with the help of Opie and Devil, two of Watcher's officers.

Without lifting his head, hoping the man had stayed close, Mason called over his shoulder. "Opie."

An immediate, "Yeah, boss," was gratifying, even as it tightened Mason's throat. That was Opie's standard response to Watcher, and hearing it while looking down at the shell of his friend was hard to take.

"We got any other injured?" First order of business, seeing to members.

"Not us, no." A hesitation, then, his voice quiet to the point of a whisper, Opie said, "Not beyond Watcher."

Mason's shoulders heaved a huge sigh of relief. "Diamante?" No screams, no sobs, no calling for God's mercy, so what Opie said next was a surprise, and not a good one.

"Fifteen out of fifty down, boss. Lalo's *número uno*, most of the rest are all members." Sand scrunched under a footfall, indicating Opie was moving closer. "Looks like they had some explosives on two of their bikes. Watcher, he wrecked through 'em, and one of their bikes caught fire. They were all standing close, pitching sand on the fire, tryin' to put it out." A pause, then a soft, "Kablooey."

"Fuck." Mason twisted, fists to one thigh. He was preparing to stand, just needing a minute before he tried. Looking down, he saw the knees of his jeans were sodden with blood. Head twisting to one side, he clenched his eyes, throat tight. *My brother's blood, an honor.* In his head, he heard the words to an old Kentucky spiritual, "Wayfaring Stranger." *I'm just a going over home.*

Business, he thought, trying to push past the pain threatening to keep him on his knees. "They got an officer left upright?"

"Chismoso." Opie bit out the word, hatred clear in his tone. "You gonna treat with him?"

"Gonna see what kind of story he wants to weave for the cops who are gonna show up any minute. I've heard a dozen cars speed past, and you know at least one of them was on the horn with nine-one-one. He wants to take the heat for explosives, that's his deal. If I gotta, I'll cop to a defense of life and property plea for the three holes I put in his men." With a last look at Watcher, he leaned over, palm to his friend's forehead, dragging lax lids closed over clouded eyes. "That's the treat I'll give him."

Wake the monster

Bones

"Do not test me," Bones told the man seated across the space, separated by only air and honor, not even deigning to bring in a table on which elbows could be propped. It wasn't Bones' intention for this man to be comfortable in any fashion. "You would be most unhappy with the results; of that, I can assure you."

Chismoso glared at him. He lifted a hand, and Bones took a breath. Knowledge of this man was hard won, but intelligence had come his way long ago that told of a certain harness spotted in a skirmish. Chismoso's fingers skimmed the side of his skull, threading through his shaggy mane to the back, and Bones decided to stall this midact. "Do not," he said, putting on a long-suffering tone. He even went so far as to roll his eyes, coming back to see Chismoso frozen, fingers wrapped around the handle of the knife strapped to his back.

Mason had continued on to Las Cruces, and was now organizing things there. Dealing with the loss of their brother and grief of the woman he'd loved, and the birth of a new Rebel chapter. Chismoso had come straight to Chicago it seemed, wanting something. It was Bones' job to determine what that something was.

"Do you not see?" Bones leaned forwards, clasping his hands, elbows on his knees. "All your secrets are known to me. All of them. From cradle to grave, you are seen and known. You—" Tilting his chin to one side, Bones indicated the men standing at Chismoso's back. "—are not the man your cousin was. Your command differs in important ways."

"His death must be answered." With slow, sure movements, Chismoso settled the knife back into the sheath.

"It was answered on the edge of the same road. Blood spilled on both sides, but you cannot say Lalo's death was not earned. He bought that with every action he performed for the last year." Bones didn't give him a moment to collect himself, pushing onwards, needing the man to give on every point. "And your boss now requires you earn your own death, sending you to treat with us as if Diamante were equals with the Rebel Wayfarers. Pull a clue from your president's pussy and *see*. With every week Diamante are bleeding. They bleed money, patches, and rockers. You change cities so often it makes one dizzy. How many have you worn?"

Bones paused to take a breath but didn't give him time to speak. Chismoso needed to see, understand, and agree. "What do you wear now? Chicag—no, not that city." Bones tapped his lips with the tip of one finger, feigning confusion. "Las Cruce—no, not there, either. Louisville, Lexington, Memphis, St. Louis, Fort Wayne—and that list of discards just spans the past months. These men care not for your life, nor the lives of any man with you. Surely they knew we would not meet on a level playing field. I have two men to each of yours, and a hundred waiting outside these doors." With a tip of one hand, he gestured towards the double-doors that led to the bar proper. "If you doubt me, then rise, and verify for yourself."

Sitting back in his chair, Bones slung his elbow over the back, kicking one leg out in front, the heel of his boot to the floor. At ease in a way that was not pretend, not playacting, and screamed a discrediting of any threat Chismoso or his men could bring to the meet. "I can wait."

Chismoso didn't respond, didn't react, and offered Bones no insight into the workings of his mind. They sat like that, stalemated for a minute, then two, the men behind Chismoso growing antsy, boot soles scuffing the bare floor as they moved. Bare for easy cleanup, and surely every one of them knew that as fact. Leather creaking, shoulders shifting, hands shoved into and pulled quickly out of pockets, not wanting to give an appearance of threat.

Finally, Chismoso leaned forwards, jutting his chin at Bones. "You are weak."

"You. Are. Wrong." Bones infused certainty into each letter. Into each pause. Into each breath that it took to push out those words. "Because I am diplomatic now, do not mistake me for someone incapable of taking care of business. I do not want to fight. But if you force my hand, I will not fight fair." The heel of his boot dragged across the cement as he sat forward, the sound loud in the stillness of the room. Scratching the side of his nose with a blunt thumbnail, he stared at Chismoso. Elbows again resting on his knees, Bones said, "I will not quit, and there is nothing sacred to me. Do not ever think that the reason I am treating with you peacefully is because I fear violence. I do not."

Bones sat back again, at ease. Lifting one hand, he pointed two casually curled fingers towards Chismoso's chest. "You fight, not for someone or something you love more than breath, but because you are instructed to do so. Do not mistake my principles for yours. Do not mistake my motivation for what drives you forwards." He thumped a clenched fist against his chest, once, twice. "I battle to protect the things and people I will die for. Such a vast difference and the true measure of a man. Fighters and warriors are not the same things." He paused, and just as Chismoso opened his mouth to speak, put those thoughts to rest. "Do not wake the monster in me."

Aftermath

Bones

Bones stared down at the list of names scrawled on the paper. Blinking, he struggled to focus on the talk still swirling around the table. "Hold, please." Silence spread through the room as, shaking his head, he repeated, slightly differently, "Please, hold." Once all talk had died down, he took a deep breath and laid his palm flat on the paper. "These are the known Diamante dead, killed by the explosion of a faulty battery." Rough laughter, because everyone knew it wasn't a battery that had exploded. "There are eight names. Seven of those were already known to us. Brothers,"—he poked at the paper, shoving it across the battered table—"those names matter not."

He looked at the men standing in the room, Rebels from four chapters, drawn here for his briefing. "What I need to know are the names not on any report. Who was there, and left, who had rolled through in the smaller group just before." He pushed to his feet, weariness making him weave for a moment before he steadied himself. "You know the stakes. You know the prize." Bones swallowed, hearing Mason's voice in his head again. "You know what I need. Now find it for me."

Turning, he motioned to Shades and Tater, taking them with him to the inner office behind the meeting room. Once the door closed behind them, he turned, and asked, "Truly, there is no word?" Both men shook their heads. "*Fuck*. Where are they?"

In the initial confusion of Watcher's death, little thought had been given to anything other than informing those who needed to know, and controlling official involvement in the event. It was hours later when Mason finally rolled up the long drive to Watcher's home so he could deliver the news to Spider and Juanita. Then in the emotional turmoil that followed telling Juanita of her husband's death, little notice was paid to what was now an apparent and glaring absence.

In the hours before Watcher hammered out his deal with Mason, that deal being the closure of the Southern Soldiers club entirely, with all members desiring a patch being offered one as a Rebel Wayfarer, Watcher had met with his near-daughter, Carmela. Met with and chastised, if one believed the tales, and then sent on her way home to Las Cruces, her role to watch over her near-mother.

Mela never made it home.

So now the search was on. She had left a campground outside Fort Wayne riding her own bike, with an escort of eight Soldiers and a lone Rebel. Myron had followed the group's route across three states, tracking them from transaction to transaction, mapping their progress until the trail disappeared. The last information anyone had was near Springfield, Missouri, where a store owner remembered the group buying fuel, Carmela's beauty so out of place amid the rough bikers, it had caught his attention. Now they were simply vanished.

This was why it didn't matter so much who in the Diamante had died, or even who was there that day. It mattered more the ones that were not accounted for, because the fear held in every man's breast was that Carmela had been taken, her escorts either killed, or accomplices. Bones used Mason's presence in Las Cruces to pick the brains of all the men there, going over, again and again, the names and loyalties of the ones dispatched to guard the Machos' princess home. Soldiers' princess, as well, because she had certainly been raised to span the divide between clubs. Then, in Indiana, she had hitched her luck to the fate of a Rebel prospect, making it a trio of clubs who would wish her safe.

Vanished.

"Bones," Shades started, shaking his head, "you're dead on your feet. At least grab some bunk time, man. Ain't no way you're thinkin' straight. How long you been up, thirty-six hours? You're toast, brother. Get some bunk time."

"If Carmela lies in the hands of our enemies, do you believe she sleeps easy?" Bones stared at him. "Watcher loved her with every breath, as does Juanita. We,"—he swept his hand out, indicating the three of them—"none of us should dare rest until we know does she lay her husband to rest tomorrow, will she bury her daughter the next."

Tater cleared his throat, then said, "You know I'm leaving in thirty. Gotta get Bella up and to the airport. Me and her got a plane to catch." Bones nodded at Tater, understanding the meaning behind his words. The redhead continued, "Bella's tore up. Red gave her some stuff, put her to sleep for a bit. Only reason I can be here now, brother. I can't hunt, you know it."

"Mica's husband gave us the use of his jet, yes?" Bones shook his head, fighting against thoughts that grew fuzzier with every passing hour. "You are taking it down?"

"Yeah, Daniel loaned us the plane. Why?"

Bones lifted his eyes, staring at Tater and Shades. "I had intentions of riding down, but that window has closed on me. I need to borrow a lift from you. What do I need to do for this to happen?"

"Nothing, brother. You show up with me, we're through to the tarmac and then it's just a license check." Tater turned to the door. "Let's go, man. You're with me. I wanna get back to Bella, and you're in no condition to ride, even if it wasn't colder than a witch's tit outside."

Bones lifted his head then, a thought trailing through his mind, chased away by his exhaustion. "It is cold outside?"

"Fuck yeah, brother. Cold and snowing. Fuckin' Chicago, whaddya want?"

Shades stepped to one side, talking to Tater, "I'll shoot you updates as we get 'em. Copy both of ya. If it's something needs immediate action, I'll go directly to Mason." Bones, still stuck in place, watched as he turned back. "Bones, come on."

"A moment, please. It is cold?" Feet unmoving, he couldn't fasten his mind to what he needed to remember.

"Bones, come on. We gotta go, man. I'll run up, grab your go bag. It won't be as cold in Kentucky."

"Kentucky?" Distracted from his thoughts, Bones was well and truly confused. "I thought we were headed to Las Cruces."

"Family gravesite is there. Remember? We went down with Mason when Danger died." Shades laughed, the sound somehow wrong in this moment. "You are fuckin' out of it, brother. Get in the truck. We'll take care of everything."

***

Bones got two hours of restless sleep in the truck. He slept in the cab as it was parked in a heated garage at Mason's home in Chicago, when the men with him decided it was better to allow his rest than wake him for no purpose. Three hours sleep on the plane, already adrift in his dreams before the pilot's voice ever came over the speaker system. The next eighteen hours were endless, arriving in Lexington to find patch brothers had scrounged and begged bikes for every man on the plane, giving them that ease at least. Bella climbing on behind Tater without a word, resting her pale forehead against the center of his back, waited for them to ready and leave. Lexington was somehow larger than Bones remembered, the trip out to Cynthania longer, the roads more challenging.

As they rode past downtown, Bones noted that the reformed Outriders had again taken back over their old clubhouse, after being ousted at one point by Diamante. He found a joyless humor in this circular pattern that was present in so many aspects of life.

Then he was engulfed in the nightmare that was watching the casket arrive, escorted by a hundred bikes. Placed on a trailer hauled behind the undertaker's motorcycle, a flag was tarped tightly around the box that carried his friend. His first glimpse of Mason's face, appearance as stricken as he believed his own. Enduring the painful grip of a handshake from a man who carried far too much responsibility for so many things, he struggled to fight back his tears. Finally handing Juanita from the car in which she had traveled, he was not ashamed to weep at feeling how her shaking body leaned into him as she cried, swollen eyes testimony to the heartbreak that had yet to leave her.

And still no word on Carmela. All he had to offer Juanita was a headshake when she asked, her voice trembling with fear and emotion. Swallowing hard, Bones stepped to the side, releasing her hand so she could embrace Bella. He nearly lost control of his emotions again, as the two women grappled each other. The fierceness of their sorrow a palpable thing, arms changing grip trying to get closer, heads bent to shoulders, sobs and cries rending the air. A Soldiers member and Tater stepped in to support the women when sadness took their legs from underneath them. Dragging his eyes away, he saw Mason's gaze on them, the expression of guilt and anguish on his face arresting in a way that wounded all who saw. Swallowing hard, Bones stepped to his side, and quietly pulled him away from the others with a question. It didn't matter what, anything to break the cycle of pain. "How is Willa?"

He'd happened on the right topic, remembering Watcher's laughing call only hours before his death, talking through great whoops of hilarity as he described Mason's regular calls to check on her health. *"Tellin' ya, Bones." Watcher's laughing voice stuttered through the words, the humor contagious in his amusement. "He's got it bad, man. Bad, bad. Like so bad I ain't never seen the like."*

In the background, Mason rumbled a rebuttal, "You're actin' like you weren't the same way with Juanita when she was carrying Bella." Still laughing, Watcher agreed, "I ain't arguing with you on that, but if you remember, you gave me all kinds of shit and grief. This is just me gettin' my own back on ya."

Now, quietly, Mason updated him on Willa's pregnancy, their second child together. "She's good, babe's good, Gar's good. She wanted to come down, but it's just...I'd rather she not, ya know? I can better keep a handle on her there, and she gets it, wants to make it easier for me."

Bones nodded because he understood. If he could have shielded all of them from this, he would have. "Who will travel home with Juanita when all is done?" A jerk of his hand indicated Tater, standing close behind Bella. "Tater and Bella?"

"Not until we find Mela. I'm nervous having everyone together here like this, brother, be even more nervous if we were spread all across hell and back. Juanita will come back to Chicago with us. She can stay at my house with Bella, and you and I can set our heads together, work all the angles we need." Mason stepped backwards a handful of paces, gesturing Bones to join him, creating a buffer of space between them and the rest of the men. "Spider's probably ten minutes behind us, he stopped in Nashville last night." Glancing around, Mason shook his head. "Spider? Off, *Jesus.* He's odd, man. Off *odd.*" Drawing out the sound, Mason emphasized the repeated word. "Juanita's leanin' on him, so we'll bring him to Chicago, too. Everyone here is comin', the compound in Wisconsin is gonna see some use, because the clubhouse will be too jammed. Mind if I stay with you, give Bella and Juanita some space?"

"You are welcome company, Mason. Always welcome. I will watch Spider. I will watch them all. I—" He paused, hearing bikes in the distance. "I do not have a good feeling about this."

"Me either, brother." Mason shook his head. "Me either. Hey, this mean I get to meet your Ester?"

Bones finally remembered what he'd forgotten.

Lost

Mason

Mason watched as one of his oldest friends lost his mind. He could see it coming, saw the flare of his pupils when Mason mentioned the name of the woman he had been chasing for more than two years. First he went still, so still, the wind ruffling the hair on his head was a novelty. In the decades Mason had known Bones, all those years the man had shaved his head. Then Mason watched as a panic seemed to sweep over him, breathing coming fast and labored, hands clenching into impotent fists at his sides. Even then he was still.

"Bones, you good?" Puzzled at this reaction, Mason made his inquiry quietly. Bones eyes grew glassy, as if his thoughts were far away. "Bones?"

With a jerk of his head, Bones snapped his full attention onto Mason. "*Yo...un teléfono. Disculpame, por favor.*" Now shocked, because in all the years they had been friends, and Mason had already noted to himself once that it had been decades, he never, not one time, could remember Bones forgetting himself enough to lapse into Spanish. Always he had spoken his stilted, formal English. A word here or there, certainly, but not a full sentence.

Without waiting for a response, Bones turned away, digging into his pocket for his phone, and the only thing Mason had heard before he walked out of range was his greeting, quietly intense, *"Myron."*

Patience

Bones

If ever he had longed for something to take his mind off the death of Watcher, Bones would not have asked for this. Torture, being made to sit and wait, to tend to the family in order to ease their pain, while trying desperately to organize a search for Ester from so far away, when the only thing he wanted to do was tear Chicago apart looking for her himself.

It started with getting Myron to dispatch someone to check on her. Bones listed out parks and times, days for the different kitchens or shelters. Not surprised when the first few came up dry, but as they worked their way through the list, fear had taken up residence inside his chest as every location was barren. As if she had fallen from the face of the earth, gone in totality, nothing to mark her passage except his terror that he had left his concern too late.

Myron had a thousand excuses for him, and Bones would accept none of them. Ester was Bones' responsibility, no matter she didn't know it was how he felt. He knew it, and had forgotten to ensure her safety. He hadn't forgotten her. No, he remembered her a hundred times a day. A thousand. But he had somehow forgotten to provide for her, which was worse.

After the success of his Christmas present to her, they had met nearly every day. She had shown him a makeshift calendar, with the column titles marked out, and in a careful, beautiful script, replaced with Bonesday. She had blessed him in a dozen ways each time, tiny touches so sweetly casual and yet he knew for her they were not. As disciplined as she was, each of them was planned, calculated to the last microsecond. She gifted him with fast smiles and even faster glances raining down on his skin.

But, caught up in club business, he had misplaced his need to see her. Presented with devastation coming from so many directions, there were many moving parts of which to keep track, and Bones had focused on the things in front of him, the men whose lives he held in his hands with each decision. Losing sight of her unknown needs. Now he wondered if she had become accustomed to him providing for her, become dependent on ways he had failed to account. Feared she was hungry. Perhaps cold, or injured. He remembered the day she had limped to him, gravel embedded in her palms, a cut on her leg needing stitches. Showing him her hands, Ester had simply asked, "Help me?" What if even now, this moment, she was seeking him out, needing him?

Bones was unaware he had been shifting in his seat, fidgeting, until Juanita reached over and pulled his hand into hers. With a tight squeeze, she allowed their clasped hands to rest on the cushion between them. Reminded that he was here for her, to support her, he was embarrassed she found it needful to try and settle him, no doubt believing his anxiety was caused by Watcher's death, when that had been the last thing on his mind. *Fuck.*

Outside, straddling the bike and waiting for the entourage to be ready to move, he texted Myron. ***Anything?*** A quick *N* his only response, he shoved the device back into his pocket, pushing it deep, instead of hurling it from him in frustration.

What you've got

Mason

"Brother, tell me." With three words Mason commanded obedience, and when he used that voice, coming from the national president, he knew Bones could do nothing except as demanded.

Swallowing hard, looking troubled, Bones told him.

"Ester. My Ester is homeless. She is beautiful and fey, gentle and kindhearted. God, Mason, you will love her, too. All who meet her do, a given. One of her many gifts." He smiled, and Mason saw how deep his affection ran in the way Bones' face softened. "She is also bullheaded, filled with a complicated and twisted sense of right and wrong, of what she can accept in assistance, and what she will not allow. I have run afoul of that line more than once and fought my way back into her graces. I see her nearly every day. She knows to watch for me, knows I will be there. Do you understand? She knows I will be there." He leaned forward, bending at the waist, nearly quivering in his urgency to communicate. "*I am not there.*"

"So, get someone to deal for you." Mason shrugged, not sure why Bones was torqued so far sideways because this was easily solved.

"That is what I have been doing for two days. No one can find her. No one has seen her." Pulling himself upright, Bones stared into his eyes. "It is February in Chicago, Mason. There has been fresh snow for three days straight. Heavy snow, and dipping temperatures. Churches have opened their basements to take in overflow from the shelters. She could be anywhere, but surely someone would remember seeing her. She is that unique, Mason. In a crowd, she would stand out. Yet, no one has seen her. She knows I will be there, and I am not. What if she is waiting for me to find her?"

"Jesus, Bones. You shoulda said something." Mason dug out his phone, and in a series of quick movements, unlocked, speed dialed, and put the ringing call on speaker. Connected immediately, he started, "Myron—"

He stopped when Bones whirled away, threw his hands up and shouted, "Do you consider me an idiot, Mason?"

Ignoring him, Mason continued, "Need you to find a chick in Chicago, Myron."

"Ester? You got Bones there? Tell him to look at his *fucking* phone, Mason. I got something." Myron sounded frustrated, and Mason was reminded of the hours the man had spent looking up information on her for Bones before, becoming invested in a way he hadn't seen before.

Bones was already digging in his pocket, staring down with unbelieving eyes as he punched buttons on an unresponsive phone. Mason filled in the gaps. "His phone's dead, you're on speaker. Give us what you got, brother."

Too damned far

Bones

Waiting for the jet to taxi out to the runway for takeoff was painfully slow, every moment seeming to drag out longer than the last. Myron hadn't yet found Ester, but he found someone who knew where she was squatting these days. From the conversations that followed, it sounded as if he had traced things through a thin thread at a time, tracking her from location to location, sending brothers as runners to nail down the next clue.

Damned persistent, and Bones was glad of that, even as he wondered at the reason. Turning to Mason, seated beside him, he asked, "When you first met Myron, he was homeless, yes?" Mason nodded, eyes to his phone, making one of a hundred connections he would make this day. And a hundred the next. And the next. *No rest for the wicked*, he liked to say, and Bones saw where this was true. As the national president of a club the size of the Rebels, there were always issues to solve. A never-ending list of things that required attention and consideration.

Reminded suddenly of Slate, Bones murmured, "I do not know how you do all the things you manage, my friend. But I am grateful you do. He seemed fine at the services, comfortable with the burden even in his grief, but how is Fury honestly handling taking on Fort Wayne from Slate?"

From the quick grin received, Bones expected a positive response, and got one. "Like he was born to it." Mason's smile took a wry twist. "I don't plan on goin' anywhere anytime soon, but it's good to know there're three strong contenders for my spot on the ladder, brother."

"Three?" Bones ran through men in his head, coming up short by two. "Slate, and who?" Mason's head tipped back, and he laughed, the first real sound of humor heard from him in days, and men and women the length of the plane turned to look. Bones was reminded of something his *abuela* said after his sister was killed, and he murmured, "Life goes on, and so too, do the living."

Mason said, "Truth spoken, brother. Wrong about Slate, though. He's hard enough to get to accept a role at all, even if he's damn good at it. Now that he's backed off, I can see only one thing that would pull him back to the forefront, and that's if I had to move Fury somewhere. Say, to nationals."

Surprised, because Fury had been Diamante, Bones asked, "Him? A known club hopper?"

"He's found a home finally that feels worthy of his time, worth any sacrifice he needs to make. Show him what he wants like that? Fuck, that man ain't goin' anywhere. Hell, every decision he made the last year he was Diamante held Rebel interests at heart anyway, so I ain't worried about him at all." Mason shook his head. "I have enough to deal with on the corp side. Gonna give up the city seat this year. We've eked all the good we can outta that, and it's a distraction I can't afford."

"I sometimes forget how many hats you balance." City councilman for a ward in Chicago; CEO of Mason Corp., the business which held all the Rebel interests; CEO of a private record label he ran with his sister, Bethany; and national president of a club with fifteen chapters, a club most felt was poised to go international, rumors of a Down Under chapter flowing like water through the rumor mill. "How does Willa feel about sharing you with so many?"

"She gets pissed and then pissy." Mason shrugged, the motion easy and relaxed. His smile was sly when he continued, "Bad moods can be fixed by being bad, that's what I tell her, and we eventually find ourselves back on track." They shared a chuckle, and Bones felt the bounce and bump as the plane's wheels left the runway, airborne finally.

"So Fury, and who else?" Curiosity drove the question from his lips, but Bones wasn't ready for Mason's response.

"You and Opie."

"Fuck you." His response was immediate and loud, pulling attention back to their conversation. Softening his voice, he repeated his words, knowing the sentiment would still be heard and understood. "Fuck you, Davis Mason. That is not a role I would seek."

"Neither would Fury or Opie, which is exactly why any of you'd be perfect. We got folks who stretch for influence, and those aren't the ones we need. Not that you're shy about talking your own virtues." Mason chuckled. "But you will never believe it your due. That's what we need. Someone who sees their own flaws and faults before they look elsewhere to find blame. Like with your Ester. You never consider there are a thousand people who could help you with her. Social workers, brothers, fuck...anybody. She's your responsibility, and you are tryin' to balance that with everything else. That's how we wear the hats, brother. We just keep tippin' things 'til we find a balance for a moment, take a breath, then find the next."

"That is a joyless life."

"No, brother. Fulla the joy. Seein' you find a woman who can bewitch you? Joy. Seein' Bella with Tater? Joy." Mason's attention was pulled back to his phone, and he scowled, features losing all the quiet pleasure he had held a moment ago. "No news on Mela. *Fuck*. Where the hell is she? Where the fuck's Hurley?"

***

"Myron?" Mason's voice held surprise as he greeted the man waiting for them inside Bones' home. "What the hell you doin' here? What's wrong?"

Bones held the thin man's stare as he followed Mason through the door. "I find myself wondering the same thing." He glanced pointedly at the door which had not been locked, and at the alarm system beside the door, currently reflecting an unarmed state.

"I set it up. I know the codes. How I got in here isn't important." Myron shook his head. "We gotta find Ester, Bones."

"Tell me what you know," Bones demanded, wondering what had changed.

"Lady at the deli said Ester's been coming in like clockwork for nearly three years. Never misses a Wednesday, until this week. Told me she looked sick last week, but laughed it off. The guy at the pizza place has the same story, said she's dependable with her rounds. I found six people who are used to seeing her, and haven't, and half of them remember her not feeling well. That crawling you said you had in your gut? I've got that a dozen times over. Something isn't right, Bones." Jaw tight, Myron stared at him, repeating his words in a way that sent a chill up Bones' spine. "Something isn't right, man."

Mason broke in, asking, "Where are these places? Where's the deli?" Myron rattled off addresses, and Mason didn't hesitate. "There's a bridge near there where you're protected from the wind in the winter. Folks huddle."

There would be time enough to explore the motivation behind this urgency. Hand to the doorknob, Bones looked back as he swung it open, already walking through. "Show me."

Needings

Ester

I coughed again, the sound tearing through the enclosed space around me, and struggled to lift my arm. Tired, so tired, I was too late to effectively block the expelling air, but just in time to capture the spray of red that accompanied it. This was nothing new. I'd been leaking like this for at least two days. I thought it was two days. It got hard to remember when it started, because I didn't know when it was now. So I held onto that idea. The one where it had only been two days since I had found myself unable to crawl out of my cardboard place. *No pumpkins here.*

"Shaddup you. Shaddup."

That order came from down the way, an older woman who was tender and horrifying by turns. Today would be the angrier end of the spectrum it seemed. *Witching hour*, I used to call it, when I had the energy to call anything by name.

I idly realized the sound I'd been listening to had stopped, so I breathed in, just to make sure I hadn't been listening to the rattle in my own chest, but that still existed so it wasn't that. The rattle and weight like an elephant, and the pain, still there. There another sound that quickly stopped, rumbling and grumbling through the underpass where we'd set up camp for the season.

Come spring, the authorities would sprint to shuffle us along, wanting the walking and biking paths to be free of any thought-provoking or uncomfortable-feeling bodies. Making sure the housed folks were free of the hidden people who looked like us, but for now, we were safe.

The grumbling sound died away, gentle at the end, like it had needed more to keep going but found itself with a dearth of whatever it was it needed. *Like me*, I thought, and needed on the wind. Needing was like wishing, but it wasn't for things that couldn't happen like crystal shoes and ball gowns and pumpkins grown into castles. Needing was for dire wishes. Needs before wants. Needing was what my mind did when it was dark out, and I was frightened. Needing was for now.

Voices, soft and quiet, respectful in their gentle approach, moving closer and closer. Not like when the police came to shift us out and away. Those were times full of loud, embarrassed voices uncaring where we went as long as we weren't here when they got back. These voices murmured, asked questions, didn't order and shout. They came closer, and closer again, and then I realized I was dreaming.

"Ester."

The dream me tried to lift her head, but it didn't move, so she tried to roll to face the tiny opening carved from the cardboard with fingernails and teeth, wedged into place to stop the wind from howling through and blowing the shelter over. The dynamics of construction at work, learned from a free workshop at the co-op on the north side of town. Two trains to get there, one train back, because later routes were different. Would I be routed from this dream? Rousted from slumber and back to pain and drowning?

The cardboard bowed in, and the witch shouted, "Leave her alone. She ain't done nothing to you."

"Ester. Are you in there?" The dream me shut her eyes in relief, rescues might be on tap for today after all. No prince in satin, but an inked man in a leather vest, riding an iron steed.

"Bones." I tried to shout this, or at least my dream self did, thinking the moment needed a profound statement of affirmation. Instead, the whisper was enough, pronouncing the rightness of his assumption.

Found

Bones

"Jesus." Bones grunted, struggling to rip the thick cardboard apart without tumbling the entire structure down the steeply sloping cement surface. Hands appeared, slapping his away, fingerless gloves not hiding the fact they belonged to a woman. Even knowing that, with her between him and Ester, he wanted this woman gone, any way he could make it happen. Frustrated, he gripped a wrist and pulled, taking her off balance, still trying to reach for the cardboard with his other hand.

"I said, leave her be. She ain't done nothing. Never does anything wrong." Pushing him, her strength was a surprise and Bones had to go to one knee to avoid falling, releasing her. She'd moved to slapping at his head now, and he put up an arm to hold her off. "She's." A swing that ended with a thump against his shoulder. "Good."

"Stop, please." He took another painless blow to the bicep, her limp-wristed attempts not hurting him, but her fierce defense of Ester stung his heart. "I know she is good. She's my Ester." Tipping his head sideways, he looked up at her, seeing wild eyes staring down at him.

"Bones." She named him, and that was chilling, knowing Ester spoke of him to this woman. "You're Bones, the famous Bones, who can leap tall buildings in a single bound. Such a good guy." He didn't try to hide his fear for Ester, and counted it a win when the woman gave it back. "Pretty Ester's Bones." A series of wet-sounding coughs came from inside the cardboard construct and the woman twisted to look at it, brows snapping down into a scowl.

"Yes, and she does not sound well. I need to get her out"—he looked at the cardboard, not certain what to call it—"of there, so I can seek help for her."

"No shit? You think I don't know that? What are you doin' out here, then? She's been coughing and waking me up. Body's gotta sleep." The woman leaned past him, and he pulled back, wary of her teeth so near his face. She pushed at a section of the wall, tugging one side in another location and a moment later the entire end of the structure swung out. "Ester learned that. Taught us all." Scowling at him, she cautioned, "Don't mean you get to come in and open everyone's house. Just Ester's, and only just cause she's sick as a dog. Don't piss me off."

"I will not." Looking in where Ester lay, he saw she was on her back, hair swirling around her face in a disheveled mass. In spite of the frigid air, sweat caused strands to stick to her cheek. Cautious of startling her, he pitched his voice to carry, calling out, "Mason, I found her." Without turning around, he heard footsteps approach at a run with his shout.

Ester never moved, not even the merest twitch, and Bones' blood ran cold.

Flattening the cardboard, careless of anything except his Ester, Bones crouched beside her.

"You got her, brother." The words were background noise for what he was doing, carefully arranging her limbs, feeling the heat from her cheek on the back of his hand. With two fingers held firmly to her throat, bitter saliva flooded his mouth when he realized how thready her pulse was, how irregular her heartbeat, slow and faint. Frighteningly so. "I'll get a bus." That got Bones' attention, and he looked up.

"No. Mason, she...no. No ambulance. No bus. My home. I need to bring her home. Not a hospital, I pray you do not make that call. Myron," Bones called, looking past Mason to where the younger man stood, eyes wide as he stared down at the unconscious woman, "where did you park your car?" They had split up to search, Bones and Mason on their bikes regardless of the bitter cold, the better to ease into tight situations. The rest in cars and trucks, which meant he had access to a warm vehicle in which to carry her home.

"I got it," was all the man said before turning and sprinting away.

"Need help getting her up, brother?" Mason had squatted on the other side of her, flicking the tip of a finger through her things. "Need to bring her stuff. Vultures'll swoop in soon as we're gone. They'll be wind in five minutes." Mason began to gather things. "Leave the food. Looks like you kept Ester pretty well stocked. They'll be thankful for that, and it's some payment for the disruption." Bones had gathered Ester into his arms and glanced around now, seeing the circle of faces watching them. Curious, angry, and confused expressions, all woken in the middle of the night by his search. "You get Ester out. I'll deal with this."

"Thank you." Such a trite phrase, scarcely encompassing the debt owed Mason, but all Bones had it in him to offer right now. "Thank you."

Mason told him, "Get her to the car, get her warm. I called Red. He's on shift, but he'll be waiting for your word."

Red was an emergency medical technician who worked for an ambulance service, but the thought of Ester in a hospital made Bones feel ill. They would not see her harmless quirks as charming. They would see them as a sign of mental illness, and they would lock her behind windows threaded with mesh. They would medicate her until the quicksilver of her personality dulled to nothing, and he would lose his Ester.

Mason must have read this on his face, because he was quick to offer an alternative. "Don't have to take her. Red'll treat her at your place, brother. Whatever you need, we will move mountains so you have it, hear me? Whatever you need."

Nodding, Bones turned and walked away, carrying a limp and motionless Ester, heat from her body baking into him even as she shivered in long undulations in his arms.

No doubts

Myron

He stood clutching the bike key Bones had shoved into his hand, watching his car pull away from the curb. Someone walked up behind him, and he felt the grip of a familiar hand on his shoulder, fingers digging in. "You bringin' Bones' bike to the house or his place?" Mason asked, knowing it was a foregone conclusion he would be doing as Bones had wordlessly requested.

"House," Myron muttered, hearing the noise from behind them, knowing it was the local residents picking through the things of Ester's they'd left behind. He didn't want to turn and watch, didn't want to think of how different the scene could have been if they'd been later. If they hadn't found Ester at all. Couldn't think of how sick she looked.

Bones had opened the tiny cardboard shelter, and Myron had stood frozen, looking down at the face of a woman he remembered only in dreams. A woman who'd been gone from his life for so long, he couldn't remember what it was like before. He hadn't been able to believe it, but he'd known. From the first time he'd seen a picture of Ester snapped on a food kitchen surveillance camera, he had known. Seeing it in the flesh, even ravaged by illness, he had no doubts about who she was.

She was the spitting image of their mother.

Dark angel

Ester

I woke up slowly, finding it in me to try and breathe one more time, surprised when this one breath came without the grinding pain in my chest to which I'd become accustomed. Warm, I was hotter than I'd ever been, yet at the same time, I was freezing. My teeth chattered and clattered in my head, filling my ears with noise that would wake the witch, so I tried to clamp my jaw closed, succeeding only in biting the tip of my tongue.

Voices from far away talked in words and phrases, which should have made sense but held no context for me, and so mapping their meaning was as difficult as surveying the dark side of the moon. That partner to the sun, the balance and fulcrum. Of course, I knew there were other mechanics at play in that balance, but it stretched my lips to think of just the sun and the moon, sharing space without it mattering who was the stronger and the weaker.

The words I could not map were strident in tone, anger and frustration ringing through far more clearly than the words meanings. "Too high. I have never seen the like."

I twisted to my back, surprised to find underneath me, where I placed all of my clothing, those individual pieces of fabric had conspired to make a far more comfortable bed than ever before, even with the addition of Bones' blanket. Thick and lush, it cradled my body with a support which, for once, was not painful. There were no angled shoulders or hips pressed into hard pavement, stones and briars carefully removed to make the surface as smooth as possible, if not soft. Not soft like this. And my shoes had surely never been this sweetly cool against my cheek.

I'd spent time in shelters and knew even their offerings didn't give me this kind of comfort. Scratchy woolen blankets tossed over bare mattresses, delousing shampoo harsh when used on skin, but at least offering a measure of cleanliness I always longed for.

I swallowed the minuscule pool of saliva that had gathered right behind my teeth, underneath my tongue. Working the thick muscle slowly, carefully, I cleansed my mouth as I wished my body could be clean. I opened my eyes and saw…everything.

Draping fabric overhead, held up by four wooden posts. Sentinels, standing at each corner of the surface like the four angel guardians the church promised would watch me sleep. Angels who, if they did watch, didn't help, not when the son of the couple crept into my bed. Crying foul when I balked and fought his touch, telling me the worst had already happened and since I was a crying baby, at least I couldn't get knocked up.

Knocked around, sure, and he proved those words true, imprinting the curvature of his palm on my face. I'd turned away, not looking, needing to be as opposite to what he was doing as the dark side of that glowing curvature in the sky, glimpsed out the window, clouds racing across as if to hide the acts from even the moon.

Angels who didn't carry me away, didn't protect me. Angels with porcelain skin, unmarked, smooth and clean and never, ever dirty. Unmarked, and above me, and beyond, so far beyond what I could be, what I could hope to be. Angels away.

"Yes, I will try that. Please, come as soon as you can." The voice, gruff with worry, rough with concern, wavering with a fear that frightened me, matched the face of my true angel. Dark, and covered by a disguise of his own making, locked inside his own jail, my angel. Bones. His face came in from the side, suspended over me, balancing me. My sun.

"I'm your moon." My thoughts, spoken in a ragged gasp that sounded like gurgling water in a pipe, half stuffed with rags, barely draining enough air to fill my lungs. Then I was suspended, held up, the comfort and warmth falling away, shivers setting my limbs adrift and making my head swim with pain. "So cold."

"I know, baby."

Sounds again of water, but this free-flowing, smelling so beautifully clean—and you might argue if you'd never experienced it, but you should, oh God you should—water could smell clean and that was what I wanted. More than anything. I wanted to be clean and warm and smell just like that.

I found myself draped over something, two somethings, straight and firm underneath my bottom, bare as the day I was born. Bare as the first day I'd met Bones. I'd always been going to thank him, because I never did, for being the man he was, but my thoughts were derailed when the pain started. Pounding into every inch of skin, a cold so brutal, a cold that bit deep, draining any thoughts from my head, washing them down an ever-tightening drain.

My voice closed off, only squeaks sounding from my chest as I fought. And fought. Until exhausted, until I couldn't lift even my eyelids anymore. I fought. And I failed.

"Help her. *Dios*, she is so hot. I have never seen someone so fevered."

No, I'm not. I'm cold, I thought, and that thought was cranky in a way that took energy, and that, along with failing, were the last things I knew for a time.

For a reason

Mason

Mason watched Myron grumping around the clubhouse office and grinned. *My bean counter got his ass handed to him.* Not physically, because even if he was slight, Myron was wiry and tougher than folks gave him credit for. No, Myron had taken a hit tonight that Mason didn't understand, and needed to. The way the man had paled when Bones laid his woman on the backseat of Myron's cage didn't say uninvolved observer.

Over the past several months, Myron had been wrapped up in finding out anything he could about this woman, Ester. More than once he'd expressed irritation when pulled away from his personal investigation to handle club business, which wasn't like Myron at all. Mason knew Myron believed Mason and the club saved him, pulling him from the world of homelessness and an aimless life. Dragging him into a place where his particular intellectual quirks could be not only put into play, but where he could be challenged and pushed every day, something that mattered to Myron.

This woman, Ester, she meant something to him. Mason had given Myron space when he'd asked for it, telling Mason that he was just curious. But today put the lie to that in a big way. His desperation to find her hadn't been hidden behind any kind of deflection, and the bald need Myron exposed was intense and deep.

Leaning back in his seat, he was surprised when Myron flung himself onto the couch near the door, tipping his head back and looking at Mason through slitted eyes. "She's my sister." Slowly lowering his feet to the floor, Mason locked his eyes on Myron, trying to keep the disbelief off his face. "I remember things, a few things. From before." Mason nodded, not understanding, but wanting to keep Myron talking.

Myron's story was out in the open in the club, sad but one that was heard all too often from kids who wound up in the system, or as Myron had, homeless. Mom and dad dead, no family to take responsibility, fucking asshole of a foster father who was only in it for the cash, which led to a too-young and too-frail boy taking to the streets. That boy pushed into unwanted things to survive, still expecting more from himself. This was one of the things that drew Mason to him the first time he spotted Myron. Clothes and shoes far tidier than expected in a homeless shelter, but the boy underneath the façade more fragile than anyone could believe.

"Mom had a different husband. My dad was his brother. They'd had a long-term affair, and she'd gotten pregnant and had me, but because she was married, I think she just expected things to play out like nothing happened. I remember the day we left, because my dad...the man I thought was my dad...pushed her out the door and closed it. Not mean. Just...firm. I was already on the porch beside the suitcases he'd set there. Told me to wait. He kicked us out. Ester was about two years old, best I can figure. We went to my uncle's house, I didn't know he was my dad then, and he took us in. A couple of years later they were dead, and I was in the system." Myron pulled in a shaky breath. "I didn't really remember Ester. I remembered the idea of a family, Mom singing while she bent over a crib, my dad...the man I thought was my dad standing next to her. Always thought it was just wishful thinking. Something a kid like me would want, having never had. Then, Bones found her, and I saw a picture…" Another shaky breath. "My mom. I thought for a minute it was my mom. Thought all the reports and everything I knew was wrong. She looks just like…" A hesitation, then Myron finished, "…our mom."

More than matters

Bones

Thin, so thin. The fever had burned away any reserves Ester had. Bones held her in his lap, cradled to his torso, letting the warm water rain down on them both. Pockets empty, he was in jeans, Ester held to him, covered with a large towel to help capture the water. Noise from the hallway, then a voice in the bathroom and he looked up to see Red staring at them from the doorway.

He hated the idea of this man's hands on Ester, but Bones knew she couldn't go on like this. In the hour they'd been in the tub, her wracking shudders had only gotten worse. Her attempts to get away from the water had been heartbreaking, because kittens had more strength. Pushing and shoving with only the barest of pressure, it still seemed to fully exhaust her.

Eyes to Red's face, Bones pleaded, "Help her. *Dios*, she is so hot. I have never seen someone so fevered."

"She coughing?" Red knelt, and as Bones nodded, he saw Red digging through a box resting on the floor at his feet. "Spitting up anything?"

149

"Not that I have seen. Just coughing like to tear her in half." He addressed the thing that made him most fearful. "But she is so hot, Red. Burning up with the fever. Even the water has not helped, she seems no better."

"Let's get her out of there." Red reached out, twisting the faucet handles and the water cut off. Once the noise was gone Bones heard Ester's teeth chattering, muscles moving in uncontrolled motions. "Hand her up."

Bones' arms tightened reflexively, even as he worked through the reasoning behind the request. *Safer*, that was the word he settled on, because if he fell trying to rise with her in his arms, she could be injured. The tub was slippery with water, and a misstep could prove disastrous. "You will take no liberties." Even as the words cleared his mouth, he knew it was a ridiculous statement. He scowled, staring down. "Of course you will not, Red. I am sorry. I find myself off-balance."

"No worries, Bones. I get it. She's fragile right now, and trusting her with someone isn't easy. You know me, though." Red's words and tone were patient as he squatted alongside the tub. "You know I would never take advantage like that. Plus, she's yours, man. You'd fuckin' kill me."

"I would," Bones readily agreed, looking up and lifting her so Red could more easily accept her weight. "I would kill you. It is good you recognize this." Standing now, Bones quickly stripped off the soaked jeans, roughly toweling himself before grabbing another towel. With a glare at Red, he removed the wet one covering Ester, and wrapped the dry fabric around her naked form, taking her back from Red, uncaring of his own nudity. The entire activity took only about two minutes, and she was back in his arms. "My room is best. That is where she will be staying."

"Lead the way," Red said, bending to pick up his kit. "Need to get fluids in her. Flu's making the rounds, but just from listening to her breathe, I'm pretty sure she's got pneumonia. She's noisy and rattlin', full of bad stuff.

We'll get her flat, let me check her out." Trailing him into the bedroom, Red stepped past where Bones stood and flicked back the bed coverings.

Three hours later her fever had fallen to manageable levels, and Red had succeeded in running two liters of fluid through an IV he'd started in the back of her hand. Not easily, because she was so dehydrated, he had to hunt for a vein and then baby it for the first hour. Adding an antibiotic cocktail to the mix, Red had stayed right beside her the whole time, anxious because Bones could tell him nothing about her medical history. "Small percentage of the population have allergies," he'd responded tersely when Bones asked what was worrisome. His words then had Bones worried, watching every breath, making certain her next one came just as easy.

At least the shuddering shivers had stopped, and instead of being shiny and dry, her skin was again slightly clammy with sweat. Her breathing, which had sounded horrifyingly wet and labored when Bones had found her under the overpass, was better, maybe even edging towards normal.

"Don't get me wrong, she's still very sick, but she's already responding to what we're doing, Bones. We keep this up, and as long as there aren't any unexpected setbacks, she'll be okay. Not outta the woods, but better." Red folded a stethoscope in his hand, leaning against the headboard on one side of Ester. Bones took up the other side, hand resting on her chest, covering the spot where Red had touched her to listen to her heart.

"The first time I met Ester, she was saving someone." Bones didn't know he was about to speak until the words fell from his mouth. Once breached, the dam seemed to give way completely, and he found himself explaining. "A prostitute had stolen a trick's wallet, and he took offense. Ester was there and intervened. He took offense at that, too. So, in turn, I intervened."

He flattened his palm against her chest, between her breasts, feeling the strong pounding under his touch. Faster than seemed normal, but so much stronger than before. Reassuring himself, he left his hand in place. "I was in Hawk's territory. Deep. Skeptics were supposed to have a sit-down with him and his crew, but they did not show, and I sent my boys on their way. I was hungry and had seen a deli around the corner, so I cut them loose. Stupid. Hawk and his Dominos knew I was there. Them not showing was a deliberate slight, so, of course, they were watching to witness my reaction." One fingertip moved, drawing the shape of a cartoon heart on her chest. Slowly he eased his hand up, spreading his fingers across her frail-looking collarbones. Heart still beating steadily, sleeping deeply in his bed, she turned her head towards him and sighed, her cracked lips pursing. *This is where I've wanted her to be for so long.*

"She saved me a beating. Showed me a ladder that led to the rooftop. She was not afraid of me, Red. Never once has she been afraid of me." He swept his thumb across her throat, pressing to feel her pulse before sliding his hand up to her jaw, thumb sweeping across there, too. "Never once have I seen fear in her eyes." He swallowed, throat suddenly thick. "Priceless and rare." Gaze fixed on her face, he watched the bare twitching behind her lids, her sight fixed inwardly in a dream he prayed was sweet.

"She deserves anything I can give her, but she does not want things. She wants me. I tried to bring her home with me more than once, and she ran. I think she was fearful of the change, the place. Maybe it was the possibility of having something she wanted that so terrified her. She punished herself for even considering it. She does not fear me, but the level of terror she feels at having things out of her control...that says so many things. Myron has assisted me, found me some of the monsters in her past, and I have dealt with them. Dealt with them for things she has survived. And I nearly lost her because I respected her fear. Almost lost her to the fucking flu, Red. When there are so many things out there that threaten her every single day, so much danger and how she lives, she is right in the midst of it. Every day. And the flu nearly took her from me.

He glanced up to see Red's eyes on him. "You see through what she is to what she could be, yes?" Red nodded. "You understand why I needed her here?" Red nodded again, eyes never leaving Bones'. "I will keep her safe, even if that means keeping her safe against her own fears. You understand what I'm saying?" Red opened his mouth, about to speak but Bones cut him off. "No, do you understand? Yes, or no?"

"Yeah, brother, I get it, but you can't kidnap her. You can't...if she's as fragile as you say, it could be the thing that severs her from reality, man." Red's head swung back and forth. "She more than matters to you, and I get it, I see it. I believe you when you say you'd do anything to keep her safe. Just—" He paused a moment, then continued, "—don't make what you have to save her from be you."

Close to hand

Ester

When I woke again, the light was gone. The cold was gone, and my muscles could have wept with joy. Back to the unbelievable soft underneath me, around me, except along my backside, where there was a giving heated hardness. A fiery firmness heretofore unknown in my existence. Testing things, I took a breath, and there was tightness, but no pain. The firmness stirred, and close-fitting iron bands already wrapped around my shoulders and belly constricted. In a voice filled with quiet and peace, Bones said, "You are awake, finally. How do you fare, little one?"

Bones.

I froze, as stuck in place as anything in the history of ever, stuck and staying right there in the moment when I knew it was Bones who lay beside me, giving me warmth from his own body, caring enough to ask me how I was. Even the nurses at the hospital hadn't asked. Never asked, they'd only assumed, taking their own wishes into account. They'd told me what to believe, and promised things that never happened. "You'll feel better," they said. "You look better every day," they told me. Lies from their lips to the ears of the angels who didn't care, uncaring still. My angel, however, demanded a response, repeating his question with the slightest of variations, adding a demand into the mix, and one that got my mouth working without my consent, as it was often inclined to do with him. "Ester, tell me how you feel."

"I was sick." More a statement than a question, it was still interrogatory in nature, and he read that, as he always read everything about me.

"Yes, you were very sick." I moved my head, nodding, feeling my cheek skim and rub against a velvet stretched over steel that felt amazing. Hot and smooth, a heating source of unknown origin. "How long were you ill, Ester?"

I sighed then, and the breath stretched my lungs and ribs in a way that felt so good, I did it again, pulling in a huge chest full of air that released all at once, triggering a coughing fit that woke the pain. Once it had passed, I confirmed what he likely already knew. "Ow."

"Yes, ow." He agreed, and I wanted to see his face because I could hear the smile he wore. I could feel the smile in the room, the air somehow lighter now, less thick, less smothering. Because he was amused. I liked that. "Do you know when you became sick, baby?"

That gift again, and it meant so much to me for him to give me that. First a sweet phrase, then my name—*my name*, making me real in that moment yet again—and then the word I wanted more than anything in the world. *Baby.* Bones' moon. "No." I sighed again, this time less largely, smaller, more controlled. "I wasn't, and then I was."

"It came on fast, then?" The surface underneath me stirred, a ponderous ship giving way to passengers. The steel under my cheek flexed, moved, and I felt his fingers skimming my face, shifting my hair out of the way so he could trace the long edge of my nose. I nodded. "Are you feeling better now?" I nodded again. As long as he was touching me, I was better even if I wasn't. I'd be better forever. "Red said it likely was influenza, but he thinks you also had pneumonia, Ester. Very, very bad. You've been here for nearly three days."

That was my daily dose of real, coming in fast, roosting on my shoulders, bearing down. "Three days?" It was too much to hope he'd made a mistake, but hope I did.

"Yes, baby. And while I do not know for certain when you became ill, I do know I had not seen you for a week. You have gotten so thin." His finger traced along my cheekbone. "Too thin. And I fear to think what could have happened if I had not looked for you."

"You found me." Evidence pointed to it being a clear truth, so I decided to talk about one of the things I feared. "My place." Something I didn't want him to know about me, even if he knew it already. Seeing where I stayed would be like painting a picture of destitution onto the face he liked to see. Hiding and covering the me he let me be when I was with him, because now there was a different definition instead of the me he wanted to see.

Maybe that was what he wanted, enjoyed that feeling of helping. Like the beskirted ladies who piled out of the church van, one hand on the Bible, the other offering food in exchange for a little time. Needing a cause to make them happier about their own lives. Putting a questioning tone in my voice, I asked for the answer I feared most. "My things?"

"I will replace whatever is needed, Ester." His words only just preceded the wave of hopelessness and sorrow, a wretched tsunami of grief and loss I tried desperately to hide.

Gone. Picked over and gone. Hands sorting through the few things that mattered to me, things kept in the pockets which came in the coat, new pockets I created with needle and thread pilfered from a shelter, clever pockets folded into the seams and extra material. A pretty necklace with a fancy letter the court lady gave me. An eah, to match my Eah-est-her. Rhinestone missing now. Unworn forever, skin gone green under the chain long faded back to peach. Clasp broken one night by a man who found himself wanting and me not giving. Still mine.

The wrist band from the hospital that proved I was a person. I had a name, an initial, a blood type, and a birthday. February seven.

The scarf. Oh, the scarf that whispered secrets to me, promising that when Bones looked at me, he saw beauty woven into the cracked fabric that was me. I choked down a sob, hating the weakness that allowed even a scrap of it to flee from my lips.

The coat. The everything that was the kindest present anyone had given me, and it traced back to and through every other thing he had given me. The coat that was just right, and I kept it that way, mending hems as they unraveled. Raveling them back together, fixing even the tiniest thread snagged by a shrub as I followed a rabbit into the woods just to watch it dig and nibble and dart into a hole, safe and sound where it found itself a place to hide. Everyone needed a place that was safe, and for me, the coat represented all the safety I would ever need. Gone.

Then, as he always did, Bones gave me back everything. "I had my friend pack up your personal items, the things you had inside your...." Here he trailed off, not wanting to offend, probably, but so unlikely to know what word to use that I offered him a boon.

"My place."

"Yes." He leaped on the phrase, well, not literally, but with his own words he filled in the rest of the gaps for me. "I asked about you. Found people who knew you. Found where you had your place. Talked to people there, found your place. And in your place, I found you."

"And where am I now?" Look at me, holding a normal conversation while lying in bed beside a man. I thought I already knew, but needed confirmation. I expected this to be the place that had come between us eons ago, driving me from his company for so long, because he wanted me to be...the crux of the issue was I didn't know what word came next. Safe. Comfortable. Warm. Fed. Sheltered.

Those would all have been fine, but I couldn't ask. Couldn't ask in case it was a different word. Like available. Or trapped. Or beholden, which was owing and I didn't want to owe, not even Bones. But trapped was so much worse. I'd avoided trapped since I was ten, and wasn't likely to give up my freedom so easily. So I'd walked away, and never again entered into a closed space with him. Denying myself his company on so many occasions it was a wonder he still sought me out.

"My home, Ester. In my bed."

Time froze for a moment. A molten freezing, because my skin wasn't cold, but hot. Fiercely bubbling under the surface was my blood, and my muscles had gone so stiff I feared sudden petrification. There'd been an exhibit in a hotel lobby once of things caught in other things. Perhaps the heat was like tree resin, melting and encasing me in a shield of something that would be hard. Not brittle, but protective, and I was afraid I needed the offered protection. Then I opened my eyes and saw the ocean of pristine white that surrounded me. White sheets, white comforter—I'd known the word but had never experienced it before, now I knew the origin of the name because comfort it did—white pillows. Added to the sea of froth-colored fabric, adrift in the midst, was an arm so covered in colors and darkness it looked impossibly real. The contrast between the bedding that was everywhere and the arm bent and folded underneath my cheek drew instant tears to my eyes.

My arms were under the covers, hands still at the ends of those arms, and I hated to lose the warmth and softness that enveloped them. But, I longed for something I had continually denied myself. Right there in front of me. Right here. Since the first meeting, thirty-eight months ago, I had allowed his touch on my skin, usually a glancing brush against my back or shoulder, a clasp of his palm to mine, the grazing caress of his thumb when I left crumbs on my lips. Since the very first meeting I had wanted, never giving in because once I started, I didn't know if I would stop. Needing, but never hardly ever touching his bare skin. The him who was so much more than skin.

Now, his arm was there, my cheek was already touching him, and I allowed it, enjoyed the contact, relished the heat and texture I'd discovered. My hand came out from under the covers, palm skimming the white sheet, better than hotel quality and I'd know, because that was my best cash job. Maids not wanting to carry the heavy bundles of laundry from the rooms to the elevator, their time better spent working in the rooms, bustling back and forth between cart and doorways, so they paid me to haul. Hotel quality was good, so good, but this was better.

My fingers hovered a fraction of an inch over his skin, and I dreamed he could feel the heat from my almost-touch like I always felt the scorch of his. Soft, so soft I nearly didn't believe I'd touched him, I traced the line of one picture from the bend of his elbow to the crook of his wrist, slipping underneath to find the base of his thumb where that line terminated. I skipped to the next line, following and tracking it up and over the back of his hand, whirls and whorls drawing me in, engulfing my thoughts and straightening my mind in a way I hadn't known could happen.

"Why am I in your bed?" My mouth asked the question, and without warning my heart wanted to know, leaping into my throat so it could be the first to hear his answer. My fingers didn't care, because I'd discovered the pulse of his heartbeat in his wrist, directly underneath a blackened rose, but within the folds of the flower's heart there was a glowing letter. S marked the spot. I was so mesmerized by the feel of his life underneath my fingertips, I'd forgotten my question, but he answered anyway, mute no more and I was glad.

"Because you are ill, little one. I wanted to keep you close."

"You're not responsible for me." *I might want you to be*, I thought, then checked myself to make sure that remained in my head.

"I want to be." That so close to his mind reading tricks, I shook my head and became enamored of the way his skin moved when I did so. So I did it again, bringing my thumb to rest in the crease of his elbow, watching the skin move with my touch. Bones pulled my entire attention back to him with his next words, so surprising and telling, I didn't know what to do with them for a moment. "I want to be everything for you."

"Why?" A simple question to cover so much uneasiness, so many fears, all of which would need to be settled before I could settle, regardless of how beautiful my fingers looked lying on top of his inked skin. Riddles written in black, drawn in blood. Promises made to himself and others, bent but not broken, names and initials marking the twisting.

"I want—" He sighed, his words halting in his throat for so long I wondered if he'd forgotten the skill of speaking. I'd seen the aftermath, of course, those who no longer needed discourse to address what they wanted. I'd never heard it in the happening. The act of muteness coming over someone. Tentacles of panic rose to choke my throat, like the woman in the alley the first time I met him, but these monster fingers didn't leave marks on my skin, just in my mind, as I tried to find a way to keep him talking. *I love your voice*, I wanted to shout, *don't keep it from me*.

Maybe. I had a thought, a memory of a prompt, like the elevator man at the hotel. *You gotta get in the car you wanna keep working. Up or down, you gotta move*. "You want…" My voice trailed off, because the word that came next mattered too much for me to get it wrong.

"You, however I can have you." Bones' voice didn't waver as mine had. If anything, the sound of it got stronger the longer he spoke. "I want you safe. I want you close. I want you to stay among the living, Ester. I want to know what you think when you look at me." His words flowed over me, tucking in close along every inch of my skin. "What frightens you, so I can slay every monster. What makes you happy, so I can bring you more.

What you want more than anything in the world, so I can become that for you."

You already are, those words longed to be air moving over tongue and teeth, not merely sparks in my brain, but I locked them down, denying the connection that could allow them to come to life.

"I called you mine, and I keep what is mine safe, happy, healthy, and with me."

His arm tensed, I could actually see the striation of muscles moving under the skin, these words meant something to him that I didn't understand. The *mine* he wanted was me, and I realized he was trapped in my responses, barred from what he wanted by my fears just as much as I was. The marks on his skin told me so many things he hadn't said. Couldn't say for fear of driving me away again. I had hurt him, the one man I never wanted to hurt. I traced the marks with the tip of my nose, finding the skin softer than anything I'd ever experienced.

Verification would help, clarity as a prompt to action. *Up or down, you gotta move.* "And that's why you asked if I'd come here."

"Yes, Ester, that's why I wanted you here with me."

"You have my coat here, nearby?" My question might be bizarre to someone who didn't know me. Bones understood, though. Of course, he did. He would know what his gift meant to me, know what it might mean if he had brought it with my body to his home.

"I will always have the things that are most important close to hand." I took a breath, and he squeezed me, tucking my body in close to his. "Sleep, Ester."

I did.

And that was how I came to move into Salvador Ramos' house, making it my home.

Never enough time

Bones

She would be well. That was what Bones had willed into being since he found her. He had anxiously waited for Red to arrive each day, his professional evaluation telling Bones what he read in her was true. Ester was healing and getting better. Still woozy and weak, but by day two she had kept down spoonfuls of soup he eased between her lips, propping her on his lap. When she spoke, which was infrequent, she was at times confused and quietly argumentative. She was also universally grumpy, which was something he'd never seen from her before. But mostly she had been quiet, moving as he asked in order to relieve herself, or shower with his support, and of course sleeping for hours at a time. Recovering. For three days he had not left her side, had been with her every moment, no matter what it required he do.

Bones had become so comfortable being with her, lying in bed beside her, listening to her sleep, that when his senses told him she had come to real wakefulness, he nearly didn't trust them. Her voice, when she responded to his inquiry, had been so weak he almost bolted from the bed to call Red. Then the rust of disuse had begun to fall away as she spoke, sounding stronger by the moment.

When she began her slow exploration of his skin, he'd frozen in place. In the time he'd known her, she had stared openly at his tattoos, had used the pad of her thumb to skim across the back of his hand a few times. Had mentioned the tattoos in passing, with a frighteningly accurate insight about their existence. But she'd never touched him like this. Nestled in his arms, her hands moved over him, fingertips gliding up and down. When his cock woke at the feel and knowledge of what she was doing, he had shifted backwards, not wanting to frighten her with an unwanted reminder that he was a man. Their conversation had frightened her enough, he had felt it in the motionless waiting she adopted, like a field mouse hoping and praying the hawk would pass it by, fly over never seeing, not knowing the hunter had already noted the racing heartbeat below.

Easing past disaster, because while she might still be weak, if she panicked it would have destroyed the hope he held that she wouldn't see him as the hawk, wouldn't see their relationship as prey and predator, but as friends and perhaps one day, lovers. Since he wouldn't let her go until she was well, her panic might have ended anything between them, left him holding her against her will. Then, nearly as sudden as it came upon them, they were on the other side, and she snuggled backwards into him, trusting as a babe. Too thin, still ill, but with him in a way he couldn't mistake. She hadn't just accepted this as a temporary arrangement, with her words, her actions, she had given herself to him.

"I will earn your trust, baby." Brushing his lips against the skin of her neck, he pressed a kiss just where the pulse of her life's blood ran underneath. It beat slow and steady. She had gone to sleep. *In my arms. Everything.*

Bones closed his eyes, rolled slightly into Ester and fell asleep, truly resting for the first time in days.

When he woke hours later, he didn't have to open his eyes to know he was alone. She was gone and pain clenched in his chest, fierce and raging. Flinging the covers back, he gritted his teeth. *Stupid fucking asshole*. He'd pushed too hard, too far, too fast...too something and she had run from him. *Me*. Yanking the denim of his jeans up his legs he cast around for his shirt. Nowhere to be found. Dismissing it, he grabbed another from a drawer, pulling it over his head as he went double-time down the stairs to the main floor.

Where he stopped in his tracks listening to sounds coming from the kitchen. Not movement, but a bright, if weak, chatter of words. Cautiously, he approached the open doorway and stopped again. Dressed in his tee, Ester sat on top of the tiny table he had positioned in the nook near the windows. Feet to the windowsill in front of her, she was staring out into the small backyard. Bowl in one hand, spoon in the other, she was eating what looked like ice cream, and a shiver of her frame told him his guess was likely right. Abruptly she leaned forwards, nose nearly touching the pane of glass, so close he could see her breath fogging the surface. "Well, aren't you pretty," she cooed, tipping her head to one side. "Pretty, pretty, pretty boy." The singsong was lilting and sweet, so sweet he could nearly taste it on the air. "Pretty, pretty, pretty boy."

Leaning back, she caught sight of his reflection, and he watched as her eyes widened, locking on the vicinity of his face. Then he was graced with the birth of a smile on her face, and watched it from beginning to middle, when she shoved another spoonful of ice cream between her lips. Swallowing, the smile still broad and beautiful, she cooed at him this time, "Well, aren't you pretty."

He couldn't help it, shaking in an instant with the hilarity that struck him, he almost missed her next words. Nearly, but didn't, which meant he got to listen to her tell him, "I wasn't being funny." Which was so funny, he also couldn't help his next movement, which was to cross the kitchen and come up behind her at the table, watch their reflections as she willingly lifted her arms to accommodate his wrapping around her, and listen as she scolded, "You ran off the squirrel." And, "Watch out for my bowl." And then he got to hear her say something he found he wanted to hear every morning for the rest of his life, "Morning, Bonesy."

"Good morning, Ester," he told her, and gave her a gentle squeeze. "You sleep well, baby?" She wasn't pulling away, wasn't fearful of him, and he tipped his head to get an up-close view of her tucking another bite of ice cream into her mouth.

She swallowed before answering, and he watched her smile when she did. "I like sleeping in your bed." A deep breath told him she wasn't finished, so he waited, and was glad he did when she gave him more. "I liked waking up next to you. You're beautiful all the time, but when you sleep, that's like beauty under glass. Energy still there, but storing up for next need. You're like your own Tesla coil during the day, all protective of what you have and full of spark and fire. Dangerous, in a controlled way. But at night? When you sleep? As if the glow of moonlight on the lake soothes you, letting your dreams ripple up to the surface but never, not ever disturbing the beauty." Another spoonful of ice cream, silver bowl of the spoon slipping out from between her lips, the tip of her pink tongue appearing for a moment, then disappearing back into her mouth. "I slept like the moonlight on the lake." The spoon clinked in the bottom of the bowl, and she glanced down. "I was hungry."

"Are you still hungry, Ester?" She nodded, and he gave her a squeeze. "Then I should feed my moon."

***

His phone vibrated in his pocket, and he glanced at Ester, then to the doorway. It buzzed again, indicating a second text and Bones knew he had to see if there was an urgency to the communication. She was better, nearly well, a little more than a week into her recovery and he had spent every moment with her. It couldn't last, this island of isolation, but he had wanted another few days, at least. *Just a little longer.*

"Ester." At her name, she glanced up at him from her seat on the rug, fingers reaching out for another puzzle piece. She had a fascination with making sense out of the things, within hours had worked her way through the first one she'd found in a closet. Red had dropped off several additional ones yesterday, and she had fallen on them on sight.

Bones needed to see what business was intruding, but knew her fear of phones could threaten the peace on her face. She smiled, and tipped her head to one side, tracing the edges of the puzzle piece held in her fingers. He told her, "I need to go into my office." She nodded. "Alone." His phone chose that moment to buzz again, and he knew she heard it when the smile faded from her face. "I will be back in a moment."

Chewing her lips, she looked at him, then her eyes darted to the floor, and then to his feet. He sat on the couch, legs stretched out and feet covered in socks she'd picked out for him this morning, complaining his toes looked cold. Eyes back to his face, Ester told him, "Okay."

He shifted, easing to the edge of the seat, drawing his feet underneath him so he could stand. "I will be back in a moment."

"Bones." Now she was smiling again, small and tentative, but it was there. "You 'member how I like pie?"

The fist which had clenched tightly around his heart eased a bit, and he took a shaky breath. "I do, little one."

"You think I'll give up an everyday menu like you give me?" Answering her own question with a headshake, she said, "Of course not. These days, every day is Bonesday." She leaned forwards and her smile turned into a grin. "I like pie too much to ever think of eating anywhere else."

Tapping the puzzle piece against her lips, those soft lips he had only scarcely tasted so far, she tipped her head down. Reaching out, she pressed the piece into place. Without looking up, she reassured him, "I'll be here."

Apt student

Bones

"Need you, Bones." Mason's voice echoed as if he were in a tunnel, and Bones twisted away from the wind battering at him, holding the phone tighter to the side of his head. He was parked on a county road near the lake, waiting for a contact who was supposed to have shown up thirty minutes ago with information on Carmela. Shades had texted earlier to warn Bones of the possibility and then called with the request while Ester was sleeping. There was nothing else that would have pulled Bones away. Ester had settled in over the past few days, but he didn't want to be gone from her for long. Add that to the bad feeling he'd had about this meeting since hearing about it. Which meant now the guy he was to meet wasn't just late, but was the definition of late, Bones had an even worse one. "Now."

"Where at?" Feet to the ground, feeling suddenly vulnerable, he sat up straight, glancing around. "I am about thirty minutes out from the clubhouse, Mason. Where do you need me?"

Static, then the echoing intensified, and he could hear overlapping words. Nonsense sounds. Struggling to pick out the directive, he finally understood one word, "Jackson's."

"I am having difficulty understanding. You want me at Jackson's?" He strained to listen, but there was only silence on the line. Looking down, he realized his signal had dropped completely.

"Fuck." Gritting out the one word, he shoved the phone deep into a pocket, starting the bike and jamming it into gear, preparing to ride to his president's need. Looking up the road in front of him, he stared at a grouping of silhouettes against the horizon. Unmistakable in outline, he could see there were three bikes positioned on top of the hill that stood between him and the main highway. Between him and his club. Between him and Ester.

Shit. If they are friendly, why would they stop just there, blocking my exit? Riding towards them would be suicide if they were the enemy. *They must be enemies.*

Bones watched as one bike separated from the other two, gliding steadily downhill towards where he sat waiting, boxed in and blocked from any movement. Readying for a fight, he sucked in a deep breath as adrenaline flooded his system, and with long practice held tight reins on every reaction. He knew it wouldn't be smart to go for his gun, because that movement alone would telegraph fear, and while he was drowning in the emotion right now, he could bide a few moments.

Closer and closer the bike came, until the rider's face swam into focus.

Chismoso.

His first reaction was disbelief, because the bastard was supposed to be in the Carolinas, somewhere. Or Florida. Or anywhere except Chicago. The bike braked smoothly to a halt about ten feet in front of him, and he stared as Chismoso grinned, fleshy lips pulling back from large, square teeth. No weapon in sight, and Bones quickly scanned the area again looking for more than the three men, not seeing any additional threats. None visible, anyway.

"You are not the man I expected to see here today." Bones made his observation dryly, raising his voice to be heard over the two rumbling engines. "In fact, truth be known, you are not a man I expected to see in Chicago again. Do you care to share why you are here, where you are...most distinctly unwanted?"

Chismoso's neck dipped, head shaking back and forth. "You wound me, Bones. You gave me an assignment. Don't you wanna hear how well I did?"

"You are now my student? All right, I will play along. Tell me what you have learned. I hope you have knowledge of the girl we seek. That would go a long way to convincing me to listen." With a flip of his thumb, Bones pressed the kill switch on his bike, cutting the rattling noises by half. His motion was followed a moment later by Chismoso, and the two men sat on silent bikes, staring at each other. "Please, by all means, tell me what you learned."

Chismoso lifted his chin. "Nothing about the girl. If she's in Diamante hands, I couldn't turn over the rock that's holding her back. But, still, I learned a lot. I took what you said to heart, my friend." The address was interesting because it was a greeting of equals, not at all close to what their last interaction would have led Bones to believe. "I returned to the fold to see."

Tipping his head to one side, Bones asked, "See? What did you see?"

"No, Bones." Chismoso shook his head. "I returned so I could *see*." The hissed emphasis meant something to Chismoso, so Bones let him keep speaking, not interrupting again. "What I saw was proof of your words. I was part of an engine driven, but not by anything that mattered to me. Not anymore." Bones stared at Chismoso, taking in the faint bruising on one side of his face, the still-swollen cheekbone and nose. "Others didn't see it the same way, got pissed when I told them I was done."

"You dropped your center?" Bones was certain the disbelief he felt was in his voice, could hear it himself, and watched through the shadows as a flare of red climbed Chismoso's neck and face. Shocked, Bones asked, "After everything you have worked for with Diamante, you dropped your center?"

"Handed 'em the full goddamned set. Didn't want any piece of it anymore. Fucking lies and distrust don't make for a good meal. Decided I wanted to lay a better table for myself." Chismoso's face had set in hard lines, skin stretching over his cheeks as his teeth clenched together. "Leaves me lookin' for a place, man. I'm a beggar now. Bones, I've been inside too long. I don't think I can run lone." He tipped his head backwards to the two men still positioned at the top of the hill. "I got twenty guys. I didn't ask 'em, fuck no. Scared the shit out of me when they did it, but they left with me. We all see the lay of the land...and when I say that, I mean we all *see*, Bones."

"You see something you want? Something you need?" Bones leaned forwards, elbows to his fuel tank, assuming a resting pose even as his nerves flared and sparked, fear curling up into his throat. "Something worth working towards?" He shifted, unsure what the answer would be, but asked his final question regardless. "Something you want to take?"

"Something I want to belong to." Chismoso corrected him immediately, and, even still on high alert, Bones knew the answer was the right one, giving him room to relax the slightest amount.

"Tell me a thing." Bones paused, waiting for Chismoso's chin lift. "Why did you remain so long in the Diamante?"

"Lalo needed me." A quick answer, sounding pat, practiced, and untrue. His disbelief must have been palpable because Chismoso tried convincing him. "My cousin, *mi famila*. My mama wanted better for her sister's boy. I spent the last three years trying to keep him alive. He had a knack for pissing off the wrong people. All the wrong people. All the time." Bones stared at him. "I know what he did, everything he had me help with. Fuck, I know where so many bodies are buried. But the whole time it felt as if we were just barely ahead of the curve, man. Like any minute the roof would come crashing down. Faster and faster, just tryin' to keep up. Just fuckin' tryin' to keep up. You don't know, Bones.

Chismoso leaned forwards, chin up, face distorted in the reflected lights from the bikes. "You've never been part of a club like that. Never seen such evil shit and feared being the target, man. It don't excuse, but it sure as fuck explains." Straightening, Chismoso indicated the men behind him again. "They know. Fuck, man, we all know. We watched Fury. Watched him figure things out, sort himself and then get himself and the men to a place where they could thrive. Not just live, not just eke out an existence, but fuckin' *thrive*. Move from bad to good, but more than that he found a seat at a table worth the work. Earned himself a meal he can savor for a change. We all want that. I need it. You got it to give, Bones. You know you got it to give."

"I cannot make that decision alone." Bones told him, not caring he gave away which direction he would lean if things came to a vote. Chismoso's impassioned plea had struck a chord deep inside him, and he knew exactly the kind of things that ate at the man's soul. "I can talk to Mason. I have no promises to offer you. I have no idea which direction he will swing. You have long been associated with our enemy."

"I know this," Chismoso said. "I know how it looks, too, me showing like this with my hand out and nothing on offer in exchange. Appreciate you listening to me."

"Not as if you gave me a choice." Bones sat up, indicating the men on the hill and his and Chismoso's positions at the bottom of it, his gestures communicating his lack of options to avoid them. "I need to go." No more was said, the two men starting their engines, then Bones waited as Chismoso turned his bike around. Afterwards, as they rode out of the area, Bones leading the pack, he was shocked when he topped the hill and saw the remainder of the twenty men Chismoso had promised. They parted to the sides of the road, and he rode through, slowing the advance of the main column until he saw all the men had turned and caught up to the tail. Twenty-one virtually unknown men at his back and his spine didn't itch, didn't tingle. Betrayal wasn't in the air tonight, a feeling he enjoyed having for a change.

Once out on the highway, they had trailed him for several miles until Chismoso surged up so their front wheels were even. He motioned to an upcoming exit and Bones lifted his chin, then offered a quick two-fingered wave, watching as Chismoso and his men peeled off and left him. Five minutes later Bones pulled into Jackson's riding solo, noting the full parking lot and catching sight of Mason's bike near the back door.

He parked, and dismounted, then stood stretching for a moment. Bones glanced at the men on the perimeter of the lot, noting their alertness. *Trouble has come to Chicago*, he thought, turning to walk into the bar. Once inside, he saw there were groups of men standing around, and a few had beers in hand, but that number was far less than he would expect for a gathering of this size. He estimated there were about sixty men inside the bar, and another fifteen outside.

"Bones, get your ass in here," Mason called, and Bones turned to look at the opening behind the bar. Mason was in the doorway, holding the door ajar, and Bones could see a handful of men in the background. Greeting Mason with an outstretched hand, he allowed himself to be pulled into a one-armed clinch, then stepped back and surveyed the room's occupants. Shades, Fury, Slate, and Tater. The elite of the Rebels' leadership.

Stepping to one side, he waited for Mason to close and lock the door, then watched as Tater set a device on the table, turning it on. "Suppression?" If this were one of Myron's toys, it would jam any listening devices, keeping the meeting entirely secret. Tater nodded, and Bones gritted his teeth. He might as well be the one to break the thick silence, and he had news, after all. "I had no luck with the source Myron found. They were a no-show."

"Fuck me," Slate muttered, and Bones glanced at him, then back to Mason.

"I did, however, have a set of fascinating visitors." From the twist of Mason's lips, Bones thought the man might already know. "Chismoso claims to have left Diamante, and took twenty men with him." Gesturing to Fury, Bones continued, "He is seeking for himself what you found, my friend. He had no word of Carmela, Mason. I believed him on that, at least. I find myself somewhat skeptical of the rest."

Settled

Ester

I lay beside him, awake in the early morning, as was my norm, watching him sleep. As often as I could, I performed this morning ritual, which set the tone for my day. On his side facing me, arm draped over his waist, his other arm bent double, hand shoved under his cheek. That hand pitched his head upwards, and I was convinced it was so he could listen behind him. Bones had learned at a young age that danger had no problems striking from behind. Cowardice only factored in posturing. In execution, his position was effective, which, in the end, was all that mattered. The scars on his back attested to this, and he'd told me of how he'd died when he was young, brought back to life in an ambulance as they rushed to the hospital. Stories from his mother of how the sirens were a muted warble from inside the speeding vehicle, and how the just-graduated EMT fainted during transport.

There'd been two additional vehicles transporting that day, less rushed, less noisy, less of a thankful outcome. His younger sister and a beloved neighbor. When he spoke of it, the sadness in his voice was palpable, covering me, cloaking the lights in the room with a watery glaze. I had become comfortable with him by then, so when he gathered me in his arms and brushed away my tears with kisses, I didn't argue the kindness.

His neighbor, he said, was a good lady. Taught him you could tell the basest nature of a person by how they treated dogs and children. I pointed out I was afraid of both, and for the same reason, showing him the bite scars on my hand and ankle. Laughing, carrying that rich sound of humor into his words, he told me I still fed both, as he'd seen the activity more than once. I allowed as how that was true, but these days I'd feed them only warily. He squeezed me, and that remained one of my favorite things about him, how he communicated his joy in our friendship in such physical ways. So with his squeeze, I knew warily was okay for him, and he still thought I was a good person.

Watching him sleep was good, but watching him wake was so much better. I held my breath in anticipation as he sighed deeply, his eyes moving in quick jerks behind the shrouding curtain of his eyelids, then his bottom lip pursed in a sweetly innocent pout. I watched as his tongue swept across his top lip, right to left, then lapping at that boundary of his mouth, a mouth which was everything except innocent. Drawing back into his mouth, his tongue curled, and I wanted to follow it, tangle my own with it, chase it inside, make a place for myself there.

Another sigh that I matched in depth and pace, and then he said, nearly the same words spoken every morning in this bed since the fourth time I woke in it, "Is that you watching me sleep again?"

How he knew this with his eyes closed, I never knew. But he was right, and I admitted it straightaway. "Yes."

"Have you gotten your fill of looking yet?"

This question was new and frightening, because if I had, did it mean he would turn me out, finally? Taking away the everything he'd gifted me? Maybe he thought me well enough to leave now, the racking coughing nearly gone unless I ran up the stairs. He'd believed me recovered enough to leave at times to tend to business, which was a compliment of the highest order, telling me I was worth coming home to. Maybe he was tired of how hard he had to work with me. I'd never tire of looking at him, watching him, studying him. A master's program in the study of Sal Ramos, Bones, my friend. I must have hesitated too long composing my response because his eyes slitted open, the barely there glint of his gaze upon me ratcheting up my anxiety.

Then he proved he could read minds, something I'd long been considering a truth, but waffling on the deciding as a finality. "Ester, peace, beauty. You are not ever going to be unwelcome in my home, in my bed. Ever welcome. Peace." The hand which had been curled under his cheek pushed out, fingers stretching towards me in an invitation I quickly accepted, threading my pale digits through and between his dusky ones, the contrast spellbinding.

"I wish you could understand what you mean to me. What pleasure you bring to my heart when you do such a small thing as take my hand without my demand. Without fear. Trust in a gesture that means all. Ester." His fingers squeezed mine, and as ever, even in isolation like that, it felt like he'd reached through and squeezed my heart so it fluttered in my chest, a wild thing looking for escape. "You bring me peace, without even knowing how or why and that"—he squeezed again, and this time I dared return the gesture, rewarded by the lifting of his cheeks under his eyes, pleasure suffusing his features for only me to see—"is exactly why my love for you is reckoned as deep, and limitless, and why you shall always be mine."

His other hand appeared, fingers spread, framing a question and I answered quickly, pushing my face into his grip, his hot palm cupping my cheek. I didn't know what he saw when he did this, his gaze roaming over every place he touched me, the feathering glide of a fingertip across my brow, the rough caress of a scarred knuckle along my chin. But the joy reflected on his face made it something I longed for, and cherished as often as it happened.

"You are settled now?"

I sighed and inclined towards him, knowing the pleasure it gave him when I initiated in this fashion. He allowed a brush of my lips against his, then also allowed my retreat as I answered his question with my actions, shifting so I rested on the pillow, facing him, our eyes level. We remained like that for a long time, at least a hundred breaths, his hand on my face, his other hand holding mine.

That might have been my most favorite of the favorite times. That half hour spent lazing in his bed. Settled.

Forged in fire

Bones

"It has been too long, Mason. We must force their hand." Bones knew his friend agreed in principle, but Bones wanted to hear the words spoken aloud. "She's missing, and this cannot go on. Juanita needs to know, one way or another." Every member feared the worst, because since Carmela and her escort had vanished, there had been no word, not even the barest whisper of a rumor that they'd been sighted. Nothing. "Weeks, brother. Three weeks."

Mason looked across the desk at him for a long minute before he responded. They were in the clubhouse office, the big window behind Mason letting in sunlight and the flashing glare of the sun on ice-crusted snow. With a sigh, Mason leaned forwards, elbows on the table as he lifted his clasped hands to rest against his mouth. Another moment, and another sigh, then those scarred knuckles shifted an inch to the side as Mason responded with a heated, "I've not been idle."

"I did not say you had been." Bones shook his head. "I know you have balanced this against a thousand things, and still kept the pressure on as you could. Without any threats or information, we might as well be whistling past the graveyard, and Diamante knows it."

"Don't think it's Diamante." Mason licked his lips as he dropped this bombshell, and Bones braced, seeing the sour look on Mason's face. "I'm looking into Morgan and Deacon. That's where I think things lead."

Bones allowed his chin to tip down, folding his arms across his chest as he considered Mason's words.

So many different pieces to puzzle over. Things had come to light in recent months, and they now strongly suspected Justice Morgan and Deacon had been teamed up for years, wreaking havoc wherever they turned their attention. Morgan was as sadistic as his son, Shooter, and the two had been plotting against Mason for nearly two decades. Morgan, through Shooter, had forced Carrie Sosa to Mason's bed. Chase, Mason's oldest son, was the fruit of that plan, but just because it sorted out in Mason's favor didn't mean anyone was okay with the original play. Morgan had also been the mastermind for his grandson Judge's abduction of the women in Mason's life, nearly two years ago. Judge, Shooter's boy. Deacon the overthrown former king of the club Mason had taken to unexpected heights. Both men carried a hate for Mason that had damaged many.

Carmela was the daughter of Raul Estavez, and Estavez *was* Machos. He was their president, but more than that he had fought tooth and nail to tear that club away from his blood brother, Carlos. Retaliation for Carlos' abduction of Carmela. Missing then, found by Watcher and Slate. Missing now.

Bones knew eight of the men on that assigned escort ride were Southern Soldiers. Watcher's men, now Mason's, but at the time still wearing the Soldiers' patch.

Hurley was Rebels, through and through, raised around the club.

"What information is available on the Soldiers who went missing?" Gaze still fixed on where his arms crossed in front of him, Bones didn't look up at Mason's grunted negative response. "So we have nothing special there. Carmela is special all in her own right, with ties to many clubs through her father, her near-father, and her *Tio* Andy." *Slate had...has been close to the girl for years, and she still calls him her uncle.* "Hurley, though. His father was not club, was he?"

"Nope. Friend, but not member. Owned a bike shop in Fort Wayne that Winger used. Got tight with the club that way." Leather rustled as Mason shifted in his chair, but Bones stayed focused inside his own head. "Where you going with this?"

"Not certain, give me a little more rope to play with." Bones waited, comfortable enough to let the silence grow between them for a moment. "Hurley seems smart. Do you feel he is loyal?" Pressing his lids shut, he stared into the darkness forced around him. "Do not answer. I know he is. The Soldiers on that run, do you have names? Something is circling my mind." An image of Ester rose, and he saw her seated on the rug as she had been a few days before, telling him in her way that she'd never leave him.

Mason rattled off eight names and Bones mulled over each. Most were unknown to him, but one name stuck out. "Diamond. Was...is he a Soldiers' original?"

"Not a founder, but one of the first after Watcher moved out there. He's been with 'em for a long time. I've only met him a couple of times. You've probably had more exposure than me. You've been out to see Watch and Juanita often enough through the years." Papers shuffled, and Mason sighed, repeating his earlier question, "What are you after, Bones? Where ya going with this?"

"Diamond. He was shot in a scuffle once, correct?" Whatever this was he was chasing felt just out of reach. Like a mostly remembered word on the tip of his tongue, it was right there, but yet not. "Andy was with Watcher at the time. This was before he came to Chicago, before we met him. Before he became Slate to us. I remember hearing Diamond nearly left the club. Is he close to any of the members in particular?" Lifting his head, Bones opened his eyes, staring at Mason, blinking against the water flooding them at the intrusion of the light. "Are there things that stuck out about him?"

"Spider. He's tight with Spider. They've been friends since before the club. I think he was the one who recruited and sponsored Diamond into the Soldiers." Mason shook his head. "Spider still ain't right, Bones. I'm worried about him."

"Call Myron. I have a hunch about something."

Mason stood, stepped to the door and opened it, calling to someone in the main room. After a moment, he seated himself again, leaving the door open slightly. They sat in silence, waiting, until Myron walked in. "Sup, boss?" Myron glanced over, and Bones saw the muscles in his jaw tighten, teeth clamped together. "Ester okay?"

"Ester is fine," Bones told him, trying to decide what looked different about the man today. Shaking his head, he dismissed the thought. "Can you look at phone records on the day Watcher was killed? Can you see what calls were incoming to a specific number, even if it is not a club phone?"

Every member who was issued a phone knew the club had full visibility into the usage of the device. Nonclub phones might not have the same capability. Only club phones were allowed to be used inside the clubhouse, and no phones at all were allowed in their closed-door meetings. Myron had built a small Faraday cage for the clubhouse, and during church, all devices were deposited there, effectively blocking any remote listening by rivals or federal authorities.

"Yeah. I can do what's needed. Whatcha got?" Myron tipped his head to the side, looping his thumbs through his belt loops in a stance so casual it looked studied.

"Diamond. He was with Carmela—"

"What do you need?" Myron cut him off. "I have his records. Lemme get my tablet." Two minutes later he was back in the room, door closed, tapping on the screen. "What are we looking for?"

"Anything to or from Diamond that afternoon, especially as we neared the time when Mason got your message." Myron had texted Mason about the approach of enemies on the interstate, hoping to guide them around the rival club. When Watcher found out who was headed their direction, he had taken off in an instant, focused only on retribution.

"I got my heads up from Diamond, so I'm on those records."

Bones jerked. "Diamond told you Diamante were headed east? What time?"

"Right before I texted Mason, why?" Myron's head tipped to the side, and he looked genuinely puzzled.

"Because that gives us a frame from which to search." Frustrated, Bones stood and bent at the waist, slapping his hands on the top of the desk. "If he saw the Diamante rolling *east*, that would mean he was *west* of where Watcher and Mason were. If he were west, but not yet to Las Cruces, then we have a—"

Myron cut him off with an anguished shout. "*Fuck*. You're right. Dammit, I didn't even think about that. Didn't put it…Jesus. What a fucking—"

"We're all in the same boat, Myron. Don't travel there. Let's see what we can do with this information." Mason's tone wasn't quiet, and the tension in his voice rippled through the room, the anguished emotion he still held from Watcher's death rolling over Bones' skin and raising gooseflesh in its wake. "Still a fuckton of highway. Tiny needle and a big fucking haystack."

"But smaller." Bones offered, and stood, turning to look Myron in the face. "What can we do with this knowledge? Can we—"

Whatever ideas he'd been about to offer were cut off again, this time with a gesture, Myron slicing his hand through the air in a sharp movement. "I can look at video, pull in traffic camera footage as long as it's not been cycled. They don't hold shit too long, even digital takes up space so they write over the top periodically. See if I can pinpoint where they were when Diamond made the call, and then we can follow them to where they went next."

"What do you need from me?" Bones stared at the man's face, puzzled because the anxious expression was somehow familiar. That made him remember the thing which had been circling his mind earlier, because something about Diamond was familiar, too. "Diamond." He paused, gathering his thoughts for a moment. "Diamond called you. He called and told you the news. Lalo and Chismoso were rolling, they were on the highway, so it wouldn't have been a set-up from Lalo. He was clueless about what was coming. As clueless as Watcher would have been without that call." Squeezing his eyes closed, Bones used the self-enforced darkness to focus. "Diamond always reminded me of someone. Mason, do you have any pictures from the old Fiends' days?"

A scuffle of movement from behind him, the creak of wood followed by the slide of a drawer. "Got a couple of pics here. Full group in one. Whatcha looking for?" Bones turned and opened his eyes just as Mason laid an envelope on the desk. "I keep 'em here, no need to show folks old history that don't mean anything."

Bones leaned across, picking up the folded cardboard and hefting it a moment. Thick and weighty, there had to be more than a couple of pictures inside. Fingers to the clasp, he bent the prongs and tugged open the flap, upending the envelope to let the pictures slide out into a tidy pile.

There, he thought, as in the top image he saw what he wanted. A long line of men, arms around each other's shoulders, scowling at the camera. Prospects were kneeling on the ground in front of them, backs to the camera, their lowly place in the organization making them not worthy of being immortalized. In front of one man, there was a boy about fifteen years old, not scowling, not smiling, just staring at the camera. The man behind him had an arm wrapped around the kid's chest, pulling him back into a hold. Their faces were similar enough it was easy to tell this was a father and son pair.

Bones pointed to the man, already knowing the answer to his question. "That is Deacon, correct? This would have been taken about the time you joined the Fiends?"

Mason reached out, pulling the picture towards him and turned it so it faced him. "Yeah." He pointed to a kneeling body, back to the camera, on the opposite end of the line from where Deacon stood. "That's me."

"And the boy in front of Deacon?" Bones gaze lifted to meet Mason's, and he saw the question in his friend's eyes, read that he wondered why this was important but Bones had to wait until he was certain. "That is his boy, right?"

Nodding, Mason held their gaze steadily. "Yeah. His kid. I don't remember his name. Not long after this picture, Deacon's old lady took the kid and booked. Kid wasn't around much after that. Summers and shit. Typical divorced family."

"You don't remember his name? Look at his face." Bones willed Mason to see, to understand. Needed him to recognize it without things being pointed out, not wanting to sway him if Bones was wrong. "Look, Mason."

Dragging the image closer, Mason finally broke the stare, angling his head down to the desk. Bones tracked the way his muscles tightened across his shoulders, saw the already square jaw become more angular, taut. "Are you *fucking* kidding me?"

"Do you see it?" Bones asked, and then jolted when there was a sudden movement at his hip, a hand reaching into view. So focused was

Bones on Mason's reaction, that until he'd moved, Myron had been forgotten. "*Jesus.*"

"See what?" Myron studied the image, leaning in to focus on the boy. "He's just any kid, Bones. What's so special about Deacon's boy?"

"Look at Deacon, then the boy," Bones offered, and waited. "Look and tell me, what do you see?" He paused, then feeling a sudden urgency for corroboration, asked, "*Who* do you see?"

"Fuck." Myron tossed the picture back on the desk, and all three men looked down into the face of a fifteen-year-old boy who grew up to become a biker known as Diamond.

***

"Found 'em." Myron's voice was hoarse and rough with fatigue. It had been nearly fifteen hours since the realization they had a time and place from which to begin looking. Fingers flying on the keyboard of the laptop he'd brought into the room, deeming the tablet underpowered for what he needed, Myron had worked to pull together video footage from a hundred different cameras. Then he'd begun running it through a facial recognition software he claimed was better than the one used on any social media websites, using images of Carmela and Hurley as their base.

It hadn't taken long to locate a video snippet of them getting onto the interstate highway just minutes after Diamond's call to Myron. At that point, they had a timestamp and a direction, but because the department of transportation's cameras were spaced far apart, it had taken some effort to track them the hundred miles to where they'd exited, heading south. Then Myron began piecing together a timeline based on video footage from bank ATMs and other security cameras near the small highway the group traveled.

Twice the group had stopped for gas, and they'd clearly seen images of Diamond talking on the phone. The timestamp placed this exchange about an hour after Watcher's death, and the phone records showed the call had been from Opie. As Mason had requested, there hadn't been a mass text message sent to all Rebel and Soldier members, each leverage member instead receiving a phone call. Bones expected when they talked to Opie—and they couldn't delay much longer, so Mason had already called for Opie to come in and wait in the main room for now—they'd find out Diamond had offered to tell the rest of the group he traveled with, probably with the stated intent to keep it from Carmela until they reached the safety of the Otey compound in Las Cruces.

"Fucking hell." Myron clipped the words, his tone harsh and suddenly more alert and awake than he'd sounded for hours. "Jesus, no."

Bones and Mason moved at the same time, gathering behind Myron to look over his shoulder. The video was dark and grainy, hard to make out individual details. Bones saw a cluster of bikes to one side, a small group of people, maybe two at the most standing nearby, and a scattering of dark objects on the ground. The video jerked and disappeared, and Bones watched as Myron clicked buttons. "Gimme a minute. Lemme save it down." The mutter sounded thick, as if Myron's throat were tight. Computer dialogue windows popped up and Myron clicked, tapped on the keyboard, and clicked again. "Okay. Jesus." He blew out a heavy breath.

The video appeared again, larger, taking up the entire screen. The line of bikes came into view from the left, crossing the frame to park where Bones remembered seeing them on the clip. "Motel," Myron offered. "This is the view from the shutdown gas station next door. Lucky they still had the electric on." One figure moved away from the rest, out of frame while the rest of the riders dismounted and stood, stretching. Clustering together. Two figures stood apart, and from the swing of hair as the helmet was removed, Bones knew one of the two was Carmela. "Motel was closed for the night. Manager lives on site, so you can ring a bell, and he'll come to the window. I already looked at this place when I started my sweep. No record of our group staying here. You'll see why."

The figure came back into the frame. "Diamond," Mason muttered the single word, and it wasn't a question, but Bones responded anyway.

"Yes, I recognize him from the back."

Mason grunted. Then at the movement on the screen, he bit off an anguished, "*Fuck*." They watched as men fell, one after the other, to become dark lumps on the ground. There was no sound from the video, and no sound from the witnesses in the room as they watched the two figures to the side merge, becoming one, and Bones knew Hurley had pushed Carmela behind him, protecting her with his body.

The camera showed no movement for at least a minute. Bones felt himself growing tenser with each passing second, then slowly, her movements tentative, Carmela came out from behind Hurley. She stood clear of him for a moment before whirling to face Hurley, her hands on his chest. They remained in this pose for a minute before Hurley stepped to the side, facing Diamond head on again. This standoff had continued for a few moments before Hurley and Carmela moved, and to Bones it looked like they tossed small items to the ground, turning to their parked motorcycles. Hurley mounted his bike, his jerky movements communicating anger and fear while Carmela gathered something from her bike before climbing on behind Hurley. Diamond moved to his bike, lifting his phone to his ear for a few seconds. Hurley pulled out of the parking lot followed by Diamond, and their bikes moved out of the frame, leaving only dust swirling in their wake.

***

Bones studied him, as chin down, Opie watched the second segment of video. It was Opie's third time to cycle through the video. Gaze locked on him, Bones watched as he reached out, tapped a key to pause the playback, and saw the shaking in his hand made his finger stutter on the button for a moment, turning it off, then on, then off again. There was silence in the room, and Bones held his tongue out of respect for a man he held in high regard watching the deaths of brothers at the hand of a traitor. The muscles in Opie's neck moved, and his jaw clenched as he swallowed hard, fighting back the emotions that held him in their clutches.

Before calling in Opie, they had skimmed through the remaining video from the gas station and Myron isolated the section where two pickups had driven into the lot. A pair of men had stacked bodies like cordwood in the back of one truck, drawing a tarp tight across their bloody cargo. They had then moved to the bikes, rolling them up the ramp and into a closed trailer pulled behind the other truck. Less than two hours after the killing started, there was nothing in the frame except the shifting shadows cast by the rising sun.

All of this had gone down the same day as Watcher, but no one had known. There were no memorials for these men, no process of mourning.

Voice shaking as much as his hands, Opie asked, "You able to follow those motherfuckers at all?" It wasn't clear which group he spoke of, but Myron answered with what they knew.

"No. Got nothing on either group. Either they turned off the highway before the next camera, or they knew enough to route around it."

Stepping back from the table where the laptop was resting, Opie settled his hips and shoulders against a wall. One hand lifted and he covered the bottom half of his face, roughly scrubbing the skin of his jaw and chin. His gaze stayed fixed on the screen where the video was frozen on an empty lot. Without looking away, Opie asked the question Bones had been waiting for. "Y'all call Raul yet?" For more than three weeks the Mexican MC had been burning up the highways and phone lines looking for her.

"Not yet," Mason told him, and then continued, "wanted to make sure we had a solid lead before we called him in. Started with the location where Diamond made the call to Myron"—Opie's head jerked around, this clearly was news to him—"and worked back from there. Wasn't expecting this, not at all, brother." At that word, Opie's jaw tightened, and Bones wondered if this was because he felt guilt at living to be given that honorific while Watcher did not.

Mason didn't have any such confusion because he cleared up things quickly. "Don't do that, man. You think just because Diamond turned, took a dark path, I'd paint you with the same brush? No way. Watch told me over and over again what you were to him. Closer than blood, you were his brother, had his back in every way he could have asked. Had his back when it wasn't a popular thing to do, and had his wife and kids in your heart when you dealt with anything to do with Soldiers. He knew, and because he knew, I know, too. Brother, you ain't Diamond. And once we tell you what we've figured, you'll see why I'm as confident of that as I am that the fuckin' sun is gonna come up tomorrow morning." He shook his head, reaching out to grip Opie's shoulder. "Don't think I have one iota of question in my head about you."

***

"There are many things to discuss, Mason." Bones leaned his head back, letting his eyes sag closed. "Did you want to finish going over anything tonight?" They'd spent the past five hours making and fielding calls, activating the network the clubs had in the southwest. That was after they made a video call to Raul Estavez.

"Naw," Mason said, his voice gone jagged with fatigue. "Opie's on his way west, and Slate'll be here by the morning. You should go home to Ester. Time enough tomorrow to deal with everything, and there's no benefit to us rehearsing what we'll say once he gets here."

"Slate is invested in the girl." Bones swallowed bile, remembering the stories he'd heard about her rescue as a child. "He has many questions."

"Watcher and him were the ones who brought her back from Mexico. Safe to say they bonded. Slate even took Ruby to meet her before he married his woman. So, yeah, I'd say he's invested." Mason's voice sounded muffled, and Bones looked to see he sat in the chair with chin tipped down, the big man's hand roughly massaging the back of his neck. "This entire thing is fucked, man. Entirely fucked. Diamond's Deacon's kid. Deacon's in deep with Morgan, and has been for years. That shit happening because Morgan ain't dead like everyone thought. And now you say Chismoso's wanting fucking redemption. Fuck, man. You believe him?"

"I want to. Badly. It would mean much could work in our favor if Diamante is poised to implode." Bones shook his head. "I do not know if I can believe. But I want to. Time will tell, Mason. As ever, time will tell."

Silence closed in around the two men in the room, friends for decades, unpatched brothers for nearly as long, patched together for a space of months. *As it has been nearly since the beginning of our path together, we are forged in fire.*

Mason's head lifted and he looked around the room, Bones' gaze tracking where he paused, seeing pictures on the walls of past members. This was Mason's private memorial to fallen friends and brothers. The club had a more public one on the wall at Jackson's, but this was Mason's office. No matter whose ass was in the seat behind the desk, it would always be Mason's office.

"I needa get Watch up there, man." Tipping his head to indicate a space directly in front of where he sat, Mason's face twisted in pain, and Bones was reminded again it had been such a short span of time since they lost Watcher. A short stretch of days, and one where none of them really had time to grieve.

"Agreed. Rituals are important. They give us closure and allow us to move on." Bones paused, careful with his next words. "Wait. Let us find Carmela." Mason's gaze swung to him, and he read the question. "We *will* find her, Mason. She yet lives, or they would have trotted her death out as a tactic. Perhaps Diamond balks because he has known her so very long. Perhaps it is their plan, and he is merely following through." Bones shook his head. "Whatever it is, I believe she lives. Wait to put Watcher on the wall until the daughter of his heart is safe."

Mason's chin lifted slightly, jaw tight with the force of his clenched teeth as he nodded sharply, once only, but no more was needed.

"And now, I should go home as you say, to Ester." He couldn't help it, when he said her name his voice softened, tone becoming reverent.

"Good you got that to go to, Bones. Glad for ya, man." Mason had noted the tone and didn't hesitate in sharing it pleased him. "I got an old lady to call, check on my boy and our bun."

Pushing to his feet, Bones asked, "You do not know the sex of your baby?" He was surprised Mason, who liked to control everything he could, didn't have this in hand. "I would have expected you to demand the information."

"Willa doesn't wanna know. Wants it to be a surprise." Mason's face softened, the corners of his mouth curling slightly. "Said childbirth is the best reveal in the world. Like Christmas morning, coming down the stairs to find out what Santa left behind." He shook his head. "She's kooky, and I dig that about her. Gonna give her this one, man. Give her anything she needs."

"As you always have." Bones tipped his chin up as he reached for the door. "You are good at that, you know?"

"Good at what?" Mason flattened his palms on the desk and pushed to his feet, muscles in his arms bulging at the effort.

Bones shook his head. "Giving people what they need."

"They feed it right back to me, man. It's a good cycle. I'm always the winner in that scenario." As Bones lifted a hand and walked through the door, Mason told him, "See you in the morning."

***

Bones stood next to the bed, slowly stripping off his clothes, careful to keep his belt from clanking on the floor. Ester was sleeping, and he didn't want to wake her. Standing for a moment, shirt balled up in his hands, he gazed at her, amazed to have this waiting for him at home. Partially turned away, her face was visible only in profile, but her beauty was blazing for anyone to see. *Not anyone*, he thought, dropping the shirt to the floor. *This is only for my eyes.*

He ran a hand over the skin on his chest, fingers lingering on a section of ink, knowing by memory what was written on his personal canvas. Tracing across the tattoo with the pad of his thumb, this was a ritual of his own he had conducted for months now, since rising from the artist's table with her inked over his heart.

Climbing into bed beside her, he waited and was not disappointed. As was Ester's way, when she accepted something, there was no looking back, no swaying from the path set. She'd determined his house was where she would be, and his bed was where she slept, and he was who she slept beside. Now, when he crawled in behind her, instead of waking in a panic, she sighed in her sleep and sought him out, her ass snuggling backwards into the curve of his hips, slotting into place as if their bodies were made for each other.

Bones got into bed, and still sleeping, Ester's neck lifted and bent, creating room for his arm to slide underneath her head. Deep breath in, and then she released it, blowing out all tension and relaxing into him. Eyes drifting closed, he nuzzled her neck, breathing deep of the scent of this woman who fate had brought him. *A woman perfect for me*, he thought, one palm drifting up and across her hip, arm wrapping around her torso so he could cup her opposite shoulder, feeling her soft breasts pressed against his forearm as he tugged her tight against his chest. *My reason to love.*

Most precious

Ester

The gunshot woke me. Sucked up from the depths of sleep and thrust into the waking world in a nanosecond. Shouting and yelling, feet pounded down and up the staircase. I sat upright in bed, a space I occupied alone, glaring numerals from the nightstand red with the information it was just past three in the morning.

Slipping from the bed, I stepped into my pants crumpled on the floor, spreading my toes inside my shoes. Ears opened as wide as possible, listening and listening, hearing only the shouting coming to an end, leaving the rushing of blood quiet in my ears. Shirt over the shirt, sweater over that. A deep wine color which looked black in the bleak moonlight gliding down from the skylight. A dark moon tonight.

A sound from the back of the closet, and even before Bones called my name, I was headed that direction, pulled there by his unannounced presence. I didn't speak, didn't ask questions. I took his hand and followed him down the winding steps I never knew existed. The door closing behind us leaving the space in utter darkness, but his feet were sure, steps never hesitating and I matched as best I could, holding on. The stairs ended, and I followed him, coordinating action to suggestion when he instructed, "A low doorway, Ester. Mind your head." Arm up in front of my face, I minded my head, ducking through, the harshness of his whisper frightening me as much as the unexpected use of firearms in his home.

"Wait here," preceded the unclasping of his hand from around mine, and I waited. Only a few pounding heartbeats, but they stretched like putty when left alone in the space, with only my breathing for company. Then he was back.

"Come." His hand unerringly found mine, and we moved forwards again, more slowly this time. Time moves differently in the dark, surging forwards at moments, and dragging at others. This was a surging, and it seemed only breaths later he stopped again, the action telegraphed by his hand to mine, signaling my feet to stop moving. "I have friends on the other side of this door, Ester. You will be safe." He hesitated, and I wasn't certain why, then he told me, "You have nothing to fear," which of course said he very much expected me to be afraid.

Pushing my shoulders back, I stood straight and waited. A metallic sound, that of a ring clicking on a doorknob, then a backwards 7 of light that grew quickly to a rectangle, that conversion something I'd never noticed before, never considered how moonlight shaped itself to the opening afforded it, how malleable the rays could be.

The door opened fully and Bones stepped through, silhouetted for a moment as if he were a retreating black figure, then he was drawing me through, and I saw he was right to warn me I would be afraid. Fifteen men stood in a narrow alley, the doorway through which we exited at the rear of the nook carved between four-story buildings, narrowing overhead so it felt the walls bulged inwards, near to touching at the top. Suffocating. Darkness behind me, not a fearful thing, since disappearing into shadows was a talent I'd long perfected. Darkness held little fear, but there had been people in Bones' home, guns discharging loudly, men's voices lifted in pain and anger and that, those things, were most fearsome.

The men blocking my advance were terrifying. Faces hidden behind fabric and beards, each obstacle masking my chance at divining their expressions. I felt my shoulders curving inwards, hiding my meager charms, lumpy fabric of the sweater clumping in unattractive prayers. Bones whirled, facing me, giving these men his back and in that instant of movement, I became at ease. Still, I had to know, needed to hear his words spoken plain, clear as the sign on a coffee cart, so everything was known, small to large, weak to strong, no haggling needed. "You trust them."

"With my most precious possession."

One man stepped up behind him, tall and broad, tattoos on his throat marking a celebratory moment in his life. Proudly carried there so people would question, ask, give him an opportunity to dispense the information. He reached out a hand, lifting his arm past Bones' shoulder, the tattoos on his knuckles telling me FREE. Bones didn't move, didn't flinch, and his words, while spoken for the man, were directed at me. "She is fragile, Road. Easily frightened. I beg you, keep her safe. She is my life."

"With my own, brother," the man told him, and Bones lifted my hand, fingertips to his lips, the barest caress against my skin, then he pressed my hand into the stranger's, and that man spoke to me, "Ester, come with me."

Bones laughed without much humor, his soft voice sounding deep as the Great Lake when I finished the phrase, and I knew he remembered our first meeting as clearly as I did, when he echoed the words, "If you want to live."

Gone to war

Bones

Bones bent double over his knees, ass to the seat, elbows to his thighs as he scrubbed hard against his face with both hands. Exhaustion had become a persistent companion over the past two days, and he fought to push past it, trying to find clarity in his mind. "When do we leave?" Rupert was again donating the use of his jet for the Rebels, and they finally had what seemed like a solid target. "Raul on his way?"

No answer was forthcoming, so he angled his neck, lifting his head to look at the man seated in the couch opposite. Slate sat, body relaxed, but his face was tense, muscles in his neck and jaw tight, eyes focused on a point somewhere over Bones' shoulder. His eyes might be open, but Bones knew his sight was turned inwards, again analyzing the stills they'd pulled from the video, Carmela's face blown up larger than life. A raw grief and terror mixed with anger clear on her expression.

"Think he told her about Watcher?"

Not the question Bones expected, but he answered it as truthfully as he could. "I do not know."

"I hope not. Hope she's not got that in her head at least." Gaze still fixed on a distant point, Slate asked, "You met Diamond, right?"

"I have met him, many times." Bones bent, grabbed a bottle of water he'd placed between his feet when he took his seat earlier, opened it and drank, unaware until that moment how thirsty he was. "I have met all of the former Soldiers." Former because even with the upheaval, Mason and Opie had pushed through with the patch exchange. Done the day after Watcher's death, when all the Southern Soldier members were at the Otey compound. "No time like the present," Mason had said, and Bones had agreed. A good message to send to members reeling in the wake of Watcher's death, the only president many of them had known.

Slate coughed shallowly, and Bones bent to grab a second bottle of water, tossing it across, seeing Slate catch it without even looking at it. He cracked the seal and lifted it, drinking as greedily as Bones had. "Fuck me. You ever think he had that in him?"

"Killing his brothers? Kidnapping his president's near-daughter? No, I would not have expected it from him." Bones heard a noise and turned, seeing Gunny coming through the doorway that led to the front room of this safe house. Since his home had been breached, the assailants a local gang known to follow the almighty greenback more than any dogma, the Rebels had gone into full lockdown mode. Family and lovers taken to the compound in Wisconsin, or dispersed to other clubhouses and chapters across the United States. Close chapters had also hit lockdown, and would remain that way until the situation was resolved. "Gunny," he said by way of greeting, not liking the look on the man's face.

"Got something for you to look at, Bones. Myron thinks he found a clue. Wants you. Said you'll have the key." Turning abruptly, the big man twisted on his heel and walked back out.

"That is my cue." Bones lifted the bottle and drained it, crumpling the plastic in his fist.

"Ain't stayin' here by my lonesome," Slate said, standing and arching his back, stretching muscles tired from a combination of hours spent riding and another handful of hours bent over maps and information on the area where Carmela and Hurley had last been seen.

In what Myron had referred to as the war room, Bones stepped to his side, knowing the man would be hard to distract. Once he dug his teeth into something, he often wouldn't stop even to eat unless forced to by others. "What do you have, Myron?"

"Take your shirt off." Myron issued the order without turning to look, shuffling through a folder full of pictures and papers lying on the table in front of him. "Need to see something."

Tipping his head to one side, Bones glanced around the room, seeing no smiles on the faces of the men standing there. "All right, my friend." He tossed the empty plastic bottle towards a trash can, not watching to see if it went in or not. Shrugging off his cut, his hands were already moving to his waist, lifting the hem of his shirt. "What do you need to see?"

"Need to see Ester." Every muscle in Bones' body locked into place, and he stayed that way, frozen, waiting. Myron twisted to him, and Bones winced to see the exhaustion every man in the room felt had etched itself so deeply into the young man's face. "Know you got her somewhere. Let me see." Red-rimmed eyes bored into him, drilling deep, and the look was one Bones had seen before. "Need to see, Bones."

"I can show you that," Bones murmured, seeing the wash of relief roll over Myron. He'd seen this before, too. Lifting his hand, Bones' fingertips traced across the tattoo, turning his side towards Myron. Once positioned, he dropped his hand, revealing her to someone for the first time knowing they knew what it meant. "This is my Ester."

Myron leaned close, one hand half lifting, then falling to his side. Bones stared at him, seeing the man's eyes darting back and forth, tracking the lines and elements of the tattoo, seeming to memorize it. He cut his eyes up to Bones' face, then dropped them to the tattoo again. That one look shared much, telling Bones that Ester meant something to Myron. "She is important to you," Bones murmured, and Myron nodded. "This will be important to my Ester, when the time is right." Myron nodded again. "For now, tell me why you needed to see this."

Myron turned back to the table, lifted a photo and handed it over to Bones who stared at it. Anger flooded him, and he knew disbelief was evident in his tone when he demanded, "What the fuck is this?"

Painted on the bricks of an alley wall, one he thought he recognized, was a stylized version of his tattoo. The tattoo custom drawn for him by a trusted artist, pulled together from listening to Bones' words describing what was important to convey. Across the bottom of the image were stacked letters, color banding from the bottom to the top, all shades of blue and gray spelling out five words. *She dies if you fail.*

Shoving it back towards Myron, he firmly shook his head and tried to deny the message, his mind racing. *They can't reach her. Road Runner has her safe. She's my life.*

Myron stepped backwards, hand up in a warding gesture. "Look at it, brother." The urgency in his eyes reflected in his tone, Myron hissed, "Look at it."

Bones held Myron's gaze for a moment, then looked at the picture again. It was his tattoo, enlarged and changed, elongated. What seemed to be random Spanish phrases scattered around and across the defacing artwork, and he felt his skin itch, as if the words were painted there, too. Frowning, he read one set of words over and over, finally deciding he knew what they meant, and did not mean. "Liar. Thief of words. Gossiper. This was not intended for me."

He pulled in a deep breath. "The attack on my home was aimed at me. Each man was on a direct path to the bedroom where I have slept for years. I cannot believe Ester factors. If I had not heard the alert that the system had been breached, they would likely have succeeded in gaining entry. I would have been alone and naked, armed with only the two guns I keep close to hand. We have assumed Diamante."

He made a gesture with the photo as he lifted his eyes, pinning first Myron, then Mason, seeing acknowledgment on both their faces.

"This *is* Diamante. This is Chismoso being called home and ignoring the demands. His failure wasn't in convincing me he wanted to change camps. His failure"—Bones tossed the photograph to the table, seeing it lying there against a dozen others, different versions of the same graffiti, the same message, same threat—"was in coming to me at all. He is fucked, brother. There is no way back for him." This to Mason, who nodded. "Do you have him?" Mason nodded again. "They fear him, and for some reason my Ester is important. Many questions. Is Silly well?" She was the tattoo artist who had inked Ester into his skin. "How did they know this was Ester? More, why would Chismoso know this was Ester? Until she became ill, she would have just been any woman, Mason. Key. Why would she be key to controlling him?"

Myron cleared his throat, and Bones twisted in place, taking in the look on his face. Guilty and ashamed, and something else, something profound in a way that made Bones chest get tight. Without looking away, Bones dismissed the other men in the room, instinctively knowing an audience would be unwelcome for whatever it was Myron was about to disclose. "Walk, brothers."

The door had scarcely clicked into place in its frame when Myron began. "We haven't found Carmela, but I think we're close. Chismoso was Lalo's cousin, you remember?" Bones didn't respond, just stared, unsure what this had to do with anything. "They're from a little village in Mexico, where Raul and Carlos grew up. Do you remember the first time Raul came to Chicago?"

Mason spoke from behind Bones, and it was no surprise he had elected to remain in the room. "I remember it. About a year after we'd had the dustup at the strip club, the Machos had lost a lotta men that day. They attempted a run at our bar, Tupelo's. Wasn't what it seemed, though. Looked like a run, but was actually Raul coming to stop an attempt by Carlos' faithful."

Slate was the next to speak, and his presence wasn't a surprise, either. "They were after me. Gonna kill me. Thought everything had turned to shit that day, came out good. Fucking surprised me. Raul gave me a marker he still won't let me clear."

Myron nodded, but didn't take his eyes off Bones, who remained silent. "They killed a woman."

"Carlos' old lady," Shades spoke, and him staying was a surprise, but shouldn't have been, because he'd had Bones' back for a long time.

"She looked like Sylvia." Myron's words fell into silence. "They were from the same village."

"You fuckin' kiddin' me? You tryin' to say Silly's part of this shit with Mela? Fuck *you*, man." Slate's outburst was loud and forceful, the sound of his boots sliding on the cement floor a signal of his agitation. "Silly wouldn't turn on the Rebels, man. *Fuck you.*"

"Didn't say that. Silverio and Sylvia were cousins. They knew Lalo, know Chismoso." He pointed to the picture lying on the table, finger outthrust without turning to see. "She drew the tattoo, knew Bones would recognize it. If Diamante came to her and pressured her, she knew Bones would see this and know where it had to come from. I think she's hoping we come to her." He held up his hand, stalling the sputtering Slate was already doing. "I don't know why she didn't just come to us off the bat. Maybe she tried. We've been a little preoccupied for the past weeks."

"Why would she pick this tattoo? Why one of mine?" Bones slung an arm out, gesturing to the men in the room. "Each of us has unique artwork drawn by her. Easily recognizable. Why would she select mine?"

"Don't know. Can't know, until we talk to her. I needed to see the tattoo to be sure. That's why I had you come here, Bones. Now we take the next step, and see what we can figure out from here." Myron shook his head, tipping his chin down. "Ester's safe, right?" Bones heard the undercurrent of fear in his voice, as if the answer to this question mattered more to the man than any other words spoken in this room today.

"She is safe. She's in Wisconsin at the compound. Road Runner is personally seeing to her safety, my friend."

Myron's shoulders lifted and fell with a relieved sigh. "Good. That's good. Means we can concentrate on this puzzle. She's good."

"Myron, is there something you should tell me? This seems a good time for...confessions." Bones kept his gaze locked on the man, saw his shoulders move, curling inwards, saw him swallow hard. Each of these movements reminded Bones of something. Someone. He'd seen the exact position change recently as Ester—his brain stuttered, trying to reset and see the possibility again. "Myron. Ester is—"

"She's safe. Carmela is not." Mason spoke over whatever Myron might have said. "We need to talk to Silly. Make it happen."

***

Bones watched as the video image cleared, coming into focus on the large screen. An exhausted-looking Raul sat at a table, a dozen men at his back. Another window appeared on the screen, and the window framing Raul's video shifted, taking up only half the previous space. On the other half was Opie and what looked like most of the members in Las Cruces.

"Where is my daughter?" Raul's question was clipped and angry, his features set in a rage. "Have you heard news?"

Seated at the table next to Bones, staring up at the monitor, Mason leaned towards the computer and started talking. He spoke for nearly thirty minutes with only minimal interruption from the men on camera. The people in the room here in Chicago knew the plan, so they waited patiently. Once Mason finished speaking, Raul paused only a breath before he nodded. That video feed disconnected, closing the computer window, and Opie and the LC Rebels' window enlarged to fill the screen.

"Whatchu need from us, boss?" Bones wondered if Opie knew he flinched every time he said that word, boss, something he had called Watcher for as long as Bones could recall. "We're ready. Fuck, we've been ready. Give us something, man."

This was something Mason had talked about with Bones and Slate at length, Shades and Myron silent observers. The men in Las Cruces had done nothing wrong, but their loyalty wouldn't let them see it that way. The fact one of their own was a traitor would be enough to make them push to redeem the chapter; they would need that chance to make things right in their own eyes. Slate had argued, mostly because he was indeed invested in Carmela, but he'd eventually seen the wisdom of what Mason was about to put into play.

"Need two teams from you. One's going deep into Mexico. We need to get to the village where Estavez is from. Need to dig, brother. There's someone there keeping tabs for Diamante, and we need to know who. The only thing we have is a name, Agustin. He knows something, and we need everything. The second team." Mason paused while Opie leaned out of view, coming back with a laptop which he opened and started tapping on, looking at the camera with a nod when he was ready.

"Second team needs to head to San Diego. Blue Line and his Malcontents have a package for us. They'll only give it up to a personal escort." Blue Line had contacted Bones via text asking for a call, and upon making that call, Bones had been pleased to learn three Diamante officers were being detained. A cop club, the Malcontents didn't do things that crossed the line, ever, and for them to have willingly participated in what amounted to a kidnapping was telling. The things Blue Line said the men had already confessed were chilling, and Bones knew the knowledge gained was the reason Blue Line was ready to wash his hands of the men. "That second team, I want you to lead, Opie."

Chin lifting, Opie stared at the camera again, waiting.

"Blue Line indicates they received coordinates on a signal Myron thinks might lead us to where Carmela is being held." Shouting burst from the men behind Opie, but the man himself was still and quiet. After a moment, he made a gesture and the uproar subsided, another abrupt gesture and it died off entirely. Mason waited until silence fell, then continued, voice firm as steel, "Might. Not a definite, and no offense to Blue Line, but I think it's thin and won't hold. On our side, here's what we got."

Bones took a breath, knowing this was his cue. "Chismoso received a message from Diamante. All over Chicago, in all the places one would expect to find covert communications. They made a mistake, however, in using something personal to me. They did not know it at the time, only thought it would be eye catching. Hard to ignore. We did not ignore it, and Chismoso confirmed their message was not lost on him. The meaning, however, was not what we had thought. The 'her' in the message we originally thought was someone close to me, but now believe meant Carmela. Chismoso was not quiet when he took his beatout, he spread it far and wide that an innocent had again been involved in club business. Part of the reason so many dropped their patches was the inference that family was not safe. Not one of us wants to think of our loved ones in the hands of our enemy." Chismoso claimed to have no information about Carmela's location, and exhibited no knowledge of Ester, and Bones believed him. That left the mystery of who had been behind the attack on his home, which meant it was not yet safe for Ester to return.

"This message leads us to believe his tale, and gave us insight into where and what your first team will be seeking. There is a woman here in Chicago who has been a friend of the club for a long time. She is originally from the same village as Lalo and Chismoso. He remembers her. Remembers her cousin, who didn't move to the States, but instead hooked herself to Carlos Estavez." Opie's already alert features became more so, eyes squinting as if through blinding lights. "Diamante knew this. The fact they were digging makes me think he has knowledge we have not yet surfaced. That is what I will be doing here in Chicago, while you are dividing your forces. I will be digging into a man's head, trying to find out what he knows, without him knowing he knows it."

"I'm thinkin' I don't envy your job, man." Opie smiled, more a baring of teeth than an expression of enjoyment.

"Blue Line has a package. You, my friend, have executive decision." Bones deliberately used a phrase he'd picked up from Watcher, knowing Opie would know exactly what he meant. The widening of Opie's eyes, visible even on the video, was proof the message had been sent and received. "Have the men report to you." This was Mason's idea, setting Opie as the main conduit, and Bones knew he would know the men the best, be able to feel out their fears and dig into anything they might be holding back. If they had to call Mother, they would cleanse every report, ensuring they were painted in the most favorable light. "I do not envy your job, even if I wish I were there to share the burden with you. I pray you find Carmela, Opie."

"As do I, brother." Opie turned away from the camera, looking at the men in the room with him. "Any questions? Now's the time to ask." As the new chapter president, that was a powerful play, Opie showing every man standing at his back that he trusted them enough to allow a voice at the table with the national president. One man spoke, pushing between the shoulders of some of the members. Spider.

"And what's Mason gonna be doin' while we're out here looking for Mela?" Bones studied the man's face, seeing the pain drawn in lines and creases around his eyes and mouth. "Huh? Sittin' on his fuckin' hands?"

"You do Carmela no favors in courting anger from this end of the call, Spider." Leather creaked as Mason shifted in his chair at Bones' hip, but held his peace, letting Bones continue talking for the group. "I see this is weighing heavy on you. The not knowing. The uncertainty. The losses we have endured there in the Las Cruces chapter of the Rebel Wayfarers." He clipped the words out, seeing Spider jolt in place as if they were physically pummeling him, knowing he hated the reminder the Southern Soldiers were done.

"Juanita is here, the uncertainty is hardest on her. Yet she is not disrespectful." She hadn't been, not once, even when Bones went to her with this information. "She knows everything you know, everything we know, and she is accepting of the Rebel Wayfarers plan." Another involuntary jolt from Spider, it looked like the fact Juanita was listening to them scored deeply.

"Chismoso has spoken of what he expects you to find if the trail leads to Carmela. He does not think Diamante would have killed her. Yet. You do your job, and if you can, ensure her safety. I have my job, and Mason's job is whatever he decides is his, and I respect that. He is my president. I stand at his side, and at his back, and do not ever—" Bones stopped speaking as he leaned forwards, getting close to the camera, knowing his face would be all anyone at the other end would see. "—disrespect him again. I will cut out your tongue, and you will thank me for it, because that would mean I would leave you living. You have one chance to get this right, Spider. Do not mistake yourself. We, every one of us, live and breathe Rebels, and that is because of Mason's drive and passion for the club."

Taking a breath, he said, "Rebels forever—," With those words, he started the motto and heard every man at his back, as well as most of the men in the room a thousand miles away finish it, "Forever Rebels.

***

"Tell me again." Bones leaned over, forehead against the backs of his wrists where they were crossed on the tabletop. "Tell me about Florida and the Feds. Tell me about New Mexico. About Texas. About Louisiana. I want to know everything from when Lalo earned Watcher's hatred."

"Jesus, man. I've been over this like a thousand fucking times." The wooden chair across the table from Bones groaned, joints sliding against the wood in which they were set, flexing with the movement of the man seated there. Chismoso made nearly the same noise, rumbling from deep within his chest. Bones didn't look up, waiting. With a heavy sigh, Chismoso began again. "It ran together, thing after thing. We left New Mexico. Duck had found Bella, and it was time for us to get the fuck outta Dodge. We hit Florida and the DEA picked up Lalo at a bar. He was out of circulation for a week, week and a half. We got him back, and he wanted to talk to Duck. No idea why. Did that, and it didn't turn out well for him. I was about twelve hours behind him. He got winged, and holed up in a motel, called me. Your man—" Bones lifted his head abruptly, and Chismoso changed his words. "—*that* man, Tucker, had a hard-on for Mason. There was a well of hate in him that drew Lalo in, moth to a flame, man. He showed at our motel, tales of causing a wreck, killing a gal. Lalo went nuts, beat the shit out of him. He was *muy loco*, man. Craziest I've...I'd ever seen."

The break in his voice made Bones look harder at him, and he was reminded that Watcher had taken Lalo with him the day he died, and many other Diamante had died as well. This was the first time Chismoso had shown any emotion for his cousin's death, and Bones suddenly found that suspect.

Lips pressed into a line, Chismoso shook his head. "Edwardo could be crazy. All my life I knew he was different, touched. I never seen him like that before. Loud. Fuck, never heard him scream like that. Just fucking screaming. Same sounds, over and over, top of his lungs. Scary as shit, and known him all my life. Our motel room was bloody, all torn to shit. Mattresses ripped, drawers smashed. With all the noise, I figured the cops would be coming any moment, so I loaded us all up into a van. The thing already had a trailer hitched up, so I rolled the bikes up and hotwired it. Took off. Made it back to Mother in Adken. Didn't even get on the lot before we got tagged. Was like they knew we were comin', just swooped in and pulled their shit. Took Lalo again, left Tucker and me sitting in a goddamned stolen van. Days later they let Lalo go, same drill as the first time. He didn't have a word to say about his time in the shit, man. Tight lipped. I don't know what they asked him. Don't know why they picked him up. Sure as fuck don't know why they let him go twice."

"Tell me about Tucker. Is he yet alive?" Bones put his head back down, wanting to concentrate on the words.

"Yeah, he's breathin'. Gringo was stupid. Came in crowing about how he'd seen a chance and took it, took Mason down a peg. I'm not sure what Lalo heard, but it set him right the fuck off. Duck's man had shot him, so he was hurtin', but it wouldn't usually make him crazed. He'd been off the charts tweaked since Fury bailed on Diamante, saw it as a personal thing. Hadn't held back, man. Nearly caused war between chapters when he took us to Fort Wayne. Fuck, my mind's wandering all over the place, that wasn't until after." The chair creaked again, soles of Chismoso's boots sliding across the floor as he adjusted his position. "Fuckin' tired, man."

"What is your given name? Your government name?" Bones didn't know why he asked the question, because it didn't matter. "I'm Sal, Salvador Ramos."

"Yeah, I know that. Lalo knew everything about you, quizzed me like a fuckin' dictator when I was here in Chicago, before you ran me out of town." There was no rancor in those words, just a plain statement of fact that Bones found interesting. Before he could follow the idea trailing around his brain, Chismoso answered his question. "Oscar Ibarra."

Sitting back, Bones stared at the man. "Edwardo Suches." Chismoso tipped his head to one side, the question plain if unstated. "Your mothers were sisters?" A nod.

"Alive?" A headshake. "Do you have other family?" Chismoso shook his head again. "In Mexico?" Another head shake, this one accompanied by a drop of his eyes. "Edwardo had family though, yes?"

"His sister is there. I haven't seen her in a while." Muscles bunching, Chismoso stretched, affecting nonchalance. "What's it matter?"

"Who is in Florida?" Bones changed directions, still not certain at what he was aiming. "Who did you see after Lalo was taken by the DEA?"

"Deacon." Not a surprise, they'd found out Deacon was the founder of the club, which went a long way toward explaining the bloody roots and warped path Diamante followed. "Just Deacon and a bunch of guys, man."

"What bunch of guys? Do you have names?" Bones narrowed his eyes, staring hard at Chismoso, trying to decide what he was holding back. It was a given that he would, a man didn't get to where he'd been in the Diamante without learning how to guard his tongue. This appeared to be simple fatigue, as Chismoso's head dropped back.

"No, I don't remember names. They were fucking soldiers. Just any guy on a bike who could hold a piece in hand and weren't afraid to use it. Guarding Mother wasn't an honor, not like with Rebels. They were fodder, not worth learning the names, not worth anything until Deacon said they were." He yawned hugely, mouth dropping open on an exhale. "Tired, man."

"Tell me about Lalo. How was he when they took him out of the van?" Bones felt like he was near something important. DEA didn't scoop a guy up and hold him for weeks, then just kick him to the curb. Not without reason, and Lalo didn't seem to present the right kinds of reasons.

"He was freaked. Called them *federales*, was all bluster and shit. He'd fucked up his stitches beating Tucker, so he was one-armed, basically. Kept asking for a port. No fucking idea what that was about. Then Deacon came out to the street. We hadn't even gotten into the driveway, cars angled all around the van, pinning us in. I had my hands on the wheel, holding tight, keeping still. Five guns on me, didn't want to give them anything to itch about. Back door opened and they dragged Tucker out into the street. Lalo, man." Chismoso paused, snorted a humorless laugh. "Fucking *loco*, he stepped out of the van like he owned the world, but then five seconds later he's screaming at them. DEA, FBI, police. Alphabet soup of agencies, and he's telling them how he's going to nut their boss." Another snort, this one slightly more amused. "DEA guy whipped him around, plastered him belly-down on the hood, laughing the whole time. 'My boss doesn't have balls like yours,' he said, 'she got lady balls bigger than you've ever seen.' Made me laugh." He grimaced, tipping his head to the side. "Cost me, because Lalo saw. When he got back, he...took me to task for my laughter."

"DEA ever show up?" If it was a female team leader, that gave them more than they had before. The Miami division had stonewalled all attempts to find out about Lalo while he was being held, but if Bones could locate the person who had put the raid together, Myron might dig out at least some information. *I don't know why it matters anymore, but it does.* "This SAC with lady balls?"

"Yeah, she fuckin' showed. Ballbuster wrote all over her. She took hold of Lalo's cuffs, yanked his arms high, not giving a shit about him bleeding all down his arm. Said something to him. He fuckin' gave up after that. *Bitch.*" His anger at being required to watch the encounter was clear, the agent had emasculated both men with one move. Bones felt a stirring of admiration. "Lalo said she knew his name. He thought the gig was up. Thought he'd been caught out for all the shit he'd done. He got back and fuckin' told everyone they didn't know shit."

"Why'd they want him, then? Deacon was there, he's the head, the mastermind—" Chismoso snorted, and Bones stopped talking, giving him a chance to explain his amusement.

"Deacon ain't no mastermind, man. That's all Morgan."

If that were true, this would be the first real confirmation that Morgan and Deacon were working together. There had been lots of speculation, but to Bones' eye, no real facts to lay out. No one had seen them together, just had reports of them being in the same locations at nearly the same time. "Morgan was there?"

"No, he wasn't there." Bones deflated a little at this, then Chismoso got his attention in a way he didn't expect. "Shooter was, though. Morgan's mouthpiece was fully in residence, and had crawled so far up Deacon's asshole it wasn't funny."

Distractions

Mason

Justice Morgan's voice rasped through the speakers, amusement evident in his tone. Whatever this was he had called to share, Mason was not going to like it, and Morgan was clearly relishing the idea of putting him back on his heels.

"Christ, son, I never took you for stupid." Mason's teeth ground together, the noise loud in his head, but he held his tongue, not wanting to give Morgan the reaction he knew the man wanted. "You seriously think your mama was the only one I took?" His chuckle was dark, full of menace. "Fuck, boy. I'm not no metro-fuckin-sexual pussyboy. You know that about me. Never one to put a bridle on my want-to, either. I see pussy I want, I take it. Don't matter where, or when...or who." Without pause, he shifted topics. "You and John never got close."

Mason made an involuntary noise, a guttural grunt like he'd taken a hit.

Morgan heard it and chuckled in response. "Yeah, you never got close, you and your brother. But son,"—at the repeat of that hated word from this man Mason's neck twisted, chin pulling to the side—"you seriously think you're the only ones?"

"Old man, you have other kids, ain't my concern. Don't surprise me, fuck, wouldn't surprise me if you had a fuckin' clan scattered ocean to ocean." Mason knew his anger was visible to the men in the room with him, felt the rise of heat in his chest and neck. Morgan had a way of getting underneath his skin, and it wasn't healthy. Nothing about his reaction to the man was healthy. "Does lead me to wonder how many of 'em want anything to do with you. Now, is this why you called me? Want to discourse on how many little Morgans you got runnin' around?"

"You always was my favorite, boy." Another rough chuckle followed this insane statement.

"Not your boy, Morgan. I'm nothing to you but a headache." Mason closed his eyes, listening carefully to the other end of the call. Noise in the background, and if he wasn't wrong, Shooter's voice not far away. "Pain in Shooter's ass. Willing to be a fuckuva lot more, y'all don't stop your shit. Ain't having a sit-down, if that's what you're calling for. You've cut any road between us so fucking deep, no damned bridge gonna mend anything."

"You know I had your mama before you were born? Course you don't, betting Irving didn't talk about that, not even when she'd come to me again." Unwelcome memories washed through Mason, the nighttime of a Kentucky holler, chill of the dew coming down.

"She didn't go to you." Voice thick with rage, Mason snapped his mouth shut a half a second too late, the words already escaping, angry with himself he'd let Morgan goad him again. "You fucking took what you wanted, without thinking a goddamned thing about what was left behind."

"Prez," Slate's voice from beside him was quiet, warning, and Mason nodded sharply.

"Told you once, I didn't know she had you and that girl." Morgan's voice was as soothing as it had ever sounded, conciliatory almost. "If I'da known, I'da took you, too. Left the girl, though. Got no use for her. Even if she's mine, gals ain't nothing but trouble."

"Jesus, man. Stop with the desperate bullshit," Mason exploded, leaning towards the phone positioned in the center of the table, he tried to shake off Slate's hand gripping his arm. "Stop with the shit, old man. You wish you'd fathered someone like me, but you got stuck with weakass Shooter. Always having to clean up after him, always having to settle the debts he saddles you with. Fuck, it's no wonder you want to spin yarns about having a passel of kids scattered around the states. No fucking wonder you want anything better than what you got."

"One thing about it," Morgan went on as if Mason hadn't spoken. "Least it don't matter whose seed laid the path for Garrett."

"I recommend you think twice before holding my boy's name in your mouth again." Mason lowered his voice and felt a chill flooding through his veins. His hands clenched, and he wished for something to throw. Something to rend and tear apart, try and kill this fury running through him. "He ain't anything to you, and you won't ever be anything to him."

"Nope, that boy is Morgan, through and through. Not a bit of Mason in him. You ever think on that, boy? What'd it be like to know Irving didn't father you? He was a right bastard, him and his congregation. Never understood his need for tender flesh. I prefer my warm and willing to be just that. Well, at least warm, and older. About Garrett, though. You sure the boy's yours? You and Shooter being blood, might have confused the testing, it looking for a difference between you and Judge. You sure, Mason?"

Mason opened his mouth to retort and thought better, reaching out instead to firmly press the button to disconnect the call. Leaning on stiffened arms, he let his head hang forwards, telling the men in the room, "Get out." Without looking up, he listened to the shuffling of footsteps as the room slowly cleared. His mood being clearly read, the men didn't speak, didn't offer him any words at all. When the door closed, without looking up, Mason asked, "You get why he's doin' that shit?"

"Yes, my friend," Bones answered, and Mason heard Slate's grunt.

"You called it. Motherfucker's desperate. He's lookin' to stir up any fucking thing he can, put you off stride." That was what Mason had told them before taking the call. Slate moved around the table, hooking a chair and dragging it to the side before he sat slowly. "He found a raw spot, or what he thinks is a raw spot, decided to dig a little, see what kind of red he could score." Mason tipped his head, glancing towards Slate, seeing a sympathetic look on his friend's face. "He scored. That's clear." Leaning back in the chair, Slate lifted one leg, propping it on the tabletop. "Fuckin' hate seeing that, but I don't know if he got it through the phone."

"He got it," Bones assured them, circling the table the other direction, seating himself much as Slate had. "He got everything. What I want to know, Mason, is why you gave that to him?"

"Fuck," Mason gritted the word out, straightening and pushing a hand through his hair. "He just fuckin' got to me. Bringing up Mama like that. He never fucking gave that first shit about her, except about how it looked when she'd run. Back and forth across the fucking country, he chased her, and she'd run. I didn't see it for a long time. Hell, she was already dead and gone, I sure as fuck couldn't ask her. All I had was Morgan's words that she'd gone to him willing." He shook his head. "The woman I remember wouldn't have done that. Wouldn't have stood beside that motherfucker, not without being bound into place. I think he used John for that. Kept her there with threats. She knew in Kentucky that at least Bethy and I had each other. Her lessons to me always to make sure I kept Bethy safe, remembered I had a brother, remembered I wasn't alone."

"Why was he looking to rattle you, Prez?" Slate lifted his other leg, crossing his ankles as he leaned back further. "Sure as shit, that was his play tonight."

"I think...distraction." Bones spoke slowly, seeming to feel his way through the words. "There is something he wishes you to not pursue. I do not know what. But I feel that is behind his call."

Mason stretched, feeling the muscles under his skin pull and burn with the movement. *Spendin' too much fuckin' time in this room.* "Bones, you know everything we got moving. You tell me, what are we hunting that might be an issue for him?" Deliberately he put behind him any thread of doubt that might have crept up on him about Garrett. *Told Willa more than once it didn't matter, and that fuckin' test showed it true. He's my boy. Our boy.* "What we got in play?"

"Easier to answer what we don't have in play, man. Which is fucking hardly anything." Slate snorted. "New Mexico, California, Utah, Texas, Tennessee. I got people moving in all those places."

"Add to that Florida and Kentucky." Mason tipped his head, looking at Bones. With a frown, Bones continued, "Chismoso's harvest is happening in Florida. We have the SAC who dealt with Lalo on the hook. She is to meet with one of our men soon."

"Got a name?" Not that it mattered, but Mason liked to know the small details. Helped him keep things straight in his head.

"Justine LaPorte. She has worked for the government since college. Appears to be a straight arrow, which makes her dismissal of their case against Lalo suspect. At least to me." Bones dug into his back pocket, pulling out his phone. "Gunny was to send a picture if he had a chance, let me see if it has arrived." A moment later he grunted and leaned forwards, sliding his phone across the table as he shook his head. Slate reached out and stopped the slide, holding the phone in place for a moment before lifting it, looking at the image in what appeared to be shock.

"Shit." His voice was low and sounded wary as he drew out the word, following it with a quiet whistle. "Bones, I'm thinkin' you found what tweaked Morgan." He pulled in a hard breath, gaze fixed on the device. "Jesus, fuck. You sure she's the one that let Lalo go?"

Bones nodded. Slate put the phone back to the table, sliding it sharply towards Mason. He got his hand down in time to halt the movement before it flew off the surface, looking at Slate, puzzled. Mason turned his gaze to the phone and drew in a breath. "Yeah, I'd say we found out what he was trying to distract me from." A grey-eyed woman stared out at him, her dark hair swept to one side, pulled into a neat ponytail at the back of her head.

Missing him

Ester

I'd been three days without waking up to Bones sleeping next to me. Something I missed more than I thought possible, but then I missed him more than I imagined anyone had ever missed anyone. I missed the way he smelled like life, full of motorcycles and beer. How he touched me like I was a bubble on the wind, set to shatter on impact with anything except him. I missed how his skin felt like steel-wrapped satin underneath my fingertips. I missed his smiles, all of them, from gentle to fierce. I missed how he kept flowers in the house for me after the single time I'd sniffed a rose at a street vendor's booth, looking up from inhaling the scent to see him smiling down at me. He'd bought every rose the vendor had that day, and since I moved into his house, he refreshed the bouquet on the table in the bedroom at least once a week.

I missed him. The everything that was him. I missed the who I was with him. I'd never known a person leaving could take parts of you with them. Everyone in my life had always been on the leaving side of the line, until him. He hadn't told me he wouldn't leave, hadn't even told me he'd be back soon. I liked how he hadn't lied to me, and I couldn't ever remember a lie from his lips. I did remember his words. Every single one of them since we'd met. And the most important ones ran through my head on a loop, like a laugh track, but without the laughter. *My most precious possession.*

I wanted him back.

Road Runner—who confessed his real name was Kevin, but had scowled when I'd called that his close friends' name, and thanked him for counting me in that circle—told me it wasn't safe yet for me to go back to Bones' home. He also corrected me, calling it my home, but I ignored that.

I restricted my questions to thirteen a day, reckoning that to be my luckiest chance at receiving the news I wanted.

He was patient with me. Kind, but firm. I wasn't allowed to leave the room he had brought me to. He was willing to restrain me if needed, reminding me this was what Bones wanted.

I knew that, but Bones wasn't here.

I missed him.

Eye for an eye

Bones

Gun in hand, Bones ran along the edge of a patio, keeping his footsteps to the silent grass. There were five men behind him, double that number approaching the house from the front. *Please, God, let her be here.*

Two days ago, Juanita had disappeared from Chicago. She had called Bella, told her she knew where Carmela was being held, and was going to get her back. Bella had immediately tried to reason with her, quickly running to Tater, phone in hand, but Juanita had already disconnected. Now, she wasn't picking up, and Myron hadn't been able to get a lock on her phone for hours. When Bones talked to Tater, he was beside himself because he hadn't fielded the call, hadn't talked to her, and didn't have any good intel.

Myron had spent hours bent over a laptop, poring over Juanita's call records, and found a pattern of communication. She would receive a hang-up call lasting only a second or two, then a text from the same number, and then within five minutes would log onto her computer. Digging through her history wasn't difficult, because she hadn't tried to hide her tracks very hard, probably only following the instructions of whoever had contacted her, so Myron had reconstructed much of the data. They had a blurry, black and white picture of a bound and gagged Carmela and Hurley, in what looked to be a cellar of some kind, the two faces turned up to the camera. They also had an address for the number that called Juanita, and from there Myron had followed a trail which led them to this house just outside Albuquerque.

Now, under cover of darkness in a spring nighttime that was as hot as the summer in Chicago, Bones eased to the wall of the house, positioning himself next to the back door. Opie pushed in beside him, leaning close to whisper, "Front team in position." Bones nodded, stretching his neck and listening hard, trying to see if there was any noise from inside.

A word, then a flurry of language. A woman's voice, unintelligible, but he thought it might be Juanita. Opie leaned in close again. "Eyes across the street says two adults, male and female. Female is standing, appears to be brandishing a weapon. Man just hit his knees." They had a spotter on top of the house across the street from their target, and Opie's earpiece was coming in handy, keeping them all up to date on what was going on. Watcher's men were more accustomed to this kind of activity than the rest of them.

On the way in the plane, Bones had considered the differences in the clubs, coming to the realization that Watcher's men worked more like a military unit, while his own had operated efficiently in a small group, but without the same level of discipline. Different strengths, he'd thought, and knew himself correct when they hit the ground in New Mexico running, with precise intelligence on where they were going.

A shout from inside, the woman's voice again, and then the report of a gun firing made Bones' blood run cold. "We go now," he told Opie and from the corner of his eye saw the man tap his earpiece, probably to relay the message. Bones had already reached for the handle and was yanking the door wide, swinging up the two steps and into the kitchen. Three strides later he was rounding an archway that led to the living room, seeing Juanita standing, feet firmly apart, a gun in her hand, aimed at a man he did not know. Before he could reach her, Juanita brought her other hand up to grasp the butt of the gun handle, and she pulled the trigger.

The man screamed and fell hard, thrown sideways by the bullet, unable to stop his fall to the floor. Blood ran red across the tile, and Bones was reaching for Juanita's gun even as she shifted, lining up for another shot. Without looking at him, she yelled wordlessly, pulling fruitlessly at the weapon he stripped from her fingers, then he felt the rush of men pushing past them and wrapped his arms around her, holding her tightly, shuffling them sideways and out of the way. Hands between them, trapped against his chest, her tightly clenched fists beat at him, each blow accompanied by her shouts and screams.

"Juanita, I have you." Bones tried to get her to hear him, seeing she was still focused on the man prone on the floor, restrained there by two Rebel members kneeling on his back and legs. "Juanita, please. Nita."

As he pulled her with him towards the back door, Bones heard her screams turn to sobs, felt her shaking, heard her voice breaking as she choked out the words, "He's got my baby. He can't have her. Watcher wouldn't have let this happen. He can't have her, Bones. My baby girl."

***

"You have information, give it up easy, and you know how things'll go. So much better for you. You make me dig it out of you, and I ain't gonna use care." Opie stood from the chair he'd pulled in front of the man. Dragged into this tightly sealed basement, they had propped him in a corner, not bothering to bind his wounds. If he had been a part of Carmela's abduction, he wouldn't live long enough for it to matter.

"You're not Diamante, but you know 'em. Know what they've done." Opie leaned over the man, reaching down to dig a finger into a bullet hole in his shoulder, men on either side holding him in place. "Know where our girl is."

Moving deliberately, Opie lifted one boot, placing it squarely on the other bullet hole the man had, this one in his thigh. Juanita's aim had been true, Watcher's teaching having stuck with her through the years. The man howled, and Bones saw his eyes roll up into his head, leaving only whites shining in the light coming from an overhead fixture. "Fuck, man. Give it to me already. Don't make me do this shit."

Opie reached back and flipped the leather locking strap off the knife belted to his hip. "Hold him." That order was to the men on either side, and Bones saw their hands move, muscles in their arms bulging as they tightened their grips. The instant the man came back to himself was marked by a change in his breathing, going from hard and labored to a panicked pant, Opie's knife poised scarcely an inch from his eye.

"You know who I am." Opie's words sounded normal, quietly conversational, out of step with the entire scene. "Know how I am. Trained by my president as I was, all my life, I am how I am. Like him, I'm definitely a guy who's gonna want an eye for an eye." He made a small gesture with the knife, the tip dipping a half an inch closer. "Yeah, I'm definitely that kinda guy. The way I see it—" Opie straightened slightly, interrupting himself with a harsh bark of laughter. "Oh man, that's funny, 'way I *see* it.' Yeah." With a dark chuckle, he bent again, closer. "Yeah. Anyway, so, the way I see it, least I can do is deal with you. Our queen shouldn't have to fucking touch scum like you, shouldn't have to waste her time on you. You're in the know. Aw, yeah, you are, ain't ya? Means if you don't wanna share, you get nothing from me. No mercy. Eye for a fucking eye."

The knife advanced, and the man's face tensed, turning white. He was already flattened against the cement floor, no retreat from the blade, and finally, he broke. Stuttering words and screams mixed with tears and sobs as Opie moved backwards, away from him, and into the light. Bones saw dark bars cast by Opie's brows, shadowing his eyes as they all listened to the dead man on the floor tell them where Carmela was.

Hey, gorgeous
Carmela

"Light it up."

That was what Carmela heard as she swam back up into the uncertain waters of consciousness. She thought she'd made this journey before, but the sounds and sights in her head blurred together. Day and night, up and down, they were all the same. *Light 'em up*, her brain supplied, not quite echoing the words of the male voice. Still swaddled in a woozy fog, she tried to move, but her arms wouldn't obey. Secured at the wrist, they were tucked behind her body, her shoulders aching from the forced angle. With a grunt, she moved her legs, feeling the toes of her boots dragging on the rough surface.

"Now?" This question came from a different male voice close beside her. Deep and rough, it gave her all the clues needed to recognize him. *Diamond.* She sucked in a hard breath to call for help and gagged as the smell hit the back of her throat. The air smelled dank and rancid, like the time the city workers failed to empty a garbage can. Full of discarded leftovers and trash, it'd been left to sit in the hot New Mexico sun, the rotting scent drawing scavengers for days. Head pounding, she sniffed and gagged again, trying to sort out the odors, overwhelmed by the smell of unwashed bodies. It wasn't until she moved again and got another wave of the stench, and realized that came from her, too. *Dios.*

Her back hurt, was tender, aching muscles already starting the windup into a scream even as she scarcely had time to recognize the pain. Exacerbated by the awkward position where she lay on a hard surface, it felt as if every muscle was in revolt, angry at her for something she couldn't remember. A sound nearby, a weak groan followed by a series of painful sounding coughs. Carmela opened her eyes, blinking slowly, waiting for her vision to resolve into something recognizable.

"Said so, didn't I?" Clearly the boss, the first speaker was farther away, keeping his distance, perhaps. Even knowing Diamond, everything in her was pinging with fear, instinctively knowing this wasn't a good situation to be in. The man was out of striking distance, no matter if she had been armed. Which she didn't think she was, but now wasn't the time to start feeling around to see if she had her pistol or knife on her. "Daddy wanted to take me out." A low laugh, then the sound of metal striking metal, suspended chains, maybe. "Both her daddies. He threatened me. *Me!* Back when he refused my trade in Kentucky. Coulda made both of us rich men, but he turned it down." *He's talking about Papa Watcher*, she thought, a chill coating her skin and settling into her bones at the words.

Memories began invading her racing mind, making their presence known. Carmela felt her body jerking at the remembered sound of the gun, the report of the shots covering the noises the bodies made when they hit the sand. The echoing silence when it was all over. Hurley's deep voice had been laced with an edge of fear when he shouted, "What the fuck?" She remembered. Scorching heat from his body when he pushed past her, putting himself between her and the fallen. Between her and the only other man on his feet. *Diamond.* Pulling in another retching breath, she remembered. *He killed them all.*

"You want it here?" Diamond's voice again, and he was close. Another metallic sound, this different, a scraping slide of metal against a hard surface. "This good?" A grunt in response, then a click like a switch had been turned on. Carmela looked around, rolling her eyes and trying to see where they were.

There was a sudden assault of light, so bright it pierced her head, and she angled sideways as she screwed her eyes tightly closed. Heat followed, and she felt the prickle on her skin as the damp caused by her surroundings dried.

"The fuck?" That mumble came from the same direction the coughing had earlier, and she wiggled, trying to turn away from the brilliance that kept her lids shut, needing to be able to see if it was who she thought. Hoped. Prayed. "Jesus H." Hurley, she was nearly certain of it.

"Camera ready?" The boss was closer now, and Carmela flinched as darkness gathered behind her lids, shadows cast by his body between her and the light source. "I'll get the girl primed for her part."

Pain ripped through her scalp, down her neck, and into her back, head wrenched backwards at an acute angle. A hand gripped her shoulder and shoved, pushing her to lie flat on her stomach, then—weird as fuck—patted her shoulder paternally. A mechanical whine and the lights dimmed slightly, becoming bearable.

"What about the guy?" Diamond asked, and Carmela blinked, still feeling blinded by the pain-fueled tears flooding her eyes. "Want him for this one?"

"No, I think the girl will be all we need."

Blinking rapidly, she tried to focus her blurry vision, seeing a man's silhouette in front of her. Both his arms were extended, and she realized one of his hands was buried in her hair, holding her head up. Swallowing hard, she opened her mouth to ask something, anything, because at this point she didn't know a single thing other than Diamond had betrayed them all. Before she could say anything, the man moved to the side, and she was blinking into the lights glaring at her from two sides. His grip angled her head to the darkness between the spotlights, and he spoke.

"You know I have her. You've known for a while now. You just don't know where we are. Can't find me, can't find your princess. Oh, wait,"—his voice went from a chilling flatness to a false concern and Carmela shook her head, testing his grip, gasping in pain as he twisted his fingers into her hair, ruthlessly keeping her in place—"Jesus, didn't think about that. Is she still a princess? If the king is dead, does the title still hold?" Knowing what Diamond had done to his own brothers, at those terrifying words which carried a threat to both her father and her papa, Carmela bucked against this man's hold, writhing on the floor. She was not aware she was screaming until a blow from the back of his hand caught the edge of her jaw as he shouted, "Shut the fuck up."

Movement from between the lights drew her attention, and she caught flashes of Diamond's face as the man hauled her back into place. She knew the growled, "Deacon, what the fuck?" must have come from him, but it sounded small, tinny, hard to hear over the ringing in her ears.

Then the only thing she saw was Deacon's face, pushed so close to hers she couldn't get away from the stench of his breath—cigarettes and coffee and beer mingling to create a sickening miasma that surrounded him, pervading her space with every clipped word.

"Dead, you keep that shit up. Shut the fuck up, bitch. You ain't among friends, and I got few reasons to keep you alive." His hand dragged her head backwards, sections of hair tearing out by the roots, abused muscles screaming at the sudden movement. "You want to stay breathing, you be smart." His face angled so he could look over her shoulder, and he snarled, "Do what I can see you're thinking about, boy, and you'll be the first one I kill. I don't need you at all, except your claim to be able to keep the bitch in line. Diamond shoulda just fuckin' killed you, too."

"Hit her again, and you're a dead man." Rough, coarse, Hurley's voice throbbed with hatred.

Laughing, Deacon twisted and looked behind him, towards where Diamond stood. "Get the fuck out of the way, idiot." Diamond stepped to the side, his body casting a shadow across the cement in front of Carmela, the darkness looking thick enough to hide her if she could only get to it. Pain at the back of her head again when his hand jerked, pulling and pushing so her neck twisted and she could look over her shoulder to where Hurley lay. "Boy, you're trussed up like a turkey at Thanksgiving. The fuck you think you're gonna do?" That was Deacon, talking to Hurley, but Carmela didn't care about his words anymore; she could only see Hurley.

One entire side of his face was swollen, eye puffed closed, angry purple and black bruises covering his skin. His other eye was opened a slit, and she could see he was focused on her. "Hey, gorgeous." Ragged and low, his voice crossed the distance between them, curling around her like a warm blanket.

Not weighed down by independent thought, or governed by any rules of logic, looking into Hurley's face, Carmela knew they'd be okay.

Never again
Bones

"Clear." Bones heard the call from his left, twisting his neck to see Opie running in a crouch to the next room. "Clear." That came through the simple earpiece they'd finally talked him into wearing, promising that while he could, he wasn't expected to speak, just listen and keep up with the reports. While most had an earwig like Bones, the former Soldiers wore more complicated setups including a single lens. Opie had used the threat of denying Bones access to what he called the "ops" if he went naked, meaning without a communication device of any kind. After the video they'd received, there was no way Bones wouldn't be in on rescuing Carmela, even if he had to wear a tiara on his head. An annoying headset and stiff body armor were small things in exchange for having a hand in saving her.

"Clear." To his right, the call came from the kitchen and dining hall that stretched across the back of the compound. The heat in southern California was stifling, even at three in the morning. Bones lifted a hand, swiping across his forehead. Mason was on his way, so was Raul, but the men already on the ground couldn't wait. The information they'd gained left little time to chance, because what the man in New Mexico had known was that Carmela and Hurley had regularly been moved, and while he was aware of their location at the moment, they were set to be moved again in only a few hours.

Now, from the quiet all around him, and the repeated calls indicating empty rooms, Bones feared they were too late. *Fuck*. Leaning against a wall, he watched as Duck moved up the hallway, alternately stooping and standing tall, running his hands over the wall. It looked like he was seeking something through touch alone.

In his ear, Bones heard a crackle and then Mason's voice. "On the ground, on my way. Give me an update."

Opie's voice was loud, heard from a room away as well as through the headset. "Nothing so far, we're still clearing, boss. ETA?"

"Myron says it'll take me forty-five minutes. *Fuck*." Mason's angry frustration ran along the soundwaves like rusty wire dragged through an alleyway. "Goddamned California traffic."

Opie responded again, "Copy. Stay on the channel. Myron can keep you patched in, you can listen."

"Clear." Some of the men had worked their way to the second floor, and had begun the process of going through each room there. Soft footsteps on the stairway, Bones heard the whine of an elevator and shook his head. Fucking mansion, and they used it to keep a woman and man prisoner.

Duck stood stock-still in the enormous room that opened onto the back patio. Head down, he seemed to be listening. Bones remembered old lady Donella's dog doing that when it heard something in the wall once, motionless with cocked head along one baseboard, and then scratching and clawing at the surface until the rotten plaster came apart. The little dog had then darted into the hole, emerging minutes later covered in dust, but triumphantly carrying a broken-necked rat.

"She's not gonna be up." Duck glanced at the ceiling above their heads, then looked down, toeing the edge of an area carpet. "Watcher's stories, how he found Juanita in a hole under a building, the women buried under that truck that blew up on his place, fuck, even how I found Bella...these motherfuckers like to bury folks."

"Then find us the basement," Bones suggested, and heard his words echo in his ears.

"Basement stairs are at the back of the kitchen prep area." Opie's voice responded and Bones realized he'd spoken into the comm system. "I'll meet you there."

Duck moved, long legs taking him across the room and Bones followed, feeling unsettled. Something about Bella's rescue was gnawing at him, and the tingle from the almost memory had him distracted from what was going on around him. So distracted, he nearly missed it. Nearly, but not quite.

"*Stop.*" His shout echoed in the room and through the headset, and Duck halted, one foot still in the air, hand outstretched to grab the doorknob. "Traps. Bella's prison and the truck, both held traps. Consequences for attempting a rescue. Do not open that door, Duck. Not unless you are assured no surprises are waiting on the other side."

"Fuck." That was Mason, echoing the growl in the room coming from Duck.

"Jesus fucking Christ. Shit. *Shit.* Everybody freeze. *Shit.* Do not take another fucking step until you look at everything around you. *Fuck.* If they boobied this place, we could all be fucked. I need Devil and Bagger to sound off." Opie paused, and Bones heard two other men recite call signs. Opie continued, "Right, I'm basement. Devil's main, and Bagger's up. *We are point.* No one, and by that I mean not a fucking soul, precedes us." An audible breath through the headset, then Opie said, "Good call, Bones. Glad as fuck you miked up. On my way, Duck. Hold, man, fucking *hold.*"

Less than thirty seconds had passed before Opie stood next to Duck. He crouched, and Duck knelt. Together they examined the flooring in front of the door, the frame of the door, the handle of the door. They shared a look and then Duck stepped back. Opie removed a thin metal rod from his pack and unfolded it, telescoping it out to several feet. He held it out from his body, twisted the handle and Bones watched, fascinated, as it bent in half. Opie did something else and a red light shone from the end, and something else and the rod straightened again. "Myron, you got eyes on my vid?"

Opie didn't have to wait for more than a moment before Bones heard, "Roger."

"Okay, feed it to Devil, yeah? Slow and steady, we'll sweep everything." Another acknowledgment through the headset and Opie put a knee to the floor. Bones waited as the rod was inserted in the tiny gap underneath the door. With minimal movement, everything appearing choreographed, Opie adjusted the position of the rod. Adjusted again and paused, then whispered, "Bingo." Opie moved, putting a hip to the floor before going prone in front of the door. "Step back, man," he said, and Duck took a measured step backwards. "Devil, I got a VOIED, spring-loaded. You got your grippers, man?"

Voice tight and anxious, Mason asked, "VOIED?"

Opie answered him, tone distracted, "Victim operated improvised explosive device. It's wedged into place behind this door. Opening the door would have caused it to explode." He shifted, moving, sliding to one side so he could angle the probe slightly differently. "Looks like alpha-alpha, Devil. I see what's probably a second location." He moved again and whistled, low. "Daisy chain. Only the first looks to be tripped." Before Mason could ask, Opie explained, "Secondary explosives are in place close enough to cause a cascade of explosions, but they aren't wired to the first. They would have depended on the heat or blast from the first one to detonate the rest of them, but it would have happened fast, boom, boom, boom, boom."

Bones heard, "Excuse me," from behind him and shifted slightly to one side, allowing Devil to enter the room. In a breath, the big man was on his back beside Opie, taking control of the probe even as he handed over several additional extendable tools. "Y'all might wanna step back a couple more," he called, and Bones wasn't surprised that Duck shook his head. Bones felt the same way. No way was he going to back off and leave these two men here alone. "Your funeral," Devil called with a laugh, rolling his head so he could grin up at the two standing.

Opie grunted, then growled, "Awww, fuck you did not." He moved, Devil moved with him, and without saying anything else Opie stood and in the same motion reached out and yanked the door open. On the floor behind the door, Bones saw a small lump of what looked like melted wax, wire and metal shoved into it from two sides. Opie bent down and fiddled, then came up with the disassembled device. Tucking the pieces into his bag, he moved into the dark stairwell and completed the same methodical disassembly of several others. Looking over his shoulder, he grinned at Bones. "Y'all comin'?" Turning, he disappeared into the dark for a moment, then was silhouetted by a flashlight as he flicked it on.

Bones beat both Duck and Devil to the doorway.

***

Staring out from his place in the shadows of the dark hallway, Bones held himself in check, wanting with every fiber of his being to burst out and stop what was happening, but knowing he had to wait for the all clear. Opie had taken one glance into the room, one stride that direction before looking down and seeing the tripwire. Neither man was willing to wait, but after coming this far it would be stupid to fuck everything up.

Four people occupied the room, two standing. Carmela, her long hair matted, twisted into a single tail thrown over her shoulder, blood on her face. Deacon, one hand fisting and relaxing, the other clamped into a tight ball of flesh at the end of his arm. The two on the floor were Diamond and Hurley, neither were moving, but Bones couldn't worry about them yet. His focus was Carmela, cataloging her injuries, evaluating her condition.

A murmur from Deacon, too low to hear from where Bones stood caused Carmela to flinch back, head moving as if struck. "*No*," she shouted and positioned herself between Deacon and Hurley. "I'm not going to let you." Deacon shifted, moving around the room and she twisted in place, keeping him in view.

"Opie, we need you to finish," Bones whispered this on a barely there breath. In another moment Deacon would be able to see them, and all advantage would be lost. "Sooner would be better."

In response to another murmured word from Deacon, Carmela again shouted, "*No!* You can't. I won't."

"One second, man." Without looking up, without giving way, Opie spoke. "One more, Bones."

"You don't have anything." Still shouting, Carmela glanced behind her at Hurley and Bones saw he was moving slightly, perhaps waking up.

The pair circling took another step, then stopped, and Bones watched with surprise when Carmela maneuvered Deacon back the other way. He didn't understand it was intentional until he heard Opie's, "Thatta girl, Mela. Keep him focused."

"Jesus, old man, you don't understand, do you? So sad. You think people are disposable. Pick up this one today, throw them away tomorrow. Blood don't matter. You think I'm going to let you hurt Hurley, then you're more stupid than I expected. He's found family, and that matters as much as blood, any day. He's my family now. Mine, and you don't have any idea how precious that is."

Deacon laughed, the sound hard and brutal, and Bones caught a few words, "...just a tool, girl. Any hand that'll fit..."

She scoffed, leaning backwards and shaking her head. "My Papa Watcher told me about you, you know. How he always thought you were an asshole, but then you proved you weren't just an asshole, but a fucking asshole. Told me you taught him a valuable lesson, though. One he's always held to. Taught him that club matters, more than nearly anything other than blood. Said he thought you understood at first, but then he saw you with your own men. Your club, and you twisted and manipulated it so the members didn't know if they were coming or going." She took another step, and Deacon matched it, his back now directly pointed to the hallway where Bones stood. "Said you broke it, took it apart at the seams, made it unrecognizable. Man like you, got no idea what's precious in life, it's sad to see you grabbing hold of the wrong things."

So focused was he on Carmela, Bones nearly missed Opie's murmur. "Clear."

When he recognized the word, Bones sprinted across the room, leather soles of his boots soundless as he raced lightly across the cement floor. Carmela never wavered, never looked at him, never gave Deacon one indication that death was coming.

"Sad and old, and the thing is, you won't ever know what you could have held in your hands. But I do, because my papa and my Papa Watcher both taught me. You hold onto what's important, hold it close to your heart, keep it safe. No matter the cost."

Bones hit Deacon square in the back, toppling him like a tree, riding his body down to the ground. Once there he straddled the man, defeated Deacon's bucking twist to try and dislodge him and then Bones wrapped his fingers in the man's hair and wrenched his head backwards, tipping it nearly to his spine before crashing it to the cement over and over. The solid, meaty sounds mixed with grunts didn't register, didn't make sense, not until he saw the blood and gray matter. "Never again." Bones lifted

Deacon's upper body off the ground before he smashed it to the ground a final time, carrying it there with the full force of his strength. He felt the body underneath him become limp, muscles unresisting.

"Bones, man. Jesus." That was Opie, he'd gone to where Hurley lay against the wall. "Deacon's done for."

Bones didn't respond; he lifted the man's head and brought it down again. Bones could scarcely make out his own words behind the grunts of effort. "Never again."

Not wanting to take any risks, he gathered the now unresisting wrists into one hand and twisted them high into the middle of the man's back as he knelt on Deacon's spine. Devil's hands came into view, and while sucking in air with heaving breaths, Bones watched as he quickly secured Deacon's arms and legs. Once they were bound, Bones looked up, seeing Carmela was crouched over Hurley, her voice a quiet murmur.

"Jesus." Duck stood next to Diamond, who hadn't moved through everything. Duck was staring down. "Dead." Glancing at Bones, Duck shook his head. "Gutted."

"Just as well," Opie said, shifting towards Carmela. "I'd have killed him slow." He stopped and reached towards his head, then Bones heard in his ear, "Secured. She's safe. Repeat, she's safe. Both targets are secured and safe."

"*Thank fuck.*" That came from Mason through the comm system, followed by calls and responses from within the house as all the men reacted.

"Boss?" That was Opie, calling a question into the comm, and Mason answered, "Yeah?"

"Just to say, Bones is one scary motherfucker. Glad he's on our side man." As he knelt next to Hurley, Opie flashed a grin over his shoulder and Bones shook his head. "He's a goddamned powerhouse." Neck twisting back, he did a visible scan of Carmela, then in a soft voice, very different from the tenseness of the past days, greeted her, "Hey honey, how you doin'? We got help on the way for Hurley. Devil's gonna get you outta here, take you to Juanita. How's that sound, honey?"

"I'm not leaving him." Carmela's voice quavered, the first such indication of emotion Bones had heard from her. "*Tio, por favor*. I can't."

"I know you don't want to, honey. But I didn't sweep the whole house, just enough to get here. I wanna...I gotta make sure you're safe, Mela. Get you out, and we can concentrate on Hurley. Go on with Devil, we'll be right behind." Opie had already turned a sluggishly struggling Hurley to his side and cut his bonds with quick movements, was now bringing him to his back as Hurley coughed and groaned.

Devil knelt beside Carmela, and when he put his arm around her shoulder, she leaned into his side. "Promise, princess."

She flinched when Devil gave her title, and Bones knew why when she asked, "Where's Papa Watcher?"

Fuck, she doesn't know.

Opie didn't miss a beat, and Bones knew he trusted in her strength because he gave it to her straight. "He went down, honey. Juanita's waiting for you. She'll talk it through with you, yeah? We need to get you to her, and I need to see to Hurley. Let me do what I need to do, honey."

"He went down?" Thin and airy, her voice sounded childish, high-pitched and filled with shock. "He's okay, right?"

Devil's voice rumbled, no humor in his tone when he took over the conversation, urging her to her feet. "Let's get you to Juanita, princess."

Standing, Carmela's gaze darted between the men, finally settling on Bones. "*Tio* Bones? He's okay, right?" Devil tugged until her torso swayed, but her feet refused to move, staying planted. "Bones? Tell me..." her voice trailed off and he could see the struggle she had to pull in a breath. "Tell me he's okay."

Making his way across to her, leaving the bodies of the enemy behind, Bones shook his head, silently answering her question. She tore herself out of Devil's hold, throwing herself at Bones and he wrapped her in his arms, holding her tightly as she sobbed against his chest.

Come home

Ester

"Honey, you need to eat." Cajoling and firm by turns, Kevin spoke to the blank wall of my mind. His hand appeared, this his right one, his knuckles telling me LIVE. I silently argued with them. Now Road Runner spoke, but not to me, into a telephone he held swaddled in his hand. For once, I didn't care. No shits given, as Bones would say. Not today.

"Gimme Bones." Every cell of my body came alert at the name, the idea he would be speaking to Bones in a moment. This I cared about. Very Much.

We'd come back to Bones' house thirteen hours ago, but it was an echoing skeleton without him to bring it to life. "Yeah, I get it. Tell him she's not eating. Tell him I'm worried."

Tell him I miss him.

Tell him to come back.

Tell him safety first.

Tell him the sheets aren't right.

Tell him nothing's right.

Kevin looked at me, then Road Runner said, "She wants him to know she misses him, but she's okay. I think she'll eat now, since that's what he'd want her to do." A patent fabrication but I wouldn't make him a liar. I reached out and plucked a blueberry from the plate of lemon-crème stuffed crêpes he'd placed in front of me earlier. Kevin smiled, and Road Runner spoke to the unseen person at the other end of the call, "Tell him it's good. Stay focused. Stay healthy. Come home. We'll be here."

Tell me your story

Bones

"So you are really my Ester's brother?" Bones pressed the phone to the side of his head, tipped his neck up, and closed his eyes. "The last time we talked you were still questioning many things about her, but gave no indication of being relations. When did this become clear in your mind, Myron?"

He and all the Rebels were staying at the Malcontents clubhouse tonight. Carmela had been treated by their resident EMT, a festering cut at her hairline cleaned up but deemed too old to stitch. It was a miracle she didn't have more things to deal with, because according to her story, Diamond had kept her drugged for most of the time she'd been missing. Blue Line's face had gotten hard when he heard that, and Opie mentioned later that Watcher had entrusted Juanita and both of their girls to the Malcontents late last summer. Without knowing what drugs were used, they'd all have to be on the watch for any lingering side effects for Carmela.

Hurley was a different matter. As soon as they'd arrived after the rescue, he'd been installed on a gurney in a lower room kept for medical treatment. Bones had watched as Mason cataloged the room and its equipment, and shared a grin with Opie, knowing they'd be seeing the same kind of set-up in some chapters where the pressure was hardest from enemy clubs. Hurley had multiple broken ribs, and the doc said his left arm was broken in two places. Nearly an hour of working on that alone, and even now Hurley was hooked up to all kinds of monitors and IV treatments.

Carmela had crawled into the bed beside him, not willing to leave, and not a soul was going to try and force her. She'd taken the news about Watcher hard, which was expected, and held it together for Juanita, but it was evident to everyone that Hurley was her solace. He needed to know she was safe and near to rest comfortably, and she just needed him.

Bones was in the common room, ass propped on a stool near the pool tables, and had decided to call Myron for a chat about Ester, and what he thought might be true. Myron had acknowledged the connection straight out, not deflecting when Bones asked. There were so many questions, still. Ideas he hadn't been in a position to ask about before. Now, however, he not only had the time but the inclination to dig out answers. Tomorrow he, Duck, and Opie were headed to West Texas, to the chapter in Lamesa, but Bones would be going home to Ester very soon, and wanted to know what Myron's news meant for her.

"Can you honestly look at the two of us and tell me you don't believe?" Myron scoffed, and Bones focused back on the call. "I've lined up family history and dates. There's no doubt in my mind that she's my little sister."

"What do you want with her?" Bones lifted his bottle and drained it, tipping it towards the prospect manning the bar. "From her?" He got a chin lift and then saw a scantily clad woman take a bottle from the makeshift bartender, swaying towards Bones with an easy smile on her lips. With a sigh, he handed over the empty, taking the full one from her, frowning when her fingers lingered on his. He wanted to get back to the call and gave her a firm head shake, then Bones watched her nose wrinkle and knew she would take more persuading. Barely suppressing a growl, he said, "I am not in the mood. Take yourself to someone else." Her hand landed on his thigh, and Bones shook his head again, this time with disbelief. Into the phone, he said, "One moment, Myron." To the girl, he said, "I am unsure how you can mistake my words." He let his boot slip off the rung of the stool, stamped his heel against the floor, and dislodged her palm from his leg. "I have an old lady."

"She here?" The woman's tinny falsetto drilled into his ears, and he felt his brows snap together at the blatant attempt at manipulation her catty words revealed. "You let your old lady run your life?"

Laughter from the phone told him Myron was a witness to this encounter and Bones winced. *Time to shut her down completely.* "How that could be your business, I do not know. One thing I do know, is I am not your business." He leaned closer, seeing a spark in her eyes, not feeling a bit of remorse that he was about to quash her excitement. "I do not want your hand on me. I do not want your company. I do not want you in my space, woman. I am not amused, and I will be certain to share my displeasure with the Malcontents. I suspect they would like to know when a guest of theirs has been so disrespected." She took a step back, but that was still too close to him, so he continued, "And I've marked three members who are watching this encounter very closely, so I suspect this is not your first infraction. If you seek a property patch, this is not a path to follow. Now, back *the fuck* off, and let me go about my business."

Turning partly away from her, he lifted his beer and took a long pull from the contents, giving her time to escape. When he brought it down, she was back by the bar, and as he expected, two of the men who had watched her persistence in approaching Bones were both headed her way. Lifting the phone back to his ear, he heard Myron still laughing. "I did not find that funny."

"It was hilarious, brother." Myron snorted, and then laughed again. "Nice tactic, pulling the old lady card."

"It was not a tactic. Ester may not know what it means, but she is mine, Myron. I would not betray her." Bones sat straighter, chin tipped down. "She is mine."

"I'm glad." Myron's voice was somber, threaded through with a vein of quiet pleasure when he said, "I'm real glad she's got you."

"Tell me your story. In talking to Ester, I may have information you yet lack." Shifting so he was leaning against the wall, Bones propped his heel on the rung again, getting comfortable. "Then we can talk about how to tell my Ester she has family."

***

"I miss you, *Papi*." Bones heard the quavering words and paused, halting in place, frozen in his tracks at the pain Juanita had in her voice. "So much." Her voice hitched. "Miss you every day. Miss your wisdom, and everything you did to make sure we were all okay. Want to know if I'm doing right, by our girls, by our family. Right by your brothers, honey.

"Wish you could have seen our Mela today. Oh, Watch, Bones said she wasn't afraid, not a bit. She was standing up to the man who tried to kill her. You'd have been so proud, honey. She learned every bit of that from you, from her Papa Watcher.

"Our Mela, so strong." With this whisper, her voice hitched again. "She's always had to be. God knows she didn't have a chance to be anything else, did she? So strong, *Papi*. So very brave."

She took a jagged, harsh breath in, blowing it out slowly and he knew from the sound that she was riding the ragged edge of control. "Girl seems to think she's got nine lives, though. You know how she's always been, looking past what she's doing now to see the next challenge. I know you're up there and got your eyes on her, steering her around all the bumps you can, *Papi*." Her voice caught, and he heard her clear her throat, the struggle to hold back tears audible.

Noise from the room, and the bedsprings groaned as Juanita moved around restlessly. "You should see to our Bella, too, *Papi*. I like this man for her, he's strong, and she's always needed strong. This Tater, he's a man's man. You were right, the patience he has with her is humbling to see. The love in his face when he looks at her." Wet snuffling noises, then the brisk blowing of a nose. "She is right where she needs to be." Another muffled use of the tissue. "I'm going to miss them both so much. Oh, *Papi*, what am I going to do all alone? Why did you leave me?"

Bones turned, putting his back to the hallway wall, needing the support to keep his knees from buckling. Grief washed over him as she continued speaking, pouring out her worries and fears to her soulmate. He knew she would never recover from the loss, knew this would be something she carried the rest of her life. The idea of what it would have been like if he hadn't found Ester in time turned his stomach, and his throat tightened at the thought. *I found her*, he reminded himself. *She's safe at home.*

* * *

Carmela

Head on the pillow, Carmela watched Hurley as he slept. *Safe*, she thought, feeling herself beginning to doze off. She jerked herself awake, afraid of dreaming. The sense of being bundled into bales of wool was beginning to recede, as the drugs waned and lost their hold. It still didn't seem real. None of it.

I lost more than three weeks.

There were pictures stuck in her head, most involving Hurley. He had protected her, cosseted and nursed her as much as Diamond would allow. She remembered him holding a mug to her lips, letting her drink gulp after gulp of warm soup. Remembered being so cold she couldn't stop shaking, and he'd wrapped himself around her, trying to make it better.

He'd told story after story, too. Words strung together to paint pictures in her head, distracting her from the fear that encompassed her days.

"You were hitchhiking," he'd said, and she'd laughed because he hadn't known she'd done that before. Ridden rides captured by her thumb. Things her father and papa never knew. *Papa Watcher*, she thought, feeling hot tears welling in her eyes.

"You were hitchhiking, and I picked you up and took you to this hotspot I knew about. A swank bar that let in people like me."

"And me," she tried to fill in, not sure if the words made it past her thick tongue.

"And you. Prettiest girl in the place." Hurley leaned in and kissed her nose. *"So, in this bar, there's a guy."*

"Swank bar," she reminded him, and he smiled.

"Swank bar," he agreed. *"And this guy, he's a big movie star. Big, everyone knows him because he was in that movie. The one with Cher about that kid."*

"Mask." She nodded, feeling more alert than she had in a long time, words coming easier. *"The biker guy?"*

Hurley grinned. *"Sure, the biker guy. Big moustache."*

"And a voice that melts women's panties."

Hurley rolled his eyes, pushing close so his forehead rested against hers. *"Sam Elliot."* She grinned. *"And Mr. Elliot has a plane out back."*

"A plane?" Carmela scoffed. *"That's kinda farfetched."*

"Did you miss the part where it's a swank bar?"

It was her turn to roll her eyes. "Okay, swank bar, famous movie star, private plane. What's next? He takes us to a castle in the mountains, and we live happily ever after?"

"Something like that. We go with him to a lodge and eat the biggest dinner we've ever had. Steak and potatoes, five kinds of cake. Anything you wanna eat, it's on that table and I pile it on your plate. Gotta feed my girl." She smiled. "He's got a bowling alley, and pinball machines, and a movie theater. Anything you'd wanna do, he's got it covered, too." Hurley brushed the corner of her mouth with his lips, kissing her softly. "Then the next day, he brings us back. But you're done hitchhiking."

"I am?" she whispered, the make-believe fading away, leaving her with the fear again.

"You are because you're gonna ride with me. Always with me, Mela." Lips to hers, he kissed her deeply, and she opened to him, tongue tangling with his.

"Always with you," she whispered, scooting a little closer to him. A cast on one arm, tubes in the other, Hurley looked like death warmed over, and Carmela thought she'd never seen a more beautiful sight.

My beauty

Bones

Bones walked through his front door, pleased to see Road Runner already gathering up his jacket as it opened. The two men met in the middle of the room, and Bones saw the flinch when his brother took in his face, knowing that bone-deep exhaustion had drawn deep creases and shadows across his features. Wrists gripped, he let Road Runner pull him into a close clinch, felt a profound relief beating into him along with the pounding against the patch on his back. Affirmation of the nonverbal type, but still his brother reminding him how much the patch mattered.

"Glad as fuck to see your goddamned face, Bones." Words muttered into his ear, Bones waited to respond, giving Road Runner another moment to communicate his relief in this way, too. "Bad shit, brother." Stepping back, Road Runner kept hold of Bones' forearm, keeping him close. "Heard you dealt with Diamond's crew."

Indeed, I did. "My call, needed to send Mason home to his old lady." Not something he wanted to do, tackle that duty alone, working as primary in charge. But also not something he had been willing to hand off to someone else. "I..." He faltered a moment, saw anguish race across Road Runner's face, hated he had put it there by exposing his pain. Pulling in a deep breath, Bones shook his head. "I did what was needful." Road Runner didn't force him to say more, and Bones was sure all members had gotten a call or text about the decision. "Judgment they already knew was coming. It simply wore my face."

"Mason's hands," Road Runner agreed, and Bones nodded and held Road Runner's gaze for a long moment. "Lighter note, Ester ate today. She's a hard one to pin down, man." With a glance over his shoulder to the stairs, Road Runner said, "Sleeping now. She has bad dreams a lot, really bad, brother. Hate like fuck being down here, but me being in there when she woke made things worse. I stay outside the room so she can come to me if she needs to."

"I am home now. Home for the foreseeable future. I will help her sleep." Bones squeezed Road Runner's wrist. "You kept her safe for me. I thank you."

"My pleasure, and when I say that I mean it, man. She's a treasure." Road Runner's grip tightened and then released, and he was moving towards the door. "See you in about a week. Not a minute sooner, you hear me? Kitchen's stocked up with my shit, and I can tell you she likes my shit, so be sure to cook." He punched a code into the alarm panel, then hit the button that would arm it when the door shut. "Relax, brother. Take a few days and get right with the world again." Turning in the opening to pull the door closed, Road Runner lifted one hand. Bones returned the gesture.

Staring straight ahead at nothing, he lifted one foot, tugging until his boot came free, letting it fall to the floor with a quiet thud. Seconds later its mate joined it on the floor, and then Bones was jogging up the stairs, two treads at a time, suddenly in a rush to get to Ester.

He opened the door, and a wedge of light entered the room from the hallway, advancing across the bed. He saw the moment Ester's eyes opened, saw the instant she recognized him, and knew it from the happy smile that stretched her lips from cheek to cheek, knew it from the way she called out to him, wordless joy falling from her open mouth.

Knee to the bed, he stretched out, intending only to rest for a moment beside her, he needed to hold her, feel her body in his arms. A moment to convince himself this wasn't a dream. Her fingers were immediately busy, untucking his shirt and pulling, plucking at it around the edges of his vest until he removed the heavy leather, throwing it towards a chair beside the bed. One hand behind his head, he reached, pulling the shirt over, tossing it away. "Beauty." *Home.* That was the feeling he had been seeking, never finding until she stumbled into his life. *My home.*

Her hands were roaming, sliding and caressing, slowly going from barely there touches followed by a firm grip as she held onto him.

Bones groaned against the skin of her neck when she opened her legs, feeling how his hips notched into her. He lifted, intending to move away, give her some space, afraid he was moving too fast for her after being gone so long. Ester had other ideas and her hand pulling him back down to her severed the last bit of control he had.

Silken and rough by turns, her tongue danced with his, pushing and twisting. Stroking into her mouth, he feasted on the taste of her. Calling his name, again and again, Ester burrowed into him, pushing as close as she could. Fast, too fast, when each moment was a memory he wanted to hold forever, until they were naked and touching, stroking and mapping each other. Mouth to her breast, he reveled in her fingers on his scalp, pulling and demanding more from him, his Ester not afraid to show him any part of her.

Beauty he had seen, slept beside for never enough nights, but for Bones, this was all sacred ground. Places to tread carefully. He wanted to discover slowly, give her time to know in her soul that this was what she wanted, too. Somehow in his time away, he'd forgotten that Ester, being who she was, would never do anything she didn't want. She held tight to her walls, her protections, but when she let him in, she'd let him into the heart of her. Now, she wanted more.

Arms around his shoulders, one hand twining up the back of his neck, she put her lips to his ear and told him everything in her heart. "I've never felt so lost as when they took you away. Lost and down the path of left behind. I needed as hard as I could, casting those out the window every day. I knew you had to go, but I was lost, Bones. Lost farther than I've been since I was six. I can't without you. Something in you matches me. All of me."

Her lips pressed to the side of his head, slid down his neck until she tucked her face against him. "Without you, it's like I'm a stained glass window when it's just a thought. An idea, all these tiny confused images and colors laid out for everyone to see, and anyone could see, any person at all, but no one sees. You, Bones, you *see*. You see me. I've been missing a piece so key, that without it, the glass couldn't hold, couldn't unconfuse. You're the mortar, the framework within which I love."

Her mouth moved back to his ear, and she whispered, "I'm not lost now, Bones. You're holding me. I'm home." Her arms squeezed him as her hips tipped up, seeking and he groaned when he felt the heat pouring out of her. "I'm home, Bones." Her hips pumped up again, and the head of his cock slipped between the lips of her sex, the wetness he'd felt earlier amplified. Slick and wet. "Come home."

"Beauty." Bones moved, shifting, rocking his hips forwards as he glided partway inside her on a slow, steady thrust. "*My* beauty." Face buried in her neck, he stilled and waited. She had gasped, tensing as he entered, arms convulsing around him, and was now silent and still. "My Ester." Tight and hot around him, a silken grip strangling his cock. She moved, and he relaxed his hold, ready to let her go if escape was what she needed, but she did the burrowing thing again, pumping up against him with her hips.

"Come home." Her breaths came quickly, gasps in his ear. Voice jagged, she told him again, "I'm found, Bones. Find all of me."

Back arching, Bones pushed, feeling her pussy part for the head of his cock, taking the length of him, enveloping him in a sensation so exquisite it was unbelievable. "I find myself without words, beauty. You giving me this, giving me you. I see you, Ester. You will never be lost again." This last was a vow he hoped she understood. "Forever found. All my life, I will hold you together." Rocking his hips, he stroked out, then back in, deeper. "You are the thing I have looked for." She'd been honest with him, so he handed her that same trust. "You see me. You see past the bars and barriers. You see me, and you are not afraid. Not distracted by the disguise. This is a precious thing, Ester." Pace building, his words came in gusts on each hard breath. "You see me like no one ever has."

"I see you, Bones," she agreed, one arm sliding so she could smooth across the skin of his back with a palm. "I've always seen you."

"Yes, you have. My Ester. My beauty." Pushing an arm under her, he gripped her hips, holding her in place as he thrust hard, pulling her down and burying himself inside her with each stroke. "Mine." She keened, stiffening beneath him, the muscles in her thighs tightening, her cunt gripping and milking his cock. Mouth to her neck, he kissed up across her jaw. "Kiss me, Ester." She turned her head at his demand, and he plundered her mouth, feeling his orgasm circling closer, urgency in each hard thrust. "My beauty." Resting his forehead against hers, he watched as her lashes fluttered, her eyes opened and stared into his. "Mine." Thighs open wide, she curled her legs around him, holding him to her, handing him everything. His hands full of her, his heart fuller.

One word undid him, pulling him to the edge and beyond, his movements uncontrolled and wild as she told him, "Yours."

Making love
Ester

On the twenty-eighth day, at four after five in the morning, the door opened and so did my eyes. I cried when he came to me, crawling in beside me, coated in fear and pain, grime from his skin smearing on the sheets and I didn't care. He wrapped himself around me, held me tight, lay on top of me so I was entirely covered in him, and that I cared about. Very much.

"Beauty." He called me, and I answered with my mouth, stealing the taste of him from his lips. "Ester." He groaned and tipped his head, branding me with his kiss. Hips pressing deep, I felt the impression of his metal belt in my skin and let my legs fall apart, welcoming him home, the hardness of his wanting pressed hard against the most intimate center of my being. He moved to lift away, and I curled my hand around the back of his neck, pulling his mouth back to mine.

That was the first time I made love.

Rescued

Bones

Hip to the kitchen counter, Bones watched as Ester busily trundled around the backyard, pointing here and there, ordering her helper around. Road Runner had bought her a couple of bird feeders but no seed, so Bones had called a prospect to make a store run this morning. Plowboy had shown up on the front steps a short time ago, bag in hand, and Ester had immediately enlisted him in her efforts to determine the perfect place for each of the three feeders.

Bones was lifting a coffee mug to his mouth when the buzzing rattle of his phone on the countertop pulled his gaze that way. Swiping across the screen, he tapped to put it on speaker, and greeted with, "Gunny."

"Bones, brother, how goes it?" Gunny's voice was rough, and he sounded as if he hadn't slept in too long. "Heard you made it back to Chicago finally."

"It goes, brother. It goes. Stopped in to see Carmela and Juanita, Bella was there. They are healing. This is good." He'd sat beside Juanita, watching the quiet interactions between the couples. Hurley, still recovering from his injuries, solicitous of Carmela in a way that said she might be more fragile in private than she wanted to let on. Bones knew

Juanita saw it, too, because the worried frown never left her face while she looked at them.

Bella was a different kind of wounded, because she missed her father more than she knew what to do with. She'd had longer to learn to cope, and Bones knew the closure of Watcher's funeral, as hard as it had been to live through, had helped her move onwards. Tater stood at her back, keeping one hand on her always, but for him, the closeness seemed less concern for her peace of mind and more something he needed.

Bones, sighed, continuing, "I have information I need to pass along. A call from a contact this morning confirmed things Chismoso has told us."

"Good news, brother." Gunny paused a moment, then said, "Me and Road got shit, too. I'm in town, so if you want, I can bring it in person."

"In person is always good. I would like my Ester to become comfortable with more of us. She knows Road Runner now, of course, a necessity. But I should like her to come to trust my brothers." Bones grinned as he looked out the window where the prospect now had a double-handful of seed and Ester seemed to be coaching him on the most likely position to lure in birds, hands to his elbows lifting them up into awkward angles.

"Lemme call Road. Think he should bring his old lady?" It was a thoughtful offer, and one that showed empathy for what Gunny knew about Ester.

"You are a different man from before Sharon, did you know that?" Bones scanned the backyard, thinking it was big enough for a dog. *I wonder what kind of dog Ester would like.* "She and your girls are good for you." *The yard is big enough for a lot of things.* "For now, let us keep the introductions to just you. She is already comfortable with Road Runner and his Aurelie, so perhaps the next time you come to my home, you may bring your Sharon."

Gunny grunted, then muttered, "Gotcha. Later." Before Bones could respond, the call had disconnected. A minute later and his phone buzzed and rattled on the tile countertop again, and Bones looked over to see a text from Road Runner. **Be there in 10**.

Movement through the windows pulled his attention back to the pair in the yard, and he watched, captivated, as Ester held out her hand towards Plowboy, two birds perched on her thumb, heads bobbing, beaks pecking wildly at the seed cupped in her palm. The smile she offered the kid was stunning, full lips stretched wide, unfiltered pleasure there for anyone to see. Similar, but different from the look that had been on her features when Bones woke her with his mouth that morning, as if he had given her everything she wanted.

I love her.

This wasn't a new thought. God knew Bones had understood her pull on him for a long time now, recognized how she'd tied his heart into knots months ago. But telling himself this now, when she was so embedded in his life, this was giving himself permission to believe.

Only one who is perfect for me.

No one else like her in the world.

Mine.

Ester glanced at the windows and caught sight of him standing there, watching her. Her smile, already so full of love, of life, became even more brilliant. Slowly raising one hand to the level of her face, she waved at Bones. The smallest crook of her fingers, followed by a wrinkled nose when one of the birds shifted, moving from her thumb to a fingertip to chase a seed trapped between her fingers. Ester's mouth dropped open at the feeling of the bird's beak tapping and pecking, and Bones read her lips when she encouraged the feathered creature, telling it, "Good job."

The rumble of bikes outside pulled his attention and Bones walked to the front door, opening and stepping to one side as Road Runner and Gunny walked inside. The men greeted him with wrist clasps and shoulder bumps, and they were walking across the living room towards Bones' office when the back door to the kitchen opened, Ester running towards Bones, prospect at her heels.

"Did you see? Did you see?" Her excitement and pleasure were contagious, and Bones couldn't have stopped his smile as he looked down at her sweetly upturned face. "Me and Crowder made friends."

"Who is Crowder, my Ester?" Fingertip to her temple, he stroked a strand of hair back, tucking it behind her ear. "One of your feathered friends?"

She stretched up, offering her lips and he took them, giving her what she wanted even as he took some of his own back, sweeping into her mouth with his tongue, eating down the soft moan the motion and contact pulled from her. She relaxed back so her heels were on the floor, leaning against him as she laughed. "No, silly. Caleb is Crowder. He's also Plowboy, which is senseless since he's from Oklahoma instead of Kansas. Of the three, he asked me to pick, and I like peas. So he's Crowder." She pulled away slightly, smiling up. "I don't name birds."

"You like Crowder?" She hadn't noticed the other two men yet, and Bones was afraid of frightening her, trying to determine the best way to draw them to her attention. "I'm glad you like my brothers, Ester. You like Road Runner, too." She nodded, answer enough for both his question and statement. "I have another brother here I'd like you to meet." Suddenly tense muscles telegraphed her unease, but he'd gotten her past meeting Plowboy this morning, his selection of the prospect intentional, the kid's physique not powerful or intimidating. He'd grow into himself in a few years, but for now, he could be Ester's little brother. *As Myron is her big one*, Bones thought, then set that aside.

Bones turned them, keeping Ester tucked against his side, arm tight around her shoulders. "This is Gunny. I trust him—"

Ester surprised him by pulling away, but not in the direction he had anticipated, not away from the two men, but towards them. "I know you." Two strides and she was in front of Gunny who had leaned his torso backwards, but kept his feet firmly planted. "I know you." She glanced to the side, tossing a casual, "Hey, Road." Attention back to Gunny, she didn't pay attention to Bones as he slid in behind her, wrapping his arm around her chest. "You're the question asker."

"The fuck's she talkin' about, brother?" Gunny's gaze remained fixed on Ester, but the question was for Bones.

"No idea." Bones leaned over her shoulder so he could see her face, noting with some surprise she didn't appear frightened, nor did she look angry. If anything, she seemed interested, like Gunny was a puzzle she needed to figure out. "Where do you know Gunny from, beauty?"

She kept talking as if there'd been no interruption. "And the dog feeder." Tilting her head, she cut her eyes to Bones. "Dogs know good from bad." Gaze back to Gunny, she continued, "He's good. Asks loud when it's important. Talks soft to the damaged ones. I like your family, Bones. I like your brothers. Crowder was patient with the birds, Road was patient with me, and Gunny's patient with the pups. That's what he calls 'em, too, his pups."

"You seen me at the shelter." Gunny's chin lifted, and then came down in a single, slow nod. "I remember, I seen you too. Didn't know you then, and you look—" His gaze drifted down and back up. "—a tad different these days." Glancing over at Bones, Gunny told him, "Know her from the animal shelter. I work with a couple of rescue groups, keep track of surrendered breeds that are gonna need special homes, try to get 'em settled before their date's up. Your Ester was a volunteer at the Chicago shelter for a while, saw her when I was comin' in and out for regional rescues."

"Until the bus stopped running that way." Ester shrugged. "No good place to stay that's close, so I had to find a different route. Different days of change. You're a good man, Gunny. I'm glad Bones likes you."

"Do you like dogs so much, Ester?" Bones' out-of-the-blue question earned him another tilt of her head, followed by a slow smile.

"You want a pup." Bottom lip captured between her teeth, Ester waited, knowing him well enough that the question wasn't something he could pretend to forget asking. When he didn't respond, the corners of her mouth quirked up, lips curling as she said playfully, "You want to have a pup with me."

"God, you're so fucked." Road Runner was laughing as he spoke, chin dropping so his grin was aimed towards the floor. "Very, very fucked."

"Road Runner." Ester's tone was scolding, humor threading through her words. "Look at him. He wants to have a pup with me." Turning to Gunny, she asked, "What kind of pup do you see Bones with? I like 'em all, so I can wash the wish, wish the wash." She raised one arm, wagging her hand back and forth. "He's all proper and hard to impress, so it'll hafta be a good 'un. Know some good 'uns?"

"You do not have a favorite breed?" Bones would be surprised if this were the case; while Ester liked many things, she didn't shy away from making her preferences clear.

"I do!" Squealing with excitement, she whirled in place, giving Road Runner and Gunny her back, facing Bones. Palms on his biceps, she lifted up, mouth to his ear and told him in a stage whisper that all could hear, "Rescue is my favorite breed."

Arms around her, Bones held her tight, face tucked into her neck as he laughed along with his woman and his brothers.

***

Retreating to the office, Bones kissed the tip of Ester's nose before closing the door on her teasing sing-song of questions. Plowboy would just have to deal with a playful Ester until Road Runner and Gunny had given him the information they held.

Turning from the door, he was surprised to see the two men standing shoulder-to-shoulder in the middle of the room. "What is it?" Stepping around them, he made his way to the desk, leaning his ass against the edge. "Gunny, you said you found something. Is it to do with Watcher?"

"Wasn't there. Didn't have a chance to catch the plane in time." Gunny started talking, then paused, drawing in a deep breath. "Heard how you killed Deacon, man."

"Brutal shit, brother." Road Runner shifted, dragging a chair close and sitting, slumping against the arm. "Beat his ass."

"Beat his fuckin' head in, what I heard." Gunny picked up the narrative. "Hurley said you cracked his fuckin' melon open, scooped out his brains and was fingerpaintin' with 'em."

"I heard you took on the room singlehandedly, pushing Opie to rush through, not carin' if you blew up the whole house." Road Runner looked up at Gunny. "Heard he rode the man for a full eight seconds. Yeehaw, motherfucker."

Gunny nodded, found his own chair, and swung around on it, arms crossed on the back. "What I heard, too. Caught that in an alley down by Gary on my way up here. Some wild shit rolling all through town about what you did. Rolling through all the towns. Myron routed a call my way yesterday, clubs in Memphis want to talk. First time since Hoss put a hurting on 'em, those motherfuckers are knocking on *our* goddamned door."

"This is good." Road Runner nodded at Gunny, then turned to Bones. "Really good."

"Fuck." Bones took a deep breath, then blew it out in a heavy sigh. "Blowback from anyone? Blowback on anyone?"

"Nada—" Road Runner began, then all three men twisted to the door when it opened.

Ester's head poked in, and she looked at Bones, face pale. The sound of her vibrating question was nearly inaudible. "Um?" From where he stood he could see her shaking, and he opened his arms, cradling her to his chest when she ran to him, her arms wrapping around him so tightly he could feel her trembling. Through the open doorway behind her came six men, all Rebels, followed closely by Plowboy who looked worried, probably because Ester was afraid, and because he hadn't warned Bones about the new visitors.

Palm to the back of her head, he held Ester to him as he stared at the men. "Brothers, I know you did not intend disrespect, but you should have contacted me."

Shades was the only current Chicago member in the room, other than Bones and Road Runner. All the rest were from Fort Wayne, and seeing so many here from Mason's adopted town gave Bones a chill—Bear, Hoss, Slate, Gypsy, and Tequila. "Good to see you. We"—with the fingers of one hand, he gestured towards the now standing Road Runner and Gunny—"were beginning a conversation about some mutual friends." No way could they continue their discussion now, not with both Ester and a prospect in the room, and the sudden appearance of the group made Bones unwilling to continue in any case. Apparently Road Runner and Gunny didn't know these men were coming, but just as clearly from their expressions, all these men knew who they'd find. "My Ester is unaccustomed to so many visitors."

"I get that, brother." Slate, with a hangdog look on his face, had the good sense to apologize. "Sorry about spookin' her. Needed to get to you in a hurry. You got somewhere *safe* you can have her hang?" The emphasis on the single word wasn't lost on Bones, and he looked at Slate sharply. "You do, then you need to get her there, brother."

Torn, because Ester needed him, that much was clear. She hadn't made a peep since she'd latched on to him, but also hadn't stopped trembling. His brothers also needed him, and whatever they had to share was either about a developing threat, or would put Ester under threat if she knew. *I cannot send her away. Not again.* With a deep breath, he gave Slate this answer. "She is safest at my side."

"Gonna be some sketch shit, man." That was from Gypsy, a man Bones didn't know well, and most of what he did know was from Gypsy's preclub life, back when he was a police officer in a Chicago suburb. The path from police to a patched member had been rocky, but Bones knew Mason trusted the man. "Sure you want her hearin' it?"

"You being here, in my home, means there is some urgency. If there were not a threat that impacted me, you would not be here, you would have called me and others to the clubhouse. My home has been attacked once, and Ester was here." She scrubbed her cheek against his chest, and Bones felt her fingers wrapping around the chain belt at his waist. Holding on, in the face of what probably seemed like a coordinated effort to remove her. "Ester knows my life. She is no stranger to doing needful things on her own. Tell me."

A moment passed, then another, as Bear and Slate stared at each other, then across the room to where Gunny stood.

"You been poking around." That was Hoss, and Bones looked at him to see he, too, was watching Gunny. "Been poking around since before Watcher went down. We think you've finally poked the bear one too many times."

"The fuck?" Clearly confused, Gunny swung out an arm, palm up. "Who you think I've been poking?"

"Got your shit in Kentucky you've been looking into. A couple of hours ago, the Outrider clubhouse in Lexington went up in flames. Word is three confirmed, likely another couple by the time it cools off enough for them to get into the place. Those three confirmed? Your informants." Gunny grunted, and Hoss continued, "Word also is those three had been seen in Chicago recently. You meet with them up here?"

Gunny's head swung back and forth, followed by a firm, "Fuck no. I keep that shit far away."

"As expected, brother." Slate shook his head. "Know you're careful. Know you keep shit from landing on our doorstep. Need to know what you're after."

"Where is Chismoso?" Bones asked the question and then marked the surprise of nearly every man except Slate. "You knew he was in Chicago, yes?" Bear and Gypsy each shook their head, glancing to Gunny, who was also shaking his. "Shades, you and Slate knew, were in the office when I talked to Mason. He never said anything to others?"

Slate shrugged, looking uncomfortable. "Shit's been busy. Know you said the man sounded solid, but with everything we have going on, Mason didn't feel it was time to push that lever. We were sitting on that, and then your shit hit the fan, then we got a solid on Mela, then Juanita hit the wind. Fuck, man. It's been chaos for a while now."

"Truth." Bones felt Ester relax slightly, her fingers running up and down his sides as her stranglehold on his belt eased. He lifted his eyes to Gunny. "Tell me about Kentucky. What did you come here to share?"

"You know the trail I been following." A statement, and Bones held his gaze, waiting. "Found fruit. Small time Chicago gangster wound up down there years ago, started working with the Columbians, blazing a path through the state for them. Seems he had a way of dealing with those distributors who didn't agree on his plans." Even knowing Gunny was skirting the topic, his meaning was clear. "If they tried to clean up, the gangster would deal, sometimes without a payday. Seemed to be working his way into an organization, but we couldn't figure out whose. Then, we got a lead on who he was working up the ladder to being. Morgan. No fuckin' surprise there. Might be tied to things with Watcher and Duck, but it's murky. Wanted to run the ideas past you."

"Okay. So then why are *you* here now?" Bones swept the rest of the men with a glance, coming back to Slate. "Tell me, Slate."

"Gunny don't know." Slate tipped his head to the side. "Myron found a pic. You know we're still sweeping anything to do with Diamante." Bones nodded. "Morgan's been in Kentucky recently."

"Why does that merit the travel of so many in unsettled times? You all"—Bones swept his hand, indicating the Fort Wayne members—"are here. There must be a reason to bring you from home and family."

Slate eyed Ester, and Bones noted how his eyes narrowed at her grip around his waist. "Sketch, like Gypsy said." Bones didn't move, didn't speak, waiting. "Pic gave us a location, found a couple of talkers there. Morgan's jawin' to a lotta folks about Cali. About you. About the shit went down there. You ain't his favorite person, Bones."

Suddenly the arrival of the men made total sense, and Bones relaxed slightly. "He is making this personal." Slate nodded, and Bones felt the corners of his mouth tip up. "You are my insurance." Another nod from Slate, followed by a chin tip from Bear. "Give me a minute." He shifted Ester to one side, letting her head stay buried against him. "Plowboy, come with us, please."

"Crowder." Ester's mumble came from somewhere near his chest, and Bones chuckled.

Our time

Ester

After that, the time I came to call our February of Absence, Bones was seldom away for more than hours at a time. The physicality that had marked our friendship was more pronounced, a change I welcomed, because each touch, each gesture spoke of his feelings. He knew the things I had told him, questioned some, and surmised the remainder. I didn't think he was far off the target with his suspicions, but since they were silent, I couldn't say yea or nay.

One night, he lay between my legs, shoulders shoving my knees wide apart, candles in the room casting flickering light reflected by the windows and mirrors. He traced the thick scar that connected my vaginal opening with my anus, gaze following the trail of his fingertips, his light and gentle touch making me shiver. Without lifting his eyes, he asked, "Does this cause you pain, Ester?"

I spoke truthfully, something he'd asked of me and I vowed to always do. *Tell me if I frighten you,* he'd said. *Tell me if I hurt you, in even the smallest of ways, my beauty. Promise me.* The last had been urgent, important enough he had paused midstroke, staying buried inside me, his heat adding to the already molten core inside me. Teased and adrift at his sudden stillness, I'd promised. I always keep my promises.

So now, I spoke the truth, for the moment, for the present, and for the past. "Right now, no. That tickles a little, but it's not painful. It doesn't hurt anymore; pains now are a nay. Pains past, yes, in the execution and realization, even in the sufferance afterwards. It's ugly." I paused, then apologized for him having to see the scar, purple and raised, writhing through a private space where I'd never considered eyes being laid, or gazes gazed. "I'm sorry."

"Why are you sorry, my love?" That first time to hear those words, my eyes drifted closed in the ecstasy of the moment. Another gift, and this one I would hold forever in my head. "Ester." His tone lacked the amusement I had expected, because he usually liked how over the top I would get when he was kind.

"Ester, look at me, please." Seeing him beyond my opening lashes, he was blurry at first, then jumped into focus, the anger on his face surprising the air from my body. Like a whip, his words lashed the air, not directed at me, but still the fury simmered over my skin from where he lay, belly down on the mattress, head canted so his cheek rested on my thigh.

A firm stroke with the pad of his thumb traced the scar, then skimmed up to press against my clitoris, causing my muscles to jump in a good way. "This is a precious part of you. That someone would injure you so is not something for which you should apologize. You should scream and shout, rend the air with rage that such was done to you." His jaw tightened, and the lines on his skin quivered with his fury. "My question was because it looks inflamed, and I want you, but I've promised you no pain." He repeated himself, the tone a vow of its own. "No pain, ever, beauty. Only joy and pleasure in my bed."

"It aches, sometimes, when we're done." I offered him more honesty and saw him accept it, not being mad because I told him. "But it's a good kind of ache, mostly. A doctor once told me there was a cream that would help keep it supple, but I didn't care then because I didn't ever want to be touched there again, not even by myself. It was thirty below, and the shelter made a health check mandatory, so I had to let him look so I could stay warm." I considered, thinking, then told him, "That was eleven, no twelve years ago."

I got lost in my head for a minute, trying to sort out the weeks and months, thinking I'd thought my way past something important. Something he'd want to know about. A day. He interrupted me, his voice growling and angry when he asked, "You bore this scar when you were but eleven-years-old?" That was when I realized I hadn't told him everything and must have worn the knowledge on my face, for him to read, because he growled again, his throat vibrating around the words, "Tell me."

I'd finished my calculations, so I could correct him, but was treading carefully, because his anger was slippery. "I was twelve, but lied and told them I was fifteen so they wouldn't call the court lady." Quickly, I finished, hoping to derail his fury, "The scar has been part of me for sixteen years."

"You were seven." He had moved, head upright, gaze boring into me, drilling down to the truth he wanted so desperately that I gave it to him, fumbling even in my rush to get it out so he could know.

"I was eight. I'm twenty-four." He took in a sharp breath, eyes narrowing when I reacted involuntarily, the muscles of my stomach jumping. I wanted to apologize, but I didn't know for what, and was afraid it would make him angrier.

That day started the period I called Interrogation by Intimacy. Bones way of making me boneless with his boner, and of course I didn't tell him *that*, but in the silence of my mind I knew it was true. He would make love to me and then cuddle close, circling me with his body. Building a wall between me and the outside, protecting me. Then, having gained a fresh perspective of the map that was my skin, he would question this line or that scar, this mark or that dimple, following the thread of a story until he held everything in his hands. Then he would make it okay, better than okay, drive me out of my mind and back into boneless, where he would hold me. Even in his sleep, he held me.

I liked that.

Make a play

Bones

"Where'd the boss go?" Opie's image flickered, then stabilized again on the screen. "Thought he needed a check-in from me?"

"Mason is coordinating something at the moment." Bones shifted to the side, letting Fury pull his chair up to the edge of the desk. "We wanted to chat with you."

Fury nodded, saying only, "Opie."

Opie lifted his chin, responding to the greeting nonverbally as he asked, "You need me to pull anyone else in, Bones?"

"No, your attention is all that is required. Are you alone in the office?" Bones knew from the scene behind Opie that he was in the barn behind Watcher's house, the only real clubhouse they had in Las Cruces. Also knew from experience that there were countermeasures in place to keep anyone from getting too close, or from snooping. Opie nodded, his face tense. "Is Juanita in the house?" Opie nodded again. She had headed home a week ago, taking Carmela with her. Hurley was settling things in Fort Wayne so he could go west and join them there. "You have someone on her?"

"Fuck yeah, I have someone on her. Got a half a dozen brothers here all the time. We aren't going to relax until we know everything's over." Opie pushed back from the table, and Bones could hear the deep breath he took, even through the computer's cheap speakers. "You looking for something in particular?" Opie's gaze sharpened, and Bones knew he had seen something on his or Fury's faces when he changed the question slightly. "Some*body* in particular?"

"Do you know where Spider is?" Fury leaned in, elbow to the desk, fingers of one hand dragging through his beard. "Right now?"

"In the house with Juanita, watching a goddamned TV show." Opie shook his head. "He's trusted inner circle, man, you know that. She's good with him inside, but not some of the other guys, the newer ones. I got two in the house, Spider and Devil, four outside, two in front, one between house and barn, one out back of the barn." Opie lifted a hand, thumbing over his shoulder. "I've got vid routed here, want me to cycle through quick and see what I see?"

"Yes, do that."

Bones waited and shook his head when Opie's face first turned confused, and then hardened with rage.

"Where the fuck is he?" A near mutter, and Opie's focus wasn't on the camera, so Bones knew it wasn't directed at them. "Goddamned bike's here. I got eyes on everybody else. Where's he at?" Suddenly Opie sat backwards, face twisting, but not with rage. With sadness. "Spider's in Bella's room. I can see him from the cam in the kitchen. Just sittin' on the edge of her fuckin' bed. What's..." Shifting so he stared straight at the camera, he asked, "What are you looking for?"

"He got a phone in his hand?" Fury voice grew intense when he asked the question. "That room got a window that aims towards the office you're in right now?"

"Yeah. I can see the screen. And the girls' rooms are both on the back of the house, so yeah, there's a window that looks out over the pool and yard." Opie's eyes closed, and his chin tipped towards one shoulder. Without looking at the camera again, voice flat, he said, "You think he's trying to listen to us."

"Yes," Bones answered. "But as long as you turned on the box Myron sent you before you made this call, he cannot hear you or us. Can you confirm you turned on the device?"

"Yeah. Thought it was paranoid overkill, but Myron's note was clear." Opie's eyes opened, and he stared at the camera. "You wanna tell me what's going on? Maybe starting from the beginning?"

***

"You think he's going to go for it?" Fury leaned back, asking his question as Bones reached one hand to the laptop, slowly closing the lid. "Man's been through a fuck of a lot, brother. Pretty sure he thought Diamond was the entirety of the LC chapter problems. Got that out of the way, lost their king in the process but got their princess back. Now you tell him a founder ain't what he seems."

"We do not know for certain what Spider is, Fury." Bones reminded him of the truth. They all had concerns, ideas based on what Myron had been able to dig up, but nothing concrete. "He could be what he always seemed to be, for Watcher. He could be loyal to the patch, not our RWMC, but the one Danger put on his back. I know it was something Watcher struggled with, the idea of setting aside everything his brother had worked so hard to create. He had more than come to terms with it at the end, had embraced the idea, much as you and I did. But Spider was a holdout."

"Myron's tied him to some shit, man. All kinds of shit." Fury reminded him of the reason for their call with Opie.

"I would disagree. Myron has uncovered some coincidences, but Spider is not yet tied to anything. That is still under evaluation, and Myron would be the first to tell you the same." Bones shook his head, sliding the laptop into a drawer. "There are tightly drawn lines, but everything is held together only by conjecture. We need something to hold to before we accuse. Otherwise there will only be division in the chapter, pitching the long-timers against the newer men. Opie will be on watch now, which was the reason for the call. So we shall see what he finds. And we shall see what Myron can unearth, too."

"Wish like fuck Mason hadn't headed out." Fury stood, pacing the length of the desk to the small window set high in the wall. It overlooked the front of Tupelo's, and Bones knew from the rumbling sounds that it was a packed house tonight. "He don't got anything solid, not sure why he's sniffing around after rumors."

"Because Deacon was good at blending, good at pretending to be something he is not. Did you hear Watcher's story of Hope's funeral?" Bones winced when he saw Fury jerk as if he'd been physically hit. With the tales circulating about Fury and Mason's sister Bethany, it was easy to forget he had thrown his hat in the ring along with Hoss at one time when it came to Hope.

Bones pressed on, "Deacon was there. He wore a stolen Legends' patch, but the nameplate was one only someone who knew the Fiends' history would put together. Plain sight of everyone and he nearly got his hands on Mason's son."

Fury swung to look at him, lips pressed into a tight line.

When he remained silent, Bones said, "Deacon and him are tied so tightly to Morgan. We have a dozen such stories, all of them showing Morgan appears to feel invincible. We know he is not, he is a flesh and blood man, and will bleed and die like any other man once we find him. We just have to find him, first. Mason is likely the best qualified to do so of all of us, because he knows not only the man Morgan was, but the man

Deacon had become. Knowing as we do how Morgan and Deacon were in each other's pockets for so long, there will be some traits shared between the men. With Shooter no longer talking to us, Mason has to follow a trail gone cold."

Fury nodded, and Bones steepled his fingers, pressing them against his lips for a moment.

"My opinion? Shooter is no longer contained. We have one story placing him in Florida, already. Another making the rounds of rallies about an appearance in Georgia. I shared all of this with Mason. Too many things point to Shooter pulling in markers and favors to gain freedom. I also shared what Myron found out about the woman in Florida. That agent is key. We just do not know what she knows. She may know everything, or nothing. We have Shooter to confirm on the west coast, and Mason's probable sister to play on the Gulf coast. He will seek out one, and see if it leads him to the other."

Faded memories

Mason

He watched her for most of a day, following and cataloging as much as he could about the woman, Justine LaPorte. Noted who came and left her house, her offices, watched how her coworkers treated her, how she treated them in turn.

Myron kept up a steady feed of information, and by the end of the day, Mason knew more about LaPorte than she may have known herself. More than once over the years, Mason thought to himself that Myron was a little scary and today underscored the skill of his diverse set of talents.

She'd gone into a bar for lunch, not to drink but just to eat a burger and shoot a game of pool. When Mason complained via text about the music she'd played on the jukebox, Myron had gotten giddy. He'd gotten into the app on her phone through the box on the wall, because she'd connected to buy credits. From there he'd found a route to her bank accounts, and with that access, Myron said it was smooth sailing to every membership she had, every financial institution she used, and he had even found a reservation she'd made for dinner tomorrow night at an exclusive restaurant in Jacksonville. For one.

Everything pointed to her being a straight-arrow Fed. She had excelled in school and aced the testing necessary to place herself in the sights of the government for employment recruitment. She had long-term friends who were loyal, and she returned that loyalty. Her family loved her, and she was paying for a niece to attend a private school out of her own pocket, even though she didn't pull down a fuckton of money at her job. In everything Myron found her morals and honesty shone through. Hell, he'd even found a video of her pulling back around into a bank drive-through to return an extra twenty the teller had put in her envelope. The only thing questionable was the release of Lalo.

Mason and Myron had a bet going. Myron leaning towards pressure from her superiors being the cause of her cutting the nutjob loose, and Mason thinking it was an external threat. That was about the time the niece moved from public to private, and the pictures Myron found of LaPorte from those weeks showed a woman exhausted, deep circles underneath her eyes, features drawn and tense.

So, when she pulled out of her driveway ten minutes ago, Mason hadn't thought anything about it, maneuvering the rental car he was in away from the curb and into traffic to follow her. About eight minutes into the journey, that was where things got interesting. Going through a residential area, LaPorte took a series of left- and right-hand turns and if Mason hadn't been paying close attention, he would have either lost her, or exposed himself as a tail. Exiting the streets filled with family homes, she got onto a state highway and drove straight out of town, this strategy having the same challenges for Mason as he followed her. Too close and she'd notice his car, but too far away and he might miss her turning off the road.

Putting his phone on speaker, Mason called Myron. "LaPorte is driving out of town headed north. You got her on anything?" A logging truck pulled onto the highway in front of Mason, and he had to slow down for a few moments before the road widened, and he could pass the vehicle. "She ran through a series of defensive maneuvers while still in the city, makes me wonder where she's headed." Pulling back into his lane, he angled his head trying to determine if LaPorte's car was still traveling in front of him. "I didn't put a tracker on the car, didn't expect to have to."

Clicking over the phone was easily identified as fingers tapping on his keyboard, and Mason waited, knowing the less he distracted Myron, the better. A moment later he heard, "Got it." Myron sounded smug when he said, "Bluetooth in her car is the same password as her phone. I got whatever you want, Mason. I can send you the route she's got programmed in if you want, but it looks like she's nearly there. Wherever there is. On your map."

Mason's phone dinged and he looked down, seeing a map application active. There were two blue dots, one traveling and one stationary.

"Her coordinates are in the middle of nowhere. There aren't even any houses nearby. It's an old sand quarry." More tapping, and Myron said, "Hold on, I got..." His voice trailed off, then came back. "Mason, it's a compound of some kind. I'll keep looking, see if I can figure out who owns it, but this ain't her first rodeo here. According to her car computer, she's traveled this route at least once a week in the past two years. She'll be there for about an hour. Return travel is more varied, looks like she's probably stopping for either a beer or food."

"Anywhere I can park, get close, see what's going on? I wanna keep an eye on her if I can." Mason saw the blinker ahead of him and grunted. "She's here, turning into the driveway." He drove past, glancing at the fence and façade he could see, noting the circumference of the clearing denoted by the edge of the forest. "Got anything I can use, Myron?"

"Half a mile, there's a logging road to the right. You can drive in and park, then either walk back out to the highway or angle through the woods. Mason, I don't like the idea of you getting close. We got nobody there with you, nobody to take your back, man." Myron's voice carried a sour note of concern, and Mason grinned to hear it. "You're effectively blind, and I don't have enough time to give you anything that makes it better."

"Yes, Mom. I know the bad men might pick on me today." Laughing, Mason turned onto the rutted dirt road. Narrow at the beginning, just past the tree line it widened, and he made a quick three-point turn, aiming the car back towards the highway for a faster retreat if needed.

"Fuck you," Myron said, then followed up with, "take your phone. I'll listen in and see where you are. At least we'll know if something happens."

"Doom and gloom, Myron. Not the best confidence builder." Car in park, Mason killed the engine, letting the silence of the nighttime dark woods settle around the vehicle. "You got anything you want to pass along before I climb my old ass outta the car?"

"Compound is licensed as a medical facility. Licensure indicates a level five, which in Florida means residential with full-time nursing staff. Officially they are an outpatient services unit, which says they aren't a hospital, but they take in long-term folks. Mental health is the most likely, but the applications I've found so far don't define the kind of care. Zoning doesn't discriminate, so it's a black hole, too." More tapping and Mason shifted in the seat, eyes locked on his phone where the two dots had merged into a single one, unmoving. "Interesting." More tapping, then, "They went through a change of ownership not long ago. Right around the time Lalo was in Florida. Wanna know who is behind the shell company that bought it?"

Wouldn't be Diamante, they were a short-term annoyance put together by Morgan and Deacon. Mason shook his head. If he were a betting man, he'd put money down on, "Outriders."

"How the fuck do you do that?" Myron snorted a laugh, and Mason grinned in the dark to hear it. "Just when I think I've got something you can't sort out, you always gotta prove me wrong. Yeah, Outriders.

Financed through a bank in Mexico, though, and I bet that wasn't something you expected. Looks like Deacon was tied deeper into the cartel than we thought."

"So it's an Outrider business, buried behind layers of bullshit, but still Outrider. LaPorte is so fuckin' clean she squeaks, but she not only cut Lalo loose twice, but now she's made a fuckton of trips to the middle of fucking nowhere to a compound owned by our enemy. You know the saying, the enemy of my enemy is my friend?" Mason didn't wait for a response. "In this case, they are all the fucking enemy. I'll be on my toes, Myron." Fingertip to the switch to kill the inside lights, Mason climbed out of the car and closed the door, using the key to lock it to keep from flashing and beeping. "But I gotta know what the fuck is going on."

Moving through the woods, Mason was reminded of a nighttime trip through the hollers of Kentucky long ago. Shaking off the memories, he cut through the trees until he could see the outline of the building. Large windows across the front probably let in ample lighting during the day, but now they were dimly lit from inside. The light was steady, not flickering, so it was sourced by something other than candles or firelight. LaPorte's car was the only one in the lot, but Mason saw a separate building off to the side, which could be a garage or a storage facility. Place like this had to have staff, and they'd have to park somewhere.

Easing his way across the yard, Mason stopped near the largest window, hoping he would be able to hear voices from inside. Leaning against the outer wall, he waited, head back, eyes closed, listening to the rise and fall of quiet conversation, trying to make out the words. Like a bolt of electricity hit him, he jolted when a voice spoke from just inside the window, the cadence and timbre so familiar it was eerie.

"Don't forget, Davy. John Morgan, you gotta remember that name, baby."

Quiet and slow, he moved, twisting so he could look inside through the window. He froze, heart pounding in his chest as he stared into the face of someone he had long thought dead. Fingernails biting into his palms, he stood and felt an icy tendril of fear crawl up his spine. *It can't be*, he thought. This was a woman he hadn't seen since he was eight years old, back during a time when he walked through the shadows alongside someone who in the decades since had existed only as faded memories.

***

"Myron, I want a list of every goddamned, motherfucking resident of the place by the time I get back to the car." Mason clipped the order into the phone, thumbed off the screen and shoved it deep into his pocket. He was crashing through the brush, skin crawling, frantic to get back to the car. Anything to get away from what he'd left behind him. Mason felt as if he'd seen a ghost, and that would have been a better answer than any of the thousand ideas rolling through his mind right now.

In the five minutes it took him to navigate the woods back to his rental, Mason somehow managed to pull his emotions back under control enough to phone Myron. Leaning on the fender of the car, he dialed with shaking fingers and barked, "Tell me," and then waited. He knew Myron well enough to know that if there were an easy connection to be made, the man would have already made it before Mason dialed the phone. He was right.

"Fuck, Mason. Did you have any idea?" That question cemented everything for him, and he heard the plastic phone creak in his hand as he clamped down on it, fingers tightening painfully at the confirmation. "LaPorte's mom's there, shoulda found this before, man. As far as I dug into her background it never even pinged, but I think there's a reason. Mason, there's another name on the list." Myron took in a breath. Mason did the same, preparing. "Getting the idea you already know who I'm talking about, don't you?"

"Yeah, saw her through the window." Shocked he'd gotten that much out, given how unsettled he was by what he'd seen, Mason paused, swallowed hard, and then said, "Read the list to me. I wanna know for sure."

"There are only five residents on the logs, and the last names don't quite fit, but there's enough here, man. Crystal Dawn Dixon, Lori LaPorte, Denise Montgomery, Julie Kellogg, and Dianne Warden." Myron took a breath, then pushed on, "In the couple of minutes I had, I was able to determine all five women are officially missing. All five women also have various aliases they've gone by. Crystal Dixon is also known as Crystal Morgan, and Crystal Mason. Mason, I never looked into your family. No reason to, not the Kentucky branch, beyond what you had me dig up on your daddy."

Mason interrupted, "No surprise. Shit would have been buried deep."

"Well, seems to be more than just that. This is wackadoodle, man. I've got Lori LaPorte also showing up as Lori Kelton and Lori Morgan. Montgomery is Smith, Kellogg is Rushing, and Warden is another Morgan. Mason, if this is what it looks like, then these women may have all been abducted by Morgan. Lori is the only one who receives consistent visitors, mostly in the form of Justine, but I found about a years' worth of video I've started churning through my software. You think this is...fuck, just the idea is messed up."

"My mom's name was Crystal." Mason squeezed his eyes shut tightly at the wounded tone of his own voice. "*Is* Crystal. Myron, you got pictures of the residents? I know what I saw, but it's dark, and it was through the glass. You got...pictures?"

"I'll get 'em, Mason."

Mind racing, Mason's muscles worked by rote as he folded into the car. Chin to his chest, he let his thoughts play out for a few moments, then made a decision. "Call Bones, get him patched in with you and me once you have some info. I want his take on this. Opie, too." He paused, then asked, "How long you think you'll take to get a photo?"

"Now that I know they're here, I took a shot, figuring they were using normal Outrider security. They are. I'm already in their system. Finding a pic depends on if they have them attached to resident files or if they are stored elsewhere. I don't have any pictures of your mom, but I put you into my system to run that vid against, and if there's a resemblance, then it should ping on it." In the background, Mason heard the sounds of Myron doing what he did best, pulling together all the assets and resources needed to give Mason what he'd asked for. Whatever it was, Myron always went the extra mile.

"You talk to Bones about Ester?" The idea of having a sister he'd never met had been eating at Mason, and was the main reason behind his trip to Florida because he had to settle his gut by knowing, one way or the other. "Can't imagine how you held that shit close to the vest like you did. Knowing, and not acting on it." Dead silence filled the phone line and Mason first thought the call had dropped, then he heard Myron clear his throat and realized he'd hit hard with those words. "Fuck, man. Sorry. I'm just...this was a shock. I'm not judging you, brother."

"I know you aren't, Mason. I know." Myron's voice was level and quiet when he responded, but the hurt vibrated through each tense word. "We don't react to things the same way. You're an action man, have to be reminded to think sometimes." This was true, and Mason didn't respond, no dispute to be made to the statement. "I'm different. Been different all my life. And me?" Myron took a breath, and Mason waited, willing to give him whatever time he needed to sort out his next words. "Sometimes I need to be pushed to action. Her getting sick, nearly dying, and me knowing what she is to me but never seeing her face-to-face, nearly losing that chance? Yes, I've talked to Bones. We're working out the best way to bring this to Ester. I gathered she's been accepting of so much, and he doesn't want to spook her more than she's going to be. Has he told you her story?"

"Some, not all." Mason shook himself, settling deeper into the car seat. "I know she's been in the system before, because he was scared right the fuck out of his head at the idea of taking her to the hospital. Afraid they'd take her away from him."

"They would have. She's been missing since she was ten years old. Been living on her own all that time, but before that she was in the system. Foster care. Her dad killed himself when she was six years old. She didn't have any family they knew about, so she hit a group home, then a family." Myron paused, and Mason didn't hear any background noises, that silence telling him he had Myron's full attention. "Some shit happened to her, shit that shouldn't happen to anyone, but it happened to her when she was eight years old. Then some more shit happened, and she got pulled from that home. Put into another one, doesn't sound like it was much better. There's so much need, and so few people overseeing the execution of everything, it's been easy for the wrong kind of people to settle into roles they shouldn't ever have. Or take on those roles for the wrong kind of reasons. At ten she had enough and just walked away from school one day. There were reports of a kidnapping, but I can't find anything to support that. From what I see, she just got fed up with people and retreated to her own head. She's smart, resilient, and fearless on some things. But because she's gotten caught up more than once in a homeless sweep, she's wary. Bones is afraid if she left and didn't want to be found, she wouldn't be. I tend to agree with him."

Myron laughed, the sound so far from humor it made Mason wince to hear it. "You know how it is on the street, you stayed there for a while. I've been there. Been in the shelters when you wake up and there's a hand under the covers, or everything you own is dumped on the floor, everything that mattered to you picked through and ruined. You had six months of it. I had a year and a half." He took a breath, and Mason braced. "She lived like that for more than a decade, Mason. Nearly fourteen years. That's a lifetime of responses and reactions that need to be reconditioned, and Bones is making headway. I hear it in every story he tells me. She'll be ready to meet me soon, and I can't wait. But I will wait, because sometimes the best things are worth it."

Mason's phone buzzed and he pulled it away to see a text from Willa. ***Miss you, my favorite honey bunches of hunk.***

Myron kept talking, and Mason heard every word, listened to the conviction behind them, too. "When she's ready, I'll be ready, too. Until then, I'll do what I have to do from here."

"I know you will, brother. You're good people, Myron. Ester's lucky to have someone like you waiting to be in her life." Mason responded to Willa. ***Better be your only hunk, woman. Miss you too, babe.*** "I'm gonna go back to the hotel. I think we know what Morgan had to hold over LaPorte, and knowing that means I need to adjust my plan. Let me know when you have something, brother. And if you need a picture of my mom, talk to Tater. He can pull one off the bedroom wall there in Chicago. I need to get in there and clear my shit out anyway, give him and Bella a chance to make their own mark on the house."

"They stayin' there indefinitely?" Myron had returned to his normal mode, and Mason again heard the keyboard strikes of his fingertips.

"Yeah. Right thing to do. I'm gonna need you do to the paperwork, so I can sell the house to Tater. Five bucks, the same thing we always do when it's club. He deserves to not have to worry about that, and Bella will like knowing it's theirs." Understanding what he was leaving behind, it was killing him to drive away, but Mason started the car's engine and rolled slowly down the gravel towards the highway in the dark, waiting until he was on the road to turn on the headlights. "But that's not urgent. We need to see which Outriders knew about this place, figure it out. Let's do that before we pull Fury in, but I'll want him on the call with Bones and Opie, so lemme know, yeah?"

"You got it."

Beauty and her Bones

Ester

At times he would come to me so worn down by the demands of the worlds in which he moved that the tiredness shouted in his silence. Bones would lie at my back, still tense and tight with everything he had seen and done that day, the things he had caused to be done. Muscles stretched taut between joints, pulling everything awry. I could see it in his gait early the next day, walking as if he'd worn penance boots full of stones to bruise the balls of his feet.

I had a plan the last time it happened, but failed to carry it out because he started touching and then kissing me, and then carrying it out was the last thing on my mind as I got carried away.

This time, when I woke to feel his fingers gripping my hip, tugging me across the bedsheets, I came to with the knowledge he needed something more than what I'd given him so far. A man like Bones, he liked to be in charge, and I knew it, and he was. But, he was sweet with me, always, taking care to be slow and gentle, even if I sometimes wanted something different. That sometimes wasn't always the same, so for now if he'd let me soothe him, I'd be contented in my comfort. His comforter.

I tested him, carefully, rolling to face him, fingers folded into a church and steeple under my pillow. His eyes opened and he looked at me. In a voice sweeping with weariness, he said, "I woke you."

I chewed my lip, saw his eyes dip, gaze going to the movement and I froze until they lifted to meet mine again. "Ester, sleep, *adorada*." With that, I knew he was in a state past tired, because he seldom used anything but English except when around the ones he called his blood family. Blood as opposed to chosen, like the men who rode motorcycles with him.

"Can I...?" For once my mouth was traitorous with silence instead of blurted secrets. The corners of his eyes crinkled, and he gave me a slight smile, a tired smile, an exhausted smile that said he wanted to sleep but he wanted more for me to have what I needed, he just didn't know what it was. "Would you let me...?"

"Ester, little one, tell me what is on your mind." He lifted a hand and I eagerly pushed my cheek into his palm, relaxing as I felt his fingers slide into my hair, lifting and stroking, soothing me even in his exhaustion. I took from him all the time. I wanted to give back. My plan, if I could just speak it aloud. "Tell me."

I reached up, cupping my hand around his arm, stroking up and down, fingers dancing across the tense muscles, working awkwardly to bring him at least that much ease. My mind reader, he knew what I wanted even without my words. "You want to touch me." I nodded, feeling the tiny catch and pull as my hair yanked through his hold. "I should like to be touched by your hands, Ester." Hooded eyes on me, he rolled his shoulders, turning so he was facedown in the bed, the trust implicit in his movements.

It only took me a moment to separate myself from his grip and rise to my knees at his hip. Then with the heels of my hands, and digging movements of my thumbs, I caressed every inch of his painted back. Ink I had seen and touched blindly, stroking in time with his movements inside me, but never seen on display like this. Remembering my long-ago thoughts, I closed my eyes, pretending to trace the lines with my fingertips like braille. "Very good." He groaned a sound of satisfaction and surprise, voice muffled by the pillow. Those two words wrapping around me, caught me as I fell, holding me close as if they were his arms.

He moved, and my eyes flew open like shutters to see him yanking the pillow from beneath his head, settling flat to give me more access. *Okay, then.* I pulled the sheet down to his waist, folded it an inch farther, dared another, seeing no fabric underneath. Down to the lower curves of his bottom, and then I swung a leg as if I were him mounting his motorcycle, settling on the round globes of his ass. He grunted in surprise, shifting slightly and then stilling. Waiting.

With a calming breath out through my nose, courtesy of the co-op's sweet yoga teacher, I gave myself leave to touch Bones as I had wanted all those months ago. Every month since. Every moment, this finally fulfilled. Fingers trailing down his spine, I counted each knob of vertebra, thumbs working the strong muscles on either side. Long, sweeping movements up, cupping my fingers over the bend of his shoulders and working hard, leaning forwards, levering my weight against the tight knots found in the bunching muscles there. Again, and again, and yet again, I followed the same path, feeling it when he began to relax into my touch, moving through the pain of those initial moments, finding comfort and, if his even breathing was to be believed, a sense of languor.

Up and over the points of his shoulder, fingers digging under the collarbone on the front side, then over one tricep, down his arm, kneading the bulges of his bicep, to his forearm, wrist, and hand, linking my fingers with his, stretching and massaging his palm with my thumbs, over and over. His other arm next, taking care to spend the same time, lest it be jealous, arranging it afterwards, parallel to his body.

Shifting backwards to reveal his low back, I returned to movements in tiny circles with stiffened arms, working the muscles of his lumbar area, and across the upper edges of his bottom. Each push and tug separated the cheeks of his ass slightly, the hair covering his buttocks springy, different in texture from the hair on his chest or arms. Without giving him pause, I moved up, reseating myself on him, changing to a slower, sweeter sweep of my hands across the skin of his back. Once more I indulged myself in tracing the stories told by the colors inlaid on him, seeing death and birth, love and loss, anger. So much of it, all that anger without a counterpart to balance it. Blazing.

Then I found it. Wrapped around the ribs on his left side, high, set under his arm and over his breast.

Not old, newer than anything else on him by months, maybe years, I found flowers; rose and lavender and peonies white as snow, the creeping vines twined around a skull and jawbone, ribs fashioned into wings, the softness of flowers covering and cradling the bones. A dark angel, and I remembered my fever dreams. This was me. He was my dark angel, watching over me.

Beauty and her Bones. I had found me, and he knew when I did, because he tensed up as I leaned close, then blew out a relieved breath when I began laying kiss after reverent kiss on the marks.

"You put me on your skin." *My angel.*

"I did. A time when I didn't think I could have you, and I wanted you with me always. So—" He shrugged, not lifting his head, but cutting his eyes over his shoulder so he could see my face. "—I made it so."

I found myself astonished at the casual way he drew the image in my head. As if it was nothing, the application of a thousand needles into his skin so he could hold a memory of me near his heart. As if in submitting to the act of receiving the tattoo, he had gotten more. I knew, of course, the ink on his skin always had a story inside the story people saw. Like the dead rose with the ember of life in the center, bearing the weight of a rebirth he wanted very much. But people saw the dead rose and assumed a meaning and he allowed that. But in putting me on his skin, not only the chosen image tailored for me, for an us that didn't exist at the time, but in the placement, in the colors, in the everything that was anything I could see, he told me secrets so far from casual I was breathless at the discovery. Seeing right through to the heart of everything. I hadn't been the only one falling, hadn't been alone since I met him days and weeks and months ago, years by now, with the multiples of hours coming at us without any desire on our part.

"Hidden but not secret, beauty carried over your heart. I see you, Bones. I see me on you." He twisted to look at me directly, eyes roaming over my face. I lowered my voice, imitating his accent and tone, "My most precious possession." His nostrils flared on an inrush of air. I remembered that night, remembered everything about it, remembered those moments in the darkness when I trusted, and he knew what that took for me.

Even as I unraveled my head these days, I still remembered how snarled I could get, and he knew it so well. He, who had pursued me even when I'd been a dreadful knot, a kitten's toy dragged through mud and dirt so that grime and bits of flotsam made untangling impossible, yet he still picked at the threads, worked tirelessly at the ends of the yarn until he found a way. But in the dark, echoes of gunfire behind us, I had followed him into darkness, and he led me out and into the light. "You love me." Given to the air, my certainty tattered in the saying, until he nodded, firming my footing on these unfamiliar shores. "You, Salvador Ramos, my Bones, my angel...you love me."

"For a long time now, Ester."

Moving in a rush, I unlocked my muscles and stretched out over the top of him, pressing myself against his back, absorbing the feel of him under me. Covering him, so he would know this was a balancing blanket he could use anytime he wanted. His moon. Hoping the everything I was about to show him meant as much to him as I wanted it to. Knowing that every single time I had wanted in the past, I'd come up in a different place, currents of revulsion sweeping me away and around the bend of the river. Closing my eyes for a moment, I needed on the air. Needed in a way I've never tried to do before, or since. I needed him to know I would never ever let anything hurt him. I would have his back, would care for him, would protect him like only his chosen family did. I wanted him to choose me, wanted to believe I could be chosen.

"I love you, Bones."

At my words, his muscles melted. Stiff and starched before, straight and edged with blades of fear, he puddled underneath me, and I laughed at the feel. "You like hearing those words from me." Eyes pressed tightly closed, he nodded, stubble on his cheek catching on his fine sheets. His hand that I could see was clenched into a fist, and I flattened my palm on the back, covering a narrow portion of his skin with my hand, bands and lines of his tattoos escaping my grip, but that was okay because his hand moved, fingers spreading and I threaded mine with his. "I'm home, Bones." I hadn't meant to give him more, but he deserved to be reminded this was how I felt. I'd gone from fearing his walls to longing for them in the space of a February, and when I was here he was guaranteed to be with me sooner rather than later, so, of course, I wanted to be inside his walls. It meant I was inside him, and now I was on his skin, too, a place even more precious where Bones was concerned. "With you, I'm always home."

He twisted underneath me, and I was suddenly chest to chest with him, the arm of the hand I wasn't holding tight around my waist. He kicked, feet shoving and the sheet I'd so carefully bundled midlength was gone, and I was suddenly *naked* chest to chest with him. Well, I wasn't naked, but I didn't have on panties, and he wasn't wearing anything. So it was more naked loin to loin, and his loin was long and hard. Without thinking, I moved, letting my legs fall to either side, and he shifted again, hips surging up and I felt the head of him probing me.

"Kiss me," his lips demanded, and I gave him what he wanted. No hardship, because it was what I wanted, too. Lips ghosting across his until he groaned, I then touched the tip of my tongue to his mouth, and his arm shifted, moving up until his palm cupped the back of my skull, pulling me down hard so our mouths clashed together and his tongue was in my mouth, sweeping side to side, thrusting between my lips as his hips moved again and that tip became the promise of more. Then that more just became more in a way that I groaned, and his fingers tightened around mine to the point of pain, but it was a sweet pain, because I was home.

"Jesus, Ester, what you give me is beyond precious." Fingers tangled in my hair, he pulled my head back, and then shoved it into his neck, the bristly whiskers on his jaw catching on my skin, each score sweetly singing about his passion. Mouth to my ear, he kept talking, giving to me while I gave to him. Thrusting up, he was far inside me, staying at that depth and grinding, then withdrawing on a glide, smooth and hard, filling me always.

"You lay your heart bare, and gift me with your love. I have done little right in this world, but I thank God I did enough to earn a moment with you. You show me every day how much you trust me, and then you show your love like this."

Our fingers were clenching, releasing, clenching, coming together in a pumping hold that was in time with every entrance and exit. The feeling was rising and subsiding, but each glide built a glory inside me only Bones had ever given me. In the past my fingers only going there in my sleep, and never to the finish line. I'd always wake and stop myself midstride. But in bed with Bones, it didn't matter if it was his tongue and lips, fingertips, or his penis, I was always pushed past the point of no return, finding the end of the race in reach, with his guidance.

I tried to always be quiet, but I wanted him to know, in case he never noticed. "You make me happy." And by happy, I meant orgasmically happy. But not just that, and I wanted him to know. "Not just the sex, but always." I'd told him about needing being like a wish, only for more important things. "I didn't know I was needing for you, but when you hold me like this, when you are inside me like this, I don't ever need to need anything else. You are everything I ever needed for."

"You make me happy too, Ester." His words had changed, morphing into more of a grunt, each word voiced on an exhale and movement and I knew what this signaled. "Baby." Another grunt, and then he stilled, and this stopping moving wasn't normal because by this point it was usually full steam ahead, so I lifted my head, staring down at his face. "You make me happy." He twitched inside me and I smiled at the insistence of his own need. Still, he remained locked in place, looking up at me. "I love you."

He immediately turned all watery, and I felt the chill of tears trailing down my cheeks. Tugging against his hand, I freed my hair and plopped my forehead against his chest. "Are those good tears, baby?" I nodded. He twitched again, and I responded in a muscular grip he couldn't mistake. Rolling us, he put me beneath him. I lost him in those movements, but he nestled between my legs and thrust, again probing and finding the perfect depth and movement. He rocked into me, my hips lifting so he could move deeper. "Do not ever doubt my love for you, Ester." Forehead pressed to mine, he made promises with his words that were supported by the look in his eyes. "Ever."

I returned the promise he seemed to need, and then I realized his words were needings he'd released on the air and I'd caught them. Needings in my heart, holding them close. "I won't." Tentative, I tried out a word that meant so much to me, not knowing if he would count the cost it took to give it back, even momentarily. "Baby."

Always he had me. Always he gave me things that mattered, because he turned right around and handed me the better words, the ones that had paved the way for this road we were on right now, rushing in a race to the finish line together. "My love."

Matching needs

Bones

"Tell me again, Mason." Bones was patient, waiting for Mason to pull in a frustrated breath, expecting a sharp retort, receiving instead exactly what he'd asked for.

"We were in my backyard, there in Chicago. I was headed down to Fort Wayne the next day, was after Ray made his visit to Mica. She'd gone home with Daniel and I was there alone, finally. Went outside and there he sat. Bold as brass, because you know we weren't on the friendliest of terms anytime, and I wasn't in the mood for his shit that night. Was a shit night, for a lotta reasons." Mason shook his head, and the background blurred as the camera tried to hold him in focus.

"We got to talking, and back then, I was of the mind that like it or not he was my blood, so unless he was actively being an asshole, or trying to kill me, I'd let him rattle on. That night—" Mason shrugged. "—I let him rattle on. He started talking about Luke, and then got on about Eddie's mom, Kimberly. How she was the only one for him, but he didn't see it at the time. That turned into him talking about our mother. He got pissed talking, could see it in his face, because he was focused on how it felt to be him, knowing his mother had another family out there who didn't even know he existed. How that galled him, tore at him until it was all he could talk about. Then, he said her being with Morgan put a target on her back. Said that was what killed her. I'd always thought she probably got sick, living the way she did between worlds. He said a Mexican club killed her. Said they caught her on the freeway and tossed gas on her car and then torched it. Said they shot her before the fire killed her." Mason took a breath, visibly distressed, and Bones wished he could do something to ease the way for his friend. "That was it. We had twenty minutes of conversation about women and Mama, and then he was gone. Didn't see him for a while. About a year later I was in the River Rider's clubhouse and he was there. Had some bangers come in and try to throw down. Willa was there with Eddie. At that point, Eddie didn't even know who I was, neither did Judge. You know the next time I saw him, in Cali, had him on his knees watching his chapter get torched. That's it, Bones. All I got."

"It is enough." Bones thought a moment, then asked, "He never named the Machos? You assumed because you knew the Outriders had bad blood between them and the Machos?"

"Yeah, pretty much. You know how it is, even if you know for sure, you still don't say names where they can be overheard. We were outside on my patio, but still the open air and no countermeasures in place that he knew of. He didn't name names, didn't call out the club, but knowing the trouble it sure made sense them killing her would either be the result of shit, or the genesis of shit." Mason's eyes were focused on the laptop camera, his sharp intensity coming through the video. "He never said, but it was implied. And he was clear about her being dead. Said that more than once. Offered just enough details to make it believable, but not so much it pinged me as a fucking lie. You think she was already here in Florida by then? That would have been five years ago, man." Chin lifting, Mason looked away from the camera. "Jesus, only five years. A lot of fucking shit has happened in five goddamned years."

"True words, my brother." Bones closed his eyes, running everything he knew of Morgan and Shooter through his head. "You said he was angry? Shooter?"

"Yeah, fucking pissed as hell. Even years after. It torqued him over there were people out there who mattered to his mom who he didn't know." Mason paused, then shook his head. "No, it was more than that. It was because those people didn't know about him. The words I heard her say, it was something she told me a lot the last time she was home. Always going on about John Morgan, wanting me to remember the name. Justice Morgan said once she'd done the same in Cali, talking about Bethy and me. Told me he knew she loved me. Said he wished for a way to make things right, claimed to not know what was left behind the last time he took her back. That was the thing. He never claimed she went willing, and I believe in my gut she didn't. Believe in my soul he took her unwilling, stole her away. If she'd talked to me about John, then it makes sense she'd have talked to him about us. He was seventeen the last time she made it home to Kentucky. Old enough to be pissed and hold onto those feelings for a bit."

"Morgan never seemed to carry any illusions about his son. I remember more than one party when he would warn people if John were in a mood. Shooter's emotions were never very predictable, but Morgan could at least tell when a bad turn was coming on." Bones kept his eyes closed, hearing Mason shifting around. A cough, and he thought it was probably Fury, dialed in from the Little Rock chapter. Opie was silent at Bones' side, everyone waiting for Bones to put whatever it was in his head together. "I remember Watcher talking about how the Outrider president in Lexington died, a questionable death that allowed Morgan to put Watcher in as a figurehead for the chapter. Shooter became a mentor of sorts, and Watcher had to keep a lid on him because he could go off the end of the pier and into deep water quickly, with little provocation." Bones righted his head, and stared at the screen, watching Mason's face. "You said even years later he was angry about your existence. Probably is still angry, knowing the man. Do you think he would have been angry enough to hurt Crystal?" Mason tipped his head to one side, considering, but before he could speak Bones continued, "Perhaps Morgan secured these women to keep them away from Shooter?"

"Thin, man." Fury spoke up, and his image popped to the top of the display, larger than life, leaning into the camera. "That's fuckin' thin, Bones."

"Maybe not so thin," Opie said. "I remember a meeting we had with Outriders, back when Judge was not much more than a boy. We got the distinct feeling Shooter was out of control, and even Judge had more on the ball than Shooter did. We know where that wound up, with Judge pulling the kind of shit he did. We already know where Shooter went with you, Mason."

Bones nodded, because Shooter's hatred for Mason was legend, and the man's failed attempts to kill his own brother had become the topic of many a church meeting in many clubs. "Shooter is capable of nearly anything, and we know that. I think we should wait for Myron to find out the dates and whatever information he can dig out of the facility records before we let the knowledge go beyond this small circle." Shifting his gaze from camera view to camera view, Bones saw everyone nodding. "Shooter should still be in prison, but we have not yet confirmed anything. Even if he is, it does not mean his reach is limited. And if he were truly incensed about something, he would not hesitate to pull in whatever markers were needed to conduct a strike, even if it meant he would spend additional time in lockup."

"Shooter's a psychopath. He'll do whatever he wants with the full expectation that everyone will agree that whatever he's done was the right thing. Fuck, Mason, if your ma *were* dead, I wouldn't put it past the motherfucker to have killed her himself." Fury moved, shifting back in his chair. "He's fuckin' insane, and everyone who's partnered with him over the past ten years is either dead, or jacked so far sideways they can't see whether they're coming or going. Hell, if Morgan did put your ma there with the other women, you can bet it was what saved her life."

"I don't doubt it, brother. Let's wait for Myron." Mason stood, leaning forward with an extended finger, preparing to shut off the laptop even as his window popped to the top of the display. "See what he turns up. Talk soon, brothers."

"Talk soon."

***

"Ester, where are you?" Bones paused for a moment just inside the living room door, listening. No answering call came to his ears, and he tensed. Calling her name again, he pulled a relieved breath when he heard a noise from one of the empty rooms overhead. This was a big home, and there were no fewer than four extra bedrooms which only had basic furniture installed. He'd never needed more than his room fully furnished.

Slipping his boots off, he casually armed the alarm, heading first upstairs to see what had so engrossed Ester that she didn't hear him come home. Feet to the treads, he sniffed, noting with some surprise there was no smell of cooking or dinner. Not that he expected it of her, but Ester had been enjoying cooking in the weeks since he'd come home, having picked up a few basic recipes from her time with Road Runner. Bones grinned to himself, remembering Road's words, and believing he had been right. Ester did indeed like his shit.

All thought was wiped from his brain when he rounded the corner and looked into the first empty room on the left. Ester stood in the middle of the floor, arms lifted over her head, swaying in place. Where he was tucked to one side of the door, she hadn't yet seen him, and he watched for a moment, trying to discern what she was doing. Head tipping from side to side, her hands moved, fingers tapping together as she lifted first one foot then the other.

Not wanting to frighten her, Bones took a step into the doorway, then another step inside the room, pleased when Ester's gaze turned his way with a smile. "Bones!" She cried his name, and he returned her smile, following it with a soft, "Ester." Another step, and still she didn't stop moving, tipping her chin to the side so she could look towards the wall. "What are you doing, my love?"

"Dancing." Said so matter of fact, the statement didn't seem to allow for any confusion, but he was still unsure.

"What kind of dancing?" Her movements could be interpreted as dancing, but it wasn't anything specific or recognizable. Without access to whatever kind of music was in her head it would be impossible to know, so he waited.

"Shadow dancing!" Joy in her voice, she called out with a musical lilt to her words, "I'm shadow dancing, Bones." Tipping her head sideways, she contorted her arm, hand flapping. "It's so beautiful." Said in a whisper, filled with reverence, she drew his attention to the wall. He stood, mesmerized for long minutes, watching as her outline danced across the flat surface of the wall. In one moment, the shadows of her hands looked like a flock of birds taking flight. Then in the next, he could see the majesty of mountains, deep valleys holding secrets.

"Isn't it pretty?" The shadows had stopped moving and his neck twisted so he could look at Ester. Her grin was so broad it stretched her lips from cheek to cheek, lit up her face, and seeing that, he couldn't have stopped himself if he had tried. Crossing the distance between them with long, fast strides, he saw the look on her face change, becoming startled, but he didn't pause, didn't slow his advance. Only when he had her pinned between him and the wall did he stop, and that was to bury his face in her neck.

Arms tight around her, he shifted, letting her feel his hard cock, willing to wait for her to catch up with him, because just seeing her, watching the beauty she created with the smallest part of herself, and then experiencing her joy, he would have stripped them both bare and been buried inside her in moments. She needed to be with him, though, and he would never frighten her, never cause her pain. *My Ester, my love.* Lips to her throat, he felt the pounding of her heart, blood coursing through her veins. *My life.*

First one, then her other arm came down, winding themselves around his shoulders. Holding tight. Fingers fluttering on the back of his neck, she lifted to her toes, pushing up even as she pulled him down. Wordless asking, always her way, and he gave her what he thought she wanted. Mouth moving across her skin, he traced the muscles and tendons of her neck and shoulders with his tongue and teeth, nipping and soothing each inch. Her quiet moan fed his knowledge of her arousal, and he ran one hand down her back, cupping a cheek of her ass, and pulling her against him, grinding into her. "Ester." All his brain cells were short circuiting, electricity flashing through his muscles, and Bones was acutely aware of everywhere they touched, everywhere her skin was on his, heated and soft, so soft.

"I won't break." Breaths ghosting across his skin, Bones had no warning before her teeth sank into his shoulder, gripping hard, the pain pushing him farther down the road to uncontrolled. "I can't hurt you. You can't hurt me. I want what you want, Bones." She bit him again, nails raking lightly down his back at the same time. "There's more need tied up in your head than you're taking from me. But you don't have to take it," she hesitated, then softly said, "baby."

Bones knew his hand was gripping her ass hard, finger joints aching with the pressure used, knew he had already left bruises on her skin. That knowing made him even harder, because he wanted his marks on her, wanted to see them there tomorrow. Wanted to put himself on her skin as a warning to all men that she was his. That she was owned and loved. *Mine.* "Ester, you do not know what you ask." Pressing deep, he rocked his cock against the core of her, felt her rubbing against him, making frustrated noises at the two layers of fabric between them. "I do not wish to hurt you."

"You love me. I give this to you. Court lady always said you can't turn down presents, even if you don't want them." She pushed up, mouth to his ear and whispered, "I know you want this one. I'm giving it to you, Bones. You can be like a scrooge sometimes, a miser barely peeking at the pocket of need. Wallow in the wealth." Her teeth came to rest on the lobe of his ear, and she nipped, then held it and tugged. "Today, you're rich." Another nip. "Wallow with me?"

"Ester, love." Bones paused, trying to decide how to talk about this. With her, each time it had been slow and sweet, making love in a way he'd never experienced before. It almost felt as if bringing in what he had done before her would taint what they had somehow, make it less precious. She could never be what the club whores were, never be what the neighborhood girls had been, either. "There have been many times in my life when I performed the act without caring. Without care, at times." How to make her understand? "Before you, there was never part of my heart held in my hands. Before you, there was never love."

He was afraid he had already hurt her with his words, as still as she'd gone in his arms, and needed to see her face. Resting his forearms on the wall beside her head, he leaned backwards slightly. Head back, she looked up into his face, trust on every feature, not hurt, not disappointment. Not fear, either.

"You know I know." Her words startled him, and he jerked again when she laughed. "I followed you, Bones. I know." Rolling to her toes, she pressed her lips against his and then settled back. "But the way the girls talked, I also knew you were kind even when you didn't have to be. Even when you'd paid to be mean, you weren't mean beyond what they wanted." Her nose wrinkled, and her brows drew together into a frown. "I don't want mean." She couldn't hide the shiver that ran down her spine, and didn't try. Voice soft as the brush of a feather, she said, "I don't like mean."

"I could never be mean to you, my Ester." He ducked his head, touching his mouth to her cheek. "I would never hurt you."

She sighed, and when he lifted back up, he saw her frown was more pronounced, chin angled down so she didn't meet his eyes. "Then you'll need more than me." Sadness radiated from her, and Bones found his hands fisting before he could stop them. "I wanted to be your everything."

"You already are, beauty." She shook her head at his words, and he searched for a way to explain. "Before my life included you, I did not have what I needed. I looked for it. Years, I searched. Never finding." Ducking his head again, he put his mouth to her ear, whispering, "I fucked women I did not love. I fucked them in ways that allowed me to keep searching, looking for what made me whole inside. Testing limits, pushing the edges, always looking and not finding. I fucked women who never saw me. They saw the man who could give them things, get them things, make their lives better with *all those things*. They did not see me, and that was why they were not what I sought. I needed my Ester to see me, to fill up all the corners inside me with herself, to make me whole. Now that I have my Ester, I do not need to look to things which did not fill me up before in order to be filled. Just my Ester does that, nothing but you, no matter how it happens. You wake with a smile, and I am full of life. If you want to explore and see if there is sometimes an edge to what we like doing together, I am very willing to do so with you. Without being mean. Never mean, my Ester. Always with love, beauty. Always. We will always be what the other needs, and you've gifted yourself to me. Now I gift you with me, too."

Mouth to her neck, he dragged his lips to her shoulder, nosing at the edge of her shirt until he could access more skin. Movements controlled, he put his hands on her shoulders, then down her arms, circling her wrists, bringing her hands up above her head. Gripping both in one palm, he stretched them further, pulling her to her toes, letting her back arch naturally. His other hand gripped firmly at her waist, then trailed hard fingers up her side, across her ribs, mouth smiling against her skin when she giggled at the touch, then gasped when he captured a nipple between finger and thumb and pinched, pulling and tugging as he nipped at the skin over her collarbone.

Ester arched more, pressing against him and moaned softly. "Bones."

"Yes, Ester." He traced her throat with light kisses, making his way back to her jaw, then her mouth, and he groaned as she opened for him, tongues tangling fiercely. Leaning into her, cock against her clit, he let her work against him, the friction of jeans and heat from her cunt a pleasurable pain that made him impossibly harder. "Take what you need, too, baby." He deepened the kiss, pulling more from her, at times fighting her for control because she was frantic for more. Fingers tracing the cup of her bra, he tugged, slipping it down and beneath the swell of her breast, palming the soft mound before pinching her nipple again and pulling, drawing and stretching with a twist, then palming her breast again, the hard nub of her nipple grazing the flesh of his hand.

Her wrists twisted, hands pulling against his grip and he took her sweet moans into his mouth, biting her bottom lip and pulling, pressing harder against her. A moment later she took flight, and he felt it come over her, heard it in the long, drawn-out call of his name as she ripped her mouth from his, face turned to the side, her voice intense and quivering. "Bones!"

He gave her a moment, then another, feeling the settling of her soul back into her skin as she came down. He couldn't keep the smug smile from his face when he heard her whispered, "Wow."

"Yes. Definitely, wow." He gave it back to her, releasing her wrists and bending slightly to scoop her into his arms. Padding softly to their bedroom, he let her feet settle to the floor and waited until she was steady before he knelt in front of her. Looking up, he caught an expression of surprise on her face and smiled. "I want to eat you, Ester. Eat you up, take my fill of you before I fill you up." Lips parting, she pulled in a shaky breath before she nodded. "This means, my beauty, we need to get these"—fingers to the fastening of her jeans, he worked to release them, tugging gently as she shimmied in place to help—"off." Dragging the fabric down her legs, he looked up again when she put one hand on his shoulder. "Step out, baby. I am hungry."

***

Ester

I lay back on the bed, head on the pile of pillows Bones had placed there, and watched him. Concentrating on me in a way that made me feel like a princess, like the most precious thing in the history of ever, he had undressed me before putting me exactly where he wanted me to be. In his bed, a place which has always been the safest of the safe for me, from the beginning of the us that was, to the us that is, and I hope the us that will be.

Before Bones, I hadn't had any pleasure to go with the girly parts I had between my legs. Now, all I had to do was look at him and heat gathered there. Steaming, like the best part of a hotel shower, I'd steam up like a mirror, and he'd take the time to wipe me clean before steaming me up again. Again and again, as if he'd never get tired, never be tired of me. This was more though, because he'd done this before, and I hadn't known he wasn't eating his fill. This time, he did, and took his time doing it, and I loved every minute.

When he rose over me, fitting himself into me, into the heat he'd pulled from inside me with his mouth and tongue and the very breath from his body, he looked down at me and gave me the words again. The ones that made me quivery inside.

"I love you, my Ester."

"You're making my nosey bits tingle," I told him, my throat tight, and wasn't ready for the response that got. Roaring laughter even as his back bowed, as his hips moved, and he glided home. That right there? Might be the best thing in the history of ever, so I'd revise any previous statements I made in my head. Him laughing as he came home.

Brothers

Bones

The tension in the room was thick and heavy, anger from the conversation in progress nearly at the point of boiling over. Bones caught Shade's gaze and nodded, seeing the same frustration on the man's features. Without a word, Shades reached out and slapped his palm to the desktop, the crack of the impact ricocheting around the small room. They were in the office behind the bar in the Chicago clubhouse, nearly a dozen men packed into a room meant for only a handful.

Mason was still in Florida, Fury in Fort Wayne, Opie in New Mexico, and one of the men Bones leaned on for advice the most had gone back to southern California, the third such extended trip Tugboat had made in two years.

Once quiet had fallen on the group, Bones slowly pushed his chair back from the table, picking up the gavel and holding it loosely in his hands. His stance combined with his confidence told every man in the room he had heard all the arguments and opinions he was willing to listen to. As with all the Rebel Wayfarers chapters, if nationals or the other chapter officers came to a clear consensus, the local president set aside any personal disagreements, and the business being voted upon would be done.

Tonight, however, nothing was clear. There were nearly as many opinions as there were men in the room, which did not bode well for acceptance of what he was about to rule upon. Chismoso and his men were up for vote, had been on the agenda for enough weeks it was necessary to push it through, one way or another. Mason had weighed in via video, as had Fury and Opie. Unfortunately, their opinions were just as varied. Mason in cautious favor, Fury opting for more observation and an invitation to hang around officially, and Opie firmly against the Rebels having anything to do with Chismoso, the man who had assisted in Bella's abduction. This vote would come down to Bones.

"Chismoso has not given us reason to doubt him since he approached us here in Chicago." Several of the men shifted in their chairs, and he paused, looking around the room.

"He has offered explanations of events, but no man here can entirely put aside the past. Not without more evidence of today's reality. A paradox, because he will be unable to convince us without us providing the opportunity for that conviction. Limited exposure means lingering doubts, and we do not need division within our ranks. Never do we need that, but even less so when we are faced with pressures as we have been these past weeks. 'Know your enemy, and know yourself,' Sun-Tzu told us." He paused again, looking around the room. "Corleone may have said it better, 'Keep your friends close, and your enemies closer.' I propose we..." He paused to let the laughter at his quoting *The Godfather* die away, then continued, "I suggest we follow this sage advice, and pull Chismoso and his men in as prospects. They have all proven the life is not a deterrent, which is usually the reason for hang around status. Anything less than prospect tells everyone we do not trust them."

He leaned forwards, tapping the table with the gavel's handle. "In order to understand the motives, we need their trust. How better to do this than to send a message that they are earning trust." He straightened, and folded his arms, letting the gavel dangle from the fingers of one hand. "This also sends a clear message to our enemies, no matter which path Chismoso takes. Either they believe we have opened the gates and let the Trojan horse inside, which gives them a false sense of accomplishment or underscores their loss of so many men to a better club."

Scanning the faces in the room, and the ones on the screen, he said, "Diligence, with no hostility. Opie—" He waited until the man gave him a chin lift, indicating he was listening. "—we will not send any of these men to you." Opie's features twisted, and he opened his mouth to speak, but Bones cut him off. "I will not send them anywhere, not yet. But, I want you here, if you can see your way clear to come in the next couple of days. Come, bring Devil." Bones' lips curved, and he felt his features soften. "I would like to introduce you to my old lady." As he knew it would, that announcement raised questions all around the table and from the speakers, because only a few men knew what Ester had become to him. "Life continues."

***

"Shit, Bones." The muttered curse came from beside him, and Bones looked down distractedly, watching as Red packed cautery powder into the wound on his leg. "Fuck. You rode here like this? You're bleeding like a stuck pig, man."

"It is a through-and-through. Just fucking tape it. Tape it up." After issuing the brusque order, Bones turned his attention back to the map spread across the table in front of him. Myron stood on the other side, tablet in hand as he tapped notes. "Are there similarities in all the hits?" Myron shook his head, reached out and angled a printout towards him, then made another note. "Which was the third?"

For the past four hours, the Chicago chapters been dealing with a running war. Businesses in far-flung areas of town targeted with drive-by shootings, each wave seeming to be tightly coordinated, with an in-depth knowledge of how the Rebels would react. So far, no clubhouses or individual residences had been hit, but each man was holding their breath, knowing it would likely come sooner rather than later. Bones had been standing outside a business the club owned on the north end of town, and taken a bullet while returning fire.

The club would be on lockdown soon, and Bones knew he would have to fight for the ability to have Road Runner be with Ester in his house, instead of her having to go back to Wisconsin like the rest of the families. She had only met a handful of men, and Road Runner was the only one she would trust. For now, she was in their home, in the panic room on the second level, accessible only from the hidden stairway or from the basement.

"Third target?" Myron asked for clarification without looking up from the tablet, making another note. Bones grunted. "Tupelo's on Cicero. They hit Ink Me at the same time. Silly's shook up, but okay." Myron's head lifted and he stared at Bones for a moment. "Whatcha got?"

"Joliet." Stinging pain in his thigh made him hiss between clenched teeth and he glanced down at Red, noting the suture needle in his hand. Looking back up, he gave Myron his entire focus. "Get some men on the Diamante clubhouse there. See what they have. The first target was north, the second was midtown, only minutes apart. This says there are two teams. Third was the first team hitting a second time, on their way back to their clubhouse. There has not been a fourth strike, this means the second team has not completed their assignment, and that first team will be sitting in their house waiting for word.

Bones lifted a hand, waving off Myron's headshake. "Trust me on this. In war, these men are as infants. We have been giving them too much credit. Credit for planning they are not responsible for. If this is Morgan, he will want to make a statement. Look at where they have targeted so far." Jabbing his finger at the map, he indicated the pins pushed through the paper and into the wood of the desk. "All of them were acquired right after Mason birthed the Rebels. Strip club, the pawn shop, Tupelo's, Ink Me. The only thing not on that map is Jackson's, which is where team two is headed right now. Every other business is less than a decade old, and did not matter to Deacon. He did not see them as a blight on his legacy. He did not see them as Mason's triumph, not like he would these four things. That will matter to Morgan. We need to call Jackson's, let those men know they are next on the list, and we need to send our men to Joliet."

Myron stared at him a moment, then tossed his tablet to the table, reaching out to grab the speakerphone and drag it towards him. Two seconds later Mason's voice sounded, demanding, "Update me, goddammit."

Myron stared at Bones for another moment, then gave a succinct summary of Bones' theory. "Jackson's is the next target. Boss, this is Diamante, pulling the shit from their Joliet clubhouse. I need permission to authorize a direct hit on that location."

Mason clipped out one word, followed with, "Approved," and then the phone disconnected.

Bones echoed him. "War." He pulled in a breath. "We do this, and he is right. It is war."

"Hope like fuck you're right, man," Myron muttered, dialing another number. "I see it, too. Fuck." The call connected, and Myron glanced up at Bones before he addressed the man on the other end of that line. "Chismoso, need you in the office, now." Disconnecting, he stared at Bones. "Feels right, sending him against Diamante. The proof is in the pudding."

"Jesus," Red whispered, then slapped Bones' leg. "Patched. Don't tear my fuckin' stitches. I'll take a van down to Joliet." That told every man in the room he expected casualties, something they all knew to be true.

A knock at the door and Red reached out, grabbed the knob and threw it wide to admit Chismoso. He took two strides into the room, glanced around and seemed to take in everything in sight. Bones gave him another second, then asked, "You left your phone outside?" Chismoso nodded. Myron picked up his tablet and walked around to where Bones stood, pulling up an app. It showed the room, with only one electronic signal, coming from where Myron stood with the tablet. Bones began talking. "We are hitting Joliet as quickly as we can put together a plan. I need to know everything you know about that clubhouse." Chismoso's head jerked back in shock, but he didn't say anything. "Do or die. You knew it would come to this. Do not pretend surprise."

"Not pretending anything. Hadn't thought about this shit coming from Joliet. Dude in charge there isn't worth a piss stain, so any surprise is about him being able to pull off this kind of shit." Chismoso took a breath and then started, "Clubhouse is three levels, with a fully converted basement as a bunker. It's vulnerable to building collapse, but not much else. House was owned by a prepper. He raised the house a foot, put in a reinforced ceiling in the basement. Word was they had food and water for a year so we won't be able to wait them out." He bared his teeth, the expression feral and fierce. "*Pendajo*, I won't cry when you kill him. He was Lalo's second in Las Cruces, the one they pulled me out there to replace. Crazy as my cousin was, this guy's just as bad." He motioned at Myron with one hand, continuing, "Get me some paper. I'll draw the space as best I remember it. You can assume they'll have the standard Diamante security in place, and I've given you that already, but let's go over it again, make sure I don't miss anything."

Bones interrupted him, watching his face carefully as he said, "We."

Chismoso cocked his head to one side, then that feral look was back, and if anything, he looked eager as he nodded, his head moving up and down slowly in agreement. "We."

***

Ester

The door at the top of the stairs opened. I didn't hear it, couldn't hear it, behind a locked door as I was, but the panel on the wall showed every level of the house, and I'd watched as first the front door opened, then closed, then opened and closed again. The code used on the downstairs keyboard showed up on the panel with the word BONES next to it, so I knew who it was.

Two men had been inside the house with me, but not with me. No one had been with me, and that was how I wanted it. If I couldn't have Bones with me, then alone was better. But now Bones was back, and the other men were gone, and this meant everything would be okay now. Meant everything would be back to as normal as it had been for us.

A knocking at the door to the room and I ran over, putting my palms flat on the surface, feeling the vibration slowly dying away. I was sure but wanted to be surer, so I waited. A moment later, he gave me what he'd promised, the surety that it would only be him who opened me back up. I sang along with the knocks, calling out my part as I returned the knocks, "Two bits."

Now came the hardest part. I reached out a single finger, one stiffened pointer, the others all tucked into my palm, protected from the panel's keyboard, looking back towards me for safety. I didn't like things like this. Didn't like them at all. I still couldn't stand the small phones everyone carried around. Every time I was around one, my skin crawled like I could feel the signals they put out, even if people always scoffed at my ideas. This, though, wasn't a phone. I pretended it was the microwave, which I'd learned to use immediately after the first time Bones brought me a bowl of the special ice cream, softened from spinning around and around inside the thing. "It's a microwave." Bones could get in from outside, but I liked him giving me this chance to be the opener, to be the accepter of the opening.

Shave and a haircut sounded again, and I glanced at the door. I'd learned how to deal with the microwave because since the reward was so sweet, it'd be silly not to. This would be sweeter. "Two bits."

Renewing the stiffening of my pointer, I said the word aloud as I typed it, pushing the green button after each number sequence, knowing without being told what they stood for. "Five, nineteen, twenty, five, eighteen."

The locks clicked, and the door opened outward, then Bones was standing there, and I was wrapped around him. His arms closed around me, and we rocked back and forth for a moment, his cheek pressing against the top of my head. "You give the best rewards."

"So do you, my Ester." His voice was gruff and taut with exhaustion. Still, he held onto me like he needed more, so I stayed still in his arms, running my hands up and down his back. "You are well?"

I knew he wasn't talking about pneumonia. He was asking where my head was, because for him, being locked up like I'd been for over a day would be torture. "It's quiet in here." Quiet was good, because it gave me time to think. So much happened outside, all the time, until it was hard to wrap my mind around how I felt or what I wanted or how to keep up with what other people expected. "This is a good thinking place." I let him know a little more. "I thought about you a lot."

"And what did you think, Ester?" Still rocking back and forth, he shifted, putting his mouth to the side of my head, lips to my ear so he could ask, "Did you think good things, my love?"

"You make me happy," I told him something he already knew, but needed him to know it was more. Pulling back, I put my fingers on his face, tracing across his lips, back and forth. "Not with your words, but with your heart. I thought about that. How happy you make me."

Pursing his lips, he pressed a light kiss against my fingertips. "I hope to always make you happy."

Leaning in, I rested my head against his firm chest, knowing under the leather, under the cotton, under the everything he had covering him, I existed there. I gave him back the wish that went both ways, the needings that we gave the other. The everything that was inside me, and on his skin.

"Me, too."

Catch the fever

Bones

"Boy or girl?" Bones saw Ester's smile at his question and knew she'd heard him through the kitchen windows. She was in the backyard refilling the bird feeders when the phone rang, and he held it where she could see it, giving her the option of staying outside longer if she wanted to avoid it.

Over Slate's laughter, he heard sounds in the background of the call, the speaker system of the Fort Wayne hospital making garbled noises. "Pretty little girl child. Means our prez joins the I'm-so-fucked daddy brigade now. He's been laughing at me with my three girls, going on and on about how life'll change in a few years. Think he expected with two boys already he'd be a shoo-in for a third." Slate made a buzzer sound, laughing harder. "Eeeehhhhhnt. Not so fast, buddy boy. Here's a girl for your ass."

"Did they name their daughter yet?" Slate was not wrong, Mason had been lording his boys over every Rebel member who had a girl in the past few years. "Garrett's little sister, he will need to grow up to be as protective as his father will no doubt be."

"Yeah, sweet name. Dolly Jane Mason. Healthy girl, her momma's good, too." Slate's voice moved away from the phone, and Bones heard him call, "Twins, get yer butts back here."

"You call your children twins?" Bones laughed, shaking his head. "Which ones are you speaking to?"

"All of 'em. Wrangling my kids is hard work, man. Glad as fu...crap Mason saw his way clear to what I needed." Slate yelled again, this time not bothering to pull the phone from his mouth, "I said get back here. Do not make me come after you." Giggles in the background followed by the rumble of a bass voice. Slate yelled, "Then effin' take care of 'em, you asshole." More giggles, and Bones listened as Slate kissed his children, their whispers of, "Wuv you, Daddy," so sweet it nearly took his breath. "Yeah, love you, too, shrimplet. Allen, 'mere, gimme a hug before Uncle Bear takes you home with him." Squeals, then the muffled sound of Slate talking to his son, "Love you, buddy. Be good, help out with KayHay."

"Bear is taking all of your children to his home? Is Eddie aware?" Bones kept his eyes on Ester as she moved hesitantly towards the door, opening and coming inside, but staying near the door. "It is good they like children."

"No fuckin' shit, man. Jase's kids are there as much as they are his and DeeDee's place. Sasha, Bear's girl, she loves Dani and Allen as much she loves Hayley and Kayley. Jesus, you look into that little girl's face and all you see is Eddie, all over. You needa come to the Fort, get a visit in before Mason goes home and everything's crazy there."

"True. Perhaps I can..." Bones let his voice trail off, because what he had been about to say was he could introduce Ester to everyone, but that would never work, not in a hospital, with so many unknown people. "I will talk to Ester..." Best to give her a heads-up he would be leaving, get her thinking about accompanying him if she could. "...and see if she is up to a visit to see the brand new daughter of my brother. Either way, I will see you soon. Stay safe." Ester's head tipped to one side, and she gave him a broad smile, nodding.

Slate laughed, and then responded, "Yeah, brother. Shiny side."

***

Bones stood in Mason's kitchen, elbows leaning against the island countertop, eyes aimed towards the living room where he watched Ester sitting close beside Willa, their heads angled in together over the top of the pink-blanketed bundle in Ester's arms. Garrett was on the floor in front of the women, playing quietly with the toy motorcycle Bones had brought for the boy. The noises he made as he pushed and pulled the toy across the rug were amusing, and Bones smiled to hear how he imitated the real thing.

"All is well?" Bones asked the question as Mason walked up beside him, settling two cold bottles of beer on the counter.

"Better than, brother. Willa's good, Garrett's good, Dolly's perfect. Chase is in a good place again, and that by itself is worth a celebration. Between you and Fury, we got the pain in our asses handled, Morgan's on the run, and Shooter's been reminded of who the fuck he is." Mason lifted the bottle, taking a long drink. "Life is good."

"Would you like to talk about Chicago?" Bones had given the debrief to Mason about their successful raid on the Diamante clubhouse, done while he was still standing in the driveway, the wreckage of the demolished building visible behind him in the video. Chismoso's information had saved lives on both sides, and the only Diamante who had died were those who knew they had no option but to fight.

"Nah, we're good, Bones. You got everything up there under control."

Mason lifted the bottle again, bringing it down abruptly when Bones asked, "Tell me about Florida?"

"Not a lot to tell." His voice, which a moment ago had been easy, was now tight, taut with discomfort, and Bones knew his words were a lie.

"You got inside. I know you did because I spoke to Myron. You got inside, and then you got out, and you had to come back here to be at the hospital." Without looking at him, Bones pressed Mason for answers, knowing that the not telling meant there was something to tell. "What did you find?"

"Office." Clipped and curt, the single word said whatever this was, Willa didn't know. Mason raised his voice slightly, calling, "Baby, need to talk business with Bones. We'll be back out in a minute." Willa looked up and nodded, her eyes on Mason dreamy, filled with an expression of love Bones might not have recognized a year ago.

Ester looked at him the same, their gazes meeting over the tiny head of the baby in her arms. "I will be only steps away, beauty." She nodded, careful so her movements didn't jostle the infant, and then looked back down, smoothing across Dolly's cheek with the backs of her fingers.

"Hooie, she's catching the fever, Bones." Mason's gruff laughter preceded them into the office he had on the main floor of his home. "Better watch out. You'll be changin' diapers instead of oil."

"Is it so bad, then? Having a child with the woman you love?" Bones grinned, knowing Mason was joking. "Seeing that in your home every day?"

"Naw, man. It for sure ain't no hardship. *God*—" Mason sucked in a breath. "—best thing in my life, meeting Willa."

***

Ester

"She's so tiny. And perfect. Even Slate said as much. You made a tiny, perfect human." I bowed in half, craned my neck around to see the flawless curves of Dolly's ears, and tugged the cap down over the tips. Holding my breath, I watched her sleep for a moment, then let it out in a rush only to pull it back in and hold it again. "So beautiful it makes it hard to breathe."

"She is gorgeous, isn't she?" Dolly's momma's voice was quietly proud and possessive, and I knew if I were in her shoes I'd never be able to let anyone else hold my human. "Our Garrett was small, too, but still so very *there*, you know?" I chanced glancing away from Dolly to Willa, and saw a sweet, loving smile on her face, and followed her gaze back to Dolly. "She's gorgeous."

"Delicate and fine, like crystal." At the sound of a quick indrawn breath, I looked at her again, surprised.

"My husband's mom was named Crystal." She offered me a smile, and I tried to give one back to her, never certain how well I did when it was forced like this. "I asked him if he wanted to use it, even for a middle name, but he had already settled on Dolly." Reaching out one hand, she adjusted Dolly's blanket slightly, pulling it up around her tiny shoulders. "I didn't ask again, but you saying that, it makes me wonder."

"Dolly is a right name, if it's what you call her in your head. If it's not, then there's no rule says you can't call her what you want with your mouth. I've always been an Ester, but my brother was given a new name." I blinked, wondering where that came from. I hadn't thought about Ronnie in a long, long time. This was something Bones didn't know about me, and my gut twisted, wondering if he would think it a secret I hadn't shared. I didn't want that, so I needed to unload this burden as soon as possible. "Can you take your tiny human back, please? I need to tell Bones a secret."

Now she was the one blinking, and I waited patiently until she caught up with me. It didn't take her long, and I knew it didn't matter what she called her baby, or what her baby called herself, this momma would always catch up. "Sure, honey. Just..." She reached out both arms now, gathering the warm bundle from my arms. I almost held on, not wanting the empty feeling I knew would follow. I'd held babies in the shelters before, watching tiny humans while their mothers showered or shat. She continued, taking Dolly entirely away, "Let me get her situated." Another moment and then Dolly woke, turning her face towards her mother's breasts, probably smelling the milk waiting just underneath the surface. Natural sustenance, and a beautiful thing to watch. "Oh, now," she cooed at her baby, adjusting her slightly, "who's a good girl?"

"I am." There went my mouth again, blurting when it should have been shutting, but at least she just giggled with me. "You feed her, I need to find Bones."

"Okay, honey, just knock before you go into the office, all right?" Glancing up at me, she gave me a grin. "Might want to tell Bones what's happening out here, so he's not shocked when he comes out."

Standing in front of the wooden office door, I lifted my hand, and then let it fall to my side. My brain had started down the what-if path, and it was hard to stop when that happened. *Maybe I should wait*, I thought, then a loud rattle came from low on the door followed by a noisy hammering. I looked down and saw Garrett standing there, grinning his little man grin up at me, hand gripping the metal and plastic motorcycle as he whaled on the door with it.

He was leaning so hard, when the door opened Garrett stumbled, falling forwards, so I reached out and grabbed him, hauling him upright. He looked up at me, gabbling away, then lifted his arms up in the universal signal of "get me off this floor" so I picked him up. Turning to face the open door, I saw first Mason, a big man with eyes that would have frightened me to bits if I'd met him without Bones at my side. Or seen him without his toddler on my hip. His eyes saw everything, and I knew he saw Willa feeding Dolly even without looking over my shoulder.

"I need to tell Bones a secret." Yes, that was my blurting mouth again. Bones was behind him, and stepped up, Mason moving to the side so I could see. "Hey there." Now my mouth was traitorous again, seeming unwilling to get to the meat of the matter. "How ya doin', Bones?"

"Ester." Tipping his head to the side, Bones looked at me. But he didn't just look at me, he saw me, like he always did, and that loosened the bindings on my mouth.

"I didn't forget, but I didn't remember, either. Not until a minute ago when Willa and I were talking about names." Garrett hit my back with the motorcycle, but it didn't hurt. Little man smile, little man strength. One day, he would be bigger and stronger, and then we'd all have to look out, but for now, he was a little man walking. "Ronnie. I had a Ronnie when I was little."

Bones had the frown on his face he wore when he was trying to catch up. Willa was already there, mostly because she'd had more time, but she was also pretty smart. She called out, "I think it's her brother's name."

I nodded, seeing understanding coming over Bones' features. Understanding and something else. A knowing. "You already knew." Bones nodded. "Okay, then. I didn't want you to think it was a lying secret." A different look flashed over his face, this more like guilt than anything.

***

Bones

"You know him." The emphasis was subtle, but there and Bones knew Ester deserved the truth from him. Always, but especially in things like this. *Honesty*, he thought, *is a good thing*.

"Yes, my Ester. I know you have a brother." Bones waited, and she nodded, silently urging him to finish voicing what she'd seen on his face. "I know who your brother is."

Staring at him intently, her expression was guarded, the tension around her eyes showing fear. "Do I know him?"

Without quite understanding the context of the question, Bones chose to answer carefully, but still honestly. "No, little one, you have not met him since you have been with me."

"Has he met me?" Her voice cracked, and Bones longed to pull her into him, but needed to give her this distance for now, letting her set the tone of the rest of the conversation.

"He has seen you. He was the man who helped me find you when you were ill." Rushing to fill the gaps, he told her, "Until he saw you that day, he did not know who you might be to him."

She rolled her lips, then reached up, scrubbing at her nose. Bending, she buried her face into Garrett's neck, and with her voice so muffled, Bones nearly didn't hear her next words. "Does he want his sister back? My Ronnie? Does he want to know me?"

"More than anything, Ester," Mason spoke and reached out, one hand gentle on her shoulder, then he tugged his son free of her grip. His other hand shoved Bones forwards with a muttered, "Catch her, man. She's falling apart." Louder, voice still gentle, Mason told her, "Myron wanted to be there for you ever since. But we've had so much shit goin' down, and I know you know it, more than most, seein' as not many folks had to deal with a shootout in their home. Bones can tell you about him, and call him, and you can hear his voice if you want. He's in Chicago, though, so you can't see him until you go home. Looks like our dinner is delayed, with Dolly gettin' some of hers first. You'll have to stay a couple hours more, Ester."

Bones looked up, arms wrapped around a trembling Ester to see Mason's gaze locked across the room. He twisted his neck to see Willa reclining on the couch, nursing Dolly. Ester took a deep breath, then on a quivering laugh, said, "Tiny human food time. I was supposed to tell you."

She moved in his arms, shifting around until she could look at Willa, too. "Aren't they beautiful, Bonesy? Have you ever seen anything as beautiful in your life? In the history of things, this ranks way up there. Top slot."

Lips to the top of her head, Bones agreed with her, and only Mason knew his gaze was directed downwards and not across the room. "Beauty."

Morgan's in Arkansas

Bones

"How sure?" Sirens sounded in the background on the call, and Mason's voice vibrated with rage when he asked the question. "How fuckin' sure are you this was Morgan?"

Bones raised one hand, holding the men in the room quiet, letting them all listen in to the call Mason had put on speaker. He and Mason had rolled into Chicago only a few hours ago, just long enough to deposit Ester at home and then come to the clubhouse.

Stan, the chapter president in Little Rock, coughed harshly, then said, "Saw him." He coughed again, and they all heard voices closer to him, asking if he were having problems breathing. He coughed, a ratcheting fusillade of sound that sounded wet and painful. Groaning, he whispered, "Know him. I know him. I'm sure."

The call disconnected and Bones stared at Mason's face, knowing what Mason's order would be even before anything was said. "They upped the ante." Stan had started the call with the information that three men were dead in Little Rock, and he was hit. "Drive-by. Like here in Chicago." Mason turned, staring out the window, head tipped back to look at the top of the business office building a handful of blocks away.

The location of that building strategic, so Mother would always be close and protected. "We got lucky here." Mason turned, staring at Bones, then shook his head. "No, not lucky. Got smart, smart enough to figure out their next move here, dealt with it before they killed anyone." Shaking his head, Mason huffed out a frustrated breath. "Upped the goddamned ante, and we'll be the ones calling on this hand. Where's Myron? Want him, Slate, Bear..." He paused, looking around the room. "Fuck. Goddamned mother*fucker*. Shit." Mason shook his head viciously, seeming to try and deny something. Bones understood when Mason gritted out, "Get me Blue Line. Need him to make a visit to Shooter."

News out of California was still muddied, but they'd gotten word from a man on the inside there was no proof Shooter was no longer incarcerated. Not that he'd been seen, nothing positive.

"Not confident that is the right path, Mason," Bones cautioned. "The idea of asking an LE club for a favor does not sit well with me. No offense to Bear"—he looked around the room, saw the same reluctance on every face—"but this man does not live in our world. He will not have the right message to give, and Shooter will know it." Bending his head to the phone in his hand, he sent a series of texts to pull together the men Mason wanted. "Did we have no information on this beforehand?" When Mason didn't respond, Bones looked up, seeing Mason staring at him.

"Who the fuck you think needs to go, then? Me? I can't fucking go, and he goddamned well knows it." Mason turned, muscles bunching in his arms as he struggled to maintain control.

"Me." With a heavy sigh Fury spoke up, and Bones turned to look at him. "I agree with Bones. Nothing settled about dealing with LEO, in whatever form they take at the moment. I agree with you, too. We do need to make a point with Shooter. But we've got fucking Morgan to deal with. It needs to be me. I don't know Morgan, so I'm less help here than I'd like to be. But I do know Shooter. And, if he's there"—he stared at Bones—"I know exactly the message we need to deliver."

Mason lowered his head, and his voice was rough when he asked, "What the hell kind of people are these? Deacon killed his own son, split his belly open. And Shooter? Fuck. Man's boy is dead, isn't that enough of a cost for him? Will it ever be enough? Doesn't he know this won't stop until he does?"

Bones nodded at Fury. "Get with Digger. He will assist with travel. Do you need to...talk to anyone before you leave?" He stepped carefully around naming the woman Fury was with, Mason's sister Bethany.

"I'll call once I'm in the air." Fury walked towards the door. "Keep me updated, brother."

"Will do." Bones turned to Mason, staring at him for a moment, then asked, "Who do you want to go to Arkansas?"

"Morgan's like the fucking plague." Turning to the back wall a moment, Mason pulled in a hard breath. "Why can't the man just fucking die?"

"We will deal with him when we can. Right now, we need to talk about Arkansas. Myron is on his way, people are being informed of what has happened. We will have Slate and Bear on video in a few minutes. They are on the way to their clubhouse now." Stepping towards the desk, he pushed folders out of the way, exposing the map underneath, one with handwritten notes for each chapter the Rebels held in the states. "We need to discuss strategy, and check in with all chapters."

Mason stared at him for a moment, then sighed and came towards him. Holding Bones' gaze, Mason stepped close and muttered, "Always got my back, brother. Appreciate you, Bones."

"You do the same," Bones responded in the same tone, reaching up to grip Mason's arm, pulling him close to thump his back, centering his fist over the patch they both wore. "Now we get to work."

"Fuck, yeah." Mason turned to the desk and stared down. "When Myron gets here, tell him I need all presidents on video." His eyes cut up to Bones, then back down. "Secure, so we can talk." A pause, then, "Fury gone yet? Have an idea."

With a smile, Bones leaned towards the door, yelling, "Fury, back into the office before you go." Eyes on Mason, he said, "He has not. What do you need?"

"Myron's got these phones, some kind of internal static battery, so even if the battery is removed, they work. If Fury can get one to Shooter, he'll expect us to hear his conversations when he's got the battery in, but he wouldn't expect us to be listening in between times. We could get something." Mason shrugged. "Or we might not, but it's worth a try."

As he'd been talking, Bones was texting Myron, using easily misunderstood acronyms to disguise what he needed. "Done." Lifting his head, he asked, "What else?"

"Hoss to Arkansas. He's got the best connection with the clubs in the area, because of Memphis." Mason trailed a fingertip across the map. "Get him an escort, let's roll in force."

"Making a statement." Bones agreed, sending another text. "Okay. What next?"

"I need to go back to Florida." Bones stared at Mason, surprised because this seemed to come from left field. "Not for what I'd like, but because we need to know why she dumped Lalo out. We need Chismoso, but we need to believe. I think she can shed light on whether his story holds up or not. I don't even have to tell her who I am."

"Brother, she will know. Like you know." Bones shook his head. "Traveling on your own is not going to happen, not with this. We need you here, not there. And with the tension we have struggled with over the past months, if you fly, you know you will be detained. Anyone with you will be detained. We cannot afford to be weakened, and you going to Florida will weaken us. Arkansas will need you strong."

"We need to believe." Mason looked over Bones' shoulder towards the door. "If I could trust his words, then I could trust him to help plan this."

"He did not lie to us about Joliet. Not a word. Not even when it might cause casualties on their side. He is no longer loyal to Diamante." Bones tried to infuse his belief into the words, hoping Mason would catch hold of it, and be easy.

"Can you say he's loyal to RWMC? Without hesitation, can you say those words, Bones?" Mason shook his head. "I can't. And because I can't, that leaves me guarding against within as well as without. He's wearing a prospect patch, and playing the part convincingly, but damn, brother, look at his face next time you ask him to do something. This is galling him, and he doesn't wear the lie of loyalty well."

Shades spoke up for the first time, and his words were a blow to Bones, because he didn't expect them. "Don't trust him. Some of his guys are all-in, some got a foot in. Most are biding. Just fuckin' biding."

Tater cleared his throat, cut a glance to Bones, then shook his head. "He's not given us a reason to trust him, yet. Not giving us a reason to not trust him is something he works at every day. But the way he goes about it feels forced. I'm with Shades, I don't trust him. Not yet."

Myron stalked through the door, ever-present tablet in hand. "Who?" He looked at Mason. "What do we know about Little Rock?"

"Chismoso." Bones supplied, then said, "And for Arkansas, we only know the smallest amount. We need you to find and feed us the information we need."

"I listen," Myron said this absently, unlocking a drawer and pulling out a laptop. He attached the battery to the device, then punched a series of buttons, beginning the boot cycle. "Fitted him out with a bunch of bugs. Since the beginning, because I wanted to be able to haul him in if needed." He angled the screen, then plugged in a cord, using the remote on the table to turn on the huge screen hanging on the wall. "He's all in, just holding back because he expects retribution for shit in the past. Guarding himself, and trying to guard the men who joined their path to his. All he talks about is how to stay here, and away from Diamante. Hates them with a passion." Fingers to the keyboard, Myron pulled up the video app they used, a software trade he'd worked with Chief, the former FBI agent and current president of a friendly club out west. "Who we need on vid, boss?" He'd made some assumptions, or been prompted by Bones' group texts to the men, because without being asked, he'd pulled in Slate and Bear, then Opie. "Chismoso is exactly what he seems to be. Don't sweat him. He'll settle if you use him more, because right now he's riding the line and feels it. That's a man—" Another call popped on the screen, and Myron paused to click it, troubled surprise in his voice when he greeted, "Retro, didn't know you had my app." Tension went out of the men when Retro moved to the side, and they all saw Hoss.

"I don't, man. Here visiting my brother and he said to answer the call." Retro waved at the camera, and Bones chuckled. He was the president of a small club in Alabama, but the blood brother to one of the Rebels' key men. "I can step out if you need me to. No sweat."

"Stay." Mason clipped out the word, then made a motion with one hand. In rapid succession, red exclamation marks showed on the four video blocks on the screen, indicating the audio feed to them had been muted. Turning to Myron, Mason asked, "When were you gonna share about Chismoso?"

"When you needed the info." Myron shrugged. "It's been busy, boss. I knew he was a rogue piece on the board. Wanted to make sure I did my bit to keep us all safe. Now we've got the info so you can place him."

Shaking his head, Mason snorted, turning back to the screen. The red marks disappeared, and the door opened and closed behind Bones, letting in Fury. Mason glanced around, then began, "Here's what we know."

***

"My Ester. I will be back before you miss me." Bones wrapped his arms around her, holding her close, rocking in place. "But with this, I must go with Mason." Closing his eyes, he let the feeling of her relaxing into him soak in, giving him something to hold on to for the next days. He would be riding to Little Rock in a few hours, and the return trip would be after the final funeral, late the next day. Five men had died in the end, almost half of the members in the chapter.

Hoss had reported the local clubs were on guard, but not antagonistic, which was good news. Then, he reported Justine LaPorte was in town, which was far from good news. That meant any ideas Bones or the other men had to try and keep Mason from going down were out the door.

"Is it safe?" Ester's shoulders jerked, pushing out the words as if they hurt her.

"Baby, it will be as safe as we can make it." He would not lie to her, and since Morgan was in the wind, not even a rumor of him since the shooting, there were no guarantees.

"Hmmm." Rubbing her cheek against his chest, she sniffed, and he cradled her closer. "You're my best needing. The biggest, too. Don't let out there"—she unwrapped one arm from his waist, and waved her hand behind her—"make you not come back."

"I will be back, little one." Wanting to calm her, he began humming softly, swaying back and forth with her. "I will always come back to you."

"You'll keep Mason safe, too?" Her shoulders rolled, fitting her body to his. "Make him come back. His Dolly needs. Even without knowing it."

In this, too, he would not lie, and felt the corners of his mouth tip up at the idea of him trying to make Mason do anything. "I will do all I can, Ester."

"My mom didn't come back. That left me with my dad, and he didn't want to be anywhere after that. Took himself away from me. I don't want Dolly to be alone. Tell Mason if she wants, she can be with me." Ester shrugged, but her body was tense. "I know what it's like to be alone."

"Ester." Bones approached this carefully, not wanting to upset her. "Do you remember your mother and brother?"

"Ronnie? My Ronnie? Of course, I remember him. I only forgot to tell you because we didn't talk there yet. The court lady told me he had a different place. I don't...didn't get to keep him. But I remember him. He was smart and silly." Her voice took on a plaintive tone. "You sure he wants to have me back?"

"More than anything, Ester. He wants that very much." She seemed open now, and with Road Runner tied up with other things, if she could allow this, it would make Bones sleep much easier. "He wondered if he could stay here while I am away? Stay here, with you?"

She leaned back immediately, blinking up at him, eyes wide and startled. "He does?"

"Yes, Ester. He very much does."

Slowly her lips parted, then curved up, the small smile growing wide and brilliant, her eyes sparkling brightly with unshed tears. Her whisper said everything. "Needings."

***

Myron

He stood on the sidewalk and stared at Ester through the front windows of the house. She sat on Bones' lap, draped as casually there as if he were her personal piece of furniture. Hands to Bones' shoulders, she leaned in to kiss him, then curled into a ball, wedging herself underneath Bones' chin.

Myron pulled out his phone, checked the text again, and opened the back door to his car, pulling out the small duffle and computer bag. Settling them in one hand, he tapped out a text, watching through the window at the reaction, Bones shifting to one side to get his phone out, Ester laughing and complaining, holding on so she didn't slide to the floor.

Then Myron got to witness his sister's excitement at knowing he was outside. In a flash she was sitting upright, slapping Bones' chest with her open palms before finding her feet. She whirled, and was running to the front door when she caught sight of him through the window. Stopping still, she stared at him, the expression on her face blank. Stared at him so long he was afraid she wouldn't know him, wouldn't want him around if he couldn't convince her that she was his sister. Then, with a shout of laughter so loud he could hear it where he stood, she ran to the door.

Myron had made it halfway up the walk by the time she wrestled the door open, and then he had to lock his knees, going back on a foot and letting out a breath of air with an oof when she hit him at a full run. "My Ronnie," she whispered into his ear, arms around his neck pulling him down for a hug that went on forever. He wrapped his arms around her, too, scarcely noticing when Bones took the bags from his hands. Myron just stood and held her, the sister he'd never given up finding.

"My sissy."

My Ronnie

Ester

Myron. I tried the name in my head before I let it trickle out over my tongue. I wouldn't have thought the removal of a space would make something seem foreign, but it did. I didn't want to make him think I wasn't accepting of the man he'd put on like a coat, even if I could see bits and bobs of my Ronnie underneath everything. Myron was a man I didn't know, but Ronnie just was. Everything I remembered of my brother, he was.

The court lady had tried to make me believe I didn't remember anything, that I was making it up out of stories and movies and tales told by people who were lucky enough to have a real family, but I never believed her. My first memory was of Ronnie singing to me.

"Do you still sing?" Bones had left hours before, and Ronnie and I had sat up in the kitchen swapping puzzle pieces of our lives apart, trying to fill in the gaps for each other. Since coming to live with Bones, I found there were more things in my head, but not in a confusing way, in an ordered progression. Red, the man who had helped me get well, had told me nutrition and sleep and safety were setting things right for me, and his words had made me think. What if all the people who needed them had food and shelter? Without the fear and rules of the shelters, just shelter when they needed it. No strings, no owing for what you were given, just something to make a difference.

Now, with my question out of the blue pulling a confused smile to Ronnie's face, I quickly figured out he hadn't followed the path to my question. I grinned at him, and reached out, dragging a fingertip across the back of his hand. "I would kiss you here, and you would sing to me." I traced a half circle there, then told him a truth. "I missed the singing a lot, but missed you most of all."

"I'm so glad you remember me, Sissy." He hadn't hesitated a moment, slipping me back into that name as if there'd been no years between the sayings. I liked it, and had told him so, which meant when I grinned at him now, he knew why. "My Sissy."

"My Ronnie." Something in his eyes gave it away, a darkening instead of a twinkling, and I knew my name for him held pain as well as happiness. Because of that, I decided to let his real name out, give it a trial run, see how it felt on the air. "Myron."

One corner of his mouth tipped up, and he shook his head. "I'm your Ronnie, Ester. I like how you held onto that."

"Did you know Mason has a tiny human?" An abrupt topic change, and I knew it, but couldn't help wondering. Bones had looked so sweet cradling little Dolly, and he was good friends with Ronnie, so maybe Ronnie would know this next question. When he nodded, I said, "Bones held her. The baby, I mean. Tiny Dolly." Head tipping to the side again, he lifted his cup of coffee to his lips, making a humming noise that said keep going. He'd done it a lot today, and it worked now like it had a dozen times before. "He liked her." His head tipped the other way, and he made the sound again. "Do you know if he likes tiny humans? Babies? Little people?"

332

"Do you like babies, Ester?" At his question, I ducked my chin, looking at the table between us, Ronnie's fingertips resting casually on the wood grains, tracing tiny lines of growth and maturity. "Do you want a baby, maybe?"

"How scary it must be, to be willing to take that on. Bring a little person into the world." I glanced up at his face, then back down, watching his fingertips make another circuit. "What if life goes sideways? Look at us, what happened. Parents can be there one day, and not the next."

"Look at us." When he agreed with me, I lifted my eyes, staring into his face. This was when I saw he didn't actually agree with me, because when he looked at us, he saw something different. "Against all odds, we found each other again. You've got a man who loves you, who would level mountains to bring you joy. Isn't adding to that joy something worth risking?"

"I don't have to decide today." Shaking off the thought, I rattled the chair with the movement of my body and Ronnie laughed. "I'm glad you're still my Ronnie."

His voice soft, he said, "If you had a baby, I could sing to it." That pulled my attention, and I stared at him, shocked. Then I smiled.

Forever Rebels

Bones

"Appreciate y'all comin' by," Mason told another group of men who had just ridden up to the Little Rock clubhouse. It had been like this all day, one group after another, coming by to pay respects to the club for their fallen members.

There was some little amount of small talk, and then as had happened in some form with every visit, the leader of the group asked, "Rebels gonna keep a house here?"

Bones sighed as Mason cut a glance over to him. They had disagreed on this topic, with Bones giving way because Mason was national president, but it bothered both men that they were so far apart on this subject. Mason nodded, giving a version of the same response he'd handed out all day. "Fuck, yeah. Of course, we are. We've been part of Little Rock for a long time. This is our place, our house, and if anyone thinks we can be run off, they got a hell of a surprise coming."

A few minutes later, bikes roared in the lot, and the visitors rode off, leaving an uneasy silence between the two men left standing behind. Bones stretched, rolling his shoulders, feeling the unaccustomed heat beating at his skin. They would be leaving early in the morning, headed north, where Chicago was still caught in the chill of late spring. Abruptly, Mason started talking. "We both know we're going to keep arguing until I can make you understand. You willin' to fuckin' listen to me this time, Bones?"

"I *have* been listening to you. For *two days*, I have done nothing but listen to you. What you say does not make sense to me, Mason. I support you, and so I support your decision, but I do not have to believe in it." Bones shook his head, squaring up with Mason, staring into his friend's eyes. "I do not have to believe in your idea to believe in you."

"*Jesus.*" The word seemed dragged out of Mason, and he tipped his chin upwards, rolling his eyes. "Just fuckin' listen to me, would ya?"

Wordless, Bones stared at him and slowly nodded.

"We lost Watcher." Bones couldn't help himself, the bald statement made him flinch. "Yeah, hits me just as fuckin' hard, every goddamned time I think about it. We lost Watcher. Same goddamned day, we lost seven men. Watcher's path was his own, and fucking impossible to understand, but still an action he chose. Those seven men, though? They were taken by a brother, someone they trusted. Doesn't matter he regretted it in the end, deed was still done. Families without closure, fuck, most of our rank and file don't know what the hell happened yet, because we haven't been able to bring our brothers home yet. That cut our Las Cruces chapter to the bone, man. Lost seven, and lost a princess. Sure, we found her, got her back, but uncovered every bit of the shit we didn't want in the process. Since then we've lost another eight men. That's fourteen in only a few months. Fucking funerals and wakes and memorial rides where those of us who are left behind have to look at each other, have to look at all their old ladies and families, and our brothers. Brothers looking sideways at brothers wondering if there's another traitor behind the mask. Not a fucking one of us believed Diamond woulda done that. Not a fucking one of us." Mason sucked in a harsh breath.

"Spider? Fuck, I remember thinking he was probably behind every fucking thing that had gone wrong. Diamond? Oh, fuck, no. Thought the man was loyal to the bone. Didn't know his bloodline." He scoffed, the sound hard and dark. "Bloodline." Taking a half step forwards, Mason spread the fingers of one hand, lifting his palm towards Bones. "You ever look in the mirror at yourself and think, I don't know who the fuck that man is?"

Bones shook his head.

"I do. And I can tell you, I don't like it." That admission was as close as a regret as anything Bones had ever heard from Mason. "Don't like looking at the men around me and wondering, who's next. I got three kids." Mason leaned close, fists on his hips. "Our brother who died in this parking lot? Stan? Stan had three kids. Three kids and two grandkids. We're in a fucking war for our lives, Bones. We can't give an inch. We give anything at all, and Morgan will find something to push into the breach. We can't let him. Have to hold, fucking hold. Make it so Watcher didn't die for nothing. None of those men died so we could back off and lick our fucking wounds. We can't give Morgan anything, man."

Mason raised a hand to Bones' shoulder, gripped tightly, his hard fingers clamped down on the black leather. "This is our goddamned house. In Las Cruces, that's our goddamned house, too. Chicago. Fort Wayne." Swiveling them so they both turned towards the clubhouse, Mason pointed a finger to the rectangle above the porch bearing the Rebel Wayfarers MC logo. "That's my goddamned house. I'm keeping my house, Bones. If I don't, then everything we have will go the same way. We can't give an inch."

Staring at the black and white sign, Bones took in everything Mason said. Times like this were what wore the fabric of a club thin. When things were unsettled, uncertainty often led men to drop their patch, citing all kinds of excuses. Every action weakening the club further. Holding the line, keeping the chapter open, this would deliver a message not only to their enemies, but also to their members.

Speaking carefully, Bones responded, hoping Mason would understand all the words spoken, and the ones left unsaid. "I hear you. I hear what you say. I do not disagree. But"—he turned to look at Mason, needing him to take in everything—"the clubhouse here is compromised. We can move members in, but that is at the risk of weakening their current chapter. Where do you propose we find the numbers to keep every line in the sand sharply drawn?"

Mason grinned and heaved a heavy sigh, visibly relieved Bones would no longer be fighting him on this. "I got something in mind, brother. I got something in mind."

***

Bones was bent over the bed in his loaned room upstairs when it happened. Looking around at the empty, pulled askew dresser drawers, he absently rolled a shirt, hands smoothing out the wrinkles, getting ready to put it in his bag. They were set to move out in about ten minutes. The clubhouse was packed because all the members in the region were in Little Rock. About half the men planned to ride with him and Mason up to the Missouri state line. That would leave about a hundred at the clubhouse to continue the wake and party that had begun after the funerals yesterday.

Bones had called home last night, talked to Myron to find out Ester had settled in quickly. When he spoke to her, the pleasure in her voice was plain. Happiness bubbled over in her words and tone, and she hadn't hesitated to share her pique that he would be away a day longer than expected, but accepted it with good grace. Having Myron stay at their home had been the right call.

Shirt in hand, he was turning to place it in the bag when the noise registered. There had been a steady rumble of bikes in and out all day.

Coming in groups of five or six, the sound had been constant, the men joking it was like being at a bike rally. Joking how Stan the Man would have liked this, grieving in their way, acknowledging the men who were gone.

So, when the noise level increased suddenly, without warning, Bones dropped the shirt and took the two steps to the window, looking out to see a massive group of bikes and bikers rolling up the hill to where the clubhouse sat. A hundred bikes that were not expected. Not Rebel. "*Fuck.*"

Shouting in the house now, he remained where he was, torn between wanting to be one of the men who greeted whoever these arrivals were, and wanting to have the advantage of high ground. Without looking, he reached back, pulling the bag on the bed closer, digging around for his spare magazine.

As the bikes drew closer, he focused on the lead riders, not believing what he saw. "*Fuck!*" Whirling, he ran to the stairs, managing to be right behind Mason as he led every member out the door and into the clubhouse lot. Positioning himself slightly ahead of Mason, he didn't wait for the bikes to park before he was shouting at the man sitting arrogantly on his motorcycle. "What the *fuck* do you think you do, coming here? Now. You of all men have no place at our club, on our lot, at our fucking *house*. No place, never have."

Shooter shook his head, tugging the bandana off his face. Without speaking, he climbed off the bike and stepped close to offer a still-gloved hand to Mason. Bones lashed out, striking it away, not even acknowledging the insult just offered his national president. "You have no place here, Shooter."

"Mason, I wanted to extend my sympathies." Shooter swept one arm out, indicating the men at his back. Even without them turning around, Bones could tell from the mixed colors of the nameplates and officer patches that this was no cohesive club come out en masse to support

Shooter. "We wanted to say how sorry we were for all the Rebels' troubles." He glared at Mason over Bones' shoulder. "Figured you'd be here. Wanted to get a look at you. See how you're holding up with all the recent setbacks."

"Message delivered." That was Opie, speaking from the other side of where Mason stood. "On your way, John."

"Brother,"—Shooter ignored Opie as he had Bones—"not a word of greeting for your blood?"

"Get the fuck out—" Bones was cut off by Mason's hand on his shoulder, pulling him to the side.

"You know what I found?" Mason asked, his voice nearly conversational. "John, do you know *who* I found?"

"Boss," Opie began, but Mason made a gesture, and he stopped speaking.

"Tell me how she died. Our mama. Tell me the story again." There was an edge to his voice now, and Bones angled his head so he could see Mason's face, keeping Shooter in view. "You told me once, and I wanna make sure I got it right."

Shooter blanched, his already jail-pallor face going even whiter. Bones watched as his Adam's apple bobbed, knew it was him swallowing nervously. "Told you how it happened. That's nothing to do with why I'm here today."

"No, you're here today to cause shit, because it's what you always do. What you've always done." Mason's fingers dug into Bones' muscles, gripping so tightly he knew it was involuntary. "Always." Mason sighed, and said, "Tell me again. How'd she die?"

"Mexicans shot her. They torched her car and fucking shot her in the face. Shot her so many times, there wasn't anything left of her. Between the burning and the bullets, you couldn't even recognize her." Shooter's words came staccato, he moved sideways, shuffling his feet. "Torched her and killed her."

"Who sold you that line of shit?" Mason's fingers gripped hard, then released slightly. "Somebody fed you a line, man."

"I saw her." Shooter shook his head. "Not something I'd ever forget."

"You recognized her? Thought you said she was shot to shit?"

"I *saw* her," Shooter said this insistently, and it was evident he believed what he was saying. "Saw her body."

"But not her face. You didn't see her. Did that action, her death, did it start a war?"

"Fuck, yeah, it started war. You don't get to kill the president's old lady and not pay." Shooter shuffled again, seeming unable to stand still. "They had to pay."

"And that war, took out the club in Mexico? Was it the Machos?"

"Fuck, no. We worked with them to end their competition. Gave us a straight line to Central America." Shooter shook himself, and then clearly tried to get back on script, saying, "Rebels took a setback this week, wanted to see you, see how you're holding up with all the shit happening."

Mason didn't follow the verbal diversion, staying on topic. "Partnered with Machos, based on the evidence of a faceless female body?"

"Based on seeing my mother's body lying bloody in the clubhouse. Burned and bloody. What the fuck are you going on about, Mason?" Two steps towards the clubhouse turned into three steps backwards as Shooter tried to keep himself under control. He leaned his ass on the bike he'd ridden in, trying to affect an ease he clearly didn't feel.

"She didn't die." Mason dropped this bomb, and waited, apparently expecting a reaction.

He got one.

"Fuck, yeah, she died. Torched and shot up on the freeway." Shooter came off the bike and was standing stiff legged, fists balled at the ends of his arms. "Daddy saw it, wasn't in time to save her. Ran 'em off, pulled her out. Too late. She was dead."

"No, she's not."

"The fuck you say!" Shooter lifted an arm, finger pointed at Mason, stabbing the air with each sharp exhalation. "She's fucking dead."

"I saw her. Talked to her. She ain't dead, John."

"Where do you think you saw her? You so stupid you didn't know you weren't talking to her?" Scoffing, Shooter shook his head. "So fucking stupid you don't know the difference between Mama and some fucking skank you saw on the goddamned street."

"You know we got another sister?" This was pure speculation on Mason's part, and Bones knew it. "You know our daddy got a girl on another woman?" If Bones read things right, this was the first time Mason had acknowledged any truth to Morgan's assertion he was Mason's father. "Two boys, two girls. Perfect family."

"Fucking shut up." Shooter's head moved back and forth in short, sharp arcs. "Just fucking shut up."

A bike near the end of the line roared, followed by a dozen more, and Bones watched as the mass of machines started untangling themselves. The first group was followed by another, and another, the sound of their exhausts dwindling down to nothing. Shooter didn't even notice, his attention focused on Mason.

"Yeah, you, then me and Bethy, and then Justine." Mason dropped the name into the conversation casually, as if he expected Shooter to already know. "Baby sister."

The last bike pulled out, turning around and heading back down the road. Bones had counted a dozen different patches, likely clubs where Shooter had held markers. Markers wasted on a call in like this, where there was no good outcome.

"Fuck you." Shooter stepped backwards, stumbling as he tripped over the pegs on the bike behind him. "She's dead, and there's no fucking bitch like you're talking about."

"I've seen her. Spoken to her. Talked to Justine. Morgan lied to you. I don't know who the woman was he killed, or why he did it, but he lied to you." Mason's fingers dug in again, and Bones began paying close attention to Shooter, seeing how his agitation increased with every word. "Stole her from you, took her away just when you needed her. Stole her and put her into a place where she's protected. Why did he do that, John? Why did he feel like he needed to protect her from you? Keep her from you? What was going on that made him think you couldn't be around her anymore?"

"Fuck you. It wasn't like that." Shooter's voice cracked, rising in pitch. "She's not alive."

"She's very much alive. I have pictures, and she's just as beautiful as ever. Our mother, hidden away all these years. Morgan kept her safe." Mason barked a laugh that sounded painful, and Bones was reminded it was his mother who had been stolen from him, too. "Kept her for himself. Kept her away from you. Didn't want you to taint her with your brand of crazy. Am I right? You were crazy, and you hated she had other kids. Hated she loved Bethy and me. Hated her enough you were going to hurt her, weren't you?"

"Fuck." Shooter leaned forwards at the waist. "You."

"Alive, and so happy to see me. Told me so. Told me she loved me." Mason's voice softened, gentled. "Told me she loved Bethy and me so much. Didn't mention you, though. Wonder if you've slipped her mind, finally."

Face red, mouth opening and closing soundlessly, Shooter stood and stared at Mason. With jerky movements, he woodenly turned to the bike and straddled it, head bowed. Without another word, without looking at Mason, he started the engine and turned the bike, back wheel spinning and skidding on the road as he roared off.

Silence settled on the parking lot as they all watched the motorcycle grow smaller, dwindling in the distance.

"Jesus. That man's batshit crazy. I'm thinkin' he won't be back like that again." Opie laughed. "You tore him down."

"And I'm thinkin' you're wrong. Won't stop him from being a pain in my ass. I'm on the fence about how fuckin' stupid it is to let him ride the fuck away," Mason said, then huffed out a breath, frustrated. "Bones, we need to follow him, see where he goes. Get ahold of Myron, have him set up a call with Fury. We need to figure out why we didn't know Shooter was out."

Bones turned and looked at the men who stood behind them. Shoulder to shoulder, they presented a united front and seeing this, it was no wonder the mismatched men who had ridden behind Shooter hadn't stayed once it was clear what the intent was for the visit. Motioning to two of the Little Rock members, he was gratified when they didn't hesitate, just nodded and moved towards their bikes. In a few moments, they were off and down the road, trailing behind Shooter.

***

"You're saying he'd been stonewalled for a whole day, and hadn't checked in?" Mason's words were delivered in an angry tone, tense with frustration and disbelief. Bones waited for Myron's response. They were inside the Little Rock clubhouse, back in the office.

"I'm saying he didn't have a chance to check in, Mason. He got held up in visitor intake at the prison, you know how Taft is out there. Access to anything is iffy, and for us, it's a definite way for LEO and Feds to isolate." Myron sounded just as frustrated. "We knew sending Fury out was courting trouble, but you wouldn't let me use the lawyers like we've been doing." The cell phone buzzed with an incoming text, but no one picked it up to check what it was. "And as to why our legal assistance didn't know Shooter had gotten released, I'm still following up on that. There's no paperwork behind it. From the surface, it looks like he's still in jail. Got no idea how the fuck this worked, but from what I've seen, there weren't any markers our men would have picked up on."

Silence in the room, then Mason sighed heavily. "Okay. Keep me updated. Not a bit of this shit smells right."

"Stinks to high heaven," Myron agreed, then disconnected.

Mason looked at Bones, picking up the phone. "Find out from Digger when Fury's back in Chicago." He read the text, then tapped out a response, saying offhandedly, "Let Bethy know." At Bones snort of disbelief, Mason lifted his eyes and glared at him, shrugging, "I can't talk her out of it. Tried a dozen ways. Her choice."

"Leave or stay?" Bones asked Mason, already knowing what he wanted wasn't what he would recommend if he were asked. Leaving now would give the local chapter the wrong message, and could position them for further conflict if anyone got the wrong idea that it was a retreat.

"Stay." Mason's voice was flat, gruff, and Bones understood. He felt the same way.

"Shooter has long been a problem. He is one that should not be allowed to remain unresolved. We have both done that in the past." Bones shook his head. "It never ends well."

"And we wind up doing the shit we knew needed to be done to begin with. No." Mason paused, and reached into a pocket on his vest, pulling out his phone. "I won't let it rock on. We need to know where he's headed, and why he's here. Out of all the places he coulda gone when he got out of prison, why did he come here?"

"I do not know, my friend." Bones shoved his shoulders back, hooking his thumbs in the pockets of his jeans. "We need that information, and to know how he managed his release in the first place." Rocking on his heels slightly, he shook his head. "I have calls to make. Do you need anything from me, Mason?"

"Million bucks and a better family?" Mason's laughter was bitter, and Bones winced to hear it. "Naw, brother. Make the calls. I want to check on Juanita, call home and check on my fam. Appreciate you putting yourself out there today. It did not go unnoticed."

"My job, to protect my president," Bones said without looking up, and at Mason's derisive snort, his eyes cut up from his phone to Mason's face. "My honor, to do this for my friend and brother." The two men stared at each other for a moment, then Bones said, "Rebels forever…"

Mason finished it, with, "Forever Rebels."

***

"You are certain of this information?" Bones asked the question, already on the move, his feet taking him down the back stairway of the clubhouse. The slapping echoes of his boot soles in the confined space did nothing to block the affirmative response on the phone. "I will be in touch. Expect us within the hour."

Rounding the bottom of the stairs, he crossed the kitchen in a few strides, pushing through the swinging doors and into the main room. Scanning the occupants quickly, he didn't see the ones he wanted and jerked his head at the prospect manning the bar. "Where is Mason?"

With a tip of his head to the door behind him, the prospect said, "Office, but they said they weren't to be interrupted." He grimaced, clearly uncertain what to do, and Bones solved it for him by moving to the door.

Knocking with one fist as the other hand turned the knob, he entered without delay. Mason sat behind the desk, two Little Rock officers seated on the couch opposite, Opie and Slate in chairs at either end of the room. "Shooter left town a while ago, riding like the devil himself were after him. LaPorte left town about an hour before he did. Shooter's in Mobile already. Mason, I think he's following her down to Adken."

Mason stared at him for a long moment, and his chin jerked up once. "Fuck, did I hang her out there today, saying that to him?" Bones shrugged, not certain how to respond. Another moment, then Mason reached out for the speakerphone before pausing, drawing his hand back and bringing out his cell phone instead. Two rings, then a sleepy Myron answered the call with a hoarse, "Yeah, boss?"

"You get eyes into the med place in Florida?" The tension in Mason's voice must have been evident to Myron, because his response was quick and affirmative. "Pull up the feed. Tell me what you see."

"Minute, boss."

Bones closed his eyes, understanding instinctively what could have pulled Shooter to Florida, even if he didn't know about LaPorte, or the facility.

Myron's voice came back, and he said, "You needa see this, Mason. Sending a screenshot to your phone."

Bones shook his head, opening his eyes to stare at Mason. Taking out his own phone, he composed a text to Digger, and paused, waiting.

A soft ping from his phone, and Mason angled it so he could look at the screen.

The single word was snarled, Mason's eyes never lifting from the image on his phone. "Morgan."

Bones hit Send.

***

Their plane was scarcely on the ground when Mason pulled out his phone. Bones heard a grunt and glanced his way, seeing Mason's phone tilted so he could see the screen. The text message displayed there was innocuous, but the person who sent it was a surprise.

Blue Line had sent three words. ***Need a call.***

"What do you have going with the Malcontents? Did you connect before we left Arkansas?" Bones stood when Mason did, entering the aisle, noting with annoyance how the pocket of space around them was left undisturbed. Mason was busy with his phone as Bones reached up, dragging their bags from the bins. Handing Mason's to him, he slung the strap of his over his shoulder, automatically adjusting it so his empty holster at the small of his back was accessible. Their weapons were in the checked baggage, and would not be returned to their normal positions until the men were in the rental car. Their permits were not valid in Florida, but neither man mentioned it.

They had hit the concourse before Mason responded, Bones giving him as much space as he needed to take care of whatever business had cropped up while they were in the air.

"Blue Line's callin' in the marker he earned with Bear." Mason let a half a dozen strides go by before continuing. "Fuckin' shit for timing, but cannot deny the man has a marker to call."

"Truth." Bones avoided a stroller sticking out from a gate seating area, smiling down at the sleeping baby strapped inside. He tried to ignore the wide-eyed stare from the child's mother, but his mind drew a comparison to how his Ester looked at him, seeing past his skin to the man hiding inside. "What does he need?"

"Need is a strong word." Mason snorted a laugh. "He'd like a representative in his area, someone he could call on when he'd like to chat. Someone who would be a direct conduit to me."

"Will you give him this?" They exited the secure area, heading to the luggage carousel, already turning and sliding along, carrying a few bags, more coming, thumping off the feeder belt every minute.

"Inclined. Thinkin' Tug would enjoy a SoCal assignment for a few months. He and Maggie have already been out there off and on for over a year, checking on his nephew. LeRoy's about ready to get out of the navy. Tug's been helping him sort out what he wants to do. Wyoming isn't a place the guy wants to live, and Tug's made some statements he'd like to be wherever that winds up being. At least for a while."

"Cannot fault a man for wanting to be with blood." Bones saw their bags and stepped to the carousel, waiting. He grabbed the handles and jostled them, distributing the weight. "Car next."

Mason grunted, already turning towards the rental counter. Ten minutes later they were in a car, guns retrieved, bags stowed. Mason plugged in the device all the Rebels used, bypassing the car's standard Bluetooth system. A minute later, Myron's greeting came over the speakers, and Mason responded.

"Made it. We'll be on-site in twenty minutes. Tell me what you've got." As he spoke, Mason jerked the car into gear, pulling out of the parking lot and getting them on the highway without needing any directions, underscoring to Bones how much time Mason had spent here in the past few weeks.

"Morgan left about an hour after you hit the airport in Arkansas. Tracked him into town. He's not far from where you are." Bones looked at Mason, trying to determine what would be next.

"What'd he leave behind?" Squinting against the sun, Mason reached up and slid his sunglasses down, covering his eyes.

"It's dinner time there. Ladies are eating. That's all, nothing odd, Mason. It looks like he was only there for a visit. Left when it was time, considerate of their schedule." Myron paused, and Bones knew something bigger was coming. "He's at a coffee shop across the street from LaPorte's offices."

"She meeting him?" Bones knew Mason hadn't approached the woman who was his half-sister, hadn't approached his mother, either, no matter what he'd said to Shooter that morning. "Got eyes on her?"

"Negatory on the eyes. But I can hear her. Nothing out of place, boss. She's just back at work after being in the field all day. Not making any evening plans, and nothing she's saying registers as off. Just another day "

"Where's Shooter?" Mason turned the wheel sharply, swinging the car through a U-Turn, taking them back towards downtown. "Know where he is, yet?"

The flight Digger had gotten them on had left minutes after they'd boarded. Given where Shooter was at that time, they might very well have beaten him into town, since he was riding down.

"Caught him on a cam about twenty minutes ago. He's headed to the coffee shop, boss. I saw you just pulled a uey. You sure that's the best course?" Bones knew Mason's increased speed had registered when Myron muttered, "Of course you do."

Bones waited, then interjected, "Mason, we do not have backup here. We have few allies in the area on which we can call." No response, so he decided to try another tactic. "Myron, what is the location around the coffee shop? I would assume open, with ample foot traffic to warrant having a shop there."

"Not really," Myron returned immediately. "It's more a drive up, or drive-through place. There are a couple of stores nearby, but not next to. The building on the other side of the road is your biggest threat, because of the number of federal employees who are officed there. There are like three alphabet divisions in the building. Fed parking is underneath and behind, though, so there are only a few who come and go from the front."

Bones reached to his holster, pulled out the pistol and checked the magazine, then opened his bag on the backseat and pulled out a spare. "I have thirty," he told Mason, who nodded. "Myron, can you send me images of the shop and the surrounding area, just so I can have a visual?"

"You got it," Myron muttered, and Bones heard the keyboard in the background. A moment later his phone vibrated against his leg.

"Want your spare?" Bones didn't look at Mason, kept his head down, studying the images on his phone, trying to orient himself on the shop building and the surrounding environment. Mason grunted, which Bones took as affirmative, so he tucked his gun underneath his leg, reaching back to grab Mason's bag, digging out and retrieving two spare magazines. He checked both, pressing the top cartridge of each against the spring to ensure it was fully loaded. He pushed them underneath Mason's leg, trapping them against the seat. "What do you want, Mason? Do you plan to talk, or do we hit the door with intent?"

"No talking." Short and clipped, Mason's answer was all Bones needed.

With a nod, Bones accepted this. "Whatever you need, brother." Mason met his gaze and held it for a moment before twisting to look out the front window again. "Myron, we need to know where Shooter is." Bones looked at the time on the dashboard clock, and then asked, "Is there anything you can do with the cameras on the building LaPorte is in? Past quitting time, so there should be only a few remaining inside, unless some of the companies have shift work. How many people are in the coffee shop? Where are they? Where is Morgan?"

"I have everything in the fed building if you want it. I can keep their security guys busy so they aren't looking out front. Mason..." Myron paused, then said, "It looks like Shooter's going to hit there about the same time. If you come through the alley to the back, and in that door, you'll have distance and surprise working in your favor, no windows on that side of the building." Bones studied the images again, seeing the alley and employee parking lot Myron referenced. "Morgan's at the table on the front wall, in the corner. You come in the back, you'll hit the kitchen first, then through the doors into the shop proper. There's one gal working, and she's spent the last ten minutes guzzling about a gallon of what looked like green tea. She just went into the toilet, so I expect her to stay there a while."

Myron paused again, and Bones heard Mason's phone ping, looked down to see a reboot screen. "I'm wiping your phone since you don't have a burner. I'll offload the backup before I wipe that. Bones, I'm about to do the same with yours." A moment later his phone vibrated and went black, then the reboot screen showed. "I'll wipe the car's GPS. I'm jacked in now, so I'll take care of that once I lose you."

Another pause, then Myron said, "When you leave the car I will have you on the cameras inside. Nothing else, Mason. Everything outside I can get at will be nonworking once you hit a block away. Inside, I won't be able to talk to you, but if I can, I'll jack into the sound system there, so I'll be able to hear you. I won't stop trying, man. You tell me what you want done, Mason, and I'll do my best to make it so."

"Gotcha." Mason's response was short, and he was focused on driving, angling the car around turns and then they were on a cobblestone alley between high buildings. "You're a good brother, Myron."

"Back atcha, boss." Myron pulled in an audible breath. "Okay. Here we go. Shooter just hit the front of the lot."

Bones saw the buildings opening up in front of them, saw a small building to his left. Mason angled the car that direction, gliding to a hard but silent stop at the back door. "We're out, Myron," Mason clipped the words as he grabbed the magazines, then got out of the still-rocking car, gun angled down beside his leg.

"Shiny side." Myron's voice came through the speakers, then there was the ping of a computer rebooting and Bones knew Myron was working his magic on the system.

With one glance at Bones, Mason reached for and opened the door, and the two men walked inside.

On the cusp

Myron

Myron hovered over the computer screen, eyes fixed on the six different camera views he had pulled up. He watched as Mason and Bones entered the building, noted how they carefully approached the bathroom door and blocked it. On another laptop, he pulled up the 911 call log for Adken, watching in case the girl had taken her phone into the bathroom with her.

Gaze flicking back and forth between the view that showed Shooter standing over Morgan, arms waving, clearly shouting, and the one that showed Mason and Bones pausing for nearly two minutes just inside the kitchen, listening. He could only watch helplessly as two men he called brother, two men he felt a closer bond with than blood, walked out into the open.

No matter Mason had said he wasn't interested in talking, that was what they did. Myron could see the mouths moving on all four men, watched as Shooter grew more agitated while Morgan straightened in his chair, attention entirely fixed on Mason. Something important was happening, and Myron frantically worked at acquiring sound, needing to hear every word.

***

Fury

Standing in the taxi line outside the St. Louis airport, Fury stared down at his phone. At the last minute in California, with a priority code via text, Myron had routed him from Taft to here in St. Louis instead of Chicago. Backpack slung over one shoulder, he was trying to check in, finding all normal phone numbers were no longer working. It wasn't unusual for the club to cycle numbers, and especially when there was a lot going on, but right now even the ones that still worked like main clubhouse phones weren't responding.

"Fuckin' blind. Gonna have to go in fucking goddamned blind." He texted another number, and almost immediately got the bubble that meant someone was responding. "Fuckin' finally."

Twenty minutes in a cab found him across the river in illinois, and stalking in the side door of the St. Louis clubhouse. Six men stood when he entered, and one of them stepped forwards, hand out. "Fury," he greeted, and gripped Fury's wrist.

Eyeing the nameplate on the man's vest, Fury returned the gesture and greeting. "Dyno." Pulling back, he asked, "Wanna tell me why I'm here?" SAA was also on the man's vest, which meant Fury was dealing with an officer, at least.

"Office," was the only response he got, so with a nod to the other men, none of them officers, he followed Dyno to a room off the back of the central area. Once the door closed behind them, Dyno swung to face him, and didn't waste any time starting. "Pike's fuckin' insane. He's spouting all kinds of shit about Mason, and I had him locked in one of the basement rooms."

Fury leaned backwards and felt his eyebrows raise in surprise. "You had your president put inside a cleanup cell?"

"He's fuckin' nuts, man. At first I thought maybe it was a bad trip, because he likes to party hearty. But then he started sayin' things that didn't make sense in a bad way. Talkin' about killin' Mason, how he hated him." Dyno shook his head. "Ain't takin' chances. Not ever again."

Shaking his head, Fury asked, "Not again? What does that mean?"

"I'm from Des Moines." The way the man's lip curled said a lot, and Fury had learned enough history to understand what he was referencing. "Saw good men die because they believed bullshit that got spewed. Wasn't taking any chances here. I figure, I keep him away from the rank and file, they don't get to hear it and wonder. I got a couple of officers on his door now." He paused, then said, "The fact that I'm not on my own in this, and called Mother right away, that's gotta count for something."

"You had to relocate to stay in the club, right?" Dyno nodded. "Hard on the family, man. I get why you want to be proactive here. Who else knows what Pike was on about?"

"Me, and two others. Nobody's asked where he is. You mention him to any of the guys out front, who don't know a fucking thing about what's going on, and you'll see relief that he's not here right now, which sucks." Dyno pulled a deep breath. "What do you want me to do?"

"Gimme a minute." Fury pulled his phone out and checked messages. Still no response. On impulse, he texted Opie and received an immediate invitation to call. "Gimme the room," he ordered, and Dyno stepped out, pulling the door quietly shut behind him. Fury shook his head, not sure why he ranked that kind of respect.

"Opie, I got a dilemma."

Without pause, Opie responded, "Hit me."

Movie mirrors

Ester

I stood just outside the office Bones had on the main floor. Ronnie had gone in there two hours ago, telling me he needed to focus on what he was doing. I knew about having to focus. Needing to dial in on something to the exclusion of anything else. I could do that sometimes, watching how a bird's wing caught the sunlight, reflecting bands of iridium beauty.

But it was time to eat now, and Ronnie hadn't come out when I called him. So I knocked. With no answer, I was left with only two options, and I wasn't about to allow fear to keep me from my brother. Bones had told me to be more forceful about what I wanted. Well, what I wanted right now was for Ronnie to eat dinner with me.

So, I opened the door. I took a single step inside, and then my feet turned traitor, refusing to retreat as I wanted. Ronnie had so much stuff in the room, I could feel the electricity running along my skin. I knew the words, of course I did. Computers, phones, tablets, monitors. I just didn't like saying them, even inside my own head.

I didn't know why movie houses didn't bother me. Just like I didn't know why the tiny cellphones did. It just was how I was and no arguing with it. I had nearly convinced my feet to leave with me when I saw something move on one of the boxes sitting on the desk. It looked like there were all these small movies, all in a row. Two rows of little movies, and one of them flickered in time with the stuttering beat of my heart.

Movement again, and my breath stuck in my throat because on the tiny movie in the middle was my Bones. Not caught in the box, I knew that wasn't how things worked, knew these were reflections of a different place. As if a mirror had been set up to relay things. I could deal with mirrors, liked them, liked playing with them, seeing how many faces I could give myself. This was like that, and it showed me Bones.

His mouth opened, and the silence that had been in the room went away. Splintered and destroyed by noise from the desk. A roaring that sounded again and again, and on one of the movies a man stood only to fall backwards, his descent taking a table with it, sprawling him on the floor like a disjointed pickup stick game gone wrong. Another movie showed a man turning around, and I saw his arm raise, stiff and thrust outward. Fire flashed, like the sparking wheel of an old-fashioned lighter, out of sync with the roaring.

Bones mouth opened again, and then he jumped backwards, as if he'd been pulled by a rope. He hit a table and fell sideways, chairs skittering away from his body. Darkness blossomed along his shoulder, and I watched as he lifted his hand, recognizing the gun he held by shape.

***

Fury

The basement steps were narrow and steep, matching the decades-old style of the house. The area had been separated into four rooms, and glancing through the open doors of the other three, Fury saw they were utilitarian: bare floors, cinder block walls, no windows, and light bulbs set inside cages like you'd see in prison.

One man stood to either side of the only closed door, and he took a minute to introduce himself, seeing an anxiety on each that matched what Dyno still wore on his face. "He's been quiet," the man on the left said, "been a relief."

"You think it's bad drugs?" Fury wasn't surprised at the head shake, because his search of Pike's room upstairs hadn't turned up anything. No drugs, and no kit, either. Meant if he were using heavy, then he wasn't doing it here, but Pike didn't keep a home away from the clubhouse. His room here was his home. "He seem unstable before?" Another head shake, this from the other man.

"He's always been hard, but relatively fair. Get some drink in him, he's harder. But, he never seemed crazy. Not like this."

Fury reached for the door, and the man on the left spoke up again. "You want us to watch your back?"

Fury paused, studying his face. "You think I need protection from one man in a closed room?"

"No offense"—this was the other man—"but he's fuckin' crazy. I wouldn't want to go in there by myself. We got your back, brother."

Dyno spoke up from behind Fury. "You ain't going in there alone, Fury."

"Then we all go in," he decided, and caught the looks of relief on all three men's faces.

Pushing the door open, Fury paused in the doorway, looking at Pike who stood leaning against the far wall. Head back, he was studying the ceiling overhead, arms relaxed at his sides. Slowly, he brought his gaze down to rest on the group, and Fury got a glimpse of what had so spooked the men. Pike's eyes were wide, whites showing, and the lines on his face were drawn, deep furrows in the weathered skin.

"Fuck." The single drawn-out word sounded hoarse, as if he'd screamed his throat raw. Slowly shaking his head back and forth, Pike lifted one hand, tips of his fingers bloody. His movement brought attention to his vest, and Fury noted the dark rectangle above Pike's nameplate. A glance at what Pike held clutched in a fist confirmed his initial impression. Two rockers, the center patch, and the president patch. Stitches picked free from the vest with his fingernails.

"Mason's not comin', is he?" Now Pike's tone was plaintive, as if Fury's being there was a disappointment beyond what he could sustain. "Can't even come deliver the beatout himself."

"You want a beatout?" Fury took two steps into the room, hearing the other three men spread out at his back. "Droppin' your patches, Pike?"

"Cannot abide the man." Pike shook his head back and forth. "He's a fuckin' blight on the life, and I cannot abide."

"What can't you abide?" Between words, the silence in the room was thunderous, and Fury felt his muscles tensing involuntarily. It felt like something was coming. Something profound.

"Heard you're fuckin' the sister." Now it was Fury's fists tensing, curling into balls of skin and bone at the derisive tone.

"What can't you abide?" *Man is fucking crazy. Dyno didn't lie.*

"Can't abide a man who thinks he's so far above everybody else, he can tell them what to do. What to think. When to do any-fuckin-thing." Pike's arm drew back, and he tossed the patches to the floor at Fury's feet. "I'm done." Arms to his sides, he lifted his hands, palm up. "Show me what ya got." He curled his fingers, making a "come here" gesture. "Bring it on. Do me a favor, though. Make it look good. Don't fuck around and miss or some shit like that. Show me what you can do."

Opie had said it would come to this. Dyno had intimated the threat had already been laid out there. Fury pulled his phone out, and saw a response had come in from Mother. It could have come directly from Mason, or from any of the other nationals. The who didn't matter. The message did. ***Do what's needful***.

Hand to his six, Fury drew his pistol and saw Pike might not be as certain as he presented himself, because the flinch at the gun's appearance was real, and huge. Shaking his head, Fury flipped his grip, grasping the gun by the barrel and handed it to Dyno. "Hold this for me, would ya?"

Advancing on Pike, Fury twisted his rings, getting things lined up just how he liked them. "You want it? Want out? Wanna throw it all away?"

Pike gave the smallest nod, mouth twisted to the side.

"You got it."

Fury swung. He did not miss.

Best in the history of ever

Bones

Seated on the edge of the bed, Bones rolled the muscles in his good shoulder, trying to stretch out the kinks. He reached up, dragging his palm across the back of his neck, digging in with his fingers and pulling at the tense muscles. "Here," he heard, and felt the heat from petite palms smoothing up his shoulder blades. "Let me help." He dropped his head backwards and Ester leaned in, letting him rest between her breasts. He looked up into her face, seeing a solemn expression on her features. Before he could ask, she shook her head, repeating her words, "Let me help."

"I always want your hands on me, little one." Her fingers and thumbs rubbed circles, working the stress away. He slowly let his head sink to one side, then the other, giving her full access to his neck and shoulders. "The sling is annoying."

"Only another two weeks, Red said." He felt her press close against his upper back, the stir of air beside his head, then her lips touched his cheek. "You can do anything."

"Does not keep it from being annoying." He knew he was grumbling, but didn't care. And Ester didn't really seem to mind. As long as she could touch him, be with him, and reassure herself over and over that he was real, he was here, and he wasn't badly injured.

Myron had told him about her reaction to the firefight she'd seen on the computer screens. Dreams of her screams had echoed in his head, because by the time he and Mason made it back to Chicago, she had been frantic to see him. To know with her own senses that he lived, that he was okay.

It had been nearly a week, and she remained as diligent of his comfort as the first minutes he had been home. Red and Myron had a few laughs at his expense, when she'd insisted in petting and fussing over him, bringing pillows for his head and a blanket for his legs, and giving him soft kisses and a whispered, "Good luckies." It wasn't until he recognized the blanket that he understood, wrestling with his own pride to allow her to care for him. It was the one she'd been wrapped in when he found her ill, the one she had taken with her after their very first date. Good luck, indeed.

Tonight was a party at the clubhouse, and Bones was determined to go, and just as determined to bring Ester with him. She had met most of the men who would be there, and he'd promised her she could stay by his side all night, if she wanted. She was giving him that, and if touching him eased her nerves, he would gladly give in to her needs.

The firefight had been brief, and deadly. Both Morgan and Shooter were killed, Mason entirely unscathed, seeming to walk between the bullets without a scratch. As he fell, Shooter had squeezed off several shots, one of which Bones caught in a glancing blow against his shoulder, breaking the collarbone. He and Mason had gotten out, leaving the dead bodies behind, scarcely managing to evade the incoming police, called in by the hysterical teenager locked in the bathroom.

The conversation he and Mason had listened to between father and son, and then what Morgan had said to Mason...all of that would require thought, and conversation. But that could come later, because they had time.

Myron had wreaked as much havoc on the video footage as he deemed wise, leaving images of the two men pulling their weapons. He couldn't do anything about the blood Bones left at the scene, but since he had no intention of returning to Florida anytime in the future, it would be unlikely for him to ever be placed at the coffee shop.

It had been touch and go for a while, getting back to where a club doc could pin his shoulder back together, but Red was confident Bones would heal. Ester was determined, too, and had taken to teaming up with Red to keep Bones corralled. If she had her way, he would be flat on his back in bed, with her spooning soup into his mouth.

Chin resting against his chest, Bones grinned at the image in his head, changing it so they were both naked. Mouth to his ear, Ester murmured, "Feels good?"

"Mmhmm, yes, little one." One of her arms wrapped around his chest and tugged. Bones went with it, leaning back against her. He felt her fingers on his chin and looked up, seeing a strange expression on her face. "What is it, Ester?"

"I was scared." This was the first direct statement she'd made referencing what she'd seen, and he watched her, seeing how her lips trembled. "I could see you, but couldn't hear you. Then you fell, and I could tell it hurt, that you were hurt, but I couldn't reach you. Couldn't touch you." She swallowed. "I was scared."

"I know." He wouldn't give her false words. No easy smoothing over what happened, or what could happen. "I am here now." He had to hope it would be enough. "I am with you."

"I didn't think you might not come back. When you left." Now the words were coming fast, tripping over themselves on her tongue in an effort to get out, expelled on the air like a poison she'd been holding inside. "I only thought of seeing Ronnie again. Then I saw you, and I knew I could lose you. I don't want to lose you. Not any part of you. When I met Willa, I thought she was brave." The topic change was abrupt, and Bones tried to understand the shift.

"How was she brave, baby?"

"She brought a baby into the world. That's the bravest thing I thought you can do. Making yourself responsible for another human being. I thought she was so brave." Ester shook her head. "But it's not bravery."

"It is not? Giving birth is hard. Knowing such an ordeal is coming, and still doing it? You do not think it brave to want that?"

"No, it's selfish. I was wrong, all this time, because it's not brave." She smoothed a palm across his cheek, cupping the hinge of his jaw, her fingers pressing into his flesh and holding tight. "So selfish."

"Why is it selfish, Ester? Help me understand."

"I knew I could lose you. Then I thought if I had a tiny part of you, it wouldn't be as bad. I could be selfish and hold onto that tiny human part of you." Her thumb stroked across his lips, and he stared into her eyes, swimming with tears. "She'll never lose Mason, no matter what, because she has Dolly and Garrett."

"Do you want a baby, Ester?" Not something Bones had ever considered, nothing he'd thought about, or thought through, because Ester was...Ester. Not something he'd contemplated before, but now the idea was in his head, he couldn't imagine a future that didn't include it as an option.

"Not today. I don't think today is the right time. But I could be selfish in a year or so. You think that'd be okay?" She blinked slowly, and he watched as tears broke free from the lashes of one eye, leaving a trailing wetness as they came together and ran down her cheek.

He reached up, curling his fingers around the back of her neck, pulling her down to meet his mouth as he whispered, "I think that would be perfect."

The end (of this story)

THANK YOU FOR READING *Bones*!

This is Book #10 in a series. Throughout this series we've been introduced to so many wonderful characters. People who live in my head in a way that makes them seem real in many aspects. I hope you fell in love with Bones and his Ester, and will continue in this saga along with me. Next up will be Fury's story, and his tale is about redemption, in both life, and love. Available now.

MUSIC PLAYLISTS

I put together playlists of music both mentioned in the book, and used during writing and editing. Want a peek into the mind of me? Be sure of your decision, it's not always normal here!

Playlist: bit.ly/bones-playlist

ABOUT THE AUTHOR

Raised in the south, MariaLisa learned about the magic of books at an early age. Every summer, she would spend hours in the local library, devouring books of every genre. Self-described as a book-a-holic, she says "I've always loved to read, but then I discovered writing, and found I adored that, too. For reading...if nothing else is available, I've been known to read the back of the cereal box."

Also by MariaLisa deMora

Alace Sweets

A dark thriller, this book is not a light read. Filled with edge-of-your-seat suspense, this intense story commands the reader's attention as it drives towards the explosive ending. Alace Sweets is a vigilante serial killer, with everything that implies and is sure to trip all your triggers. Be ready.

At seventeen, Alace Sweets turned a corner in her life, taking the wrong shortcut home from school.

Resisting the harsh knowledge her attackers will never be made to pay for their actions, Alace takes a stand. Justice must be served, and if fate's scales are out of balance, she's determined to set things right as best she can.

When the laws of men fail, the rules of Alace prevail.

5-Star Reviews for Alace Sweets

"deMora has a superb story-line and exceptional character development. All of her characters have such depth that will intrigue the reader..."
~Turning Another Page

"Hot, sweet, dark thriller."
~Beth D

"It will keep you on the edge of your seat and give you chills."
~Escape Reality Book Blog

"Disturbing, haunting, sickly; yet hot, sexy and heart racing!"
~Amanda L

"From the first page [deMora] pulls you into the world she has created and you do not even try to escape..."
~Little Shop of Readers Blog

"A must read for all those dark, gritty romance fans out there."
~Sweet & Spicy Reads

"You will find yourself so drawn into the story that the outside world is blocked out and your locking the doors and turning on all the lights."
~Danena F

"Don't judge me for bonding with a vigilante serial killer, she's more than what she does."
~iScream Books

"Thrilling...chilling...full of suspense, nail biting edge of your seat excitement."
~Tracey H

"Every time MariaLisa deMora picks up her pen (or opens her computer), she creates characters you want to believe in."
~Gail S

"Intriguing dark storyline, beautiful love story and nail-biting conclusion, what more could a reader ask for?"
~Manda M

"This book takes you a dark and twisted ride that is gripping..."
~Renee Entress' Blog

"This book is dark and gritty and I literally had to take a day off from reading it because it's that intense."
~My Girlfriend's Couch

"This is my favourite book so far from this author ... I recommend this book if you enjoy dark romantic thrillers."
~Cheekypee Reads and Reviews

"There's not enough stars to give this book and 5 just doesn't really do it justice!"

~DeLane C

"I couldn't put this book down from page one! Tried to stop & go to bed but couldn't sleep thinking about Alace and got up & finished the book."
~Debbie M

"MariaLisa DeMora, wordsmith that she is, made this a story of the enlightenment of a woman and finding love in a life where she has had none."
~Kat W

"Whatever deep dark trench [deMora] pulled a character like Alace from should be revisited again and often."
~Confessions of a Serial Reader

ADDITIONAL SERIES AND BOOKS

Please note that books in a series frequently feature characters from additional books within that series. If series books are read out of order, readers will twig to spoilers for the other books, so going back to read the skipped titles won't have the same angsty reveals.

Rebel Wayfarers MC series:

Mica, #1
A Sweet & Merry Christmas, short story #1.5
Slate, #2
Bear, #3
Jase, #4
Gunny, #5
Mason, #6
Hoss, #7
Harddrive Holidays, short story #7.5
Duck, #8
Biker Chick Campout, short story #8.5
Watcher, #9
A Kiss to Keep You, novella #9.25
Gun Totin' Annie, short story #9.5
Secret Santa, short story #9.75

Bones, #10
Gunny's Pups, novella #10.25
Never Settle, short story #10.5
Not Even A Mouse, short story #10.75
Fury, #11
Christmas Doings, #11.25
Gypsy's Lady, #11.5
Cassie, #12
Road Runner's Ride, novella #12.5

Occupy Yourself band series:

Born Into Trouble, #1
Grace In Motion, #2 (TBD)
What They Say, #3 (TBD)

Neither This, Nor That series:

This Is the Route Of Twisted Pain, #1
Treading the Traitor's Path: Out Bad, #2
Trapped by Fate on Reckless Roads, #3 (TBD)

Other Books:

With My Whole Heart
Alace Sweets
Hard Focus

More information available at mldemora.com.